Norah Hoult was  8.
Her mother, Margar   ic
and her father, Powi: :h
parents died when sh   ld
her brother to be educated at boarding schools in England.

Hoult began her writing career in journalism, working for the *Sheffield Daily Telegraph*, *Pearson's Magazine*, and the *Yorkshire Evening Post*. Her first publication, the collection of short stories *Poor Women!* (1928), would be rejected nineteen times before being accepted by newly founded Scholartis Press. That collection, which explored the consciousness of women in different walks of life, was a critical success.

Between 1931 and 1957 she moved from Dublin to New York and London, before finally settling in Ireland. A prolific writer, Hoult published twenty-four novels and four collections of short stories between 1928 and 1977.

Deeply concerned with issues of religion, sexuality, and the economy, Hoult wrote extensively about the cultural experience of being a woman in twentieth century Britain and Ireland. For her treatments of these themes, ten of her books were banned by the Irish censorship board.

She spent her final years living in Greystones, County Wicklow, where she died in 1984.

Praise for Norah Hoult

'Her short stories are far away the best I have read this year – in fact, no comparison is possible, for I know of nothing written of late years with which to compare them. They are the unique manifestations which genius always gives us.'

H.M. Tomlinson (1931)

'Hoult has a dark sense of humour, and the stories are written in strong prose, … nuanced and subtle, lending themselves to more than one interpretation, and would hold their own in any literary company.'

The Irish Times, on Cocktail Bar (2018)

'Miss Norah Hoult's *Poor Women* is a remarkable book. It is remarkable not for its themes … but in being, of its kind, almost flawless … Hoult discovers a pathos which is none the less acute for the restraint of her writing; each picture is built up of an infinity of small strokes, its tragedy never, or hardly ever, actually expressed, but implied by each concatenation of circumstances.'

The Times Literary Supplement, on Poor Women!

Also by Norah Hoult

Novels

*Closing Hour/
Time, Gentlemen, Time!* (1930)
Apartment to Let (1931)
Youth Can't Be Served (1933)
Holy Ireland (1935)
Coming from the Fair (1937)
Four Women Grow Up (1940)
Smilin' on the Vine (1941)
Augusta Steps Out (1942)
Scene for Death (1943)
There Were No Windows (1944)
House Under Mars (1946)
Farewell Happy Fields (1948)
Frozen Ground (1952)
Sister Mavis (1953)
A Death Occurred (1954)
Journey Into Print (1954)
Father Hone and the Television Set (1956)
Father and Daughter (1957)
Husband and Wife (1959)
The Last Days of Miss Jenkinson (1962)
A Poet's Pilgrimage (1966)
Only Fools and Horses Work (1969)
Not For Our Sins Alone (1972)
Two Girls in the Big Smoke (1977)

Short Stories

Poor Women! (1928)
Nine Years is a Long Time (1938)
Selected Stories (1946)
Cocktail Bar (1950)

Farewell Happy Fields

Farewell Happy Fields

Norah Hoult

Introduction by Louise Kennedy

NEW ISLAND

FAREWELL HAPPY FIELDS
First published in 1948 by William Heinemann Ltd.
This edition published in 2019 by
New Island Books
16 Priory Office Park
Stillorgan
County Dublin
Republic of Ireland

www.newisland.ie

Print ISBN: 978-1-84840-737-4
eBook ISBN: 978-1-84840-738-1

Typeset by JVR Creative India
Cover design by Catherine Gaffney
Printed by L&C Printing Group, Poland

New Island received financial assistance from The Arts Council (An Comhairle
Ealaíon), Dublin, Ireland.

New Island Books is a member of Publishing Ireland.

Introduction

Louise Kennedy

A few years ago I was thinking about doing a PhD and struggling to find a subject that would both sustain and engage me through several years of study. I bought a copy of *The Long Gaze Back*, Sinead Gleeson's 2015 anthology of stories by Irish women, to distract myself from the quest for a research topic. A couple of paragraphs into Norah Hoult's 'When Miss Coles Made the Tea' I knew I had found one. The story was deeply ironic, often funny, and quietly heartbreaking. Here was a natural storyteller with a sharp eye for detail, an ear for dialogue, and a way of looking at the world that seemed years ahead of her time. Despite having produced a considerable body of work over five decades, she had been virtually ignored by academia.

From the outset, I encountered problems in obtaining copies of Norah Hoult's books. Even with the help of a delightful coterie of specialist booksellers and publishers, notably The Second Shelf, Arlen House and Persephone Books, several of her titles still elude me. Not only has Norah Hoult's name been omitted from the canon; it seems her books have literally vanished. *Farewell Happy Fields* is among the elusive ones. A recent search for it yielded a single vendor in Denmark who had just sold his copy. One cannot overestimate, therefore, the role of recovery projects such as the Modern Irish Classics series in preventing fine writers such as Norah Hoult from sliding into obscurity. It is humbling to have been asked to write this introduction.

Farewell Happy Fields was published in 1948 when Hoult was fifty. It was her sixteenth book. The title comes from Book 1 of John Milton's *Paradise Lost*, the epic seventeenth-century poem that tells the story of the fall of man and the temptation of Adam and Eve by the fallen angel Satan. The quote from Milton does much more than provide a title; it informs both theme and structure. The passage from which the quote is taken contains the lines:

> The mind is its own place, and in it self
> Can make a Heav'n of Hell, a Hell of Heav'n.

The novel begins on the day Adam Palmer is discharged from an 'asylum' and sees him resolve to dedicate his life to 'the purpose of rebelling against the will of God, and destroying entirely that immortal soul which in his youth he had been at some pains to nurture.' Adam blames God for his misfortunes, for falling for a married woman and losing his mind, and vows to send himself to hell. He is a devout Catholic – in order to believe in the devil, one must first believe in God – and his faith torments him. His private thoughts are addled with catechism and religious rhetoric.

This fervour features often in Hoult's fiction, from the novels *Holy Ireland* and *Coming from the Fair* to her short stories, in particular those with Irish characters. This preoccupation may be explained by her background. Her mother, Margaret O'Shaughnessy, came from a strict Catholic family and on the day of her twenty-first birthday eloped with an English Protestant who was twelve years her senior. Her father cast her out of her family and disinherited her for marrying outside her faith. Privately, however, Margaret's mother maintained contact with her daughter. After the death of Margaret's patriarchal father, the O'Shaughnessy family voluntarily made a financial settlement to Margaret; she and her husband were in poor health and struggling financially. It is also worth noting that Powis Hoult, Norah's father, was an ardent theosophist, so it is possible that the young Norah was exposed to religious fervour at home too.

There is a pattern in Hoult's books of presenting male characters who are weak-willed, sometimes emasculated, and *Farewell Happy Fields* is no exception. Adam is unable to shake off his religious conditioning or control his obsessive thoughts. His friend from the asylum is an exhibitionist (a flasher, frankly) who is kept by his wife. The acquaintances Adam makes when he returns to Ireland range from vain to ineffectual to sleazy. Hoult herself had poor experiences of men. There was the grandfather who barred his house against her mother. The father who died when she was a child, leaving her in the hands of relatives she barely knew. The brother, her only sibling, who survived the trenches only to commit suicide a few weeks after the Armistice. The husband to whom she was married briefly and unhappily.

The Edwardian England Hoult moved to as a child was thrown into social chaos by the First World War, with traditional gender roles upended and class boundaries blurred. Much has been made of the lack of men in Britain in the interwar years, often linking it to the scale of the slaughter at the Front. In reality, the country had been bleeding men to the colonies for decades and there had been a surplus of women since the 1850s. The men who did come back from the trenches, however, were altered by what they had seen, and unprepared for the post-war life to which they returned. Elaine Showalter, the literary critic, described the war as a 'crisis of masculinity'. *Farewell Happy Fields* reflects this; it is not that there is a lack of men; it is rather that the men themselves are lacking.

On the back cover of a later edition of *Farewell Happy Fields,* Adam is referred to as the hero of the novel. He is a compelling character. Hoult makes us privy to his warped reasoning and we can follow the logic of the choices he makes on the path to spiritual annihilation. But much as we are drawn to Adam, we stop short of cheering him on. It is through Kathleen, the dowdy middle-class girl who marries him out of pity and love, that we get to the heart of the novel. Rather than commit a mortal sin such as murder, Adam chooses a slow route to hell that he calls the 'Little Way', by inflicting small cruelties on those around him. For Kathleen, it is akin to death by a thousand cuts. He demands that she cancel arrangements to meet her friends, leaving her isolated and cloistered. A couple of days before their wedding he persuades her to sleep with him, and is offhand with her afterwards, as if it meant nothing. Perhaps most cruelly of all, he deliberately sows seeds of anxiety about the health of the child she is carrying. Her forbearance is what gives the novel emotional heft.

Hoult's first book, a collection of short stories entitled *Poor Women!,* was published in 1928, twenty years before *Farewell Happy Fields*. In some American editions of the book, she included a note. She had set out, she said, to portray women who were struggling to maintain their self-respect, who were dependent on or had to 'conciliate the man'. Retrospectively the note reads almost like a credo. Themes of shame, financial insecurity and emotional poverty recur throughout Hoult's work. Kathleen's mother is dead and her father has remarried. He gives her a paltry dowry and is relieved to have her off his hands. She leaves England to live in Ireland with a man who feels nothing for her. She could be one of the 'poor women' of Hoult's early stories.

Here, as in her other novels, Hoult's storytelling is so confident, the narrative so readable, that one can overlook the fact that her work is deeply political. Yet on feminism she is difficult. She once wrote, 'I am anti-feminist rather than feminist in my view, since I believe that feminism has done, on the whole, more harm than good to the true welfare of women.' This contradicts her sympathetic treatment of the women who inhabit her pages. The statement had been made in 1955, before the second wave of feminism had begun; before that, women seldom claimed the label. Hoult may not have embraced the term, but the work speaks for itself.

Hoult led a peripatetic life, particularly during the thirties. In some accounts it is said that she spent the early part of the decade in Ireland, researching her mother's story for the book that would become *Holy Ireland*. In fact, her husband had found work in Dublin. After the marriage foundered in 1933, she rented a flat in Rathmines for a short while and spent some time in Connemara but was mostly based in London. In 1937 she travelled to America, where she toured extensively and wrote two novels. When war was declared in September 1939 she returned to London and remained there for the duration of the conflict. She experienced bombing raids, evacuation, blackouts, rationing. Hoult's descriptive powers are strongest in *Farewell Happy Fields* when she evokes England; the quiet of a country railway platform, the shabbiness of a Pimlico street. The Irish setting is less convincing, but she circumvents this by confining the action largely to the domestic sphere, behind the walls of a rented flat. She calls the Irish location Inishkill. It is difficult to ascertain where it is, although some clarity is added by her reference to a walk along the Dargle, which seems to locate the book in north Wicklow.

Hoult was unapologetically a realist writer. She once reviewed a book by Jean Rhys and pronounced it 'a work of art, which is to say it creates life and experience'. That this is Hoult's view of what constitutes art is worth noting; the book is about 'bed sitting rooms' and 'getting off', the same territory into which Hoult ventured in her own writing. A woman of modest means obliged to support herself, this was a world she knew. Perhaps the thing that makes Hoult unique is that she endeavoured to tell the stories of the lower middle class, the class with the least class solidarity and consciousness, the one to which no one admits membership.

In 1948, the year in which *Farewell Happy Fields* was published, Hoult wrote to a friend that she was having trouble finding a publisher for her next novel. She persisted, producing another twelve books. Towards the end of her career reviews of her work became less favourable. The young Roy Foster acknowledged the quality of her writing but bemoaned a 'streak of extreme sentimentality'. What had passed for social realism between the wars seemed less gritty in the sixties and seventies. Norah Hoult was beginning to slip out of fashion.

Her fictional universe is not that of the Anglo-Irish Big House or the farmhouse kitchen; nor did her writing sit entirely comfortably within the British interwar canon of middle-class novels by middle-class women. Ironically, though, if her hyphenated identity made her hard to place in the canon, it is assisting in her recovery. Both New Island Books in Dublin and Persephone Books in London have reissued her work. Hoult herself was not concerned by issues of identity. To paraphrase Virginia Woolf, as a woman she had no country.

PART ONE

— ONE —

I

WHEN Adam Palmer went to say farewell to the Medical Officer-in-Chief of the asylum from which he had been discharged, he took with him a resolve which had grown through the year of his incarceration. This resolve was to dedicate his life to one purpose: the purpose of rebelling against the will of God, and destroying entirely that immortal soul which in his youth he had been at some pains to nurture.

Not as mighty Lucifer had fallen did he propose to fall. No, indeed! He had a better sense of perspective than that. No splendour of the angelic beings was his, but at least he had brought into the world some capacity for perceptive intelligence. Was not the Medical Superintendent saying as much at that very moment? Adam made the effort, for such was his excitement that it *was* an effort, to listen, and heard:

'... so in your case there is every prospect of success. You were a literary journalist. Well, I see no reason why you shouldn't resume your career. After all you needn't mention ...'

Dr. Maydew stopped with a wave of his hand. Adam said: 'You mean I needn't mention in what fashion my career was interrupted.'

He stopped, realising that there had been irony in his voice. And that was something he had rarely permitted

3

himself during his terrific daily struggle to convince
everyone, nurses and patients as well as doctors, that he
was as other men, better educated, more intelligent perhaps than the majority, since it was a rate-aided institution,
but like them docile, sheep-like, ready to share a little joke,
to enjoy a pipe, an hour in the sun, even, more lately, to
take part in the weekly dances and socials. His remark
had been the first conscious pin-hole he had made in that
cloak of gentleness and amiability which he had gradually
contrived with such care that he thought it would accom-
pany him henceforth almost as much a part of him as a
skin. So he looked quickly into Dr. Maydew's eyes to see
if he were translating his speech as token of bitterness. The
least shade of bitterness, he knew, was considered by him
and his like as dangerous. A bitter man, a man with a sense
of grievance, was very likely, they considered, to injure,
not merely himself, which was comparatively unimportant, but others. When fine words were swept aside the
asylum existed and had its being upon that social founda-
tion: to keep in prison, but without, Adam had thought
yearningly, the blessing of a cell of one's own, all who
might prove a source of danger, or even of mere social
inconvenience, to other people. Most of his companions,
he knew, had that sense of grievance, against their wives
or relatives, against the State, against the bosses, against
dark powers who were persecuting them; and would
talk or rave against the source of their trouble as they
conceived it. He alone, being more logical, and from his
childhood better instructed, bore no grudge against any
creature or institution, but against the First Cause, the
source of all creation. It was God, and God alone, who

was responsible for the degrading humiliation he, Adam Palmer, had endured, by being placed in that most appalling form of human segregation, the lunatic asylum as it existed in the nineteen-thirties.

But not one word had been allowed to escape of this knowledge, as elementary as A.B.C. to anyone who believed in God. If he had talked, he would have been filed off as a religious paranoiac, and that hurdle would have taken a long time to jump. He was thankful now for the instinct which had prompted him right from the very beginning to disclaim any particular religious beliefs. He had admitted, since his mother would probably have told them so, that he had been brought up a Catholic, but had told them firmly, and for that matter truthfully, he was not a practising Catholic, and desired no priestly administrations.

But now Dr. Maydew was speaking, and it was evident that his interpolation had been treated as the merest commonplace.

'Yes, I am sure you have it in you to do some good work, and perhaps you will send me any articles you may write. I shall be most interested. By the way your mother, Mrs. Palmer, wrote that she was expecting you home, and had sent you the money to cover your travelling expenses. That is correct?'

'Quite correct.'

'But she is not coming to meet you in London?'

'No. You see she is an elderly woman somewhat troubled with rheumatism, and she would find the two journeys over fatiguing.'

'You propose then to cross to Inishkill in the next day or two?'

'That is what I plan.'

'I wouldn't leave it too long, you know. The first few days in the outside world are naturally inclined to make you feel a little strange. You need quiet, but you also need society. You don't want to be alone.'

Oh, but how I want to be alone, cried out Adam's heart. But he answered with a nod: 'No. Quite.'

Dr. Maydew didn't seem quite satisfied. He was looking at Adam's papers again in a frowning way. After a few moments, restive ones for Adam, he said:

'I wish you had had visits from relatives or responsible friends. There was, of course, that man, Davies, who came once or twice. But they complained that he turned up, well, rather ...'

'An old journalistic colleague. Yes, he was very drunk when he came the second time,' said Adam smoothly. 'I told him not to bother to come again, as he kicked up rather a shindy.'

'And no one else has come. But you have an unmarried sister?'

'Yes, but she lives with my mother. And as for the other relatives, it's unlikely that they have been told. You see in the old-fashioned circles in which my mother moves, and they are very old-fashioned still in Inishkill, it is considered rather a disgrace to admit that you have a relative in an asylum.'

'But that is very wrong,' said Dr. Maydew warmly. 'How is it that they cannot see that a mental breakdown, especially when it is temporary as in your case, is a misfortune that might happen to anyone? And yet the very ones whom one might expect to co-operate, the educated middle class, are the ones—speaking generally, of course—who fail to visit their friends or relatives or consult us about them.'

Adam thoughtfully observed Dr. Maydew's large sallow-skinned face. The Kindly Dyspeptic he had christened him to himself long since, a well-meaning man, but prone to get irritated at the vagaries of a world which in so many cases failed to toe the lines he had laid down for its salvation. In his heart he replied to him with: 'It is very hard, my friend, for the respectable to enter the Kingdom of Heaven.' But this must be translated into a form more suitable for the Puritan intelligence. So he said gently:

'It is very hard, I suppose, for people of any status to get rid of the notion that insanity in their family reflects in some way on themselves, their earning capacities for instance. If it has happened to a brother, or even an aunt, might it not happen to them? It must be an unpleasant thought if one has gradually worked up to earning say a thousand a year, and is living in *Mon Repos*, Surbiton, or some such place, with son and daughter to educate, that, at any moment, one's memory might fail to function, or that the temptation to throw oneself out of an open window might prove irresistible.'

'Yes, yes,' said Dr. Maydew. 'But ...' he stopped, frowning down at his desk.

The 'Yes, yes,' because Dr. Maydew himself was of the *Mon Repos* class who played golf on Sundays, after a week of hard and exacting work. The 'But', because his study of psychiatry had convinced him that insanity was an illness due to certain specific psychoses or neuroses which with goodwill, patience and the co-operation of the patient could be cured, and were therefore in no different category from a duodenal ulcer. The pause, because Dr. Maydew was necessarily a creature of routine, and had no time to go into all that now! His gaze had gone to the clock, and Adam immediately stood up.

Dr. Maydew also stood up. 'Well, it's a very fascinating topic, and I hope we may be able to resume it on another occasion. I mean if you are in this neighbourhood at any time it would be a great pleasure if you'd drop in on me.'

'Certainly. I shall bear that in mind.'

'And in your case, I can take it, we have made it clear that it is a fool's trick, and a coward's trick, to jump out of any open window?'

Adam said slowly and with complete truthfulness: 'Yes, you have made that completely clear. I am very grateful to you.'

'That's fine.'

'I must thank you,' said Adam, now embarking upon his prepared farewell speech, 'for all your kindness to me. I was indeed fortunate to have fallen into such good hands, and I am sorry for all the trouble I must have given when I was not quite *compos mentis*, rather dreary in fact.'

'Not at all, not at all,' said Dr. Maydew warmly. Now he was experiencing one of those moments which he believed to be the happiest in life, when a patient of the asylum, cured and in his right mind, gratefully acknowledged his debt. Of course most of them, poor fellows, were not gentlemen, and therefore one could not expect from them the habits of a gentleman. But this fellow, Palmer, was different. 'You haven't given us any trouble to mention, and if it had been left entirely to me …' he paused, seeing that his warmth of heart had led him into an indiscretion.

'I quite understand. Dr. Canning has always given me the impression that he feared I might at any moment have a relapse. I confess I have rather wondered why.'

'Ah, well,' said Dr. Maydew vaguely, 'you must recognise that as an enthusiast, and, of course, quite a young man, Dr. Canning feels that … well, that still waters may run deep.'

'So he likes to go on fishing in them. Oh, I quite understand when you put it that way.'

'And after all, best to be on the safe side. I'm sure you don't regret this last six months, do you now?'

'Not at all. It has been most kind of you, really.'

'Good-bye then, and all the very best.'

'Good-bye, and once again, thank you very much.'

'And don't forget about sending me any articles you write.'

'I won't. Good-bye.'

It was over. The dismissed schoolboy had been given his last kindly word, and he was walking out of the Superintendent's house and along the path which led to the building where his own ward was. Now he had only to collect his bag and his mackintosh, and walk out of the place for good. But he still felt tense: when he put his hand to his forehead to push back a lock of hair which had fallen forward he found his skin was damp with perspiration. So I was more strung up even over the last words of the Maydew, he thought, than I had fancied. The poor decent man!

Now there was only Kenneth Cooke waiting to say good-bye: Cooke who had become sentimental about him these last few days, and had refused to go out with the others for exercise this mild spring morning on the plea that no one, even in an institution, could be hard-hearted enough to deprive him of the last sight of his friend, his best friend, his only friend. And there he was waiting, tall, dark, warm-skinned and handsome, and, of course, as usual, *molto simpatico,* for the more lush Italian phrase seemed to fit his personality.

'How did you get on?'

'All right.'

'What did he say?'

'Nothing really. At least that is what it amounted to. As do most conversations.'

'But he must have said *something.*'

'Oh, he wanted to read my future articles. It was just like leaving the dear old Alma Mater. Well, I must be off.'

'You've heaps of time, though you did stay longer than I had expected. Listen, I'm not going to stay here any longer than it takes to tell my wife to expect me. That's what I've decided.'

'Well, you can please yourself. You're one of the volunteers, not a conscript like myself.'

'I know. I must have been mad to agree to come here. That madness is over anyhow. And so you must come and stay with us very very soon. Promise.'

'I'm going home, you know, pretty soon.'

'But not yet, oh, not yet. Please!'

Adam glanced at the attendant waiting to see him off the premises. 'Well, we'll see. I must go.'

'Oh, just a moment. I feel in such a state that I shan't be able to walk with you to the gate. My heart, you know!'

'Bad luck! I'm sorry. You ought to lie down.'

'So I shall. But I'm so unhappy about your going. That's what has brought the terrible palpitations on.' Kenneth put his hand on his heart, winced, and then smiled bravely, as though through tears. 'We've been through so much together, and now I am the only sensitive and ... I'm not a snob, but you know what I mean ... well, I can't help being unhappy. So do promise.'

'Of course. Good-bye. I really must go.'

Taking up his bag Adam put out his other hand, half turned towards the door. But Kenneth wouldn't let go his hand.

'You haven't got me quite right, Adam, you know. You don't think I have brains as well as you. But I have. And I am going to prove it to you.'

'I'm sure you have.'

'Oh, now you're angry with me. Please don't be! I'm so unhappy about your going: it's making me ill. Of course I'm glad for your sake. But ...'

He must be interrupted: he'd talk for ever. 'I know. Good-bye now. I'll write, and send my address.'

'Oh, will you? Promise!'

'Of course. Cheerio.'

It was over. Kenneth was the sort of man who made you in reaction talk like a man who sold motor-cars. Had he really said *cheerio*? He had! But he had also slipped five shillings into the hand of the man who had locked the door behind him, and in that gesture he had regained his liberty as a free citizen. Now he was in sight of the main drive, and the only person he could see was the gardener, a mental defective, who was leaning on his twig broom, staring in front of him with that grin which never totally disappeared from his face. Avert his eyes; say good-bye to him in his heart. Now there was only the man at the lodge who would peer out at him suspiciously, and probably have to be informed once more that his name was on the discharged list, now and for evermore.

But a car had turned in, and was coming up towards him. Adam looked steadily down at the gravel as he walked on, but he felt a sick presentiment, which was verified when he sensed rather than heard that the driver was slowing up.

'Hello! Thought it might be you, Palmer! You're leaving to-day, of course?'

'Yes, I'm just off.' He nearly added: 'I looked for you to say good-bye,' but stopped himself. No need now for unnecessary lies.

'You're going to the station, I take it. I can give you a lift. Jump in.'

If he had only been through the lodge he might have said: 'Thanks but I prefer taking the bus.' As it was ... well, anyhow he had said 'thanks very much', and had got into the seat beside the driver.

'Sure, I'm not delaying you, because ...'

'No, it's all right. I've plenty of time before I'm due. Throw your case behind.'

He was taking him back to the asylum! Of course there was a reason for that. He couldn't turn till he got to the end of the drive. But a bad omen. It was another trifle to put down to the account of his Guardian Angel, who knew perfectly well that if ever he hated a man, it was this man, Dr. Edward Canning.

Canning backed and turned. As they went through the gate, Adam had a glimpse of Hunt, the lodge-keeper, looking out in surprise, and thinking presumably, oh, so that loonie, Palmer, is being taken for a ride. He had crossed the Rubicon, and not on his own two feet, but petrol-driven, speed destroying any real sensation, as it always destroyed any sensation. He turned for a last look at the high brick wall that bounded the asylum grounds. But Canning's profile interfered: he was a plump-faced, fair-skinned, spectacled man with thick light-brown hair, and that expression Adam knew so well of mingled good temper and intelligence. The salt of the Anglo-Saxon middle-class earth! But it was salt lacking in savour for the derisive Celt: too much good sense! A man who drank in moderation, but rarely got drunk; a modest man, too, no doubt, but one who would never fall on his knees crying in agony: God be merciful to me a sinner. Certain to be fond of his wife, and invariably courteous to women, who would find him attractive. But in his turn, could one imagine him overtaken by the desperation and degradation of lust? No, for out would jump the censor with his observation, not that it was wrong, but that it was such bloody waste of time, and so the yearning would trickle away with golf shots, cold baths, hard work and helping others 'less fortunate than himself'. As indeed he had most estimably made it his business in life to do.

As Adam's mind leaped along the well-worn tracks of finding justification for his dislike, he heard Canning say in his pleasant voice like one of the more mellow of the B.B.C. announcers: 'Well, I expect you're glad to be out of it all, Palmer?'

A question that didn't need an answer. By raising his eyebrows, and the shoulder adjacent to Canning, Adam hoped to make the effect of having been asked a banality. But unheeding, his eyes ahead on the road, the doctor continued: 'Let's see. You are going back to Inishkill right away, aren't you?'

'Probably.'

His tone would surely shut him up, and in another two minutes they would have turned off at the station approach. But the car was slackening: of course, a red light. Canning was looking at him directly now. 'By the way, you are quite all right for money, are you? I mean it's a nuisance to be short of small change if you're making a journey.'

'Oh, didn't you know? My mother very kindly sent me twenty pounds as she thought that I'd probably need a new suit besides my expenses crossing. I think she surmised that I would probably have gnawed the one I am wearing to ribbons.'

Canning said nothing. But he'd certainly heard, for he smiled faintly. So he was determined not to take offence, but remain kind and patient to the end! What he ought to have done was to have said in a whining voice: 'If you have a fiver to spare, Doctor, it would come in very handy.' He wouldn't have known how to take that.

The car shot forward. Canning said unexpectedly: 'If I were you, I'd marry. Find a nice sensible girl, and settle down.'

'A *sensible* girl. Of course. That is what I need, you think?'

Ah, at last he had drawn blood. The cheek beside him had flushed ever so slightly. But still it had flushed. The man had his share of sensitiveness. That was what, of course, made him dangerous.

'I merely meant that I think it's a good thing for most normal men to marry, and particularly the highly strung, and perhaps ultra-sensitive, as I think you'll agree you are.'

Answering back, was he? Adam said smoothly: 'Quite, quite. As a matter of fact, if it is of any interest to you, that is exactly what I intend to do: find a nice sensible girl, settle down and have children.'

'Splendid!' said Canning briefly. One finely-shaped long-fingered hand attracted Adam's attention as he indicated to traffic behind that he was turning: his hands, Adam told himself, were inherited and somewhat above his degree, forming no true index. That 'Splendid', for example. Canning always finished their interviews with clichés; his blue eyes might peer interestedly out above the old school tie, but they were fairly myopic.

Relaxed he saw the station just ahead. Then he heard Canning say in a low voice: 'And, by the way, I wouldn't, think too much about religion and theology. In the long run we can only do our best. We don't really *know*.'

Ah, so, thought Adam, sitting up, alert and angry as at an unexpected sting from a rapier. But no better retort came to him than his usual specific of mild agreement.

'No, indeed! As you say, we don't know.'

No, you don't know, his wounded mortified heart cried out. But I do. Blessed are those who have not heard, but who have done. Blessed are the ignorant and well meaning, for undoubtedly they will enter the Kingdom of Heaven. I am sure you will, my excellent enemy, receiving a special award as one who has laboured in the vineyard at the promptings of your own decency, or, as we should say, by the light of your natural grace.

But the car was coming to a stop, and his racing mind must steady itself. Mechanically he put his hand on what he thought was the door handle, but which was really the window lever, and tugged vainly.

'No, the other one, old chap,' said Canning. 'Here, let me.' He reached in front of Adam, gave a quick turn, and the door opened. Adam got out, and then attempted to reach for his bag. But Canning was before him: he had got out, he had set the bag down for him. At least he hadn't turned the engine off, so he wasn't coming, or was he, on to the platform?

'Well, I mustn't stop. I must get back to the daily round. But I do wish you the very best of luck. And though I know you don't like me, I wish you would try and feel that if at any time you want to let off steam about anything, and think that I might be the faintest use, well, drop a line, or phone or something. You know where to find me. Good-bye now.'

He was holding out his hand. Adam placed his own loosely and limply in it. 'Thank you so very much for the lift,' he said directing his gaze just past the glittering spectacles.

'Not a bit,' said Canning in a smiling way. He got back into the car, raising a hand in salute.

Adam nodded vaguely, and walked towards the booking office. But his ears were attentive to the beat of the engine. When he judged it safe he strolled casually back, and stood on the edge of the pavement. Yes, there was the blue car shooting fast ahead: he watched it broodingly out of sight.

Well, at least he had had the last word. Thank you, he had said, for the lift, disregarding Canning's kind little speech. Canning would understand that he hadn't thanked him for anything else. His 'I know you don't like me' had gone quite uncontradicted. Nor had he said 'good-bye'. He didn't wish God to be with Canning. Or did he? For after all God was now an enemy, as was Canning.

He went to the booking office, and bought a single third-class ticket for London. The clock on the platform informed him that he had a good twenty minutes to wait. If

Canning hadn't butted in the bus would have brought him with just five minutes or so to spare. He remembered how pleased he had been to find that the bus fitted in so well with the time of the train's departure.

Canning had spoilt all that, as he had spoilt things before. He had spoilt the savour of these first moments of freedom. Why? Adam considered as he lit another cigarette. Because, of course, the swine had got in that bit about religion, proving that he, Adam Palmer, hadn't diddled him quite as completely as he had thought to do. These psychiatrists had something: they had their book of words. A man had only to pronounce the name of God, not even with reverence, but with some slight gradation of tone as the heart or mind paused before the immensities involved, and the eyes behind their spectacles glinted with suspicion. At some of the word games Canning had tried to make him play at the beginning, before he had refused to catch those particular balls, he must have given some reaction.

Well, it didn't matter now. He needn't think about Canning any more. Other people were coming on to the platform, and he wanted to watch their eyes, to see if their casual regard of himself quickened to interest. Ex-convict, or ex-madman, must share the same thought. Do we give ourselves away at first sight? But the elderly husband and wife evidently going up to Town on some shopping expedition were certainly concerned only with themselves. Would the train be punctual? Would they get a nice lunch? Would they get tired?

He turned to stare back at two smartly-dressed young women whose glance upon him he had felt. No, their regard had dismissed him immediately as of no interest: too old and too shabby. Nor was the business man with the black leather bag interested either in him, or in anybody else. A little tired, a little worried about something or other, his gaze was turned inward, planning, speculating.... The two matrons with shopping baskets had looked towards him twice, but with them he decided it was because they liked to place people, and he was not perhaps so easy to place sitting there smoking, with his shabby overcoat and wide-brimmed black hat. They wanted to know where he had come from and where he was going. That was all.

He heard the click indicating that the train had been signalled. Picking up his bag, he moved farther up the platform away from the other passengers, and there he waited straining his eyes till he saw the first plume of smoke from the advancing engine.

II

He knew exactly what he was going to do when he got to Victoria. He must turn to the right, after he left the station, and walk up Wilton Road, turning right again into that dreary region known as Pimlico. He had never lodged there before, but now its very dreariness, the monotony of its squares and rows of porticoed houses, would be soothing to his over-taxed nerves. You don't look for a nice place, a bright place, a fashionable place when you come out of prison; you look for a dull unobtrusive hiding place, as the fox escaped from its pursuers goes to ground.

But what he had not anticipated was the effect of being suddenly surrounded by so many people. They confused his head and made his heart beat more rapidly. So that outside the station he paused to collect his bearings, and so attracted the attention of a man selling flowers from a barrow.

'Daffodils, sir? All fresh this morning!'

'No. Thank you very much,' said Adam, and walked quickly on, his cheek flushing, because he felt the man had given him a sharp look. He had made a blunder of some sort. Of course there was no necessity for him to have spoken at all. He ought just to have shaken his head. He'd have to pick up the unwritten rules of the outside world all over again. What one had to remember was that really no one was watching, no one cared about you so long as you appeared to behave like anybody else. No one wanted to notice you. It was the reversal of life in the asylum when one was being observed—or might be—all the time; when you therefore must dissociate yourself from the other inmates, and make it clear that you were not like them: that you didn't laugh too long and on a high-pitched note; that you had no odd sexual inclinations; that you had no grievance and didn't cry or wave your arms or refuse to answer intelligibly when you were spoken to. Briefly, you had to insist all the time that you were normal, and just like the doctors or the male nurses with their interests, so far as you could adapt yourself to such interests. But he mustn't try and convince people any longer because, of course, if he did, they would begin to suspect that there was something wrong.

He looked anxiously at the faces that passed him, and found reassurance. For none looked back. Except a thin girl with a white face and yellow hair under an extraordinary, as it seemed to him, hat. She looked back all right, and her footsteps slackened, so that he increased the pace of his own. He felt his heart beating while he assured himself with some contempt that he needed reassurance on the obvious. She was a prostitute, of course. You always encountered them around the big railway stations.

He looked again at other faces, and this time he was really reassured by the blankness which met him. It was all right. Oh, the blessed anonymity of London which he had forgotten! It was drink to a parched man, and he drew from it refreshment.

At Gillingham Street he turned, his eyes attracted by the sight of a square ahead. Of course it was Eccleston Square, and he might go in there and rest a few moments on a bench. There was an hotel, and he half paused. But, no, it was too grand a place for him, too full of people and waiters, and commissionaires and reception clerks, even if he hadn't decided to make his money stretch a while, and allow him a respite in London before returning to his mother.

There was surprisingly no bench in the gloomy square. As he walked slowly, puzzled, some boys broke through the bushes in front of him with loud shouts of triumph at having avoided the permitted way of entry, and forced the unpermitted. Their cries, the feeling that he was an object of derisive attention from them even if it were merely because he represented the defeated authority of the grown-up world, brought back his self-consciousness. He seemed to feel Canning's interested eye upon him, almost he heard him remark: 'You see, as soon as he arrives in London, and still carrying a heavy suitcase, he starts to prowl round and round a London square. Is that a sign of normality?'

As if goaded by the prick of a whip, he left the square hurriedly, and turned northwards, looking sharply at every house he passed to see if there was a sign advertising a vacancy in furnished rooms. But when he did see one such sign, he passed on, because he saw an old woman observing him from behind a curtain on the ground floor. It was really more difficult than he had imagined, this business of walking up to strange people and asking them if he could come into their house. He ought to have had a double whisky at the buffet at Victoria Station. Why not look for a pub? But Canning stopped that, too. Canning didn't say anything this time: he just observed him swallowing his whisky and shook his head.

Ah, here at the corner was a small newsagent's shop, and at one side of the door was a glass case containing cards. Now recollection came to his aid, and he stopped to read those headed: 'Room to Let' or 'Flat to Let'. One or two sounded promising, and setting down his bag, he searched for a pencil. But he hadn't got one. Quite simple: go into the shop and buy one.

'Yes?'

Why was the man looking at him and then at his bag so suspiciously?

'I want a pencil.'

'Certainly.'

'Haven't you a sharpened one?'

'No, sorry.'

There was a pause. He might have the decency to offer to sharpen it. No doubt he expected that Adam would have a knife of some sort. He didn't know that inmates of asylums were not allowed pocket knives. While the words asking if the pencil could be sharpened for him hovered on his lips, he perceived that the man's attention had left him, going to a woman behind.

'Good morning, Mrs. Watts.'

'Good morning, Mr. Peaker. And how are you to-day?'

To hell with them! Adam shook his head, mumbled something, and walked out of the shop. Outside the case, he paused to memorise two numbers, and found the first address fairly easily since he perceived the name of the road just ahead of him.

A stout grey-haired woman in a blue apron opened the door. Adam raised a hand to his hat.

'Good morning.'

'Morning,' she muttered, and she seemed suspicious, too. 'You advertised a furnished room with a gas-fire and ring at fifteen shillings?'

'Oh. Well, I did. But it's gone.'

'Oh, I see.'

'Where did you 'ear abaht it?'

'You have a card in the shop over there.'

'Oh, you mean Peaker. 'Asn't 'e taken it out? I told 'im the room 'ad gone. Last time I was in, I told 'im.'

'I'm sorry to have bothered you.'

'Oh, it's all right. But if you're passing, you might tell 'im, will you? I mean it's not fair wasting people's time, is it?'

'Quite. You don't happen to know of anywhere, do you?'

'Sorry, I don't. Not that I could recommend, that is.'

'Thank you. Good morning.'

'Good morning.'

The door closed almost before he had turned. But somehow he felt his spirits rising slightly, as when one recognises the name of a tune one had long forgotten. Of course, people were like this, suspicious and antagonistic when they first saw you. Some people inspired confidence from their very looks, but he did not belong to that happy breed. Nevertheless he had learnt that the suspicion of the English was more apparent than real. You merely had to counter it with apparent open-heartedness.

You raised your hat to some women; others you called, 'dear'. You said: 'Sorry to bother you,' or 'Could you tell me, mate?' Then the blank stare disappeared, and they did, yes, on the whole, they did what they could to help you, because they had placed you, and understood your request was, as it had to be, of course, a reasonable one. That woman wasn't really cross. She was just one of the more self-centred ones.

But now he couldn't remember the name of the other address. Was it 56, Gloucester Street, or was it 57? He had to go back to the newsagent to confirm. And by this time, his bag was beginning to weigh very heavily. He heard a clock strike twice. That must be half-past twelve, and of course he hadn't had anything to eat for some time.

If he didn't click at this address, he thought, when he'd found it, he'd go and get some lunch. He had noticed a café in Warwick Street. There was no bell on the door of the second house, so he knocked in a peremptory way which satisfied his sense of now being able to cope with affairs.

A schoolgirl answered the knock. She could not have been taken for anything else with her stout black-stock-inged legs, her navy gym tunic and white blouse, and her spectacles. You imagined her immediately equipped with exercise books under her arm or with hockey stick.

The grave glance she turned upon him, a glance as free from suspicion as it was from coyness, afforded Adam, more tense than he knew, immediate relief.

'You advertised a bed-sitting-room, I think?'

To his disappointment she said: 'I'll tell mother,' and then remembering her manners: 'Will you come in?'

He stood on the red-and-green patterned linoleum in the hall awaiting her return from basement regions. The floor was highly polished, as was the old-fashioned hall rack. And there was a painted container for umbrellas. A gloomy hall but a clean one belonging, he decided, to an old-fashioned lower-middle-class household. If they would only have him, how glad he would be to stay here in the proximity of that stout schoolgirl, and make the place his clearing station.

He heard steps on the stairs, and braced himself. A fat short sallow-skinned woman in a brown dress came towards him. She looked good-natured, even naturally a smiling woman, but over this good nature she wore the circumspect veil which her upbringing and experience of life had taught her to draw.

'Good morning! You were requiring a room?'

'Yes.' He saw that her gaze had gone to his suitcase, so he added: 'I've only just arrived in London from the country, and I want to get fixed up.'

'I see. You want it straight off. Well, it's ready. But how long would you be wanting it for?'

'It's difficult to say. For some days.'

'Oh! Only a few days? You see I really wanted a permanent. The last young lady I had stayed for six years, and another young lady I have now is going on for three years.'

Lives plodded steadily on in this house, and he was merely a transient not worthy to join the procession. He hastily improvised:

'It would probably be at least a month. My plans are rather unsettled. You see I've been ill. I had an accident and have only just come out of a convalescent home. I am supposed to rest for a while.' He smiled depreciatingly, hoping to appeal to her maternal sense. She remained considering.

'You're not in a job then?'

'Not yet.' His mind ran about seeking to clutch a job that would appeal to her, and he remembered the school-girl. 'I'm a schoolmaster actually.'

He could feel that she was impressed. After a moment she said: 'Well, perhaps you would like to see the room. It mightn't suit you.'

The room on the second floor was fairly large and very clean. In his perturbation he took little in except the existence of the brass bedstead which commanded the scene. And there was an arm-chair. Also a gas-fire and ring. What more did anyone want?

'Very nice, very nice indeed.'

'The bathroom is on the first floor.'

'I see.'

'There's a shilling-in-the-slot meter. Here.'

'Oh, yes.'

A pause came. Adam remembered the necessary question: 'And how much would it be?'

She had thought that over. She answered immediately: 'Well, it's usually a pound, but, as you're not a permanent, I should have to make it twenty-five shillings.'

He nodded. She asked: 'Would that be all right?'

'Quite all right.'

Apparently his alacrity had not given a favourable impression, for she still stood in thought, and he regarded her anxiously. She had, he decided, probably been brought up in a Dissenting household. Or for that matter he had often caught sight of such plain, but yet attractive because they looked both kind and sensible, faces underneath the bonnet of the Salvation Army. In either case she would have learnt, and might still believe in, the existence of Hell. Did her nostrils then detect a whiff of brimstone about him? Did her spiritual perceptions realise, as it might be far off, that one who had said:'*I will not serve*' had entered her house.

She moved. She said: 'Well, then, if you think it will suit you?'

'Indeed it's just what I want. I have to be quiet for a little while, you see.'

'Oh, it's a very quiet house. I don't think you'll be disturbed. There's just one young lady on this floor, and she's out all day. We have the first floor. I don't take more than two extra people.'

He bowed his head in pleased understanding. 'Shall I give you the week's rent now?'

'If it's convenient. Thank you. I'll send Mary up with the receipt. Could I have your name?'

'Palmer. Adam Palmer.'

'I'm Mrs. Hammond. Let me see. You want a towel, don't you? And you must let me know if you're not warm enough. There are three blankets on the bed, and though it's old- fashioned, I mean a lot of people must have divans these days, mustn't they, it's a comfortable mattress.'

'I'm sure I shall be quite all right.'

But she lingered. It was as if, with his money in her hand, she felt she must be sure that her part of the bargain was accomplished.

'I suppose you haven't any crockery. I can lend you a kettle, and a tea-pot and a cup and saucer if you like.'

'Oh, I can buy them. But thank you. It's very …'

'There's no necessity to buy. I am a bit short of bread, but …'

'Oh, I shall be going out to get food, and to buy a few things.'

'Very well then.'

She went, and after a moment Adam sat down in the chair. He was waiting for Mary to come. She came in a very few moments, carrying a tray with crockery, while over her arm was a towel.

'Mother said to tell you that the water in the bath-room is quite hot, and it's on the floor below, next their front bedroom.'

'Thank you very much.'

'And this is your receipt.'

She indicated a piece of paper on the tray.

'Oh, yes. Thank you.'

Now she went over to the wash-stand and hung the towel on its rail. As she walked past him to the door, he looked at her hoping to receive a smile, but she went by him gravely without looking in his direction.

But she came out of a room when he went down to the hall on his way to get some lunch.

'Mother said you'd want this.'

She had handed him a key. He had been given a key of his own. His mind paused on the thought, and hugged it while he ate some poor food in a cheap café in Warwick Street. Further than that all capacity for thought had disap-peared. The hunted fox had found cover, and all he wanted was to get back to it. He could hardly bear to delay in order to buy a loaf of bread, some butter, a pint of milk and a quarter-pound of tea. The moments waiting to be served in the little shops were almost more than his now overpowering feeling of exhaustion could stand.

At last he was back without meeting anyone. At last he could turn a key in a lock, and taking off his boots, and removing the white counterpane, fling himself on the bed in a room to which he had the sole right. Very soon he was fast asleep.

— TWO —

I

THE next few days were spent chiefly in bed. It was a luxury to doze through the afternoons, to awake, and savour his isolation. There was no one in the next bed; there was no next bed. He was no longer hemmed in; he need no longer exercise eternal vigilance, for the reason that no one was watching him. He need no longer speak, for there was no one to speak to, except the woman who came in to clean in the mornings, and who made his bed and dusted the room. She generally came up the stairs at about ten-thirty, and went to the other lodger's room first, so if he break-fasted about nine he could be out of the way by the time she knocked at his door. He would loiter down towards Victoria Station, gazing at the contraceptive shops on the way, find his way to the Public Library, occasionally treat himself to a glass of beer in a dirty public-house, and then do his shopping on the way home. It was a beautiful life, he thought, a life that lacked only one thing for its full appre-ciation, and that was an increase of physical energy. As it was, his very bones ached with the tiredness that now like a stream that had been long dammed up seeped through his whole being.

Nevertheless the exterior pattern of the household in which he found himself gradually became plain, and, as far as he thought at all during those days of much needed respite, his fancy played about it. Mr. and Mrs. Hammond, their daughter Mary and her younger brother Donald, occupied the ground floor and the first floor; also Donald slept in one of the two attics, and came pounding up the stairs every evening about eight. There were the two bedrooms, or bed-sitting-rooms, on the second floor, and these were, of course, occupied by himself and the other lodger, whose name was Miss Bartlett. It was clear that Mrs. Hammond was no professional landlady, but merely let rooms in her house. She was not dependent for her livelihood on 'letting'; her husband had an upholsterer's and furniture repair business, and the house, Adam decided, was probably their own. It was well furnished in the late Victorian fashion of heavy mahogany, antimacassars, sofas, table runners, and thick dark curtains which shrouded the windows. The effect was of solidity and cloistered stuffiness. The household was in fact one of the few survivals in Pimlico of an earlier more rooted way of life than was represented by the drab shelters for transients and near slums which lay all about it. Mrs. Hammond shouting up the stairs: 'Donald, you'll be late for Sunday school,' put the finishing touch to Adam's satisfaction. So the children went to Sunday school! Here at least Queen Victoria was still on the throne, and here reigned that respect for standards which provided the sense of security of which he felt in need. His Guardian Angel must have guided him here anxious to provide him with a healing setting. And for the moment, so spoke Adam back to his Guardian Angel, I will take what is given. *For the moment!*

It took him longer to place the other lodger. She was out all day but in her room most evenings, except on Saturday, when a girl friend sometimes came to tea, and later they would go out together. But he felt they were going on no expedition squired by boy friends. No, their destination was probably the pit or gallery of a theatre which showed one of the more thoughtful attractions. And afterwards, over a coffee at a Corner House, they would discuss what they had seen, letting their senses be pleasantly stimulated but not stirred by roving glances, by the voluptuous strains of the orchestra.

For after he had caught a glimpse of Miss Bartlett coming out of the bathroom as he descended the stairs, had heard the uneasy 'Good evening' she gave him with averted eyes, his imagination started to play about her. A quiet pale girl, unremarkably dressed, who was at least no man-hunter. 'Our Miss Bartlett has returned,' he would whisper to himself, as gazing out from his bed at the pale spring twilight he heard her soft quick step on the stair, and then the opening and closing of her door. Now she would be starting to make her evening meal; then she would settle down to a book, or to darning stockings. After he had made himself some supper, having added a frying-pan to his equipment, he would go back with relief to his blessed bed, and there as the moments ticked on he would again imagine what Miss Bartlett's night thoughts were as she lay on the other side of the thick wall. Her dreams, he decided, would be romantic rather than practical. She would think of someone who was gentle and understanding, not too young, and his hand smoothed his own greying hair, because Miss Bartlett who worked so hard for her living would have a paternal complex, and desire someone who would look after her. And does she wonder what I am really like, as I wonder what she is really like? Only with this difference that as regards this world I want very little but a slice of bread thinly covered with butter, and she expects quite a lot, since she is young.

Then one morning he awoke to find a letter had been slipped under his door, the first he had received since he had been in the house. It bore the Inishkill postmark and was, of course, an answer from his mother to a brief note he had written three days ago. Feeling unreasonably irritated because his seclusion from the outside world had been disturbed, he opened it. It read:

'MY DEAR SON,

'I received your letter, but am sorry to hear you have a cold, and have decided to stay on a while in London. You will surely be much more comfortable here than in a lodging, and can have a good rest when you come. Maureen has made your room look very nice, and it is all ready. As I have told everyone that you are coming back after an illness which has made it impossible for you to continue your work at present, it will look odd your not arriving. Also I feel responsible about you to the Medical Superintendent who wrote so nicely, and said you were coming home at once, and would be quite all right with rest and company. He seemed to expect some relative to come over, but you know that in my state of health I cannot travel, and Maureen couldn't get away from her job.

'So please let me have a definite date from you as to when we may expect you. I hope you have got a new suit as it would be a pity if the money I sent you for that purpose was just wasted on your board and lodging. Especially as you can be so much more comfortable at home. I am well enough, but the rheumatism is very painful at times. Maureen has had a cold. She sends you her love. And I send mine with the hope that I may see you very soon now.

'From your loving mother.'

Frowningly Adam pushed the letter away, thought for a moment, and then re-read it more slowly. Then he lay back in bed, hands behind his head, his mind setting to work on its favourite employment of dissection. Not one loving phrase. She wanted him back merely because she thought it would look odd to the neighbours if he didn't come. For all her secrecy, there had probably been rumours, half suspicions, which, if he didn't come, would revive. She had prepared his way for him, and he must walk on it.

A woman, of course, who had no ease with the pen. She couldn't even chatter as did other middle-class matrons, putting up the appearance of warmth. But she didn't try. This was the woman who had immediately urged the lunatic asylum for her only son, without one attempt to harbour him herself. Although her religion taught her, and she professed to be a good Catholic, that one of the temporal works of mercy was to harbour the harbourless.

But his dissection was not logical. It was merely making him angry. Long ago he had accepted his mother with her limitations, and he might have anticipated such a letter. It was God who had sent him to the asylum, not his mother. To cry out against her, to cry for the fatted calf that some mothers might have killed for the Prodigal Son returning from Bedlam, was to cry for the moon. What had gone amiss with him that he was so illogically hurt?

What had gone wrong with him, he decided, after he had been refreshed by his morning tea, was that he had relinquished himself to the drifting tide too easily, too happily. He had been in this place some ten days, had spent approximately four pounds of his twenty pounds, and had committed no little sins, not even of thought. Would the Little Flower, Saint Thérèse, proceeding painfully on her upward ascent, have let ten days go by without sanctifying any of them by some act of grace, some aspiration towards holiness. No, she would not!

And it was no real excuse to apologise to his new master, the Devil, and say: 'You see, I've been very tired!' The Little Flower had also been very tired. It took half an hour for her numb hands to undress herself when she returned to her cell at night. But in spite of all her physical sufferings she went on, she went on and up with her smiling face lifted to God.

He lit another cigarette. What fools they were who had said that the descent to hell was easy! Hard indeed to mount upwards. But equally hard to go down for poor human nature which had thus been impaled in the dilemma of its own lukewarmness and desire for short cuts for two thousand years, when One had come who had told them plainly that there was only one way, and had added in His prescience that there were few that found it, for it was strait.

Yes: the path went down, and the path went up, but there were long tracts in which it was difficult to observe whether would-be-good was going up, or hardened sinner going down. It was no light task this, to follow the Little Way of Saint Thérèse in the reverse direction, follow it as steadily as she had followed the steep ascent.

He lit another cigarette. How much easier, he thought, because his soul had sighed at that infinitely wearying prospect which had opened, how much easier if he could reach his goal at one stroke, say, by killing the young girl who had opened the door of this harbour to him. Kill Mary Hammond, who was surely destined to lead a worthy if apparently unspectacular life. He could go into her little bedroom one night, and suffocate her with a pillow. Then the police, prison, the trial... but, by Heaven, when they learnt that he had just come out of a lunatic asylum, and Canning no doubt would be kind enough to give evidence on his behalf, he would be reprieved from the hangman, and sent most probably to Broadmoor.

No, the quick stroke, the kill, the mortal sin, was not for him! Though the matter was grave, though he, the murderer, had a most clear knowledge of the guilt of that action, and there was full consent of the will, it was not for him. In the first place he knew it was impracticable, for a man like himself, who hesitated to kill even a threatening wasp, could not at such short notice undertake to dispose effectively of a healthy girl, aged about fourteen. In the second place, he could not be sure that his soul would not betray him by making some act of repentance, feeling sorrow, perhaps when the mother screamed out in her first agony. And if so, there would be no way out from the infinite mercy of God, who would receive back from injured society the soul of cold-blooded murderer, only to proceed with its purification. The souls in Purgatory, so the nuns had told him, so the Church taught, could do no good for themselves; they were dependent on the prayers of the living. But neither could they work ill any more, and there would be those, if not his mother, certainly his sister Maureen, who would pray for him.

The damnation of his soul would then be jeopardised by any large deed, such as murder. There remained the Little Way, in which one took the hours as they came, marring them as opportunity allowed. Step by step to go plodding down to hell, never to allow one's determination to reach the goal to be weakened by slackness, as the saints had never allowed their determination to reach the Beatific Vision to be weakened by slackness. It was no easy thing, this he had set himself, to pit his own will against the infinite love of God, and also the infinite patience of God.

A knock at the door interrupted his depressing thoughts. He drew a deep breath before he said: 'Come in.'

It was Mrs. Padgham, with dust-pan and brush. 'Oh, you are in, sir! If you was out I thought I'd do your room first this morning because the young lady is in bed poorly.'

'It's all right. Come in. I'm just going out. I didn't know it was as late as that.' He got up quickly. There were his shoes to find, his shoes to put on. As he sought for something to say, his mind recollected her words.

'So the young lady's ill, is she? I'm sorry.'

'Got flu by the looks of her,' said Mrs. Padgham, proceeding to strip the bed. 'Said that when she went down to telephone the office she felt quite giddy like. So it's best for 'er to stay in bed, isn't it, sir?'

'Much the best.' Adam had sat down to unlace his shoes, and was struggling with a knot.

'You don't look very well yourself, come to that. Mrs. 'ammond told me as 'ow you'd been ill before you come here.' 'Yes, I was. But I'm much better now, thank you.'

'Well, you do look better than what you did. Your new gentleman, I says to her when I first see you, 'e looks a proper ghost, 'e does.'

Adam forced himself to smile back at the big not unhandsome rosy-cheeked woman who was regarding him with frank speculation. Of course all this time she must have been full of curiosity about him, and his avoidance of her had only whetted that curiosity. He ought to have told her something about himself.

'What was it you suffered from, sir? Somethink serious?' He spoke at random. 'A kind of spinal trouble. I had a nasty fall on my back.'

'Your spine!' Mrs. Padgham gazed at him with intense perplexity, waiting for more. 'Your back looks straight enough now, but …

'Oh, yes, I'm much better now. It was just a weakness. I had to lie up, you see.' He had succeeded in untying the knot, and in a minute he'd be able to go. 'I was in a convalescent home.'

'How did you get your fall? Was you run over?'

Too dramatic! He'd have to invent a long story. 'No, I just slipped on some stairs.'

'Fancy!' She was gazing at him, expecting more. But Adam took up his hat, smiled at her, and went through the door.

Was it his mother's letter? Or was it the grim turn his thoughts had taken, or was it Mrs. Padgham's curiosity and desire for a chat that had made him for once observant as he strolled along? A man and a woman came towards him, attracting his attention by the earnestness with which they were talking. His arm was in hers; she was looking at him, vivid sympathy on her face. Listening, listening to a recital of some wrong done him, though the only words Adam overheard were: 'I wasn't going to take that, of course, so...'

Adam pondered on women. It was no wonder after all that men sought them out. Women with their extraordinary lack of critical standards, particularly where their affections were involved. That applied, of course, also to men. He of all people ought to know that. But men were driven by their lust, and lust passed. But women, amoral and instinctive, could be such a perpetual cushion for a man. They interposed their acquiescence as a cushion between him and the harsher judgments of their contacts in daily life. Home to the little woman who said: 'What a shame, dear!' And: 'How clever of you, dear!' Such a cushion would be very useful for him to take back to Inishkill with him. Of course he had thought that he would find such a girl at home. But Inishkill women were a sharper-angled breed. Now he searched women's faces with interest. At every girl, who he felt was a nice girl, a sensible girl, he looked eagerly. And from every painted face, from every young head held high in the disdain of youth and prettiness or in imitation of a film star, he turned impatiently.

Still bold, still in experimental mood he made his way to the Park, and sat down on a tuppenny green seat, where he continued to divide girls and women into the sheep and the goats. But the sheep, the nice girls, he soon found, were going to be difficult of achievement. Those who experienced his regard looked away quickly one girl, the girl in fact who had drawn him to choose that particular seat, rose and went away, as if she were frightened when he cast a third glance in her direction. And well may she flee, thought Adam defensively. For sooner or later it is the fate of her like to be exploited by some man who takes more than he gives, who acts the flaunting peacock or the crowing bullying cock of the walk. With downcast eyes and hurrying steps they seek to avoid their fate. But nevertheless it is the bold meaning glance that stirs the pulses of the timid, the cunning who make the shy their prey.

He began to feel cold, as well as snubbed. Well, he thought, looking at his watch and deciding to move, there was always our Miss Bartlett whose acquaintance at least it might be amusing to make. Miss Bartlett has flu! So next morning, he might allow himself to knock on her door and ask her if he could get her anything, bread or what not. In fact that very evening he might make a beginning by slipping the evening paper under her door. And, failing Miss Bartlett, there was Miss Bartlett's friend, who also looked a nice girl, though perhaps the more common-sensical kind.

II

'Of course,' said Kathleen Bartlett, 'I don't believe in God.'

She looked across at him, hopefully alert, and then took a puff at her cigarette, which she smoked self-consciously as do women with whom the habit is not automatic. As he made no immediate reply, she felt less confident, and went on: 'I mean the Orthodox God.'

'And what is your idea of the orthodox God?'

'Oh, you know. I mean …' she hesitated a moment before the long word that was coming, and then plunged, 'the anthropomorphic God, who rewards and punishes, and who, they tell you when you are little, is always watching.'

'Oh, so you did receive some religious instruction when you were a child?'

'Yes, of course. Scripture lessons at school, and sometimes pi-talks from the headmistress. When I was fourteen or fifteen I was really quite religious for a while, and loved listening to the organ in church, and looking at the stained-glass windows, and so on. The beginning of adolescence, I suppose.'

She laughed on a rather mirthless note. Adam tried to rouse himself, perceiving that his non-committal attitude was making her self-conscious. He had been at some pains to draw her out about her childhood. It was quite interesting to hear about the villa by the sea, the mother of whom she was so fond who had died, and then being sent to boarding school. Her father was the managing clerk in a solicitor's office, so she would qualify as 'middle class' he was thinking, when she unexpectedly brought up the subject of religion, which, as interpreted by her, was not likely to be at all interesting.

'I suppose it was,' he said kindly.

'You don't believe in God, do you?'

'Yes.'

He had thought his tone was light enough, but though he smiled at her, her face remained grave.

'Not a … a personal God?'

'Yes, I'm afraid I do. You'll have to forgive me!'

'But you don't belong to any of the set religions. I mean you're not a Christian?'

He blew smoke out through his nostrils before he answered: 'You see, I was brought up a Catholic.'

'A Roman Catholic?'

He nodded.

'Oh. Of course you were born in Inishkill, I'd forgotten. But you don't believe in all the things they believe in, do you?' He answered her truthfully, since in any case she wouldn't be very interested. 'With one reservation. The Church teaches that the soul is indestructible. I am of the opinion that just as by the grace of God we can make our soul, so we can also possibly destroy it entirely. Browning's, you remember, *"the soul doubtless is immortal where a soul can be discerned."*'

She pondered on this for a moment, and then returned to securer waters. 'But you don't believe in all the other things?'

'What things?'

'That a priest can forgive you your sins, and that everybody who isn't a Catholic goes to hell?'

'You've got it wrong. A priest has been given by the words of our Lord authority to forgive sins, but there must be true contrition, satisfaction, and the desire for amendment. As to hell, that is really reserved for the Faithful, since Catholics believe that for the most part those who are not Catholics are in a state of invincible ignorance and will not therefore be damned.'

'But ... I say, what superiority! I was going to say blasted superiority.'

He smiled. Kathleen was attractive again now, forgetting her cigarette, forgetting her self-consciousness, leaning forward eagerly, her brown eyes bright, prepared to embark on what the young believed was a Serious Discussion. It would be quite pleasant to kiss her, to watch the blood penetrating those pale cheeks.

'You are not a practising Roman Catholic, are you?'

'No.'

41

'I thought not.'

'Why?'

'Well, the two Sundays you've been here, you didn't go to Church, and R. C.s have to, haven't they? Like me you didn't get up till late. I wondered the first Sunday if you knew about the char not coming in on Sundays, so that we make our own beds.' She stopped suddenly, realising that she had betrayed an interest in his movements, and he admired the profile presented, as she turned her head away. Really the girl was much more attractive than he had first thought. If she used a little more make-up …

'You don't say anything.'

'What is there to say? I was feeling flattered that you did spare a thought for the strange lodger. No, I am not a practising Catholic.'

'But you do believe that there is a personal God?'

'Yes.'

'But why? What proof is there?'

'Well, there are the five proofs as given by St. Thomas Aquinas. But don't let's bother to discuss them.'

'Why not? I'd like to. I'm not such a fool as you think me.'

'I don't think you're a fool at all. I think you're a very charming girl.'

He watched while she lowered her eyes. And yes, he had made her flush. Good! He must have said it convincingly. These were the waters in which he wished to fish. It was high time he kissed her.

As he made a movement towards her, she drew back, and said, looking him straight in the eyes. 'I wonder if you mean that.'

'Of course I mean it.'

'Do you know what I think about you, that you are a mystery.'

'In what way?'

'Well, you make me tell you all about myself, the dull story of my conventional upbringing, of mother dying—I mean that's not very interesting to *you*—and daddy marrying again, and my leaving Eastsea, and getting transferred to the Civil Service here. And becoming just another of those girls, not so much of a girl either, since I am twenty-seven, who live in bed-sitting-rooms, and cook on a gas-ring. It's pretty tedious, isn't it?'

'No, it's not.'

'And you don't tell me anything about yourself. Mrs. Hammond told me that you were a school teacher, but then in Kew Gardens you laughed when I said that, and told me you had only said it because it was the first thing that came into your head. If you are a writer, why didn't you say so?'

'Just a slip of the tongue. Besides I'm not a writer any more. One has to be something for these people.'

'So that's why I think you are a mystery. Why, I don't ...' she paused, looking down. He realised she had been going to say 'I don't know if you are married,' and said: 'I'm not married, if that's what you were going to say.'

Looking up she was about to disavow, but, as she caught his amused eye, laughed, and said instead: 'It is rather interesting to know that about people. As a matter of fact I certainly thought you were.'

'Why? Because I have that harassed married look. Besides being middle-aged. I'm nearly forty.'

'No,' she said doubtfully. And then very quietly: 'I do think that you look as if you'd been through an awful lot.'

So there was the cue, he thought, sitting back and lighting another cigarette. She was one of those sympathetic girls, and when he had told her his sad sad story she'd be still more sympathetic. And pity begat love, and she might agree to marry him.

Which would be quite a good idea. She was really a very nice girl. And if the prospect of marriage with her, or with anyone at all, made his heart desolate with the long long prospect of boredom, then that boredom was due to an atrophy of the will. He must take up his bed and walk. He must in fact strengthen his will to serve his new master. But if he looked squarely down the long and grey prospect ahead of him, he couldn't do anything at all. *One step enough for me!*

'Do you mind my saying that?'

'Not at all. You're very sweet. The fact is, well, I've been ill.'

'I know. But is that only what makes you look so unhappy? You looked so unhappy just now.'

'Did I? I didn't know I did.'

He heard the reserve in his tone and, as he saw her turn away, rebuked himself for it. But damn it all, there was something indecent at the alacrity with which women with hearts rushed to put them at the mercy of the butcher. They loved sob stories, doted on them.

'I expect it was just that you were sleepy. I know I am.'

She was getting up, she was hurt, and she had pride. Good girl!

'Please don't go yet. Are you cold? Let me feel your hand.'

As she sat back, still unsure, he leaned over and took her hand. Then he began to stroke it gently. It was really quite a pretty hand, he thought. And the skin was soft to his touch. 'You are cold, poor child. Why don't we light the fire?'

'I'll do it.' She rose, withdrawing her hand. 'Have you a match?'

He produced a box, and taking it from him her fingers avoided his touch. He commented to himself as the fire popped into existence, so she isn't quite ready; a modest withdrawing girl. That is how it should be, of course!

She turned back to him with an unexpected question: 'Have you always believed in God?'

'Yes, always.'

He watched her as she seemed to ponder on the answer. 'Why?'

'I just wanted to know. I don't think there are many people like that.'

Her gaze was going round the room in an abstracted fashion. She said suddenly: 'Oh, I must wash up our tea things.'

'Don't bother. I can do them, as I told you before. Why are you getting restless?'

'I'm not restless: I just want to do them, that's all.'

She gathered the cups and saucers and plates from which they had eaten earlier, and took them on a tray to the bathroom. Too indifferent to follow her, he yet found himself perplexed. Why had she asked him that question? Now she would think him religious because he had told her that he had always believed.

And how much better, how much easier it would have been, he thought, his consciousness deepened by the silence her departure had left, if he had not believed. But he had known always. From a very small boy he had been cursed with this gift of faith. Behind and through the gold and green and blue of the summer mornings through which he had run quickly to school there was God; in the pale spring twilight; in the crimsons and rich colours of autumn; in the steel black and white and grey of deep winter. It was in the slap of cold on his face when he had hurried, with sick feeling in his empty stomach, to Holy Communion on many a biting morning. Sometimes God withdrew, but again He made himself felt almost unbearably, as during those hours in the night when he had watched by his dying father in the hospital ward. He was very near as he, Adam, heard the silence broken by the heavy gasping breathing of one drawing with pain and effort the last breaths of mortal life. It was a relief from that pervasive Presence when someone coughed, or the nurse came hurrying down the ward. Yes, God always there in the rise and fall and turmoil of man struggling his hard way out of the wrappings of the beast, and becoming cruel or whining or disheartened to death in the process of that desperate struggle.

And there had been a time, Adam thought, a half-smile of contempt on his lips, when his desire to help to fulfil the will of God on earth had been warm and quick with life: he had imagined himself as he lay in bed at night another Father Damien among the lepers, another Vincent de Paul among the convicts. He had thought of so sacrificing the flesh that he would take his place among those who had the strength to take the short cut to Heaven, saints, prophets, martyrs, monks, priests and nuns. What a vain conceit! As it had proved.

He lit another cigarette, and looking deep into the glowing orange and blue of the asbestos wondered uneasily if he were still imagining a vain thing, now that he had turned in the opposite direction? Then he ground down the inconvenient query, as one puts down a heel on a lighted match blazing merrily on a pavement, hastily assuring himself that the answer was 'No', because he had now come so far from love and joy and innocence that his soul must already have become a meagre starving thing. Also he wasn't underestimating the difficulties of destroying in it all vestige of life: a long way, a hard way, a thorny way! The Little Flower took only a few mortal years to ascend on her thorny path; he was prepared to devote all his middle years, all his old age, if there were still any sparks left by the time he was an old man.

The hardening of his will by this reflection made him eager to start. When Kathleen came back into the room again, a little timidly, a half-smile on her face, he stood up to greet her.

'How kind of you! You must be an angel in disguise.'

'I'm not. Shall I put on the light? Do you know you are sitting in the dark?'

'No, I didn't.'

She switched on the light. 'You must have been deep in thought!'

'I was. I was thinking about you. Sit down and be comfortable. Tell me about this friend of yours, what's her name?'

'Oh, Eleanor. Well, she's a very nice girl.'

'Is she like you?'

'Oh, not a bit. She's competent, and I'm not.'

'In what way?'

'Well, she takes the lead, because she always knows what she wants to do, what play she wants to see when we go on a Saturday afternoon. She's planning our holiday this year. She wants to go to Switzerland. Have you been there?'

'No.'

'I'd rather go to Italy really.'

How characteristic, Adam thought, watching her musingly. Of course Italy would suit Kathleen better, sunlight, and scents and dark smiling men. Perhaps if she went, she would be seduced and that would make a woman of her.

'Eleanor's fair, isn't she? I think I saw her once on the stairs.'

'Yes. She's good-looking, isn't she?'

'A trifle heavy in the figure, I thought. But yes, quite good-looking.' Perhaps Eleanor would suit him better than Kathleen? But she evidently had a tendency to bully.

'I am, too.'

'No, you're not.' But there was a certain sturdiness about her hips, he had observed, thinking that that was all to the good when it came to child-bearing.'

'I've put on weight lately. It's all this sitting in an office, I suppose.'

'Some Italian would be sure to make love to you if you went to Italy.'

'Of course not.'

'Why not? But you must remember they are mostly stupid Papists there.'

She said hurriedly in order to avoid the personal touch he was introducing:

'You've got me wrong. I don't object to Papists. It's just some of the things they … you believe. Like, like worshipping the Virgin Mary.'

'Veneration is the word. But never mind. To us, you see, it's very odd that heretics should not have a great devotion to Our Lady, since she was the Mother of God.'

'But in herself she was only an ordinary woman.'

'Ordinary? How could she be ordinary?' He looked at Kathleen's lips, half-parted as she looked towards him, and reflected that in one minute he would put out his cigarette, get up, and kiss them. Meanwhile … 'Haven't you heard that when Our Lady wished to dry her linen, she laid it out on a sunbeam? And when in the evening she wished to light a candle, she called down a star?'

She smiled uncertainly. 'That sounds charming.'

'But you don't believe it's true?'

She looked down at her hands. 'Well …'

'All poetry is true, you know,' he said, getting up and putting out his cigarette, and going over to her. And although her heart sank in her breast like a stone, she was glad.

Under his lips, his seeking hands, her senses stirred. But the gladness went. Never mind, she thought, returning his kiss: it was his unhappiness, his tiredness, that she was taking in to herself. Maybe he didn't really love her yet, but oh, she did love him because he had been so hurt, because he said beautiful things, because of the deeply grooved lines from his nostrils, for any and every reason. It had just happened, that was all. And so it was sweet fulfilment to dare to trace delicately the lines across his forehead, to try and smooth out the permanent puckers, to dream of soothing away all the cares which pressed so heavily upon him.

III

So, thought Adam, the first part, really the chief part, was achieved. Kathleen's eyes were mistily bright when she talked or listened to him. An unexpected encounter on the stairs or landing sent the blood racing on her cheeks. Timidity and boldness struggled, expressing themselves in self-conscious movements, in retreats into silence, or in unnecessary laughter, and, when they first met, an uncharacteristic chattiness. All was sailing on a favourable wind if he had merely wanted an *affaire*. But as his intentions were honourable—he smiled cynically at the word—as he wanted marriage, there must be the preface of confession, even if it were only a partial confession. He needn't tell her more than a few of the essential facts, but his rehearsal even of these was intolerable enough. By nature reserved, because always insecure among his fellows, and deeply aware of their infinite capacity for betrayal, for distortion, for misunderstanding, the year he had passed in the asylum had increased his sense of apartness. His inner life now dwelt in such a deep groove that even to convey in matter-of-fact words something of the experience he had undergone would be torture.

He would not, he decided, make his confession as they sat alone in his room or her room because her reaction would be too close, and the importance of everything underlined.

But neither would a crowded place, one of the Corner Houses or an hotel lounge, serve. Others ears might overhear, a face turn curiously in his direction: he had to tell her something, but, by God, he would tell no one else, not even a complete stranger to whom an overheard confidence was merely, if comprehended at all, in the nature of an oddity.

Why must he tell her at all? Not at the bidding of his conscience, certainly. No, he could be assured on that point. If he didn't tell her, and if she accepted his proposal of marriage, why then there would be his mother ready in Inishkill to supply the deficiency. Maureen too! He had to do it as a safety precaution: it was quite different from whipping oneself up to the confessional because that was the *right* thing to do.

A pub then would be the best place. Some quiet corner in a saloon bar fairly early in the evening. She could sip the gin-and-limes she favoured, and he could steady himself with beer, glorious beer! Having made the decision he intercepted her on the stairs as she was going to work.

'Can you meet me at six o'clock at the Duke of York's, you know that pub in the alley off Victoria way?'

'Oh, well ... no, I'm afraid not. I promised to go with Eleanor to the pictures to-night. You see, I put her off on Saturday because of you.'

'Surely you can go with her another evening, say tomorrow?'

'She'll be hurt. I mean she won't understand.'

He looked at her impatiently. This was the first time she had not acceded to any request. His expression flustered her.

'Is it so very important?'

'It is, I think. Probably wrongly. But if you'd prefer to go to the pictures.'

'It's not that. But I promised her.'

'She can have you on Saturday.' He touched her arm, looking at her pleadingly. 'Please come.'

She looked at her wrist-watch. 'I must go or I shall be late.'

'Then you'll come. Six o'clock, or as near as you can.'

'I'll try. But if I don't turn up, you'll understand.'

'You must turn up.'

'Will you be outside then? I don't like going into a pub by myself.'

'Oh, all right. I'll wait outside. Only don't let me down.'

She nodded, and sped on. It had been a victory, but one for which he had to plead in the same unscrupulous way as women pleaded, by physical appeal. He passed the day in a state of irritation, unable to read, unable to settle to anything. And when Kathleen coming breathlessly to the rendezvous saw his frowning face turned towards her, her heart sank. Tired herself, feeling guilty because, of course, Eleanor had not taken the last-minute cancellation of their engagement lightly, but had used it as a peg for a lecture on the importance of character and integrity, assets which she feared Kathleen lacked, she experienced the first savour of that dark doubt which most women have felt at one time or another. Were men worth it? Were they *worth* all they put you through?

After the first exchanges they sat in silence while she observed a thin disagreeable smile hovering about the corners of Adam's mouth. The smile was there because he was reflecting that, while he hadn't wanted heroics or spotlights, the setting of this small dirty and gloomy bar was a trifle too denuded of any inspiration. At a far table an elderly man sat reading his paper over a glass of stout: at the bar two men, probably commercials, were talking quietly and gloomily together. The smell was of stale beer and dust. Yes, there had been one attempt at brightness: the grate on his left held an ugly vase of faded artificial flowers. Naught's here for cheer, he thought and, if he were a satirical artist, he might picture the private Judgment taking place in similar surroundings devoid of all platform props, all cosiness, all charm. One went up before the Heavenly bar, having been given full knowledge of all the sins one had committed, but hoping that one's sensual memory would aid in the recital of all the extenuating circumstances. Alas, that memory had gone: it was rotting with the body in the grave, or become an infinitesimal particle of the residue of charnel that remained when the crematorium fire had done its work. 'Yes,' one had been prepared to say, 'that was so, but at the time, I seem to remember … Agreed all that futile waste of time encompassed tracts upon dusty tracts of my life, yet that was surely when …'But one's voice would die away because one could no longer find remembrance of the excuses, the partially, at least, extenuating reasons. The accused in that dock would be mute, having no brilliant counsel primed for the defence of those recorded sins which one had never truly realised, and therefore, even if one had been a practising Catholic, never truly repented. In that silence one had merely the knowledge of the Recording Angel's unanswerable: 'What I have written, I have written.'

Kathleen said timidly: 'It's nice here, isn't it?'

'Do you think so? How odd of you! Was Eleanor very cross?'

'She was rather.'

'So now I expect you are cross with me.'

'No. At least, to be truthful, I do hate breaking a promise. But I told her you wanted to see me for a very special reason.'

'Quite.'

She was looking at him expectantly. Damn it, why was he feeling nervous? He didn't owe this girl anything, any more than he owed anybody anything. 'I think I'm going to have a whisky. This beer is awful. Shall I get you another gin?'

'No, thank you. I've only just started this one.'

The woman behind the bar, whom he hadn't taken in before, was plump, middle-aged, and not at all bad-looking. She wore, he noticed, a wedding ring. But there were other barmaids, not too young, matey, with plenty of experience in handling men, who weren't married. He would have done better to have chosen one of them, he thought, much better than a nice middle-class virgin. Of course he wanted children; that was the only point in favour of Kathleen's type.

As soon as he sat down Kathleen heard him ask: 'Do you like children?'

'Yes, I do. At least I haven't had a great deal of experience of them. Though when I lived at home I had a friend who had the sweetest little girl. I used to take her out and play with her. She was a pet.'

'I am sure she was.' He took a drink and found it good. His mind, which, of course, wanted to delay this tiresome recital to Kathleen, dallied with the speculation of how comparatively easy and pleasurable it would be to kill his soul by drowning it in alcohol. On the other hand his stomach was not a very strong one, and would probably keep rejecting the anæsthetic. Moreover the process was an expensive one. He was in the position of a would-be suicide who hadn't enough pennies for the gas-meter. So he had to use a knife and use his will and cut off bit by bit, or flake off bit by bit, the growth, not a malignant growth but a heavenly one. And in cold blood!

'Dorothy,' said Kathleen, breaking what seemed a long silence, 'that's her name, says such funny things.'

'Yes. Children do, don't they?'

She must have caught the irony in his voice, for she had flushed and tightened her lips. It was all getting worse and worse. He clenched a hand and forced himself into speech. 'Well, what I wanted to tell you, or what I thought I *should* tell you, was that I have just come out of a mental hospital, an asylum.'

She wasn't, thank God, looking at him, she was looking down at the table. He raced on hastily: 'I don't mean that I am dangerous, that you need lock your bedroom door or anything. I was never in a padded cell; I wasn't homicidal. I was just a simple depressive, a temporary case.'

'Depressive?' she said, half-looking towards him, as he raised his glass once more.

'Yes, of course, you don't quite know what that means. Well, roughly speaking, depressives just sit round and don't take much interest. Sometimes we bite our nails. We don't concentrate very well. We wander about the grounds by ourselves, and we are very backward in taking our part in the Saturday night dances which the authorities have in order to cheer us all up. In fact we are the dullest and drearriest kind of patient. The hysterical cases are much, much more entertaining. We are psychotics, you see, and they are neurotics, usually with delusions of persecution. Or they are exhibitionists. I had a friend, a man called Kenneth Cooke, whom I am sure you would like as he is extremely good-looking and a great ladies' man. You ought to meet him some time.'

He stopped for want of breath, and forced himself to meet her eyes, now looking straight at him. She said gently: 'I felt you had had a terrible time. I am so very sorry.'

How nice, how kind, he thought detachedly. Somewhat to his surprise he heard himself saying in return: 'By the way, I'd rather you didn't tell anyone. You see, one has one's living to earn unfortunately.'

'Of course I shan't. Never.'

Mildly indignant. So full of loyalty and compassion! He was glad to see her glass was empty, and reached over for it. 'Let's have another.'

'Thanks very much.'

When he came back and sat silent Kathleen said: 'But what caused it? I mean what made you a depressive?'

'A depressive psychosis is frequently caused by an emotional shock,' he answered in a pedantic voice. Now to get this bit over. He exhaled cigarette smoke, looking away across the room. 'I suppose it can be said that my emotional shock was the consequence of disillusionment. I was very much in love with a woman. Or, more accurately, lusted after her. She was married, and would never have married me in any case since I had very little money and was a nobody socially speaking. However we were intimate. Then I found that I was not the only one. That was all.'

'Don't talk about it if you'd rather not.'

'It's all right. It doesn't hurt now.'

That was true. How distant and unimportant it all seemed now. The wound bled no longer. One picked oneself up and went on. It just happened one was changed, and sometimes went in a different direction.

'You loved her very much.'

It wasn't a question; it was a pitying affirmation.

'You can put it that way. But ...'

'And the shock upset you so that ... I understand.'

He looked at her. She did understand, but her understanding was inevitably in the terms of Hollywood. A fair false woman had ruined his life: he went into an asylum because he had lost all confidence in himself and his fellow creatures. A faithful heart now broken! Perhaps it was only vanity but he had to add something that would mitigate the crudity of that conception. Not only vanity, but self-preservation, for a woman like Kathleen fancying that she held the pieces of a broken heart in her hand might be over-assiduous in trying to mend them. And that would make her a bore.

'It wasn't quite like that. I wasn't so much disillusioned in her as in myself.' He took the cigarette out of his mouth reflecting how he could make clear to her in her terms that painful ascent he had once endeavoured, the achievement of that high ambition: *'Be ye therefore perfect as your Father in Heaven is perfect'*.

'You see I had a notion, absurd as it must seem to you, of trying to lead the good life, of trying to be a saint, of freeing myself from all concupiscence.'

'What's that word mean?'

'The claims of the flesh and the predominance of the sensual in the mind. Of course when one is young it's not easy. Throughout my twenties I kept falling in love, as you would call it, but mostly running away. When I succumbed I knew I had sinned and went with beating heart to Confession. It must all seem quite bizarre to you, but there are some young men like that.'

'It doesn't seem a bit bizarre. Where did you live then?'

'I was at home in Bailey. I started as assistant in a library. It seemed to be the natural thing for a bookish young man. But what I really wanted to do was to write. I had a certain amount of success free-lancing, and then I got a staff job on a new weekly to which I had contributed. So I came to London. Like many another young provincial. Not so young at that. I was thirty-one. Now I am thirty-nine.'

'And it was here that you met this woman?'

'Not for some years. I lived quite chastely most of the time, with only bouts of drunkenness to make a change. Quite a happy time really.'

Not really true, he thought, lighting another cigarette from the stub of the last one. He had become a little queer from loneliness. He had lost his sense of the presence of God in dwelling upon his dislike for those of God's creatures whom he found himself among. He had been contemptuous of one man's shallowness, another's go-getting. He hadn't been popular because of his weakness for saying unpleasant things, or odd things. Then there had been the strain of his work. Not that it had been arduous, but for an over-conscientious and highly-strung man like himself any work that had to be approved by others, that had to be reduced to terms of the common understanding, was a strain, an incessant nagging strain.

'Of course I missed the mountains, and being able to walk,' he said aloud.

Yes, the grey pavements had got him down, had thinned his blood, and made his outward gaze sharp to note defects. The splendour of God had been hidden by the murky veil of his own dullness. He no longer looked for God, and therefore it was inevitable that sooner or later he should succumb to the exaggerated admiration of a creature. Cynthia represented a neon light, at the time how welcome.

'Well, anyhow, at some literary party I met this woman, Cynthia. She took me up as a sort of curiosity at first. She was, is, I suppose, the wife of quite a well-known man. The name doesn't matter. Anyway I escorted her to one or two dinner parties, wore evening dress quite often, went to the play with her, and so on.'

'Didn't her husband mind?'

'Not a bit. He was interested in another woman. They both went their own ways, as the phrase has it.'

He smiled at Kathleen, and received her nod of grave understanding. Oh, yes, all banal enough! But at the time, how it had wounded him, this so-called civilised life, whose desires were not struck spontaneously from the ardent longings of the flesh, but were directed by the calculating mind so as to extract the maximum savours. It was then he had known fully the meaning of self-disgust, had sampled each one of its shames.

'Was she intelligent?' asked Kathleen. 'She must have been, or you wouldn't have bothered about her.'

'Very intelligent in certain ways. That is, she was an adept in playing her part of the refined harlot. She liked me to read poetry to her. Donne's love poems were great favourites of hers. She liked music too. We went to concerts and we would listen to the radio with perhaps one softly shaded light in the darkened room. She was quite an epi-cure over the titillation of the senses. She liked spice in the way of quarrels, too, and then the makings-up. And she had quite a pretty hand with the pen. Enigmatic letters that said just so much, you know, and left you wondering.'

'I can see that you must have found her wonderful,' said Kathleen.

The unexpectedness of the comment made him look at her with raised eyebrows. She looked back at him frankly. 'I mean that I understand how it was difficult for you to resist her.'

'Can you? That's interesting.' And interesting it was, he thought cynically, since it proved that it was women who admired sirens with the admiration of the amateur, the would-be, for the professional. Mean women disguised their jealousies under sour belittlements, or took refuge in moral disapprobation. Kathleen was not mean. Her values were tainted as were the values of practically all women, certainly while they were still young, by their essential subjugation, under Nature's provision, to the flesh. He looked away from the rounded line of her cheek to the plump creased sagging face of a woman who had come in and was sitting down at a table close to them. With what gusto she was raising the glass of black foaming stout to her lips. She had reached that maturity when the beverage was more consoling than any amount of the *grande passion*. Such a woman could be trusted at long last to call a spade a spade.

Suddenly she met his eye. He had expected a half-smile at least, reflecting the camaraderie of fellow drinkers, but she looked away immediately and, he felt, dismissingly. Oddly discomfited, as if he had been rejected by a connoisseur of life, he said to Kathleen:

'You are too generous, my dear. Actually a more experienced man wouldn't have thought very much of Cynthia; they'd have found her bag of tricks somewhat obvious. My trouble was that though I was well on in my thirties I was just a dreaming country lout.'

Kathleen, he observed, looked back at him fondly, as if she didn't agree. She had, no doubt, already firmly fixed Cynthia on the pedestal of the other woman, a beautiful impossible She.

'Of course I hate her for having hurt you so much,' she said. 'For not being faithful. I think that was the unforgivable thing.'

'Do you? But why should she have been? It was not her metier. Just as it was my unfortunate nature to take it hard. No one to blame, really.'

Yes, poor devil, he had taken it hard, he reflected. Standing night after night under her window, writing her such abject appeals. He had experienced the hell of unfulfilled desire, manifesting itself in such pettiness of word, thought and deed, that even now he shrank from the recollection of all the humiliations he had undergone. And then the retching had started, till there had seemed nothing at all left to vomit up. He needn't tell Kathleen about that. He needn't tell her about his discovery in *flagrante delicto*.

'What about another drink?'

'It's my turn,' she said, standing up quickly and taking the empty glasses.

He let her go. Well, it was practically all told now. All that he had to repent was the return of a familiar misery in the solar plexus. Talking of old times had aroused self-pity. How despicable! He averted his attention to watch Kathleen standing patiently at the bar, waiting to be served. Should he propose to her that night? Was she warmed up sufficiently? Or had she in reality experienced a revulsion?

He started talking quickly as soon as she had set their glasses down. 'I'm afraid I am making a long saga about nothing. But there isn't much more to tell. I lost my job, of course. Plenty of days I was too ill to turn up. So I just stayed on in my flat till I had spent the cheque they sent me. When I hadn't my rent I told the woman I was going, and packed my bag and walked out. I slept out for a night or so—it was quite mild, this time of the year—and gave up eating. Then the police got hold of me for wandering about without visible means of support. I didn't bother to tell them anything, and at the police court I was remanded in order that my state of mind should be inquired into. I kept mum because I didn't care any longer. I had laid down my cards.'

She said gently: 'Did you think of committing suicide?'

'No. You'll think it was probably because I hadn't the courage. More that I hadn't the energy. In any case suicide is for Protestants, agnostics, atheists, Jews, and what-have-you. As a believer that way out was closed. I had lost all will to live, but I hadn't lost those tiresome convictions of faith: I felt—this will be odd to you—my soul still existed, blackened and perverted as it was, and therefore that soul was doomed to continue existence on the other side of the inhaled gas, or severed artery, or over-dose of morphia. To put it briefly, I had that in me which still preferred to fall into the hands of man rather than into the hands of God.'

She was looking intently at him, perhaps too intently, for he had no intention of ever providing her with anything in the nature of a real clue. He hurried hastily on. 'Of course I wasn't quite sane, and it must all seem very extraordinary to you. In any case, that was the outcome: they decided I wasn't quite sane, and somehow got hold of my mother. I forget how they got her address. She came and quite agreed with them about me.'

'But how could she? I mean surely she should have taken you back home, and looked after you?'

'How romantic you are! People are really not like that. They don't want to be bothered. Why should they? It would have been such a disgrace. Besides, I must make that clear: she didn't have me certified. I was only a temporary patient.'

'What does that mean quite?'

'It means that you go in willy-nilly for six months. I should have played ball, and then I could have gone as a voluntary patient, but I wasn't ... co-operative is the word, I think. Well, the six months can be extended for another three months, and then for a further three months, depending on the condition of the patient. There was no reason at all why I shouldn't have come out at the end of my six months, but one of the doctors there, a fellow named Canning, took it into his head to prefer the longest sentence. He took rather an interest in my case, you see. And that was odd, because I was just a common or garden depressive!'

'They can't make you go back, can they?'

'Not unless I am regraded, or certified. And I should have to do something violent for that.' He turned reassuringly to her, 'I promise I shan't become violent. I hope you believe me.'

'Of course.' She put her hand on his. After a pause she asked in a low voice: 'What are you going to do, if you don't mind my asking?'

'I shall have to go back to Inishkill, because my money is giving out and I must get a job. It will be easier to get a job there. The mother will be able to pull a few strings.'

'But your writing? Will you give all that up?'

'Journalism? I'm afraid I've rather blotted my copy-book there. These things get round Fleet Street, you know. Besides I couldn't compete with bright young men. I'm rusty.'

For even a poor bloody journalist, he thought, had to be interested in life alert to its appearances, quick to recognise who's in, who's out, to provide Mr. Everyman with his daily ration. And if the salt had lost its savour?

'Oh, I do so wish I could help you. I wish there was something I could do.'

How warmly and eagerly she spoke. This must be the tinder on which to strike his match.

'But you have. Think how patiently and sweetly you have listened to my dreary recital!'

She shook her head. 'That's nothing.'

'I do so wish I could take you back to Inishkill with me,' he said holding her eyes with a long gaze.

She looked down at the table. 'I don't suppose I could get a job there.'

'Oh, I could give you a job all right.'

'What job?'

'But of course you wouldn't take it. And I have no right to ask,' he said, looking sadly away, and feeling the weight within lighten as he appreciated his own bit of acting. Yet not all acting. He did want her to marry him. Only the words, the gestures to be gone through were so tedious and so trite. He turned back to her. 'You must want some food. Let's go.'

She rose obediently. He was aware of her, as they walked, like a gentle nurse at his side, watching him anxiously, waiting for him to speak lest she should say the wrong thing. She was also the sacrificial lamb waiting to be offered up.

'You've been wonderful,' he said as they waited for their food to be brought in the little restaurant they had patronised before.

She said: 'I'm proud that you should have given me your confidence. It's made me feel somehow as if I was part of real life. As a rule ...'

'Yes?'

'I don't know. As a rule I feel I am outside everything the whole time. My work is so dull, and I don't really help anybody or do anything that matters.'

'Well, you have done your good deed for to-day anyhow. Giving up the pictures with your friend. And not getting much in exchange.'

She looked at him in reproach. But with a sideways jerk of his head he indicated that they had a listener: an elderly woman who was staring at them with interest. He added: 'Tell me what you do do at your office actually.'

She told him haltingly. After all, he thought, as he half-listened, she would really be making a good bargain if she married him. She had no career to sacrifice: she was not remarkable in any way. Perhaps a Prince Charming would come along. But in how many cases did a true Prince Charming arrive?

They came out into Eccleston Square, and he took her arm. 'How I wish you would come to Inishkill with me.'

'I've always wanted to go.'

'But you wouldn't come with me, would you? No, of course you wouldn't.' He stopped suddenly. 'Listen! Do you hear that blackbird? Isn't it extraordinary how birds sing through everything: through people going mad, starving, taking their dogs out for exercise, buying cigarettes, committing suicide and adultery, working for examinations, and selling newspapers?' Turning his head as they walked on he surprised her looking at him with tenderness in her eyes. He spoke quickly: 'But you wouldn't come, would you?'

'Your mother would be surprised at your turning up with a strange young woman,' she said trying to speak lightly, but aware of disturbance, as one seeing a bright picture of a far-away country becomes aware suddenly that one could, after all, go there.

'She would be delighted. She has always wanted me to marry and settle down with a nice girl. And you are a nice girl, aren't you, Kathleen?'

'Is this a proposal then?'

'But of course,' he said, and 'of course,' he added strongly, thinking as he looked about him that in the good life this would be quite a solemn moment, so that he would probably always remember the rouged face of the tart on the pavement opposite, and the two approaching young men with their faces set in a slightly scornful would-be men of the world air, and the black cat slinking into the area, and the pieces of a broken milk bottle flashing up from the gutter. And the blackbird still singing.

'Be careful! I might accept.'

'I wish you would. But now you know how little I have to offer.'

'But you don't love me, do you?' she said in a simpler more matter-of-fact voice than he anticipated. 'I'm not at all important to you.'

'But you are!' And so she was. Important as getting furniture for your new house was important. You *had* to have furniture, hadn't you? He imparted a tone of faintly hurt indignation to his voice: 'Why do you think I lacerated myself in telling you my grimy past? I don't give confidences as a rule, I can assure you. I just thought it wouldn't be fair to suggest a deeper relationship between us unless you knew all about me.'

'Oh, I do understand how awful it was for you telling me.'

They were near to their lodgings. One last appeal *ad misericordiam*. 'I need you so much,' he said, and started to walk faster, feeling the desire to get away from her. It was up to her now. She could take him or leave him, damn her! Inserting the key into the door he said: 'I think I shall lie down for a bit. I have a headache.'

Had she heard? She seemed so quiet and grave now. Yes, for she said, as they came to their own landing: 'Let me get you an aspirin?'

'I have one. Thank you very much.'

For a moment they stood uncertainly together. Then Kathleen said in a low voice: 'I do want to help you. I like you so much. But we must think it over.'

'You mean you must think it over. Of course. But don't keep me too long in suspense. Good night.'

She's hooked, he decided without triumph. Then he threw himself on the bed, and darkness encompassed him about.

The trouble was, he thought much later, struggling back to the acceptance of pain, the telling of half truths stirred the roots, as one tearing at a handful of weeds is made conscious of what remains. Kathleen now would always believe that it was Cynthia's betrayal that had sent him out of his mind. But that in itself was such a little thing. It was *because* it was such a little thing! He had betrayed the Holy Ghost for a bauble, a glittering hollow toy which any man serving mammon, sowing his wild oats with care where they would give an abundant crop of satisfaction, would have discarded as not worth his while. It was self-contempt that had sent him temporarily out of his mind, or off his rocker, whatever euphemism one might care to use.

But the punishment had been too great. Much too great, he reminded himself firmly. God has not tempered the wind to the shorn lamb. He had afflicted him far more sorely than He had his servant, Job, for what were plagues and loathsome diseases and financial ruin compared to spending a whole year in a lunatic asylum with madmen for daily, hourly companions? Oh, yes, he had read the book of Job in the asylum and knew verse after verse of it by heart: *Why hast thou set me as a mark against thee, so that I am a burden to myself? And why dost thou not pardon my transgression and take away my iniquity, for now shall I sleep in the dust; and thou shalt seek me in the morning but I shall not be there.*

Job had become reconciled to God, had turned aside from Satan. But not so his one-time servant, Adam Palmer. God might seek him in the morning, might seek him every morning, but he would not be there. He would go *'even to the land of darkness and the shadow of death …'*

IV

The letter Adam received from his mother said:

'Of course I was very surprised to hear your news, and naturally, since I am your mother, and only wish the best for you, a little worried. I cannot feel that you have known this girl long enough to be sure that you are doing the right thing in becoming engaged to her. You ought carefully to consider your present state of health which I am sure can't be very good. I don't want to interfere at all, and you know I *never* have done. You have always gone your own way, but surely the trouble you had in the past, and though you refused to confide in me I naturally guessed a good deal, should make you very careful. It was that made you so ill and strange, and should have taught you that it is better to look before you leap as the saying goes. You may despise these old sayings, but believe me there is a lot of truth in them as I have found in my own life.

'If you are so interested in this girl, and I understand you are grateful to her for being so kind to you, as you say, though, of course if you had come straight home there would have been no need to make chance acquaintances, but why not ask her to come here on a visit? You say she works in an office so she will be sure to get some holiday in the summer. That would give you a chance to get to know each other better. You don't say if she is a Catholic, so I suppose that like most English girls she is a Protestant. You know the Church is against mixed marriages, and it seems such a pity when there are so many good Catholic girls at home here, that you would now have a chance to meet. However if she wants to be received into the Church I am sure Father John would make it easy for her. That is if you are both still set on being married after becoming better acquainted.

'It isn't, my dear son, that I am against your marrying, indeed I am sure that when you have found a job here it will be a very good thing for you and help you to settle down after your long exile from us. So let you fix a date with Miss Bartlett for her to pay us a visit, and do you come home now. I note that you ask for more money, and say that you have spent nearly all the twenty pounds I sent you. But money does not grow on trees: you know that I have only my annuity, and can just get along with Maureen, dear girl, helping out with what she earns. So don't take it amiss if I enclose just the four pounds for your fare, and say that I can do no more until we meet. I must do what I feel to be right, and I cannot feel it right for you to be living in London in a room with no proper care, except what the kindness of a stranger gives, especially when the Medical Superintendent wrote that you would need rest and attention. So let me have a line by return to say when you are arriving, and Maureen will I am sure be at the station to meet you.

From your ever loving mother.'

Adam restored the four pound notes to the registered envelope. The letter, he thought, was the sort of disgruntled production he might have expected, but he had hoped that at least she would fork out a tenner. The problem then was how to acquire money. Kathleen had said she would marry him, but couldn't they wait a while? And supposing he went off now and left her, she might change her mind. Well, that evening, when they met, she would have to be told that the financial situation was beginning to be acute.

His sense of failure made him greet her coldly when she came out of her office, and crossed the pavement to him.

'Hello!'

'Hello!'

'I'm not late, am I?'

'No, I was early.'

'Where shall we go?'

'Wherever you like. But not, unfortunately, the Savoy or the Ritz.'

'Don't be silly. Where do you suggest?'

'I'm afraid I have no ideas at all.'

Kathleen turned up the collar of her coat, for a few rain-drops were starting to fall. She tried not to feel hurt, but she had spent the whole day in a warm glow of expectation which now, at his cold words, dwindled to nothing. She told herself, however, with determination that she must expect him to be a creature of moods. After everything he'd been through!

'What about the Corner House?'

'Oh, *not* the Corner House. Please spare me that.'

'Sorry. Well, then ...'

The rain began to fall harder. She said, as he made no move, but stood gazing past her: 'There's that vegetarian place. Eustace Miles, it's not far.'

'If you like it.'

'I don't like it specially. But we must go somewhere.'

'I suppose so.'

As they started to walk, Kathleen bowed to someone passing. Adam raised his hat, and then asked: 'Who was that?'

'Oh, that's Mr. Young, one of the cashiers.'

'Really.'

'He's a darling. Some of the girls don't like him, because he is always telling funny stories, and some of them are a bit, you know. But he's always so friendly and cheerful.'

'How different you must find him from me.'

She said nothing, but he saw that her lips were compressed.

'And he looks so well dressed, too!'

She turned into the restaurant still without replying. As soon as they sat down he bent towards her and said: 'I feel I should apologise. It really must be very mortifying for you to be seen with someone as shabby as myself.'

'Please don't be silly.'

'But I am shabby.'

'If you are, so am I.'

'Oh no, not at all.' He stopped himself from saying: 'You look like everybody else', which was at the moment the impression he was receiving. She was wearing the plain 'summer' coat that most hard-up business girls affected. No different from their winter ones except that the winter one had a fur collar. It was grey, and her plain felt hat was also grey, but with no striving for smartness. No one would really look at her twice, he reflected. If she had been ugly, or at least had some sort of unusual plainness, he might have got very fond of her, he decided with malice. 'You look very nice,' he said aloud taking up the menu.

'You don't think that, really.'

'But of course I do. But I think I like you better without your hat. Do take it off.'

After a moment's hesitation, and then because it seemed stupid not to please him over so small a thing, Kathleen obeyed. 'You have such a nice forehead, so smooth, and then your pretty hair,' he informed her with detachment. 'It's a shame not to show it.'

'Well, I am glad you like something about me.'

She hadn't intended to snap out like that, and took up the menu with a pretence of absorbed interest. She decided on something, and he chose something else. As soon as the waitress had gone he said smoothly: 'I don't advise you to expect much. We shall both be filled up with proteins, and, like much that is good for us, the taste is disagreeable. But, as the Book of Proverbs says: "Better a dinner of herbs where love is than a stalled ox and hatred withal."' As she made no reply, he insisted: 'Don't you agree?'

Goaded, she said bluntly: 'Since you don't love me, it is not likely to be better for you. We had done better to go to Simpson's.'

With lowered eyes, playing with his fork, he examined the little tinge of pleasure her words had given him. It was a pleasure, he decided, akin to that of a cat when a mouse makes a dart towards freedom. He was glad she had showed so much spirit. But it was a pleasure in which he could not afford to indulge. He must get the habit of directing his malice only toward essentials. It was no part of his plan to bait Kathleen, whose role was to be that of the necessary background figure concerned with his kitchen and his children. Besides if you quarrelled a lot with someone you forged a bond, since increasingly they diverted energy and occupied your mind.

Under the table his foot sought hers, and he said: 'Do forgive me. I know I am behaving badly. You see I've had a letter from my mother, and that has depressed me.'

'Really?' said Kathleen withdrawing her foot.

'Yes! Do you know she only sent me four pounds, the bare price of my fare back? She hasn't even the decency to send your fare, though I told her all about you, as you know. She thinks it would be better for you to pay us a visit later.'

'That is very understandable.'

'Understandable?' He affected surprise.

'She doesn't like the idea of your marrying me, I suppose. And she is probably right.'

'But of course she isn't right. Here, you had better read the letter. It will show you what a conventionally minded woman she is.'

He passed the envelope over as the waitress brought them their dishes. As he started to eat he watched her face unobtrusively. It was certainly not a letter that would endear his mother to her, and she had better start by assuming her role of his ally.

Kathleen passed it back without a word, and took up her fork.

'Well?'

'If you are short of money I can lend you some or give you some. I have about sixty-five pounds in the savings bank, part of a hundred pounds my mother left me.'

'Don't be ridiculous. As if I would take your money.'

Oh, thought Kathleen suddenly, as she tried to swallow the dry food, if only he would take *all* her money, and go away. She'd gladly give up the holiday abroad she and Eleanor had planned. Life would be empty for a while, but then peace would come back to her again.

'The letter just shows what a mean old bitch she is,' said Adam noting with pleasure that he was breaking the Fourth Commandment. He repeated deliberately: 'A mean bitch.' As Kathleen said nothing, he went on, slightly annoyed because she hadn't rebuked him, 'I am afraid she's taken away your appetite. Why don't you order something else? This isn't bad … better than yours, I should think.'

'It's all right. I'm not very hungry.'

'When we get to Inishkill you shall have a steak with butter sizzling on top in our local Ritz. The cooking can be quite good. Or aren't you interested in food?'

'Not particularly.'

'You're too young, I suppose. I think I shall have apple tart next. What about you?'

'I'll just have a coffee.' Kathleen laid down her knife and fork, and stared away.

'Are you punishing me because I admitted my financial embarrassments?'

'No. I told you I'm not hungry.'

'I'm afraid the mother's letter has annoyed you?'

'No. I was just thinking. I can quite understand that she'd prefer you to marry a Roman Catholic. Don't you think you'd better …'

She stopped because the waitress had appeared, and as she took up his empty and Kathleen's half-full plate, he gave the order: 'Two coffees and one apple tart.' And then to Kathleen: 'You're sure you won't change your mind?'

'What about?'

'You won't have a pudding?'

'No, thank you.'

The waitress went away. He said: 'Let's see. What were you saying?'

'I was commenting about your mother's disappointment because I am not a Roman Catholic.'

'Do say Catholic, if you don't mind. Redundancy is always tiresome.'

'I don't know what you mean.'

'Never mind. I only mean there is only one Catholic and Apostolic Church. Well, why not become a Catholic? That would spike her guns.'

'I have no intention of doing that, whatever happens.'

'Why not?'

'Because I don't believe in it.'

'That's the point. You are no Newman struggling on from one stage of belief to another. You don't really believe in anything in the way of religion, do you?'

'Well,' started Kathleen, and then stopped as the waitress brought their order.

'No, you don't,' said Adam starting his apple tart with every appearance of enjoyment. 'You think there *might* be a God, that's all. At least that's what you said the other evening.'

'Well?'

'Well then it would be merely a matter of form. It wouldn't hurt your integrity or whatever you proudly call it, in the slightest. You needn't become a practising Catholic, but it will smooth things over with the mother. Don't look so serious. I can assure you it's done every day.'

'That doesn't make it right.'

'Right hardly enters into it, as you don't believe in anything. I admit it will be rather a nuisance for you having to be instructed.'

'I do believe in something. I believe it would be wrong to pretend to believe a lot of things I don't believe in.'

'I see,' he said dryly, pushing away his plate, and starting to stir his coffee. 'Have a cigarette?'

'Thank you.'

His silence made her uneasy. She said at last: 'Honestly, I don't quite understand why you should want me to do something in which you yourself can't really believe, as you don't practise it.'

'I do believe in it.'

'Well then, why don't you go to Mass and all the rest of it?' He smiled back at her, thinking of the impossibility of making her understand. There was for her Right and Wrong, two main tarmac roads, duly mapped and making in diametrically opposed directions. Whereas the kingdoms of Good and of Evil had their charts, but they were charts not obtainable save by much seeking, much knocking, much experience. One could, indeed one *should,* shape the whole of one's life to that search. There were hints, of course, which illuminated. Such as Saint Bonaventure gave when he said that first there was Purification … words which had once been familiar to him echoed in his mind: *So we must first pray, then live holily, and, thirdly, we must look long and attentively at the manifestations of truth; and, so attending, we must rise step by step, until we reach the high mountain where God of gods is seen in Sion.*

Easier to say than to do. But he had tried; he had spent his youth in such laborious ardours. With his imagination fired by the goal of the Beatific Vision he had essayed a few steps. Fewer than he had thought. For he had fallen. And now?

Kathleen watching him saw the tolerant smile which he had turned toward her flicker out, and be replaced by a momentary look of such desolation that her heart contracted. 'What is it?' she cried, all her resentments forgotten.

He looked at her blankly: 'What?'

'You looked so unhappy suddenly.'

'Did I? It was nothing. Oh, I had a twinge of indigestion. I ate that stuff too quickly. You were wise not to have anything. But you must be starved.'

'I'm not. You don't mind about my not becoming a Catholic: I mean you don't *really* mind, do you?'

'Of course not.' Surprised at seeing her so quickly warmed and troubled, he added with conviction: 'I was stupid to bother you about it. It was just my mother's silly letter. Only ...'

'Only what?'

'You won't mind if the children, if there are any children,' he was speaking humbly and apologetically now, and she listened to him with an unreasoning compassion, 'are brought up as Catholics? Because in a mixed marriage they do, well, I'm afraid they insist on that.'

'You mean *you* would like that?' she asked, dismissing with interior scorn the 'they'.

He nodded, still apologetically. She said, giving him this toy, this fetish, if he wanted it, since he had looked suddenly so pitiable: 'Of course. If you are really so keen about it.'

'I've got a devout sister, you see, too,' he said more firmly, more dismissingly. It was to the darkness within that he was now apologising, explaining that it was no part of his bargain not to allow others at least their initial chance.

'That's Maureen, isn't it?' she said, her elbows on the table, leaning over towards him. 'Tell me about her.'

But he felt too tired to talk about Maureen, or to talk about anything. 'Oh, you'll be seeing her. Let's go to the pictures, shall we?'

'If you like.'

'It's what you like,' he said, looking away. 'But I think I should like to. There's a sort of security, if only the security of a pause, about two young lovers, at least you are young enough for both of us, sitting holding hands in the warm darkness with the improbable story of an improbable happiness holding our eyes. And outside the rain falls, I expect it's still raining, raining on the thousands and thousands of roofs and miles and miles of pavements, and policemen holding up the traffic.'

'So it is, nice and cosy,' agreed Kathleen gazing round for the waitress, for now she wanted to give him everything he wanted.

And that mood persisted right through the movie show, even though she felt that since it had turned out to be quite a good and intelligent picture he ought to be giving it more attention than he was, instead of sitting there brooding and not following the story. But she was still tolerant when, on their way home on top of the bus, he said: 'I've got such a good solution to our financial problems.'

'What? I've told you I've got some money.'

'Your money, my poor child,' he patted her arm. 'Hold on to it. No. You remember I told you about a comparatively rich man I met when I was ...' he hesitated, feeling the presence of maybe listening ears, 'in that place from which I have lately come?'

'No. A rich man?'

'Kenneth Cooke. Anyhow I can borrow a tenner off him. That will give us another week or two here. And show the old lady I needn't scurry to her whistle.'

She smiled kindly at him, deciding that if he seemed absurdly triumphant over trifles, it was part of what he had had to endure. He hasn't got his sense of perspective back, that's it, she thought, gazing out of the window at the black and glistening pavements, at the bright lights, at the strained faces waiting for buses. She made a resolution to be very good and very patient. Because love meant giving and not getting. And she was ready to give. She wanted to give.

— THREE —

I

IT was June. The sun streamed through the window of the third-class carriage where Kathleen was sitting opposite Adam, and looking out she felt something shining tugging within her. The shining thing was happiness and it tugged and fluttered uncertainly because having been suppressed for some long time it was still uncertain whether it might venture forth. Come to think of it, she reflected, and, of course, she shouldn't come to think of it because it was disloyal, she and happiness hadn't had much to do with each other ever since Adam had come into her life. Excitement, yes; pleasure, yes; but nothing that stayed.

And yet she had stupidly imagined that being engaged would be one of the happiest times in her life. For once in her life she would know the fulfilment of being able to tell someone else all the silly little things that made up one's day, and that someone else would be really interested, not just pretending to be interested. And he would tell her all the things that had made up his day, and, oh, she would be so glad to hear. And he would quote his favourite poems, and she would quote hers, and on Saturdays they would go for long walks into the country—day return tickets from Waterloo—or in the summer they would go on the river. Of course if he had a car that

81

would be glorious, but if he hadn't, if he was just a poor clerk, that wouldn't matter, since whatever they did they would be happy together. Indeed the way she had hoped it would be was contained in the words of an old song she remembered her mother singing:

'Some Sunday morning when the weather's fine,
The song birds singing and the world in chime …'

It would always be a Sunday morning, and the sky a clear blue, and the fields green and the buttercups yellow and the brooks chattering, just as beautiful as it was now outside the carriage window. And she looked over at Adam hoping to see a reflection in his face of that tentative happiness rising within her.

Adam was reading the *Spectator*, reading it with concentration. Kathleen wished for a second that instead of buying the *New Statesman* and the *Spectator* at Victoria, he had bought, say, *Punch*. But she accepted that Adam was not the sort of man who would ever buy *Punch*. And certainly he looked less tired and less strained than he had looked for some time, in fact ever since she had known him. He had cheered up since he had received the warm invitation from Kenneth Cooke to come and stay a week with him at his cottage in a Sussex village, accompanied by a cheque for ten pounds. He had said: 'Of course we'll go: that will show the bitch!'

The bitch was his mother, whom now he always referred to thus, so that looking apprehensively into the future Kathleen feared that he really must hate and loathe her, and that she must expect a lot of family quarrels.

Also she tried to brush the thought away that the only time she had ever seen Adam really pleased was by the thought that he had triumphed over somebody. Oh, that couldn't be true. Or rather, on such a lovely afternoon as this, it couldn't go on being true.

She looked out of the window again, and then, daringly, touched his knee to attract his attention. 'Do look!'

He looked. In the foreground there was the moss-grown roof of an old barn, and red-and-white cattle browsing; behind through dark trees was the square tower of a church, there was also the beckoning glimpse of a narrow white road curving over a stone bridge and leading over the hills and far away. To Kathleen it threw back a reflection of English peace, English tradition; for ever that hamlet would be sunning itself in security as an old man drowses on a bench, all passion spent.

But what did the picture say to Adam? She watched him brooding over it with no lightening of face, and ventured: 'Lovely, isn't it?' He nodded, and settled back in his corner. But now he wasn't reading.

Thinking then? Of what? Happiness left her as she thought of the long years ahead in which she would see his face compressed in thought and have no clue to that thought. Oh, no, surely not! He was a sick man; he would recover; he would smile again at joyous things.

For in a flash of understanding beyond her years she was recognising that the lack of someone with whom to laugh, whether it be friend or lover or neighbour, made for more loneliness than anything else. With practice one could learn the trick of keeping one's woes to oneself; by laughter we joined hands with our fellows, separated ourselves from the beasts that perish, and approached the gay and careless gods.

Adam was recollecting lines from *Paradise Lost: Farewell happy fields where joy for ever dwells.* How did it go on? *The mind is its own place, and in itself can make a Heav'n of Hell, a Hell of Heav'n.*

For him no more happy fields. He must be careful to dismiss the faintest uprise of pleasure in such matters. For these were the ways by which God first engaged your attention, by revealing the splendour of His footprints on the earth. A man must be a fool, said St. Bonaventure, who remains unmoved by such splendours. Well, for the rest of time, he must be such a blockhead.

He looked at his watch, and said to Kathleen: 'We shouldn't be much longer now.'

Kathleen felt the uprush of shyness. She wished she knew more of these strangers among whom her lot was to be cast, and said: 'Let me see: you said Mr. Cooke was good-looking, didn't you?'

'Extremely so. Just the type most women fall for. I expect you'll be thrilled by him, and want to have an *affaire*.'

Kathleen stared at him steadily. Of course, she was telling herself he couldn't *mean* any of the things he said. He couldn't attach so little meaning to her love, to any love, as that. She must learn to take him lightly, and stop herself from being so unreasonably hurt.

'I expect Mrs. Cooke would probably object.'

'Oh, I can't tell you anything about her. She's got the money, so I expect she's one of these jealous possessive women.'

'Is he in love with her?'

'I should say Cooke is in love with nobody but himself, never has been and never will be.'

She ventured anxiously: 'Still, you do like him? I mean he wrote you such a nice letter, didn't he?'

Adam raised eyebrows. '*Like?* That's a long word, you know.'

But if he didn't like him, *why* then borrow money from him? *Why* go and stay with him? She said because there didn't seem anything else to say: 'Well, I'll go and make myself presentable.'

When she returned from the toilet she was gratified by the welcoming smile he gave her. He was indeed pleased to see that having added lipstick and a fresh coating of powder she looked quite attractive. For there was always that faint irritation caused by Kathleen's lack of feminine tricks, of feminine guile. Admittedly Cynthia had snared him thus. Women should beckon, and then pretend they hadn't beckoned. For thus they became part of the tantalising quality of life: a secret stirring as one walks by a hedge at night; a door shutting suddenly, and one wonders who has shut it and why; a solitary footstep along a city pavement as one lies awake before the dawn; the dream which one cannot recapture; the set mouth and wrinkles of an old woman's face which hide such secrets of pain and endurance.

Kathleen said: 'I hope Mrs. Cooke won't be very smart and very frightening.'

'I shouldn't think so. Or else Kenneth as an egotist would not have been likely to marry her. A dowdy woman devoted to him, that's how I picture her.'

Why did he speak in that sneering way? In time would he refer to her devotion in that same contemptuous fashion? Men wanted women to become devoted to them, and then despised them for it. Of course Cynthia hadn't been devoted. Cynthia certainly knew her onions, reflected Kathleen wryly.

'What did Mr. Cooke do before he married her?'

'Oh, I gather he was always a rolling stone. Lots of jobs. He used to teach. Then he gave it up because they wanted him to teach something he didn't believe in. The authenticity of Holy Writ or something, I suppose. He's chockful of principles. Then he had a job in some Socialist book-shop. Oh, and his last was being secretary to a Pacifist society. He had to give that up because of a certain idiosyncrasy which makes him liable to the attentions of the police. But he is sure to tell you all his neuroses. He talks about them very well.'

Adam looked at his watch again. 'We're due in now. I hope he'll be there to meet us, and not suddenly succumb to a heart attack or something. Neurotics have a nice sense of timing so as to inflict the maximum inconvenience upon their friends. Well, I'll be getting your bag down.'

He stood up, and reached up to the rack. Kathleen opened her handbag, and gave her nose a final powdering. She realised with apprehension that she was about to set foot in an unknown world in which it was unlikely she would ever become a native.

II

Being a timid girl with no particular idea of her own importance, and one moreover whose bent was to incline toward the sun rather than the shade, even if a little doubtfully, Kathleen belonged to the class which counts its blessings before its dissatisfactions. And she was thinking as she sat having tea in the front garden attached to the Cookes' cottage that she had much to be thankful for.

In the first place Mrs. Cooke, a big fair woman in a cotton smock over an extremely old skirt, and with no stockings on, could certainly not be considered either smart or fashionable. Her face, flushed by having baked a cake in a small hot kitchen, was unpowdered, and she sat ungracefully with her knees far apart. Kathleen, indeed, if she had not been the modest person she was, might have felt she showed to advantage dressed in a becoming green linen sports frock which Adam had approved. But she was merely grateful that Mrs. Cooke, whom she had been told to call Myra, and who addressed her as Kathleen, was not intimidating.

In the second place Mr. Cooke besides being tall, dark and handsome which she had expected, was unexpectedly deferential, even humble in his manner toward her. Kathleen, who had always had a prejudice against good-looking men as likely to be conceited, felt herself warming toward him. I expect he's really a good kind man, and Adam is just prejudiced, she thought, and then felt slightly embarrassed at catching Mr. Cooke's eye, for whenever she looked toward him he seemed to be ready with that appealing rather sad smile.

And though of course they are intellectual, it's the good side of being clever, the trying-to-improve-the-world side, that matters with them, not impressing by their brilliance, her thoughts determinedly went on. For Kenneth had been talking very earnestly about the necessity of a world federation for peace, and she remembered the many yellow covers of the Left Book Club which adorned the bookshelves of the living-room. Jung and Freud were also well represented besides other books on psychology. I should read books like that, she thought, glancing over at Adam. Mrs. Cooke probably has read them all in order to do her best for her husband, and if I read them then I might be able to help Adam more.

'Of course,' Mr. Cooke was saying, 'if all the young men would refuse to fight?' He looked at Adam.

'Ah, if only they would!'

'You don't believe that's likely?'

'No, I don't believe that's likely.'

'We know there must be education and propaganda of course. That's the point.' As Adam said nothing he said more sharply: 'You don't agree?'

'I don't think the propaganda of cranks has any result but that of the creation of more cranks,' said Adam equably.

'You think it's cranky then to try and stop people from killing their fellow creatures,' said Myra with definite hostility in her voice, as Kathleen noticed with some alarm.

'If people generally are told and believe that it is a righteous war, I mean it is only the cranks who will stay out. And those who set some extra value on their own skins,' said Adam. He spread a hand, and added deprecatingly: 'Like myself, for example.'

'If war comes you're going to stay entirely out of it then?' asked Cooke.

'Certainly. Kathleen and I are going to live in Inishkill, where there won't be much chance of bombs coming our way, or our children's way.'

Feeling the Cookes' glance toward her, Kathleen felt herself flushing.

Myra said, in her abrupt rather deep voice: 'Isn't there something in the New Testament about he who seeks to save his life losing it?'

'There is. But I am rather surprised to hear you as a pacifist quoting it.'

'I'm not thinking of *my* wretched life. I'm thinking of all the thousands, probably millions of other people, including women and children, who will be killed and maimed.'

'That will certainly happen,' nodded Adam.

'We just can't understand your indifference, you see, old man,' said Kenneth as Myra sat back with mouth compressed.

Bravely Kathleen spoke up: 'Adam isn't indifferent. He just doesn't feel he can do anything about it.'

'I am afraid you are too kind,' said Adam. Kenneth said quickly: 'No, she's not. It's no good pretending, old man. You are as sensitive as the next person. After all—Kathleen won't mind my saying this, because I know you have told her everything—both of us, you as well as myself, wouldn't have been in a mental hospital if we hadn't felt more than the rest.'

'Speaking for myself,' said Adam taking his cigarette case out of his pocket and passing it over to Myra, who shook her head, 'I was in a mental hospital because …' he lit his cigarette … 'because of my own suffering, if you like to dignify it as such. Not at all for other people's. I didn't give a damn for other people's pains.'

Kenneth shook his head with a sad and noble understanding expression on his face. Myra got up, saying: 'I'll just clear away these things.'

Kathleen sprang up. 'Let me carry something.'

When they were out of earshot, Kenneth said with a faint touch of reproof: 'Do you mind not sounding quite so cynical in front of Myra? She is a person who takes strong likes and dislikes.'

'You mean I mustn't speak frankly?'

'Not too frankly. Don't be offended! I understand your mood of … never mind! I must admit I feel I can breathe so much better myself when she's not there.'

'Really?'

'Well, you've seen her. A dull plain woman who, of course, has got everything she wanted out of marriage with me. But as for me, it's like living in a strait-jacket. My dear! The incessant conflict that goes on underneath. All the time! The strain. Never mind! Because I mustn't be disloyal. No, I mustn't be disloyal.' Squaring his shoulders Kenneth sat stiffly upright, gazing in front of him. Then he relaxed and said in a different voice: 'By the way, I didn't drop a brick just now in mentioning the asylum in front of Kathleen? You *have* told her everything?'

'Yes. You asked me that before tea.'

'Of course, I just wanted to be sure. Such a sweet girl!'

'She hasn't any money to speak of, by the way.'

'Quite. I wasn't accusing you of anything mercenary. For that matter I didn't marry Myra because she has a little money. I really loved her. I do still in a way love her. Can't you understand?'

Before Adam replied they heard footsteps approaching. Kathleen came up, and said shyly: 'Mrs. Cooke, I mean Myra, won't let me wash up with her. She said she'd rather I took Scottie for a walk if I felt energetic.'

'But what a good idea,' said Kenneth, who had risen with alacrity. 'I'll come too. What about you? You'd rather sit and laze, old man, I expect.'

'Do come, won't you?' said Kathleen appealing to Adam.

Adam smiled. 'I don't think I will. Let Kenneth show you round, and I'll keep the garden safe for you.'

'Splendid,' said Kenneth. 'And if you want anything just tell Myra. Oh, I'll leave you those cuttings of my articles to look through, if you don't mind. I shan't be a moment, Kathleen.'

Kathleen said in a low voice to Adam: 'Are you really feeling lazy? I'd rather you came.'

'It would be too unkind to deprive Kenneth of showing off in front of you. You'll have to excuse me this once. Every dog must have his day.'

Kathleen turned away. He was separating himself from her. Of course he didn't love her; he didn't, she felt at that moment, even like her. So she mustn't expect anything of him. Mustn't she ever expect anything of him? Behind her she heard Kenneth return and say: 'I've got them. Here they are. I shall greatly value your criticism as I fear Myra is prejudiced in my favour. Of course they don't amount to much really.'

Kathleen watched Adam take the sheaf of papers held out to him. She had a feeling that his fingers-tips revolted from even touching them while he said tonelessly: 'I'll certainly read them.'

Kenneth was the first to break the silence between them as they turned from the main road up a lane. He said in an intimate faintly caressing voice: 'Can I be candid with you?'

'Of course.'

'Well then, I am rather worried about Adam.'

'Are you? Why?'

'I feel he doesn't take enough interest. I should have expected him to be in better spirits after his wonderful luck in meeting someone like you.'

'Oh, but … I mean it isn't as if I'm anybody. I'm rather stupid really, that's the trouble, I think. I keep trying to imagine what he went through, and it's difficult. It must have been awful for him in that place.'

'It was awful for all of us; it was awful for me,' said Kenneth, unable to resist the short cut to the centre of his world. 'Remember it wasn't my first visit; it was my seventh.' He accented the last word with the pride with which some women refer to the number of their operations. 'Yet one never gets used to it. The ghastly humiliations! And, of course, the plight of the other poor patients.'

Drawing on her courage, Kathleen asked: 'Did Adam… I know how he must have suffered … But did he show it?'

'Oh, no. Depressives don't. They sit around in somewhat sombre fashion. But what I felt was that Adam *humiliated* himself unnecessarily.'

'How?'

'To put it bluntly, he used to suck up to the doctors and the nurses. Anyone who gave him treatment.'

'I can't imagine Adam sucking up to anybody … He did have treatment then?'

'Oh, electrical treatment. But he wasn't really co-operative; he wouldn't help the doctor who was most interested in him, a well-meaning if rather clumsy chap, Canning. He just went round pretending there was nothing wrong with him. Now I told them *everything* about myself that might be of help.' He looked at her sideways. 'I suppose Adam told you what my trouble was.'

'Oh, no, he didn't.'

'Didn't he? Well he should know that I wouldn't mind. Not to someone like yourself who is broadminded and sympathetic. Exhibitionism!'

Kathleen nodded. 'Exposing myself,' added Kenneth just to make sure there was no doubt in her mind.

'It must have been frightful for you.'

'Yes, and still is. Because, of course, they haven't cured me. They can't cure me, it seems. For even now I get the most frightful temptations to telephone respectable people, spinsters, dowagers, clergymen, you know, and say the most shocking things to them. I've done it, too,' added Kenneth with some pride. 'You see, Myra knows so many respectable people. She does a lot of work for the Village Institute. Of course it's rather hard on her.'

'It must be.'

'And yet, and yet, Kathleen, if she'd only be a little more truly understanding; if she could only realise what agonies I am suffering. Agony is the one word that describes what I go through.'

'It must be awful. But I am sure she does try and understand.'

'She *tries*. It's just not in her to understand mental torture.'

'But when she married you she knew all about things, I mean how they were with you?'

'Oh yes, and she still loved me. She does now, poor woman. Believe me, I'm very sorry for Myra. And I mustn't be disloyal! I'm shocking you.'

'It's only that Mrs. Cooke, I mean Myra, has been very nice to me, and it doesn't seem quite fair ...'

'I know. I know. What a good sweet loyal little soul you are. We'll leave Myra out of it. But I want us to be friends, so do you mind if I tell you a little about myself?'

'Not a bit.'

The little turned out to be a lot. While cattle grazed the last sweetness of the day from the cud; while road-menders plodded cheerfully homewards; while the secret

honeysuckle at last yielded some of its heady scent to the
evening air, and wild roses spread themselves like earthy
stars on the hedges, Kenneth went on talking. He spoke of
no ecstasies of the flesh but of its dark and furtive motions;
where others extracted pleasure he apparently had extracted
only pain. And yet, he was careful to emphasise, it was no
sin in himself, no corruption, that had turned his steps into
murky places; he himself was indeed a splendid fellow full
of noble aspirations to leave the world better than he had
found it. Unlike Adam he loved his fellow creatures, he
grieved for them; in spite of his own continual trials he
remained solicitous for their welfare.

It was the only mention of Adam in a recital which
continued while the sun turned to gold and the western sky
flamed into crimson and green and mauve. Kathleen feeling
her heart grow heavier and heavier within her watched
the splendour as if through a glass darkly. If she had been
alone, she thought with some resentment, how she would
have enjoyed herself. But the words that were being spoken
interposed so that she saw sky and green fields and the very
stones of the ancient track on which she trod, as her forbears
had trodden before her from generation to generation,
blanketed by her companion's account of furtive hidings
in basement areas, of the touch of a policeman's hand upon
a trembling arm, of a man sitting in a Black Maria while
policemen alternately jested or reproved.

'But I am boring you?' said Kenneth with the com-
placency of one who believes that whatever is his hearer's
reaction it cannot be boredom.

'No, of course not. I am so sorry. I see you have had a
terrible life,' said Kathleen with sincerity.

'You are so understanding and sympathetic.' Looking about him Kenneth observed that they were nearing home, and felt that Kathleen deserved her turn. His hand encircled her arm. 'May I tell you something? I so much admire the bravery you are showing in making up your mind to throw in your lot with poor Adam. It's noble.'

'Noble?' questioned Kathleen. 'No, because, you see, I am very fond of him.'

'He's lucky. To have love with understanding. My life might have been different if I had only had the luck to have both.'

Kathleen said nothing. She was feeling very tired and very depressed, and was glad to see the tower of the village church as they came into the road.

Kenneth released her arm with a last lingering pressure. 'If I only had had the good fortune to meet someone like you,' he said and sighed deeply.

'That's nonsense. I'm a very ordinary person,' said Kathleen beginning to walk a little faster. 'By the way, where's Mac?'

'Don't worry: he'll have run home before us. He hates walking slowly, and, of course, with my heart I can't walk fast.'

Kathleen slackened her pace obediently. She heard Kenneth say: 'Are you happy, darling? Please forgive me for calling you darling.'

'Yes. I mean I am quite happy.'

'Do you mind if I say I don't quite believe that? We'll talk again, but I do want to say that if ever you need a friend I am here. Just think: "Kenneth is there. I can tell Kenneth, and he will never give me away."'

'It's very kind of you,' said Kathleen. She observed with relief that the dog was running towards them, having taken up an observation post at the cottage gate. 'Oh, here comes Mac!'

And Kenneth was really very kind, thought Kathleen as she stood that same night before the window of her little room before undressing for bed. It was wonderful of him to remain kind and not be bitter considering what appalling things had happened to him. But she wished he wouldn't disparage Myra. Yet he was probably really very fond of her. Look at the way he had hugged her as soon as they had come in from their walk, and made a lot of fuss of her for the rest of the evening, drawing her out, making her talk about the play she was getting up for the Women's Institute.

There was a knock at the door and Adam came in. 'Hello: I just thought I'd look in to see that you had everything you wanted.'

'Yes, thank you.'

'How did you get on with Kenneth on your long walk?'

'Oh, all right.'

'I suppose he told you the sad story of his life?'

'He told me some of the awful things that had happened to him.'

'Quite. And did he try and make love to you?'

Kathleen hesitated. 'No, not really.'

'I understand. He just held your hand, as all might, or so very little longer, to quote Browning.'

Kathleen turned back to the window to draw the curtains. She took a last long breath of the night air, faintly scented with hay. And how still and beautiful stood the trees. 'Oh, it *is* a beautiful night,' she exclaimed involuntarily. 'I wish …'

'You wish what?'

'I wish people wouldn't spoil it.'

'And why do you think they spoil it?' asked Adam, coming to stand by her, and look out with her.

'I suppose,' answered Kathleen slowly, 'it is because they are so hurt and unhappy and restless.'

'It is because we are wounded creatures, wounded by sin.' After a pause Kathleen said gravely: 'Yes, I think that's true.'

'You are beginning to learn,' said Adam looking at her with interest. He gazed up at the sky to the silver crescent of the half moon, and then to the strong line of the downs in the far distance. 'And some of us,' Kathleen heard him say in a low voice, 'are more mortally wounded than others.'

She looked at his profile, pale and bleak. He meant himself, of course, and a surge of sympathy and repudiation rose up in her heart so that she linked her arm in his. 'But you're not. Of course you're not.'

He said: 'Yes, I am.'

And the words falling like stones made her realise that he really meant it. The intuition aided her mind to ponder upon an enigma: Adam, so realistic in his judgments of affairs, of other people, was a Romantic about himself. He really thought he was a much greater sinner than the rest, and therefore set apart as something special. He had fallen into one of the more cunningly hidden pits which Pride sets. Some understanding of this made her repeat warmly: 'Of course you're not. My silly darling!'

But Adam shook his head. Like the centurion he had realised that he was not worthy that his Lord should enter under his roof. But he refused to add: 'Say but the word, and my soul shall be healed.'

III

Adam and Kathleen returned from Sussex on a Saturday evening, and went to bed early. In the morning he awoke to the sound of bells, and lay a moment confused, wondering where he was.

No, it was all right! He wasn't in the asylum; nor was he in Sussex. He was in Pimlico once more, and this was Sunday morning. Turning his face to the pillow, the steady clang of the bells sent his mind on a far journey to those other Sunday mornings of his childhood and youth, when Sunday morning first and foremost meant Mass. It might be an early Mass when he would go up to the altar rails; it might be a sung Mass; it might be the short last Mass because he had overslept, or wanted to do something else before, or to avoid someone. Or he might meditate the adventure of hearing Mass in a different Church. In any case some part of his mind or heart was under the spell of preparation, preparation for the tinkling of the bell which announced that God Himself had come down among them. O mystery beyond comprehension of the Church on earth joined with the Heavenly choir of Powers and Dominions, of Angels and Archangels, of Cherubim and Seraphim to sing Sanctus, to sing Hosanna to the Eternal God. What mingling of joy and awe had then shaken his soul!

But now, he thought, burying his head deeper into the pillow, trying not to listen to the bells, I can look back quite coldly on that callow young man I used to be; I can view him as a grown-up looks back on childish excitements, say, a circus when the lady bareback rider was so beautiful and so brave, and the high-stepping horse so proud; or when the German band that used to play in our road when I was very little broke into a Sousa march, and everything went to the beat of triumph and gallantry. So many times there had been when all the Sons of the Morning had shouted for joy. Ichabod, the glory had quite departed!

As the bell stopped, he moved restlessly, and turned to lie flat on his back. For it occurred to him that though he had lost joy, and surely lost it irretrievably, he had not yet lost Faith. Faith which, so St. Thomas had said, was the first movement of the soul toward God, the first bridge, and therefore the last bridge to be burnt on his retreating course. And that bridge, he accepted, would take a long time to burn. An aversion from God in itself implied faith in Him. So then he must make himself utterly null, come to that point where he forgot his cherished enmity, come to disbelieve in his divine adversary. That, he feared, would only be when he had expunged his soul entirely, or almost entirely. Slow and steady must do it. There's a long long trail a'winding ... a slug's trail.

He turned on his side, pulling up the blanket, closing his eyes, sickened by his imagination of that downward course into noisome slime and final corruption, but unable to resist probing the final conclusion. At what moment did a man, drawn slowly down till the morass bubbled stickily over his head, give up the ghost? Was it when the slime rose up to his nostrils so that he could breathe air no longer but suffocated and choked, the corrupt not putting on the incorrupt, but becoming merged in the corrupt rotting earth, no longer mother, but vampire? *And there shall be weeping and gnashing of teeth.*

He heard a movement and opened his eyes to find Kathleen standing by his bed. 'Did I wake you? I knocked, but you didn't answer. I've brought you a cup of tea.'

'Not civet to sweeten the imagination. How kind of you! Thank you!'

'How do you feel?'

'Fine. How do you?'

'Oh, I'm all right. You look rather white.'

'Do I? I slept rather well, as a matter of fact. You *are* energetic, aren't you? All dressed.'

'Yes, I thought I'd go out and get the Sunday papers. What do you want?'

'Oh … The *News of the World,* of course. In Inishkill we shan't be able to buy it. It's banned by the Government as a filthy English rag. Let us gather our rosebuds while we may.'

'All right. I'll draw the curtains, shall I? Doesn't everything seem stuffy after the country?'

He watched her impatiently. She was really rather overdoing this ministering angel stuff, he thought. As she turned suddenly she caught the expression on his face, and for a moment it arrested the words on her lips. She said: 'I'm afraid I'm disturbing you. Did you want to go to sleep? I was wondering if we might go out somewhere. It's really quite a nice day.'

'Later, if you don't mind. I'm going to be lazy this morning. It's so wonderful not to meet host and hostess, not to have discussions about Auden, Spender and Isherwood, the wickedness of Franco, and the best method of saving the world to make it safe and secure for Kenneth.'

'You mean you want to be left alone all day?'

Now he had hurt her. 'Of course not. We'll do something later. I know. We haven't been to Hampstead Heath together. We could get some dinner at the Spaniards'; then we needn't bother much about lunch. Would that suit you?'

'I don't mind where we go. I'd rather like to talk to you some time, though.'

'Of course. We have heaps to discuss. But later. I have a bit of a headache. Those church bells. How right Keats was: "*Calling the people to some other prayers, some other gloominess, more dreadful cares, more hearkening to the sermon's horrid sound.*"'

Kathleen came to stand by the bed. 'You haven't a temperature or anything, have you?'

'Why on earth should I?'

'You just sound rather excited and queer.'

'It's considered a mark of education to quote poetry; it doesn't mean that you are sick of a fever.'

'Sorry to be fussy. Well, good-bye for the present.'

'Good-bye.'

A little later he heard her steps ascending, but this time she didn't knock. He watched while she pushed the Sunday newspaper under the door. Much later he gathered energy to get out of bed, make himself fresh tea, and return to bed to read with absorption. Before his intent eyes there spread a panorama of mothers murdering their unwanted babies, of girls dying under illegal operations, of men committing bigamy, sodomy, rape, assault, desertion, confidence tricks, of runaway lasses and defiant lads being committed to Borstal. He also read not only his own horoscope but that given for those born under other stars. When Kathleen came in with coffee and a boiled egg for his lunch he used his knowledge to make conversation:

'There's going to be an unexpected change in your environment. You are going on a journey.'

'Am I?'

'Yes, of course. It says so here. You're born under Venus and Taurus, aren't you?'

She took the paper, read where his finger pointed, and put it down without comment. Then she went away. She was evidently going to be difficult, he thought resentfully. He had a good idea of what she wanted to talk about. She wanted to break it all off. And he'd have to try and ingratiate himself so that she would soften once more. More degradation ahead! He set his teeth. She must be allowed these maidenly flutterings.

When, later in the afternoon, she knocked once more on the door, there was no reply. She opened it gently, and going up to the bed found that this time he was really asleep. For a moment she watched him: he looked drawn and tired, she thought. Well, that was nothing new. Even the sun and good air had done little to mitigate the pallor of his sallow skin. But in sleep he looked—as, of course, everyone did—so defenceless, and moving in that defencelessness. That was one of the differences between animals and human beings. No one pitied a cat or a dog dozing on the domestic hearth, but once the heart had made a true movement in charity—which is to say a movement whose primary source is not self-interest or self-love—toward another human being, how his or her temporary unconsciousness tugged at the strings of pity. Uneasiness, too, as if there comes a moment's sub-conscious realisation of the common responsibility of our human frailty. She went out noiselessly with her heart softened, though she had not wanted her heart to be softened.

How different when he was awake and on guard, she thought wryly later, as, having dined, they sat on a bench on the Heath looking down over London. How difficult he made it for her to break the ice and become personal when he continued to talk of impersonal things, which didn't really affect *them,* such as the way Myra gave Kenneth a feeling of social inferiority. 'She makes him feel that he is not a gentleman, so of course he has to prove that he is so much more interesting than any gentleman with a stiff upper lip could be.' And then the war, and its impending horrors which seemed, she could not help thinking, to provide him with a strong feeling of satisfaction. The Germans, he thought, would be the ones to start bombing. Much later the British or the Americans would evolve some bomb, some gas that would kill thousands where the Germans had killed hundreds. 'Then they will hold up hands dripping with blood, and say, "dreadful, but, of course, we had to do it to shorten the war."'

'You think we are hypocrites?' she said politely.

'No, not at all. You are perfectly right. It is only that the Anglo-Saxon reasoning powers are, if not more subtle, at least different from those of the lesser breeds.'

As she was silent he stole a glance at her averted profile. Oh, yes, he knew she wanted a discussion. And how much he didn't want one. That, he thought, was one of the main differences, separating youth from middle age: youth thought everything could be resolved if one opened one's heart freely, and talked oneself out; middle age had done that so many times and found that nothing was resolved, so that one was wary of words, fatigued in advance.

'The Germans, you see, have to justify themselves with some such aphorism as we had in the last war. "Might is

Right". The British are never, could never, be so crude in their tactics.'

Still she said nothing, but continued to stare at the distant prospect. He followed her eyes, thinking of those first days in London when he had come up here, and looked down over the City, and dreamed of its conquest, not of leaving his name writ large, but making at least some faint impress. Of being a minor notability among a few thousand other minor notabilities. That, of course, was all over now. He hadn't achieved even the mild satisfaction of seeing Adam Palmer written in *Who's Who*. Well, his ambitions were otherwise now. Vaster, though nobody would know of their realisation, *if* he realised them, save his Creator. The thought gave him the impetus to be about his business, so that at last he gave Kathleen her opportunity.

'Oh, by the way! Have you written to your father and stepmother about us?'

'No, I haven't,' she said, without looking at him.

'Really? Well, that's as you like. But you ought to give in your notice at the office to-morrow, oughtn't you? How long do you have to give them? Is a week enough?'

'I should have to give them longer than that. At least a month.'

'Oh, that's a pity. Because it looks as if I shall have to go back not later than the end of the week. My cash won't hold out longer. Never mind! I'm your John the Baptist: I go to prepare a place for you.'

She gave him no answering smile. She said after a moment: 'I've been thinking, Adam. Do you think it would really be a good thing for you to marry me?'

'But of course. Surely …'

'You see, I accept that you don't love me, but …'

'Oh, golly, don't harp so on *love*. It means so little. If you only knew how little it means outside Tin Pan Alley and sick lusts and dreary desires, and sore hearts aching in monotonous circles.'

She waited a moment, and then went on steadily. 'But I thought I might be of use to you. But since we stayed at the Cookes'—while we stayed there, I began to feel that I couldn't help you at all. For one thing you're clever, and I'm not at all clever. I should get on your nerves.'

'Please don't call me clever. Whatever I am, I am not that. You make me feel as if I were one of the young men who write for the *New Statesman*.'

'There you are! When I say anything, you make me feel that I've said the wrong thing, that I'm stupid and clumsy. Well, maybe I am, but …' She stopped, for to her horror she felt tears stinging the back of her eyelids. How awful if she broke down and wept here publicly with people passing on the path below them, with other couples passing. They would think that she was going to have a baby, and was imploring Adam to marry her!

'I'm sorry.' She felt him seek for her hand, and touch it lightly. 'I don't at all feel you're stupid and clumsy. If you only knew how your sincerity and honesty showed up Cooke's self-dramatisation, and Myra's tedious and conceited missionary endeavours, you would never say that to me. It's just that my manners have been shot to pieces. I'll improve as time goes on. Honestly.' As she still said nothing he added: 'Satisfied now?'

'Not quite,' she murmured.

'Well, out with it. What else have I, do I, do wrong?'

'It's not anything that you do wrong. It's just that I think, what's the word, I think you are a perfectionist. That you can't get on with ordinary people. After all, the Cookes aren't so bad. They both wanted to be kind. But you have no toleration. You haven't even any toleration for yourself, I don't think.'

He looked at her sharply. Out of the mouths of babes and sucklings! 'That's perfectly true. *Mea Culpa*. But how have you discovered it?'

'I was thinking about you and ...' she made the effort, 'that woman. Well, other people have fallen in love, or whatever way you would put it, and ...'

'And perceived that they dreamed a dream, and woken up finding that the faerie gold had turned to dead leaves. The fate of those who follow after rainbows! But nevertheless they take up their bed and walk. Is that what you mean?'

'Something like that. Of course you put it much better.' He meditated. It seemed that he must tell her some of the truth. Together they stared in front of them, at a prospect fair enough, but now wrought upon by their minds' eye to reflect dejection and loneliness. The silver birches were loaded with a mute sorrow, the people who strolled and laughed along the sandy tracks, and called to their dogs, strangers for ever, as remote as puppets.

'The difference is,' he said in a low voice, 'that I was a believer; and I broke all the Commandments, or nearly all.'

'Do you mean the Ten Commandments?' she hazarded, fearing a smile at her expense.

'Yes. I broke them all for nothing. I coveted; I cheated; I lied; I committed adultery. And all ... came the grey dawn,' he added trying to speak lightly, trying to suppress that surge of misery that had risen in his heart.

Now she touched his hand. 'I do understand. More than you think. It was worse for you than for most of us who don't believe much in anything except in trying to be kind. But you do want to start again, don't you?'

Start again? There was the rub. Did he want to start again? His case was that of Macbeth: *I am in blood stept in so far, should I wade no more, returning were as tedious as go o'er.* No doubt her guardian angel was joining hands with his to soften his heart. He spoke rapidly and at random: 'You don't know what it was like in the asylum. There was a man who followed me about so that he could masturbate in front of me. There was an attendant who pushed me into a bath of scalding water so that I screamed. Yes, I screamed out before him.' She made a little exclamation of pity and put her hand on his arm.

'I didn't know. I thought from what Kenneth had said …' she stopped, realising her mistake too late. He had turned on her. 'I know what Kenneth told you: he said that I had played up to the doctors, he told you that I gave the attendants the cigarettes Maureen sent me as bribery to ingratiate myself with them, that I tried to be helpful, and do some of their filthy work for them. It's quite true.'

'Oh, no. He didn't say that. Honestly, he didn't.'

He turned away. 'It doesn't matter whether he said it or not: it's quite true,' he said, and feeling his heart beating, drew out a cigarette. Yes, he was thinking, that was what he couldn't obliterate from his mind, from his account with God. The other things were nothing. Brutalities can be overlaid as time goes on, only recurring perhaps in nightmares. But the despicable *crawling,* the servility, the incessant pretence, because I was terrified, yes, terrified out of my life that I'd be certified, *that* I cannot forget or forgive.

'Listen,' she said, 'we won't talk about it any more.'

'No, we won't talk about it any more,' he agreed. He lit a match and noticed that his hand was shaking. 'Oh, I'm sorry. Will you have a cigarette?'

'No, thank you. I just want to say that we'll try, won't we, darling? We'll try and forget all that, and be happy?'

'You say 'we'. Do you mean 'we'?'

'Yes,' she said bravely. 'Yes, I do. I think I understand still better now. It's only that I wanted to be sure that I could be a help to you, and not a hindrance.'

'Oh, you can be a help all right. But you make me feel that I am taking advantage of your sweetness.' And so I am, he thought to himself. So I am!

'Don't think of it that way.' As he said nothing she went on, putting brightness in her voice: 'I've got it all planned out. You go back one day this week; I must do some darning for you, or else your mother will think you are marrying an awful slut who doesn't give a damn. And I'll give a month's notice to the office, and then follow you. How's that?'

'That's fine,' he said. 'And very good of you.'

She looked at him searchingly. No, she mustn't take any notice of the flatness in his voice. She saw him shiver as he thought, more *crawling*.

'It's cold. Let's get back to our nice gas-fire. It's quite late.'

He rose, and they made their way down the bank, and on to a path. Kathleen's hand tightened on his arm; she stumbled once on her high heels as she walked, for the sky above them was darkening.

PART TWO

PART TWO

— FOUR —

I

MRS. PALMER did not look at Kathleen while she talked, but Kathleen realised that her conversation was directed to her, for whenever she lowered her own eyes, or gave a brief glance round this strange room, she was immediately conscious that Mrs. Palmer was aware of her momentary defection of attention, that her own eyes then rested full upon her. So now there was something of strain in her listening as the long story of why Mrs. Palmer's foot was bandaged proceeded to its crisis:

'... a good enough young woman as a rule, and maybe it was my fault, for truth to tell she has cut me my corn many and many a time and no harm done. No harm done but a good deal of good, so that I usually go out with an airy feeling in me, the way you have after making ... but you wouldn't know about that. But yesterday, whatever was in it, but I might have been nervous or something, or have let my attention wander, but I moved my foot, and with that she cut out a whole piece of it!'

'How terrible!' said Kathleen with genuine sympathy, thinking that the climax had come. 'It must have hurt like anything.'

'Do you know what she did?' said Mrs. Palmer ignoring the interruption. 'When she saw the blood pouring out, she

111

clapped iodine on, cotton-wool soaked in iodine. And with that I let a scream out of me that you could have heard in the next street.' She leaned back triumphantly.

'Good Heavens,' said Kathleen, looking at Adam to find him staring indifferently ahead of him.

'You see, it stung as if I'd been bitten by a wasp. "What are you doing to me?" I said. "Well," she said, "I've taken a piece of your foot off you"—those were her very words—"and if I don't disinfect," said she, "it might go and get septic on you."'

'I see. But wouldn't peroxide or something have been better?'

'That's what she did. And, of course, in a way I couldn't blame her, for it was myself moved my foot, thinking of the Lord knows what. Anyway she bandaged my foot the same as you see it now, so that I had to get a taxi home. Taxis are very dear here. I wonder if they are as dear in England?'

The sudden change of subject took Kathleen unawares. She looked at Adam for help. 'Well …'

'Not having had possession of much or any money lately I haven't been in an English taxi for some time,' he told his mother. 'By the way, haven't we some sherry or something to offer Kathleen after her journey?'

'We have, as well you know. But I didn't know if Miss Bartlett drank, so I was leaving it to you to offer.'

'Oh, don't bother, please.'

'Kathleen doesn't drink to excess, Mother, but she can take a glass of wine.'

'Of course, naturally. I'll go and get it. I thought Maureen would have been back by now.'

'Can I go? Or can't you ring for Bridie?'

'Bridie's out at Confession. And anyhow I wouldn't let her have the key of my wine cupboard. It isn't that I don't trust her, but it's wrong to let a young girl be led into temptation. Don't you agree with me, Miss Bartlett?'

'Oh, call her Kathleen, Mother, and have done with it.'

'Certainly, if Miss Bartlett doesn't mind.'

'Please do,' said Kathleen to the retreating back as Mrs. Palmer hobbled to the door and shut it behind her. There was a moment's silence after she had gone; then Adam said: 'Well, how are you feeling?'

Her feelings were so many and so mixed that there was no possibility of putting them into a sentence. It was better, she could have said, that Mrs. Palmer should do the talking: at the same time she felt cheated of those questions she had anticipated about her journey, whether she was tired, and so on. Was she then just a rambling self-centred old woman? Not altogether, certainly, for there was her sense that she herself had been summed up, that all the while she chattered Mrs. Palmer had been forming certain judgments, and that these judgments were not sympathetic. She replied: 'Your mother is a handsome woman, isn't she?'

This was true. Mrs. Palmer was a brunette whose black hair was plentifully streaked with white, and whose full white face was now sagging. But one could see the proud good-looking girl she had once been. That was when she talked with the animation with which she had been talking, though, Kathleen had felt, the vivacity was a cloak for disapproval. Going out of the room her mouth was pulled down into an expression of mingled bitterness and resignation. Mrs. Palmer, Kathleen's intuition told her, had had to compromise with life, and had fought, perhaps still fought, a necessity which she found to be gall.

Adam had shrugged. He was still looking at her questioningly. Her eyes glancing round the room rested on a coloured picture of the Sacred Heart. The red wound seemed to her a fantastic melodramatic touch in this Edwardian drawing-room with its faded flowery chintz covers, its polished little tables, and the pretty empty watercolours hung in narrow gilt frames.

'She's very religious, isn't she?' she said in a low voice, her ears alert for the opening of the door.

Adam shook his head. 'No! I wouldn't say that she really has it in her to be religious. But in her old age I find she has taken very heavily to piety. The gaining of indulgences is a profitable, as she thinks, hobby, which takes up a lot of time which would otherwise hang heavily for her. Actually, of course, she is erecting a barrier for herself which she will find very hard to pass.'

'To pass?'

'To pass into the Kingdom of Heaven,' said Adam, smiling at her. Of course Kathleen didn't understand him. She had no key to the perverse satisfaction which had filled him at, so he thought, encountering in his own mother another soul treading a way of damnation, the way of piling up credits for oneself which in effect obliterated any sense of humility. The smile went, as to himself he added the rider: but, of course, she doesn't know what she is doing. God would forgive the pious, the smug who hardened their hearts, because they knew not what they did.

The sound of voices in the hall distracted Kathleen, and she looked apprehensively at Adam.

'That will be Maureen,' he told her. 'Now Maureen is a different matter.'

The door burst open, and a tall girl with a beret clapped on to curly untidy dark hair, and a smiling fine-skinned pinkish face with rather too much lipstick placed carelessly on a large mouth, came in.

'Hello, Kathleen, how are you? What sort of journey did you have?'

'Fine, thanks,' said Kathleen, rising while Adam murmured unnecessarily: 'This is Maureen.'

'I was raging that I wasn't here when you came,' said Maureen wringing Kathleen's hand after a second's worry whether she should kiss her or not. Perhaps being English she wouldn't expect it: all the same she wanted to show her that she was welcome. 'But did Mother tell you: we discovered at the last moment that we'd ran out of coffee, and I wondered whether you took coffee for breakfast the way all the best people do in England, don't they? And I thought well, it would be a terrible thing if Kathleen didn't have what she was used to on her first morning in a strange country, that she'd start off thinking we were all Yahoos …'

'Maureen, would you open the card table for me?' said Mrs. Palmer in a patient voice behind her. 'Then I could put this tray down. Oh, thank you, Adam.'

'We're all going to have sherry,' said Maureen in a voice full of gratification. 'And wine biscuits. Do you like sherry, Kathleen? I love it.'

'Sit down, Maureen, and don't talk so much,' said Mrs. Palmer. 'Kathleen can't get a word in edgeways.'

'I know, I'm sorry,' said Maureen seating herself against the wall. 'Well, I'm glad you had a nice journey. Did you see anyone you knew to talk to?'

Kathleen shook her head. 'No.'

'Maureen imagines,' said Adam as he passed glasses and plates, 'that the world is made up of people who live in England and Inishkill, particularly Bailey, who are continually crossing the sea that divides the two places. To her London is Paradise, except that she didn't see as many Bailey people as she wanted to on the one occasion she went there.'

'Don't listen to him, Kathleen. I love London; I wish I could go again. I saw *The Maid of The Mountains* and the Tower of London, and Kew Gardens and Hampton Court …'

'Please spare us, Maureen,' said Adam. 'It's not very interesting, you know.'

'I suppose not. It was just interesting to me, because I'd never been anywhere, and of course we're very stick-in-the-mud here. Have you been to Paris?'

'Yes, once.'

'How wonderful,' breathed Maureen. She took a long drink, brooding now over Kathleen in silence, as if seeking for some outward sign of worldly grace which had accrued to her.

'My friend and I were there only for a week,' said Kathleen, apologetically.

'Your friend?' said Maureen with interest. 'Were you with a girl or a man?'

'Oh, a girl,' said Kathleen, joining in the laughter which followed, though Mrs. Palmer's laugh was more a snort than a laugh. And she said reprovingly: 'Of course, it was another girl, Maureen. What will Miss Bartlett, I mean Kathleen, think, you talking that way of her?'

'Maureen has a novelette mind,' said Adam. 'She reads only the very worst books.'

'But I didn't mean anything bad,' said Maureen, flushing. 'Men and women in England do go away together, don't they, Kathleen?'

'Yes, of course, they do.'

'And no harm in it, is there? I only meant that you'd feel rather dowdy going round a place like Paris with another woman. At least I think I would. Of course you can't tell.'

'As you can see,' said Adam, 'Maureen is a highly expectant virgin.'

'Adam!' said Mrs. Palmer sharply.

'What?'

'That's enough of that sort of talk.'

'I don't mind,' said Maureen. 'It's not quite what I am, because I've given up being expectant. I mean I'm not hoping any more now that I'm thirty-five.'

Kathleen smiled back at her, but couldn't think of what to say to break the disapproving silence which flowed from Mrs. Palmer. She finished her sherry, saying as she restored the glass to the table:

'I enjoyed that. Thank you so much.'

'Have another,' said Adam, rising.

'No, thank you.'

'Oh, aren't you, Kathleen?' said Maureen disappointed, and plainly expressing her feelings that if Kathleen didn't she wouldn't be able to.

'Not just now.'

'Another biscuit, Kathleen? No, well then,' said Mrs. Palmer, 'perhaps you'd like Maureen to show you your room and the bathroom and so on. I'd come myself, only the way it is with my foot so bad …'

'Oh, of course, you mustn't,' said Kathleen, getting up quickly. Maureen got up more slowly, with resignation in her air.

'It's not a very good room, I'm afraid,' she said to Kathleen as they went up the stairs. 'You see, Adam took back his old room that we'd been using as a guest room while he …' She stopped.

'Yes, of course,' said Kathleen hastily. 'Oh, I'm sure I shall be very comfortable. It's very good of you to put me up.'

'What else would we do?' said Maureen. She added enigmatically: 'You mustn't mind Mother. I used to mind her, but now I don't.'

She opened the door of a pleasant attic bedroom, and setting Kathleen's suitcase down went on: 'Don't you think we should get out of the way of minding about people too much? I mean I used to, and I underwent agonies. But now …' she sought for an expression and with some pride found it, 'now I'm snapping out of it.'

'I expect you're like Adam in that you're very sensitive.'

Maureen seemed to consider this rather more earnestly than Kathleen felt was required. Looking round the room, and seeking to turn the conversation to more conventional lines she said: 'Oh, how lovely! I'm sure I've got you to thank for these.'

Maureen's gaze followed hers to the bowl of red roses that stood on the polished table underneath the window. Momentarily she was gratified for she had arranged and

118

rearranged them that morning. And the evening before both Bridie and Mrs. Palmer had been called in to admire the decorative touches she had added to the room, to note how well she had polished up the table, how brilliantly the varnished boards now shone, how wonderfully ammonia had restored the colour to the faded square of brown carpet in the centre of the room, and how her own bedside rug which she had sacrificed practically matched the blue curtains at the window. For the past few days this room had indeed been the centre of Maureen's life, to be thought of at the office, to be rushed up to the minute she had eaten her high tea. But now it had taken its place with other finished jobs; the spotlight had shifted from the room to the girl standing by her. For Maureen lived in the present, with excursions, if the present were dull, into a future that would surely contain compensating gold. Kathleen then partook both of the present and the future for, though she had looked rather disappointingly quiet and serious-minded at first view, already Maureen was prepared to exchange glamour for hidden depths. She hoped they would become great friends, and to become great friends they had, of course, to exchange confidences.

'Yes, they are lovely. I do hope you'll like it here. Of course your own flat will be much nicer for you. But I've left that mostly to Adam. They've already started the distempering; he was along this morning. I suppose he told you?'

'Yes.' Kathleen had knelt down, and was starting to open her suitcase. She felt she needed a wash, and wanted to find her sponge bag. Maureen came eagerly to her side. 'I expect you've brought some lovely things with you. I'm dying to see your clothes.'

'I haven't got many. What I have are mostly in the trunk we left at the station to take to the flat later.'

'Oh, what a shame. Still it's something to look forward to.'

'Honestly, I've nothing very exciting. You'll be disappointed. Daddy gave me ten pounds for a wedding present, and that doesn't go very far toward a trousseau.'

'But how mean of him!'

'Well, you see,' said Kathleen, standing up and flushing slightly, 'he married again, and my stepmother isn't very interested in me: I think they were both glad to feel I was getting married and would be off their hands.'

'How dreadful of them,' said Maureen plunged deep into sympathy, and her sympathy going to her head she asked: 'Is that partly why you married Adam then?'

'How do you mean?'

'I mean to get away from your unhappy home.'

'I didn't live at home; I lived in London. Where I worked.' There was a slight stiffness in her voice, but sympathy, curiosity, and the unaccustomed sherry combined to make Maureen disregard the danger signal. She rushed on: 'Did you agree to marry Adam then out of real love?'

'Why do you think I agreed to marry him?'

'Well, there could be several reasons, couldn't there?' said Maureen sagely. 'Now that I've met you, and seen what a nice girl you are, I should think it could have been out of pity.' Perhaps Kathleen's subconscious recognised the measure of truth there was in this, a truth which her conscious mind had no intention of admitting, stiffening itself into anger against the tactless Maureen. She snapped the lid of her suitcase shut before she replied slowly: 'It seems to me that you probably don't altogether understand Adam. I admit he's not easy to understand.'

'No, he's not,' agreed Maureen instantly and innocently. 'He's a funny one, isn't he?'

'By funny you probably mean clever. He is very clever.'

'No, I don't mean just clever. Even I have met clever people, though I'm the fool of the family.' She paused: what she wanted to say about Adam was that he was bewildering because she had found him since his return wilfully unkind. He wanted to make her feel, for example, that she was badly dressed, gauche, ignorant, that he expected her to say something stupid every time she opened her mouth. She said instead: 'Don't you find him very critical?'

'He's an idealist, you see,' said Kathleen with a slight touch of the schoolteacher in her voice. 'He wants everybody, including himself, to be perfect. And then when they're not, he is much more hurt than ordinary people like ourselves can understand.'

Maureen nodded. 'Yes, I see. Do you think then that's why ... why he had his nervous breakdown?'

'In a way, yes. I know all about the woman, if that's what you mean,' said Kathleen. She felt that it was Maureen who had made her mention Cynthia, and her heart hardened increasingly against her.

'Oh, I didn't mean about her,' said Maureen quickly. 'That's all over now, isn't it? She must have been a real bad one. But you mean that he must have put her on a pedestal and then when she tumbled off ... but even so, Kathleen, I don't quite understand it. Because, after all, other people have been disillusioned, too. I mean life as well as books is full of it. We all have our spots of trouble that way. And I can

understand people even committing suicide over it. But …'
Maureen frowned and rubbed her chin reflectively.

Kathleen's control broke.

'You mean,' she said in a tense voice, 'that just to suffer
so much and so unbearably that he was incapable of looking
after himself, so that you and your mother immediately had
him clapped into an asylum, that seems to you, I suppose,
rather petty. It's not enough for you, I suppose!'

No dreamer was ever awakened more abruptly than was
Maureen at that moment. Baffled, terror-stricken, she gazed
into the bright angry eyes confronting her while a castle in
the air came tumbling down, and its wreckage loaded her
heart so heavily that she could only stutter out, clasping her
hands in appeal:

'Oh, Kathleen, please … we're not as bad as that. Truly!
I'm not as bad as that. I wasn't at home when it happened,
and Mother couldn't get hold of me quickly. That's why
she had to go to London … all by herself. It was awful. I
kept writing to him, and sending him things, but he never
answered. I see what you think. That's why he hates me
now he's come back. But Kathleen, please try and understand. I didn't mean to be horrid. I was just stupid. It's like
Adam says. I never open my mouth without putting my
foot in it.' She tried to smile, blinking back the tears that
wanted to force themselves under her eyelids.

But Kathleen gave her no answering smile. 'I think it
would be better if we didn't discuss Adam,' she said coldly. 'If
you wouldn't mind showing me the way to the bathroom.'
She added in a polite voice, turning away from Maureen's
stricken face: 'I've been travelling since quite early this
morning, and I feel dreadfully dirty, and must look it.'

'Oh, no, you don't. But, of course! I'm sorry. It's this way,' said Maureen almost in a whisper.

Downstairs again, both brother and mother commented on Maureen's unusual lack of speech. Smiling feebly, and carefully avoiding Kathleen's eye, Maureen said she was always really much quieter than people thought. They all went to bed very early.

II

Adam noted the outward signs of Kathleen's loyalty toward himself, which displayed themselves in attentiveness whenever he spoke, and a sweetly proprietorial attitude which became her, since it imparted a self-confidence she usually lacked. The trouble, as it seemed to him, was that such loyalty tended to become contagious. One Monday morning when Kathleen was out he found himself challenging his mother: 'Well, what do you think of your future daughter-in-law?'

Mrs. Palmer, who was hastily patching a sheet before it could be added to the wash, went on threading her needle without replying. Then, without looking up, she said: 'What did you say?'

'You heard what I said.'

'No, I didn't.'

'I asked you what you thought of Kathleen.'

'Kathleen? Oh! Why she appears to be a very nice girl.'

'She not only appears to be a nice girl: she is a nice girl.' Mrs. Palmer bowed her head over her stitching in silence.

'I suppose you find her very English?'

'Well, she is English, isn't she?' Uninterestedly Mrs. Palmer glanced toward the window. 'Oh dear, I hope it's not going to rain.'

'Of course. Do you consider her reserved?'

'I'd say she is a reserved type,' said Mrs. Palmer mildly. 'Quite right, too. Why shouldn't she be?'

As Adam looked at her baffled she went on: 'I'm sure she sets Maureen an example. It's dreadful the way Maureen blurts out everything that comes into her head. I've told her time and time again, "not unless you're with your best friends," I've told her, and the dear knows that we none of us have many of them.'

'Do you mean that Kathleen has snubbed Maureen?'

'Oh, I don't know anything about that, my dear. If she has, I'm sure Maureen well deserved it. Of course after Maureen doing all she could and ransacking the house to make Kathleen's bedroom fine and fit for her, she might have been a little … that's so nice of Kathleen, too. Making her bed every morning and dusting. I've told her she mustn't do it. After all we have Bridie. And when you and she are in your flat she'll find she has plenty to do, so now is the time she should be taking a rest.'

'So you do like her, and you're glad I'm marrying her?'

'As to that it's you that are marrying her and not me. The only thing …' Mrs. Palmer looked up from her sewing and sighed.

'What only thing?'

'Well, of course, you'll say it's just an old woman being ridiculous about her religion, but it did go to my heart when Father Fitzgerald told me that as it was a mixed marriage the banns wouldn't be called. Ah, I know it naturally doesn't mean anything to Kathleen, and not you now that you've turned against your religion: it's only an old-fashioned woman like myself that feels it's not the same as a proper marriage.'

'Well, you knew I was marrying a Protestant: we can skip all that. What I want to know is, have you anything against her apart from that?'

'Nothing in the world. Haven't I told you?' There was a pause, then Mrs. Palmer added detachedly: 'I was a bit surprised in a way at the choice you made; I don't mean that Kathleen isn't quite nice-looking, but when you were at home here it was always the smart lively girls I'd catch you throwing sheep's eyes at. Oh, that was a long time ago, and you have more sense now.'

'What you really mean is that you're disappointed because I didn't bring some common slut back here, so that you would have real cause to complain about her. You're mad because I haven't made a fool of myself, that's what it amounts to.'

Mrs. Palmer looked up at him coolly. 'That's not a very nice thing to say to your mother, do you think? I wouldn't say that's a nice thing to say at all.'

It wasn't a nice thing to say, but there it was: his mother had made him lose his temper as she generally did, and generally had done in the years that had gone. 'Oh, you win as you always do,' he threw back at her, and then to his relief heard Kathleen's knock at the door, and went to let her in. 'Here you are at last,' he said in a loud voice so that his mother could overhear. 'I was afraid you'd got lost: I was just coming out to look for you.' And then it was that he found himself patting her arm, and taking her parcels from her, and helping her off with her coat and guiding her into the room and pulling out a chair for her as if he had been the most infatuated of lovers.

It was when that evening he sat with her in the pictures, her hand in his, feeling two against the world, or at least against Mrs. Palmer, for Maureen didn't really count, that he suddenly realised that his feelings were dangerous. My God, he thought with horror, I believe I'm getting really fond of her.

Kathleen noticed that a few moments later his hand gently withdrew from hers, and decided that he was probably giving more attention to the movie, which was approaching its climax. Actually Adam was paying no attention at all to the G-men who were closing in around their prey: he was seeing himself the prey, if not of love, at least of liking.

And out of the past he remembered a poet telling him, as they sat in a pub discoursing of religion, that he himself believed that if once you really *liked* a person why then you were saved.

At the time he had felt immediately and intuitively that there was truth in this. You liked, and there was a breach in the walls of the heart. *Harden not your hearts* was a supreme warning. Was not the immediate and most efficacious result of the duty of prayer which the Church urged upon the faithful, prayers for the dead, prayers for the souls in Purgatory, prayers for those whom we loved and prayers, too, for our enemies, that of softening the heart? No man or woman could kneel down and send up an entreaty that God should be mindful of one person other than themselves without practising the grace of charity.

In the semi-darkness, he closed his eyes tightly. Charity was not for him: never, never, never, if he lived for another forty years, until he was eighty years old, could he allow himself one thought of kindness. There was Hans Andersen's tale of the Snow Queen, of little Kay and Gerda … how well suddenly he remembered it. The Snow Queen had asked Kay if he were cold, and then she had kissed him, and the kiss was colder than ice, and for a moment he felt he was going to die.

And sitting there in the warm stuffiness he too felt he was going to die, not from cold but from nausea in the pit of his stomach. Never, never? he asked wonderingly. And NEVER, the voice replied. And to try and avert his attention from that sickness he went on listening to the voice, which must be his own directing reason, and which explained, now less sternly and more blandly, that, of course not, and didn't he remember all the texts in the New Testament about nothing profiting without charity, so that obviously the first thing he must do was to eliminate charity, since nothing must profit him? And, of course, it would probably get much easier as he went on. Since he had remembered the fairy tale, didn't he also remember that the next moment, when the ice had fully penetrated, Kay felt quite all right, and didn't notice the cold all about him?

Kathleen, looking away from the screen as the Tommy-guns cracked out, touched his arm: 'Do your eyes hurt, darling?' she asked anxiously.

He looked at her as from an immeasurable distance. 'What? Oh, my eyes! Yes, they are rather tired.'

'Do you want to go? Or …' she looked at the screen, 'can we just wait till the end? It won't be long now.'

'Of course.'

He stared for a moment at flickering grey and black-and-white. What was it so enthralled her? The police were tumbling into cars shiny black, malevolent; sirens wailed as they raced along past brilliant electric signs cutting across the empty spaces made by the warning cross-road lights ... he closed his eyes again; when he opened them they stared at the interior of a luxurious apartment; as the sirens screamed and there was the grinding of brakes from outside a man said to a beautiful girl in evening dress: 'So you've framed me,' and slapped her across the face, once, twice, hard so that she staggered and fell, and the man had a gun and was going to shoot her when the door opened, and one of the cops said: 'What's going on here?' while a plain-clothes man gripped the wrist that held the gun, and the gun went off in the air, and there was a yell, and now the man with the gun had got away and was holding the crowd as he stood by an open window, and there were more shots and then he had jumped straight through, and now the audience were whisked to another apartment and saw through the eyes of a man and a girl who were standing motionless with linked arms a man falling past their window, falling down, down, down past the lighted windows of sky-scrapers ... he averted his eyes, and thought 'what nonsense! what nonsense!' but without conviction, for he knew at the same time that a man killing himself was never nonsense. Beside him he heard Kathleen sigh deeply.

'Well, that's that,' he said as the screen became one patch of blinding light.

'Yes, we'll go, shall we?'

They walked up the thickly-carpeted passage-way between rows of white faces and dark clothes; as they were caught in the pressure of other people towards the exit doors Kathleen said: 'It was exciting, wasn't it?'

'Oh, undoubtedly.'

For a moment her heart sank, for there was the old sneer in his voice. But when she saw his face as they stood waiting for the tram that would take them home her newly-won confidence revived. He was tired, that was all.

In the tram on the upper deck they were separated. But from where she sat she could see his profile, and pressed her devotion toward it. And her understanding. Of course she realised it now: it had been a mistake to go to a gangster film: he had probably identified himself with that hunted man; some of the ugly scenes had aroused old memories. That was why he had taken his hand from hers; that was why he hadn't wanted to look. His mother and Maureen wouldn't have understood something like that. But she did; she was prepared to be infinitely patient with him when he slipped back into one of the old dark moods, be prepared for him to say unkind things ... all by herself she was going to nurse him back to happiness.

Maureen, looking up as they came in with a polite: 'Did you enjoy yourselves?' on her lips, wondered why, when Adam had on his scowling withdrawn expression, Kathleen looked, on the whole, rather pleased with life.

III

Adam said at breakfast the next morning: 'To-day I'm going to show Kathleen our mountains, as we call them. We'll have a picnic, shall we, Kathleen?'

'Lovely.'

And Maureen said: 'A great idea. I'll go and cut you some sandwiches.'

When she'd gone, and Mrs. Palmer had also wandered off, Kathleen said guiltily: 'Oughtn't we to ask Maureen? I mean to-day she's off from the office.'

'Definitely not,' said Adam. 'I want you to myself.'

Now they were going up a narrow lane bordered on one side by purple heather and golden gorse, with a stream running deep below the opposite hedge. Soon they would reach the high places where low stone walls marked the divisions of rough grass land and bracken stretching away to the mountains sloping above. Now and then they paused, once to look into the yellow eyes of a tethered goat, again to admire the still blue smoke from a turf fire rising straight from the thatched roof of a white-washed cottage drowsing in the sunlight. Just inside a small farm there was a pond with ducks swimming upon it, and Adam had to murmur, more to himself than to Kathleen:

'Four ducks on a pond,
A grass bank beyond,
A blue sky of spring,
White clouds on the wing:
What a little thing
To remember for years—
To remember with tears.'

Kathleen said: 'Exactly the same except that it's not spring, but autumn.'

And Adam said: 'Exactly,' and sighed, and then cursed himself for sighing. What a nuisance a literary turn of mind was, he thought, since like an undertaker it embalmed for ever matters that were best out of sight and out of mind in the grave of one's past. How often as a lad, as a young man, had he not trodden this self-same path up to the mountains, mostly alone, sometimes with another; once it had been with a student who was training for the priesthood, and the thought of his friend's vocation had at once mellowed and saddened the whole day's excursion with a nostalgic autumnal tinge. Not many more days, he had thought, for the other to lie carelessly on the heather and watch the drift of clouds, the black clothes, the Roman collar, the respect of the laity barring him for ever from the lonely self-sufficient untamed joys.

And once he had brought a young girl, named Margaret, whom he was beginning to love. They had kissed once and once only. She had gone away suddenly to England. And he hadn't written, because if he wrote and she didn't reply, then it would prove that it had meant nothing to her at all. And that would have been harder to bear than just leaving it as it was:

What a little thing
To remember for years—
To remember with tears.

He closed his heart with determination against these echoes from the past which the familiar earth threw up at him with every step. He would talk; that was always a way out:

'Aren't you glad Maureen isn't with us?'

Coldly he heard the falsely caressing note in his voice, turning his head for Kathleen's reply.

'Well, I am, of course. But I am a bit worried about Maureen.'

'Why?'

'I have the feeling I've been rather unkind to her. But …'

'I know, I know. She started to criticise me the very first evening you came, and you wouldn't stand for it. It's a pity in a way. Maureen should amuse you as a foreigner. I suppose she rates a trip to Paris and a pilgrimage to Lourdes about equally high.'

'It's a pity she didn't marry, don't you think? Perhaps she still will.'

'I doubt it. She didn't tell you about her romance with a grocery assistant, did she?'

'No, she hasn't told me anything. Why, did she really love him?'

'Oh, yes, they both loved each other. But, of course, a grocer's assistant was below the Palmer standard. Mother was disgusted and frowned, and I scoffed and jeered. So I suppose poor Maureen couldn't quite stand up to us. We're frightful snobs in this country, you will find.'

'You do really like Maureen, I believe.'

'Used to, used to. When she was a bright little girl. But her arms and legs are too fat for her figure, and she is really unbearably gauche, don't you think?'

'You are so critical! She's really quite nice-looking. Do you think she's still in love?'

'Oh, I shouldn't say so. There was somebody else afterwards, but I forget about that, only that there was an impediment.'

'Poor Maureen!' said Kathleen. Hearing of Maureen's ill-starred if somewhat, as she was young enough to think, ludicrous romance, she felt her anger against her vanishing.

She stopped to take a deep breath and look around her. 'Oh, I wish she was as happy as I am happy,' she exclaimed.

He watched her glowing face. Yes, she was happy. She was falling in love with him, as he was, or had been, falling into liking of her. That must be stopped, my girl, he told her in his heart. If he didn't look out he'd have her singing about the house next! So easy it was really to make a woman happy! A little kindness from some man they liked was all it came to. And the shadow of his resolve rose up and stalked before him.

'Come on. I want to find a spot where we can be sure no one will disturb us,' he said. 'When we get to that stone, do you see it, we can turn off the beaten track.'

She nodded, bright eyes brightening still more. As they went on, she asked him softly the usual feminine question: 'Are you happy?'

Angels rushed in, where fools might fear to tread, he thought, turning his head away from her and looking back to where a donkey grazed. Best to go on talking: 'Of course! Maureen, you know, needn't really be pitied. She'll probably end up as a religious woman.'

'Like your mother?' said Kathleen with a note of contempt in her voice.

'No, not like my mother. She is, as I think I told you before, merely a pious woman.'

'Pious or religious they have both behaved extremely badly to you,' said Kathleen emphatically.

'You must remember that as my mother looked on it, and as most people look on it, to have a lunatic in the family is a disgrace. It reflects on themselves they think.' He stopped, thinking, I've told someone that before, oh, yes, old

133

Maydew, when we said our farewell. 'The son from whom she had hoped so much, and then he must go and do a thing like that!'

He spoke equably and lightly, but satisfaction stirred in his heart, because his memory was letting in dark things. Whatsoever things are of ill report, think on these things. That was a good rule for the Little Way.

'Well, I think, and shall always think, it was beastly of her.'

'Now, if we turn here, and go down this slope, we shall find what was once a quarry of some sort: it makes a good hiding place,' said Adam touching her arm to guide her.

He could feel her warm to his touch. He must also warm sufficiently to ensure the mechanical success. One help would be to think of her as … no, not as Cynthia, that was all fordone, if not forgot. He would think of her as Margaret, the love that had beckoned in the distance and then withdrawn for ever. It could be a romantic dream in which Margaret came back. That hunger and ache of the body which made the heart sick and unsteady with longing, that was surely all over for ever. Such lust was a part of love, however much the reason and the spirit might reject. Unless it were there one might admire and like someone; might indeed imagine oneself into love, but something was lacking. A fire had not been lit. And if it were there, how easy for the mind and the spirit to be drugged to acquiescence; indeed more, to take a lively part in that act of creation by which man differentiated himself from the animal, creating a god or goddess out of some to others very ordinary creature, cherishing every gesture, every inflexion of a voice. Quite often it worked; the melody lingered on; indeed if there were any sort of goodness there it worked, and so made a true sacrament out of marriage. It had just been unfortunate that in thinking back on Cynthia he could find no recollection of any honesty, any true sweetness, any kindness for anybody or anything but her own pleasure. He had worked overtime to create not out of straws but out of the dung of a complete falsity.

'I see where you mean,' cried Kathleen at his side. 'And look, I believe there's a foxglove.'

'Willow herb, I expect,' he said. And so he couldn't forgive himself, and what was of greater matter, he couldn't forgive God.

'Are you hungry? I am.'

'Well, we can sit down here for our picnic.' And: 'What have we got?' he asked, humouring her, as she opened the neat parcel Maureen had made.

'Egg and cress. Goody! And ham. Which are you going to have first? And I'll pour out the milk.'

She waited on him; if it had been Cynthia he would have waited on her. Now what he must remember was that Kathleen was not Cynthia but Margaret.

'How nice you look to-day!'

'Only to-day?'

'Always, of course. But I haven't seen you for a long while.'

Her heart leaped. He must mean that he was beginning to see her, not, of course, as she really was, but in the way people in love saw each other. Her hand made an instinctive gesture towards him, but he was looking away, so she said instead, following his gaze: 'Of course you must have come up here many times. Tell me the names of the mountains.'

He told her, ending with a little unconscious sigh. For, of course, those names were a litany that must never be said in his heart again. Such love and, when he was first working in London, such sorrowful desire had been generated by their images.

'Why did you sigh?' she said quickly.

'Oh, did I? I suppose coming up here again after so many years is like looking at an old album. You smile but you also shudder looking at faces dead or gone for ever. The banquet hall deserted sort of thing. And unless you are a sentimentalist you put the album down quickly.'

'But these hills, all this ...' she made a gesture with her hand, 'they're not dead. They're always here.'

'Are they?' he asked, crumpling the sandwich papers and bag and throwing them away. A spot of desecration! But Kathleen said: 'Oh, we mustn't leave our litter here! I'll hide it somewhere.'

A nice girl with nice instincts, he thought, watching her as she recovered the rubbish. But he mustn't think of her as that ... *Margaret, Margaret*. And he lay face downwards on the grass, summoning an old forgotten dream to warm his senses, as the sun was warming his body.

After she had come back he said: 'Let's go along to the quarry now.'

'All right. But aren't we going to go on climbing?'

'No, I want to make love to you.'

He took her arm to guide her, and when she started to speak shook his head, and said: 'Hush!' She mustn't be allowed to speak; she must do nothing to pierce the frail fabric of the dream he had fashioned out of long ago and far away. And she submitted to him with joy and with fear, looking to him for reassurance, for comfort, for tenderness, when in the darkness into which she had entered she could feel nothing but pain. At first, when she was still in his imagination Margaret, he gave her some caressing words, then, when his desire was strong enough to mount and ride alone, the image he had summoned vanished, dismissed.

When it was over, and Kathleen had disappeared for a while, he examined what he had done with the satisfaction of an accountant balancing the ledger. In the first place he had sinned before God, since owing to his early training he believed, and would always believe, that sexual intercourse outside marriage was wrong. In the second place he had sinned before the old gods of the earth since he had taken his woman without fleshly joy or fleshly tenderness making her merely the instrument of a cold fabricated lust. No pipes of Pan had played. And that sin was in itself part of a greater sin, a sin against the spirit which was love. He had given no love, as on his side there had been love in his liaison with Cynthia, when he had given all he had, spirit as well as flesh. God would surely note that there were no extenuating circumstances in this deed, the so-called act of love.

He was smoking, looking at the ground, when Kathleen came back to him, face powdered, hair combed, seeking still in her vast uncertainty that reassurance which he had denied her. Now surely he would put his arms about her and tell her all was well.

He said: 'Have a cigarette.'

'Thank you.'

'Are you tired?'

'I am a bit.'

'Well, what do you say to climbing no farther, but to making our way across country to a pub I know, where we can get a drink. One of the good things in this benighted country is that we can get a drink most times in the day.'

'If that's what you'd like.'

'I'd better lead, as it's rather rough walking.'

They went mostly in silence. When they sat sipping whisky in the tiny parlour of the remote public-house at which they were the only visitors, he threw her words meant to be friendly as one rewards a useful dog with a bone.

'When we are settled in the flat, you must have your friend, Eleanor, over to stay.'

'Why? I thought you didn't like her much.'

'I don't dislike her. Why should I? Oh, I remember. We felt she didn't like me much. She was jealous of my taking you away.'

'I don't think it was that, so much as …'

'As that she thought you were exceedingly indiscreet in agreeing to marry me at such short notice?'

He watched her inwardly assent to the truth of this. He noted how pale she looked, how her mouth drooped. Poor child, he thought with an objective pity. She is thinking: is this all it is? And for the rest of her life, unless she leaves me for another man, that will be all. Of course it will become easier for her; she may even derive some physical satisfaction from it. But in essence that will be all. And since she isn't coarse-grained, since she isn't a natural fornicator going to it as easily and instinctively as rabbits, and also as do many men and women, as underneath all the dressing-up dear Cynthia did, for example, I have cheated her for her whole life, maybe. Note that, God, as I am sure You are doing.

'And how right she was, wasn't she?'

She looked at him now with appeal. A few words, that was all it needed, and Eleanor wouldn't be right. As he didn't say them she looked away, stared hard at the runner on the round table set in the middle of the little room: 'I don't know really; I don't think I know anything.'

'And what do you mean by that?' he asked her gently. Since she said nothing, but drank her whisky with a sort of determination, he said: 'We'll have another. You need it.'

'Ought I?' she asked him childishly. 'It's very strong, isn't it?'

'Yes, it's good whisky,' he said, rising and going to seek the landlord.

Left alone she looked at her face in her handbag mirror thinking, as many another girl has thought before her, I don't look any different! Then she thought, I expect I've disappointed him. Still, he knew she had had no experience.

He came back with the two glasses. 'When you've drunk this you'll feel a lot better.'

'You treat me as if I were a sort of invalid.'

Without replying he lit a cigarette first for himself, and then for her. Then he asked curiously: 'Have you any feeling we ought to have waited?'

'Waited for what? Oh ... Till we were married, you mean. Well, we are going to be married in a few days, aren't we?'

'I hope so,' he assured her with a smile. 'That is, unless you run away.'

'I shan't run away,' she told him, and then there came a rush of feeling that threatened tears. That was one thing it did to you: it did make you feel that you belonged to someone. Even if that someone didn't specially want you to belong.

'But perhaps you don't want to now?' she said bravely, lifting her head. 'I mean I was rather stupid ...'

'Don't be silly,' he said, roughly interrupting her. And in that roughness, in the way he immediately changed the subject and started to speak of their plans, that it was a nuisance he had to start on this new job in the Library that his mother had found for him by pulling a few strings, so that they wouldn't have any proper honeymoon, she did extract at last, with the warming aid of the whisky, some of the reassurance she had been seeking. Perhaps it was all right, she kept telling herself as their talk flowed on easily enough to future events. Or perhaps if it wasn't—for she couldn't quite cheat herself—all right yet, it would be.

There was a point when going down the hill towards the bus stop, towards houses and people, he made a crack in that hastily assembled reassurance. She had said, looking back towards the dim shapes of the mountains, fading away from them now as the light faded from the sky, sensing how remote they seemed, how self-contained and apart:

'We'll come up here again, won't we? Quite soon?'

'Shall we? You forget winter's coming on.'

'That won't matter, will it? We'll still go for long walks.'

'You forget, I shall have a desk to attend to every day.'

'But there'll be week-ends?'

'I expect I shall mostly fall asleep at week-ends. Remember, I am middle-aged, my dear, and will become so more and more.'

But he wasn't thinking—his face, as she looked at it sharply, told her that—about being middle-aged. He was thinking of something as remote from her and her grasp as the mountains which sank into the dusk behind them. About them lay the peace of the evening and the homely sound of the noisy rooks as they wheeled their way to the great elms. But he was outside that peace, and therefore depriving her of its balm.

When they came in, Maureen noticed that this time it was Adam who looked quite pleased with himself while Kathleen seemed very tired.

IV

Adam Palmer rose from his knees after his gesture of saying the penance the priest had given him, and strode down the aisle of the nearly empty City church. In the street, among the restless Saturday night throng making their way homewards from cinema, chapel, public-house, sports gathering and theatre, he examined his sensations and found to his relief that triumph predominated. Perhaps not yet a completely emerged triumph: the burglar who has made a safe get-away with his booty still needs time to assure him that the heavy hand of a policeman is not about to descend.

But for him there was no human policeman. He could and did look boldly into the faces he passed; sniff in the odour of drink from a group of noisy gesticulating men standing on a corner, cock his ear toward an argument that was starting between two women: 'You did!' 'I did not; you're a liar.' He looked so hard at a newspaper boy selling the last edition that the lad thrust a sheet into his hand, and he had to pause for a moment to find the coins demanded. The tiny incident heightened a sense that he was taking part in a masquerade in which all significance, all solidity had been erased from people, houses, shops, the lighted trams and buses, bodies bent over bicycles, speeding, hooting motor-cars, the policeman directing traffic … he was walking in a world that had no landmarks, in which movement was aimed at no goal.

A pageant, a play without meaning, just as his action in buying a paper he didn't want was without meaning. He saw it so, he decided, because he himself was a playboy having reduced the Sacrament of Penance to a mummery. It had all been so unexpectedly easy, going according to plan. He had come late, he had seen to it that he was almost the last penitent outside the particular box he had chosen; he had started with a lie saying that it was nearly a year since his last confession while all the unshriven years of sin and despair lay heavy on his soul, and quite glibly gone on with the recital of venial offences: a few lies, over-indulgence in drink, loss of temper, missing Mass a few times … just another borrowed and spurious handful of the small change of human frailty to rattle into the priest's weary ears, weary surely to the point of satiety after listening that day perhaps to a hundred similar recitals. Certainly he hadn't probed; nor had he given any homily. Little did the man the other side of the grille know that for the first time surely that day he was listening to a sacrilegious confession. And to one act of sacrilege, that of making an impious and dishonest confession, he was about to add another, that of contracting marriage while he was in a state of mortal sin.

With his reckoning of this twofold sin against the laws of the Church, Adam permitted himself to savour fully his triumph. Whatever colour his other sins wore, he mused, as he stood waiting for the bus that would take him home, sacrilege would have its own garb: black against scarlet? Or purple, since the soldiers who had scourged Jesus had put on Him a purple robe. Now he was joined to those mocking soldiers who had cried: 'Hail, King of the Jews!' as they placed a crown of thorns on His head, and smote Him with their hands.

But even among the soldiers he stood apart, for they knew not that they blasphemed, and so were included in that prayer of Divine charity from the Cross: *Father forgive them.* He had known, and he knew perfectly well at that moment, what he had done. Moreover he was contemplating the extent of his sinning with cold pleasure as at last a fitting sacrifice to be offered to the foul fiend.

A bus drew up before him, jerking his thoughts momentarily away. But it was not his bus, and seeing a rosary protrude from the handbag of a woman who had dismounted, his mind took another track. Maybe he wouldn't feel so triumphant over his fake confession if he had gone to a London church, walking as it were out of line and out of step from people from whom faith had been drained, as blood drains from a wound leaving the flesh cold and dead. But here the greater part of the people had as yet seen no reason to dissociate one great saying of the New Testament from another, to blue-pencil here and there: still believing that the Word made flesh had said to His apostles, *Whose sins ye shall forgive they are forgiven,* they went in humility to confess their faults and their sorrow for those faults. Again he stared eagerly at the faces of those who were more than likely to be fellow believers: that pretty girl would turn from me in horror if she knew of my purple sin; and so would

143

you, sir, though now you merely think of me as another man waiting for a bus. And as his bus rounded the corner towards him he drew a deep breath of the damp autumnal air, wondering if perhaps a leper who had been a connoisseur of living did not experience some such subtle pleasure as he was experiencing in knowing that he was a ghostly outcast among his own.

Maureen on her way to bed was intercepted by him.

'Have you by any chance a copy of the Penny Catechism?'

'Yes, I think so. What do you want it for?'

'Just, my dear sister, to refresh my mind about something.'

'I'll bring it down to you.'

'Thank you, darling.'

He was not usually so free with his 'darlings', she thought as she turned away. Probably it was an unthinking continuation of the almost demonstrative affection he had shown to Kathleen since his return, the jesting half-affectionate attitude toward their mother, and then his earlier announcement that he was going to Confession. Maybe this unusual high-spirited mood was the outcome of his receiving Absolution for his sins. But why then did he remind her of a schoolboy who had robbed an orchard successfully? There's something more wrong than right about him, thought Maureen, her heart heavy as she hunted up the little book.

She looked him squarely in the face as she gave it to him, and noticed how dilated were the pupils of his eyes. He looked as if he might have been drinking, she thought, but there was no smell of drink off him.

'Good night, now.'

'Good night, and thank you. Bless you!'

In his own room Adam found what he sought. It was a sacrilege to contract marriage in mortal sin, and: '*Instead of a blessing the guilty parties draw down upon themselves the anger of God.*'

Kathleen, of course, was not a guilty party, dear Kathleen, whom he had found almost touching to-night in her innocence and in her ignorance! He would really try and make the poor girl quite a good husband, or at least a passable imitation of one. On himself alone let the anger of God fall!

And if, he thought later, lying in bed, it was only a beginning, the wilful breaking of the Commandments of Holy Church, still it was a beginning. Any theologian would admit as much! A beginning of the Little Way!

PART THREE

— FIVE —

I

To the highly strung and the nervous, no job, however easy, is easy at first. But this morning, as he sat at his desk in the Public Reference Library, Adam Palmer congratulated himself that he had at last got the hang of things sufficiently to relax. He knew now what were the books most people were likely to demand and their whereabouts; he knew, too, that he had little to fear from his chief, Mr. Ferguson, who was a mild non-interfering sort of man; still less from the fussy little Mrs. Doyle who was in charge of the down-stairs lending department; he knew she didn't care for him, that she was one of those women who were repelled rather than fascinated by his personality. But there was no rea-son why he should spend time, precious time, ingratiating himself with any of his colleagues. They couldn't hurt him, and since their ways crossed infrequently, save in the way of inter-house telephone calls, for this or that, he couldn't hurt them.

For that was really the main part of his mission in the service of the fiend, he was thinking, as ostensibly he stud-ied the English *Times*, from which it was his duty to make certain cuttings every morning. In so far as he was capable he must in the words of the prayer said after Low Mass unite himself under Satan with 'the other wicked spirits who wander through the world for the ruin of souls'. It was souls that he must attack, not their flesh and blood, nor their temporal possessions, nor their wives, nor their maidservants. In any case these matters were to a considerable extent under the protection of the laws of the State: people who took what wasn't theirs sooner or later were likely to go to prison; violent assaults on the person were even less likely to go unavenged, punished according to their degree of ferocity. It might be the gallows! As for lechers, they had to have their wits about them—and usually lechers didn't, poor devils, have their wits about them—to escape such inevitable consequences as humiliation by some loud-mouthed virago, drains on their purses that went on and on. Yes, the little sinners against property and propriety paid the price here and now, filling the prisons, the casual wards, the slums. Like Lazarus they received their evil in this world.

Raising his eyes he discovered that at that moment there was in his vicinity a true Lazarus in the person of an old and unshaven man sitting in a very dirty brown coat at a desk in the most remote corner of the room, pretending to be reading the *Economist*, actually surreptitiously conveying morsels of food to his mouth from paper bags hidden under the desk. He had noticed him some days before when he dozed. For, like other men, after he had eaten he liked to relax, to rest, perhaps to sleep. But unlike other men he lacked a comfortable chair, privacy or, most important of all on a cold day such as this, warmth. So he had done the best he could for himself finding a corner next to the hot-water pipes in this silent room provided by Mr. Carnegie and supported by the rate-payers. But neither the founder nor the ratepayers intended the room to be used for the benefit of those who like himself had probably been compelled to leave his doss-house at an early hour that morning.

If therefore he, Adam Palmer, did his duty by those rate-payers, and by the Corporation Committee who paid him six pounds a week for doing his duty, he should now descend from the majesty of his large desk, walk over to the old man, tap him on his shoulder and inform him that he must not consider the library to be, like an inn, a place in which he could take his ease.

As if he felt the gaze of authority upon him, the old man's head half turned in his direction, the champing of the jaws ceased, a page of the *Economist* was turned. Adam dropped his own eyes back on to his newspaper.

I don't think I shall disturb you, he told him in his heart. If I rebuked you, if you shambled forth to eat your garbage in a doorway or on a bench, no doubt the Recording Angel would, looking at you in pity, jot down another credit to your assurance of eternal bliss. My business is not to harry God's poor; Pharisee and policeman do that; but to give a little further push to those who have a canker at the heart, who are at least in some danger of retribution at the Judgment.

But then, he reminded himself, affrighted, might not this very abstention on his part count as an act of mercy, freshening, if only infinitesimally, his arid soul parched for lack of grace. If he had been by nature a conformer, believing, as a Protestant would probably believe, that his duty as a librarian was obviously to see that the rules of the library were kept, then he would be committing no sin in reminding the old man that the Reference department of a Public Library was intended as a place of mental activity rather than of physical rest. But, alas, what he really and truly believed

151

was that beyond and above all rules and regulations, even, it might be—though this was another question—beyond and above the Commandments of Holy Church, there was a primary duty of charity. The letter killeth, the spirit quickeneth. The old man was harming no one; therefore he not only could but *should* be left alone.

He squared his shoulders, he rubbed his hands together, preparing himself reluctantly to rise from his desk, for no spirit must quicken within him. Then he saw that someone had come in at the door and was approaching his desk as if to ask a question.

The next instant he recognised someone he knew, James Norman, one of the new band of Inishkill writers, whose first novel had won a good deal of praise from the English reviewers. An ex-schoolteacher, he had only lately returned to his native country with the ambition, so Adam had summed him up as the result of a previous meeting, to make himself a personage. Of medium height, fair-skinned, and brown-haired, with a slight moustache, spectacled, wearing no overcoat but a thick scarf over his brown tweed jacket, Adam decided that he looked more like a clerk affecting Bohemianism than anything else. He half rose from his seat, stretching out a limp hand, pretending cordiality.

'Nice to see you. The inquiring public is, as you see, conspicuous by its absence.'

They both glanced over at the old man, who now, Adam saw, was resting his head on both arms, apparently asleep.

'And what a specimen!' said Norman surveying the spectacle. 'Do you, by the way, allow tramps in here?'

'Ah, that's the problem with which I was actually concerned when you came in. At present, of course, he is disturbing no one, but if he started to snore, disturbing any serious student—and here we have one, I think——' he added under his breath as a stout, well-dressed man came in, and took down a volume of an Encyclopaedia, 'why then, I suppose … what do you think, really?'

'Well, he's not a very edifying picture is he? But then,' he darted a keen look at Adam, 'there are a number of things in this country that I don't find particularly edifying, do you?'

'Quite,' said Adam, disappointed that the conversation had moved away from the particular. He shook his head, as Norman thrust his open silver cigarette-case towards him. 'Sorry, neither public nor librarian are allowed to smoke in these sacred precincts. You were saying … for example?'

'What a bore for you, not to be allowed to smoke. For example? Well, I should think examples cry aloud to any of us who have known other countries. That tramp is much filthier in his person than an English tramp, just as our streets are dirtier and shabbier than English streets.'

'You think so?' said Adam. He was going to add a reflection on the dreariness of those tracts of consciously respectable slum which like patches of dingy grass among wild herbs militate against the colour of the weeds, and avow his preference for slums that were slums, but restrained himself. Not for him, a humble librarian, to suggest the aesthetic viewpoint to one whose function it was to be an artist. 'Well, perhaps you are right.'

'And then—we all come to it sooner or later, don't we, here? Religion! I don't want to tread on any corns, but you're not a practising Catholic, are you?'

'By no means.'

'So I suppose you'll agree that the superstition in which the people are plunged isn't any help. Mind you, I'm not anti-Catholic, but the trouble is that unlike Continental Catholics who are civilised, Inishkill Catholics over-do things. They can't really be trusted with religion at all; they turn it into an affair of slobbering piety, making it an excuse to avoid their first duty to be decent responsible citizens.'

Adam could not resist saying: 'You remind me of the ending of a prayer which I heard on the radio the other day: of course it was a Protestant service: *"and let us ask Jesus to make us more sensible and useful people."'*

'Well, why not?' asked Norman, with a slight pucker between his brows. 'Of course,' he rushed on, a little angrily, 'I am quite aware that we imagine ourselves to be much more highly spiritual than anyone else, any other country.'

'Quite, quite. All nonsense, of course,' said Adam soothingly. He was aware that the man with the Encyclopaedia was glancing toward them, and that a girl who was standing in front of the quick reference shelves had also turned her head. Observing the other's uneasiness, Norman said: 'I know this isn't the place to discuss these things. What I really …'

'My wife would so agree with you,' murmured Adam hastily. 'She is an English girl, and that is her reaction.'

'Really? Louise, that's my wife, so wants to meet her. That's what I came in about, not to raise a brawl. Would you both come to a small, very small, house-warming party we are having, next Tuesday evening? About eight or so.'

'We should love to. I am pretty sure Kathleen isn't engaged then.'

'Then we can get together and have a real talk,' said Norman turning on his heel. 'By the way, I also wanted to look up a quotation: you have Bartlett's, I suppose?'

'Certainly. It's over there. But do let me show you.'

Returning to his seat Adam watched Norman's bent back and intent spruce profile. A vain man, he thought with satisfaction. Can be narked in a moment if there is not instant encouragement. And his vanity leads him into a certain amount of indiscretion. He took me for granted rather too easily. Of course he's younger. About thirty-four possibly. And because he has got a few good reviews, because, as he told me, his third novel is due out next month, he feels the world his oyster.

Envy touched him, as he took up his scissors to cut out a paragraph which concerned an increase of wages in the textile industry, which item might, or more probably might not, be the occasion of a question from the inquiring public. If he had started earlier, he thought, if he had not wasted so much time in his youth dreaming of God, of beautiful chaste women with whom he might he, a sword between the twain, resisting or, finally, not resisting temptation, of the old dark legends of long ago and far away when poetry walked the earth instead of being confined between the covers of a book; if he had but coined the vision when it shone instead of looking for a living and stepping-stone out of unrewarding journalism which staled the head and sucked away the vitality, why then he might be sitting as smugly as Norman did now, master of his own time. My mistake was that in the beginning I took too literally what the good nuns taught me, that I was here not to make a name for myself, not to enjoy myself or get rich, but simply to know, love and serve God. Look down now, God, and judge between us. If I had served the Muses as faithfully as I once tried to serve You, would incarceration in a madhouse have been my reward?

He bit his knuckles savagely, looking gloweringly across at the unconscious Norman, who was making a pencil note on a pad. Seeing Norman close his book with what seemed to him a self-satisfied air, his thoughts darted down another passage. All the same, it is quite possible, my fine fellow, that God may see you, as equally He sees me, in danger of damnation. But *you* don't know where you're going, and I shall do my best to speed you on that downward path.

The library was filling up now with the first comers from the lunch-time interval. Norman went out with a wave of his hand to Adam, to which he was careful to respond with nod and smile. And then he observed that the old tramp, temporarily forgotten, had begun to snore, that heads had turned in his direction.

Without giving himself time to think he got up and walked over to his corner. His hand touched the arm in its frayed sleeve. No use. He gripped the arm firmly, giving it a slight shake, and the old man's face lifted, eyelids opening on dimmed blue eyes.

'You are not allowed to sleep here: I think you'd better go, hadn't you?'

He saw the discoloured veined hands grope protectingly over two brown-paper parcels lying on the desk, perhaps containing uneaten food, like a squirrel guarding its nuts; then one hand slid the *Economist* towards him as if in propitiation.

'You must go,' he repeated coldly, aware that heads had turned their way.

Without a word the old man, understanding this time, gathered his belongings together, pushed back his chair, and shambled out with downcast head, and yet with the noiseless furtive effect of those accustomed to make themselves scarce either at the voice of authority, or before the voice of authority can speak.

Adam returned to his desk, and to the covering protection of *The Times*. It was as if he had whipped the old man, as he might whip a schoolboy. But the old man wasn't a schoolboy: he was one of those defeated by the hurly-burly of life, and therefore one to whom as much courtesy as possible should be showed.

Reading but not absorbing lines of print, he presented his sin, and waited hopefully for the feeling of triumph which should therefore be his reward as it had been his reward when he had fornicated coldly and lovelessly. It did not come. He merely felt sick and shaken.

If he could only smoke; his hand groped for his packet of cigarettes, and then he glanced impatiently at the clock on the opposite wall. He had still some moments before his relief, Dickinson, was due to take over while he went out to his lunch. Meanwhile he must reason with that feeling of guilt. It existed simply because he had forced himself to do something wholly alien to his particular temperament. He could not expect a path, just because it led downwards, to have no stony places over which he tripped and bruised himself. The other matter had been easier to encompass, probably because his bent, like the bent of other natives of Inishkill, was anti-woman, whom they had been taught to regard as a source of temptation. He had been in a way revenging himself upon the whole sex. But he had never had any feeling against the very poor and the outcast: still less now, when in the ghostly way he was doing his best to identify himself with them. He had so much more in common with that old man than with that smug young woman who had stared, he sensed approvingly, when he turned him out. His hand clenched, *God damn her!* As perhaps He would!

He folded *The Times* neatly, and started to clear the desk, reproving himself, as he did so, for his thoughts. No, no! This outcry must not be permitted. For actually he had learnt something. He must not spend too much time in the enlargement of those sins which came easiest. If we love our friends, what thank have we? *But I say unto you love your enemies!* Through all his folly and sin, a gentleness natural to him had stayed; he must ungentle himself.

The door behind him opened, and young Dickinson appeared a full three minutes before he was due.

'Here I am!'

'Oh, hello!'

'Been busy?'

'No, not particularly. Up to about twelve, hardly anyone. Oh, I had to turn an old tramp out who has come before. He was snoring rather loudly.'

'Oh, I know who you mean. He always takes the *Economist* as a screen. I doubt if the bloke can even read. He's a nuisance, isn't he?'

Adam darted a quick glance at the rosy-cheeked, fresh young face. A nuisance to whom? To nobody but a few dullards trying to extract something from print as a dog roots in a dustbin.

'You agree I should have turned him out then? I was wondering if I'd been too harsh.'

'Oh, no … I mean. Well, they leave fleas and things, don't they?'

That was another point of view. It was a pity he himself was not hygienically-minded.

'Filthy morning. It's started to rain now,' said Dickinson seeking a change of topic, since the half-smile that twisted Palmer's mouth made it seem as if he had said something foolish.

'Has it really?' What a pity, Adam thought, he hadn't realised that circumstance. If he had, it would have increased his sin: turning the old man out into the wet as well as into the cold. And he had no overcoat.

'Haven't you got an umbrella? I think there's one in the office you can borrow.'

'Oh, that's all right. I never use an umbrella. I have only to go round the corner to Richards' café. Well, if you stamp these new books that have just come in I think that's all.'

'Rightio.'

Dickinson, settling himself into the chair, felt some relief as Adam disappeared. This new chap might be very clever and all that, as he was supposed to be just because he'd been a literary journalist in London, but he wasn't the sort that you could get on with very easily. He was overdoing things, too. What was the idea of turning old Economist out? Why couldn't he have just woken him up, and told him he was snoring and disturbing other people? That was the obvious thing to do. That was what he'd have done. And nobody's feelings hurt!

— SIX —

Not having gone to many literary parties in his native town, Adam and Kathleen arrived too early at the Normans'. They had to learn that in Bailey if you were invited for eight it meant that you turned up any time after nine. With the consequence that there had been rather too much time allotted to putting Kathleen through her paces. Chiefly by Norman, while his wife, Louise, and Adam had listened and thrown in a word or two. For Louise was certainly less talkative than her husband. A warm-skinned, dark-haired girl, with fine eyes, she had also the ingrained suspiciousness characteristic of the native of provincial Inishkill. And this, though she had nodded with approval when Norman had asked Kathleen if she didn't find a lot of pettiness and narrowness in Bailey after London.

But then, Adam had decided, Louise was at the stage, would probably never move away from that stage, when everything that her husband thought and said was likely to be to her ears marvellous and profound. A devoted wife! And a maternal wife, he added in his mind when an old friend of Norman's turned up in the person of a Scot, Macdonald, a painter, whom she didn't know very well. For when Macdonald contradicted something that Norman had said, her brown eyes grew sombre and she regarded the lanky dark young man with disapprobation.

More devoted than Kathleen, Adam was thinking, half-envying the other his possession of such unqualified hero-worship. Kathleen had failed to rise socially to the bait thrown before her. She said as regards Inishkill that she really hadn't enough experience to judge; when asked what plays she had seen in London she had mentioned a Noel Coward piece; and after a cataract of disapproval had been launched on Noel Coward and his works by Norman, she had replied gently and firmly that all the same she was afraid she had enjoyed it. And that, though he, Adam, had nodded assent to the strictures and added a phrase or two of his own.

In fact, though self-conscious and not at home, Kathleen goes on speaking the truth as she sees it, thought Adam. Whereas others strike attitudes. She won't be a success in this company so. They'll dismiss her as very English. But he himself had to make his mark. He had to achieve a position from which to plant seeds of distrust and enmity.

So he was pleased to be found talking with some fluency and more precision of phrase on the topic of D. H. Lawrence when Colin Rowton, attached to the leading local paper, arrived. For Rowton, a pleasant-mannered chubby-faced man with glasses, and a Northern accent, was in fact much cultivated by Inishkill's intelligentsia. Rowton had the power to see that their names, even their photographs, appeared in print. Those who had had a book, even if only one of those slender volumes of poems, published were not infrequently invited to fill a column under their names for which they were paid two guineas. It was not the money but the local kudos to which they aspired. If there was any job in the town which Adam coveted it was Rowton's job with its opportunity for playing one person off against another, and thereby promoting such manifest works of the flesh as cited by the Apostle Paul in his epistle to the Galatians: immodesty, enmities, contentions, emulations, wraths, quarrels, dissensions, sects and envy. He determined to introduce himself further to Rowton, seizing an opportunity, others having come into the room, to catch him standing alone busy helping himself to whisky.

'That's a good idea! I'll join you.'

'Take it quickly,' said Rowton, 'because there isn't very much. Actually I was prepared for James to underestimate our thirst, so I turned in at a pub on my way here.'

So he obviously had, thought Adam with satisfaction. Already, to judge by his glazed eyes and a slight slurring of speech, he was well oiled.

'What do you think of the party?'

'Too many highbrow writers, and not enough booze. As I said. Sorry, hope you're not a writer.'

'I certainly am not. I was a journalist; now, alas, merely a humble librarian. I've never had a book published in my life.'

'And you're none the worse for that,' said Rowton with conviction. 'But why have you got out of journalism?'

'Too tired. I got ill actually. It was pretty tough going where I was, you know.' He gave details of his job. 'And then the old mother wanted me to come home. And, of course, I knew I hadn't an earthly to get in with your lot, so I took up the old trade of my youth once more in order to keep a roof over my wife's head.'

'Bad luck … well, I'm 'fraid I can't hold out much hope at present. On the editorial side, you see …'

He mustn't become wary. Adam interrupted: 'My dear chap, of course not! I didn't dream of it. One misses the song of the printing presses occasionally, of course, but …'

'We might take an article from you now and then. If you'd care to send in something?'

'That's very decent of you. Of course, remember I'm not a novelist, or a poet, or anything like that. I never wanted to be, as a matter of fact.'

'Could these bloody poet-novelists turn out stuff the way we have to: a readable and grammatical column about nothing or something in half an hour? I tell you what they are, bloody amateurs and nothing else, whom any editor would kick out after a week.' Rowton paused, put his fingers to his lips, and looking round added with a grin: 'But don't go and tell them that I said so, will you?'

'I wouldn't dream of it,' said Adam with sincerity. Since he wanted to play ball with Rowton, no indiscretion concerning him must cross his lips.

Mrs. Rowton, who had just come, fussed over to them. 'Excuse me, Mr ...'

'Palmer,' supplied Rowton. 'This is my wife, Palmer.'

'How do you do! Do you mind? I just have to tell Colin something?'

'Certainly.'

Adam turned quickly away, and with glass in hand considered his surroundings: all very suitable, he thought ironically, yes, all: the rows and rows of books, the cream distempered walls, the pictures, few, and quite excellent reproductions hung low, the open grate burning peat and wood; perhaps that lamp-shade was a little too ornate, too crinkly, representing Louise's taste, but the green carpet and the matching green brocade curtains could not be criticised, and incidentally must have cost Norman something. That chap must have saved from his teaching, he thought enviously, remembering how he and

Kathleen had had to furnish mostly with cast-off's from Mrs. Palmer, and to be content with a few rugs and a lot of varnish for their floors. And his eyes went toward the owner, whom at the same moment he overheard saying: 'Let's look him up in *Who's Who.*'

Now that was interesting. For if *Who's Who* was on Norman's shelves, an expensive book, and one to be consulted at any library, did it not strongly suggest the probability …? Anyway he could soon satisfy himself. He had strolled over, and was standing near Norman when the latter had shaken his head over a blank.

'You've got the new one very soon. Ours has only just come in at the Library.'

'Well, you see,' said Norman, turning to him not without pleasure, 'I thought I'd spring a few bob, as they have put me in this year. Besides, it's quite a useful thing to have around.'

'Of course. May I have it a moment?'

Norman gave him the book, and Adam looked up the entry concerning him. He was attentive particularly to the hobbies, which told those interested that James Norman favoured 'Drinking for Talking's sake, and Talking for Life's sake'. How young he is, he thought. And was it not probable that a man as young as this entry denoted was, since he had well passed thirty, likely to remain immature for the rest of his life?

He turned the pages. For there was another man in the room, the poet, Kevin O'Hara, about whose possible inclusion he was concerned. No, he was not there. He looked across at the large fat red-skinned man who at that moment, with head thrown back, was laughing contentedly with the other older man with whom he had come in. Yet O'Hara was a genuine poet, almost the only genuine poet that Inishkill had produced of recent years, and one who had laboured a deal longer in the vineyard than had Norman.

O'Hara found Palmer, the new Reference Librarian at the Central Library, by his side when he was filling a glass from a now almost empty bottle. He had had a few drinks with him in a pub once, but had found him, as far as he could remember, rather too solemn a chap, so he nodded rather curtly. 'Hello! If you're after a drink, I fear you are unlucky. Not much left.'

'Oh, that's all right. I was here early, and have had my fill.'

'I shall have to give this to Masterman, that's what's upsetting me. But damn it, you can't bring a butty to a party in the expectation of some liquor, and then have to turn down an empty glass.'

'I see the predicament. One of the first magnitude,' said Adam. He was aware that they were being watched, and turning his head found Louise Norman moving in their direction. He gave her his most appealing smile. 'I'm afraid we've drunk you out of hearth and home.'

'Is the bottle empty? I'm sorry. I'm afraid there's no more whisky. But we have some gin somewhere, I believe.'

O'Hara ducked his head in embarrassment, murmuring: 'It's all right.' For Louise's voice was not particularly inviting, but Adam said: 'I should just love some gin, if it's not giving you too much trouble.'

'I'll fetch it,' said Louise moving away.

O'Hara was now looking at him admiringly. 'Brave man! Did you see the look on her face, though?'

'I don't know that I greatly mind.' And that was true, he affirmed inside himself. He was not going to waste time ingratiating himself with his new friends' women. He had hardly bothered to glance at Mrs. Rowton. After all, you couldn't do much to persuade women further into sin, except in the one obvious and so unsubtle way. As Browning had it: He for God only, she for God in him, or something of the sort.

'She's a bit of a ... isn't she?' said O'Hara shaking his head.

'Actually I don't know them well. It's my first time here.'

'My first time, too,' said O'Hara.

Louise returned surrendering a bottle of gin into their hands, and moved back to the Masterman-Norman circle.

'Tell you what, we'll keep this to ourselves,' said O'Hara, holding out a glass to be filled. 'You be barman, and I'll take this to Tommy Masterman. I'll be back in a sec.'

When he returned Adam said in a confidential voice: 'What actually do you make of Norman?'

'Do you mean his work. I know nothing of it?'

'But himself?'

'Well,' said O'Hara. He took the glass Adam gave him and saying: 'Cheers!' drank deeply. Then he became aware that he hadn't answered some question. 'Norman? Well, I think he's a bit of a ...'

'Yes?'

'A bit of a ...' repeated O'Hara with satisfaction. It seemed to him he had found the perfect formula which at once said nothing, and said everything. 'Yes, he's a bit of a ... Come over and meet Tommy. He's the best man in the room.'

'What I can't understand about him,' said Adam detaining O'Hara with determination, 'is how he's wangled himself into *Who's Who*. Of course I'd expect someone like yourself to be there. But, after all, he's only written two books. And novels at that. Realistic ones, I believe, though I haven't read them either.'

'The lowest form of art,' said O'Hara with some violence. 'In fact not a form of art. The snooper at the keyhole of human nature, that's all it is.'

'How I agree!' said Adam, noticing with satisfaction that now O'Hara was glaring over at Norman. 'In any case I find it doubtful whether a man so desirous of promoting himself is likely to be an artist.'

'Bugger them all,' said O'Hara. 'Let's go over to Tommy where the salt wind blows free and fresh.'

Public-house winds, reflected Adam, as he was introduced, looking at the red-faced large-featured, shortish man who nodded back to him. Masterman was older than most of the others in the room, being probably in his middle fifties, and there were heavy pouches under the blue eyes. What was surprising was to find Kathleen with him, a Kathleen who now looked as if she were enjoying herself.

'I've just been trying to entertain your wife with a few of my chestnuts. She is young enough to find them new and ... well, I won't say piping hot because I've done some editing.'

'Mr. Masterman knows London very well indeed, and likes it,' Kathleen informed Adam with an effect of triumph. 'But he's shocked that I don't know some of the places he knows.'

'Rule's,' said Masterman. 'You know it, of course?'

'That's Rule's in Maiden Lane?'

'Rule's in Maiden Lane is correct. You know the story of the pretty, but perhaps not extremely well educated in the scholastic way, lady who took up with an erudite gentleman who knew all the classical tags. Always adaptable, she did her best to learn, poor girl, and one day directed her cabby "Rule's in Virgo Intacta Lane."'

After the laughter Masterman added: 'I bet at that the cabman understood all right. Smart fellows those cabmen in the days of my not so gilded youth. A friend of mine, poor old Montie, dead now, God rest him, came to join me in Romano's one dripping cold night to have a drop of the stuff that won Bannockburn for the other people. A minute or two after, the porter brings in the cabman with something shining in his hand. "Beg your pardon, Gov, 'aven't you made a mistake?" And he showed him a sovereign ... those were the days, you see, my dear, when the yellow boy was the true coin of the land. "Oh, so I have," said Montie, on to this bit of luck, as it seemed, like a bird on to a crumb in a weary frozen land. "Here's half-a-crown for you, and what will you have?" Well, when the cabman went off refreshed, says Montie to me: "There's an honest fool for you. Now what'll you have, old chap?" But when he tendered the yellow one in payment, the barman told him gently but firmly that they didn't take Hanover Jacks ... Hanover Jacks,' added Tommy, turning again to Kathleen in explanation, 'being the name by which we referred to coins that didn't ring true, that were in fact upstarts and not true Jacobites.'

O'Hara took the floor with a Bailey story of an old-time jarvey, capped again by Tommy Masterman. And now Adam, with his glass refilled, listened but vaguely to the points of the stories; instead his imagination lingered upon that old-time Edwardian London which they evoked. It was a London in which one could be poor but merry, starting with chops and champagne for breakfast, and, though pursued by the cunning of bailiffs and duns, not letting such furies detain one from attendance at maybe Henley regatta, maybe a friend's house-boat at Maidenhead, certainly Brighton and Goodwood and Epsom and Cowes, and ending up not infrequently with a conquest ... though there were perils here: Adam caught a phrase that Tommy was chuckling over: 'Said she to me in the way of advice, "never let the counterpane know who's sleeping between the sheets."' It was the London of Marie Lloyd and her wink, and the imperturbable Arthur Roberts ... Masterman exhibited his stick given to him by Arthur Roberts ... it was a London which, it was true, has its seamy side, in the way of doctors and litigation, but even here a laugh could be obtained. For now Masterman was retailing the remark which was made by one, 'Drummy', to the famous surgeon, Sir James Paget. 'After an intricate operation, the medico had stepped across the room to the washstand in order to rinse his hands: Well, his gaze met that of the patient, and he smiled reassuringly, as doctors often do after half-killing a man. "You may well smile, sir," said Drummy, "but you probably won't think it so damn funny when it comes to the suit of Paget *versus* Drummond for your fees."' Now he was on to a Jew story, and Adam thought: Yes, that was part too of that Golden Summer of putting a pony on a horse, of toppers and all that ever went with evening dress, one could tell Jew stories then unselfconsciously, without being labelled anti-Semitic or Fascist or something or other; no concentration camps in the rear interrupted one's view of Gay Paree …

Louise Norman interrupted his meditations with: 'Do you mind if I take the gin? Mrs. Rowton would like one.'

'I'm afraid there's not a great deal left,' said Adam, rescuing the bottle for her. Her disapproving appearance made him aware that he was spending too much time in this charmed circle sacred to the memories of a Bohemia that would never come again … How right was Sir Edward Grey in 1914: *The lights are going out all over Europe,* he thought, moving over to where the Rowtons and one or two others were listening—in Rowton's case rather reluctantly, for as soon as Adam appeared and he received his drink, he edged his way towards O'Hara and Masterman—to Norman holding forth.

Seeing Adam, Norman said: 'Ah, here's a man who will support me, I think. You believe there's going to be war, don't you, Palmer?'

'Undoubtedly.'

'And when it comes, it will be a very nasty affair?'

'Very nasty,' said Adam. 'Thousands and thousands will die, many thousand others will be maimed; churches, priceless buildings and common public-houses will go up in flames: instead of taking the tube to Richmond and 'appy 'ampstead, people will huddle on the platforms trying to escape the bombs. Whether they *will* escape the bombs is another matter. They will put out the lights, of course, the lights that have only been spuriously lit after the last war, a not so gay interlude, for Noel Coward is really not so gay as Gilbert and Sullivan. There'll be darkness over London, Paris, Berlin and Rome.'

'And New York?' questioned Macdonald.

'Probably New York. Anyhow, Britain will win in the end because of American dollars. America will come in on the moral side. So that freedom shall not perish from the earth!'

'You don't sound very hopeful about freedom not perishing from the earth?' suggested Macdonald.

Adam fixed him thoughtfully. He was aware that he was rather drunk, that he was speaking as if he were rather drunk, and that they were all looking at him with perhaps too much attentiveness. But he also felt that he enjoyed saying these things, and wanted to go on saying them.

'Peace when it comes, as it seems to me, will rise on a grey dawn, came the dawn, as the films say, a dawn which will light with greyness the shambles of broken cities, of graveyards and wasted lands where once corn grew. And will any man about town sport a gardenia in his buttonhole?' He glanced over his shoulder towards Masterman.

'Well, you think the British will win, anyway?' said Norman, as if drawing a neat line.

'Oh, they'll win all right. But our Lord will have descended into Hell again.' Adam closed his mouth abruptly. Yes, he must be drunk.

'I agree with you about the peace,' said Norman. 'That's what I've been saying. I think the English should go on compromising with Germany, and avoid a war that will bring calamity on the world, and hold up progress indefinitely.'

'Well, I dinna agree,' said Macdonald. 'What comes after isn't the point. One step at a time. The British are right to fight if only to stop the persecution of the Jews.'

'Surely,' said Norman impatiently, 'an act has to be regarded by its consequences as well as its intention toward good. And as we all seem to be agreed, including Rowton …' he glanced round and noticed Rowton's defection toward the group that every few moments laughed, he considered, too loud and too long … 'that the chief consequence of this war is going to be the devastation of Europe and civilisation, it were better avoided, even at the price of allowing Germany more elbow room in the Balkan States.'

'It wouldn't stop at that,' said Macdonald. 'All right, I know that's not the point. I'll try and tell you how I see it. All that poor humanity can do is to struggle and even fight the other fellow if that's the only way to stop him doing wrong. Put it another way. Suppose a man rescues another man from drowning: the man is a homicide, and the next day he goes out and kills a few people. It was still right that he should have been rescued from drowning. The only way we improve is doing the decent thing under our noses.'

'You're a man then that believes in progress toward the good, on the part of humanity?' Adam asked him.

Macdonald swung round on him. 'I do. But don't mistake me. I don't believe in that straight line up and up, and on and on, that the nineteenth-century philosophers were optimistic enough to predicate. It's a spiral movement. You go up a bit and then you slip back before you go up a wee bit again.'

'A crawling slipping movement,' suggested Adam, and Mrs. Rowton, bored by the conversation, laughed, throwing him a glance of approval.

'As ye say,' agreed Macdonald placidly. He added: 'And through slime for the most part. We havna got as far out of the slime as most of us think. That's the main part of the trouble. We're all a bit like the Germans: we've gone daft with pride, and got above ourselves.'

While Adam brooded, Mrs. Rowton caused a scurry of movement by announcing that they really must go. Aware that Macdonald was about to speak to him again, Adam got up and moved over to Kathleen. He wanted to get away from a man who seemed to know the answers. In any case, what did he really care about the coming war? He could leave that to the Prince of Darkness. First see that the mote is in thine own eye, he told himself. He had his own private war to conduct. Mrs. Rowton was telling a reluctant husband that 'Darling, we really *must* be on our way,' and Masterman, turned to Kathleen, was concluding a story about Sir George Jessel, who lacked aspirates and also loathed a sanctimonious judge: 'Whenever he encountered Selborne in the Courts he'd mutter: "'Ere comes that 'oly old 'umbug 'ummin' 'is 'orrid 'ymns!"'

To make an apparently happy man less happy, could that be done? Adam interrupted Tommy's chuckles to say: 'By the way, it was stupid of me not to recognise you before. You are a Masterman of Masterman and Son, Lisle Street, posh solicitors in the days of my youth.'

'Well, I'm the son and, as you can see, it's no longer a posh firm, for it's only represented by me, and I was a Prodigal Son. Now if I make seven and a tanner a day it's a beautiful day! By the way, these are the old man's trousers that I'm wearing. They belonged to his dress-suit, and I've had them for twenty golden years. Shows they're good stuff, doesn't it?'

'Don't you think it's monstrous that a man of your entertaining powers shouldn't be able to buy twenty pairs of trousers?' asked Adam.

'You're too obliging, sir. I can tell a story now and again, because I've known a few characters in my time. But as to monstrous … when I had the money I spent it, so what do you expect? I garner a few crumbs, that is to say a few glasses from other men's tables now and again. Though the other evening when asked the usual question and I said "brandy", a friend of mine told me very seriously: "Tommy, I'm afraid you're living beyond our means! Make it a beer." So a beer it had to be.'

'Are you a practising Catholic?' inquired Adam, and Kathleen looking at him hard wondered whether this irrelevancy, and surely impertinence, was because he had drunk too much.

'Certainly I am. I perform my Easter duties. It's a good time to go to Confession, you know, because there are so many, and you can cut it short. "Drunkenness and adultery," I say, and the last time the priest said to me: "Can't you marry, my son?" "Can't afford it, Father," I said.'

Rowton was at Masterman's elbow saying: 'Listen, Tommy, we can give you a lift. The wife's got the car outside.'

'I'll be glad, thanks. The legs are a bit weak,' said Tommy chuckling again, as he found some difficulty in hoisting himself from his chair. 'Put not your trust in legs, as the psalmist probably said somewhere …'

'We'd better go, too,' said Kathleen to Adam. 'I should think we've missed the last tram, as it is.'

It took longer for them to make their farewells, for Norman insisted on showing Adam a first edition, or alleged first edition, that he had picked up on a barrow and asking him his opinion of its authenticity. Of course in his mind I'm just a librarian, thought Adam resentfully, for he was aware that this learned chit-chat was losing him the opportunity of being asked to make one of the car party, which included O'Hara, for he had overheard him telling Tommy that they could be dropped off for a last one at Jimmy's bar. 'I know the password … trust a poet to know the password.' But he didn't want to offend Norman, since he was aware of him as a prospective victim, and first the spider propitiates the fly.

'Well, how did you enjoy it?' he asked Kathleen as they walked through the deserted streets.

'I didn't think I was going to at first. But after Mr. Masterman came it was grand. He saw that I was sitting all by myself not saying a word, and so he introduced himself, and started to entertain me. I think he must be a very kind man.'

'He's a notorious boozer, you know. I remembered about him afterwards. In his palmy days he had to be sent home in a cab every night, he was so drunk.'

'I don't care. I think he was the nicest person there.'

She waited for a contradiction, but as none came she added: 'Except you, of course.'

'You are catholic in your tastes, at least. I should think—in fact I'm quite sure—that of all the people there he was the most unlike me.'

'You mean because he's happier than you are …?'

'Yes, possibly, because as Yeats has it, "*the good are always the merry save by an evil chance*."'

'Well, in your case, an evil chance happened, didn't it?'

'You're always so kind,' said Adam. 'But I think there's more to it than that.'

There was more to it than that, he thought, as he lay in bed a victim of that wakefulness which often follows unaccustomed potations. Hang it all, Masterman had no right to be so cheerful when, by his own account, he could hardly keep his head above water, and spent his leisure cadging his drinks, wearing a cast-off pair of his father's trousers. And it wasn't as if he had been a saint or near saint either. He admitted cheerfully to the fleshly vices.

Into his mind came the remembrance of a little book he had rescued from the books of his youth which his mother had faithfully kept all through the years. It was *The Scale of Perfection*, by John Hilton, fourteenth-century Augustinian Canon, and he had started to re-read it, hoping to glean hints that he could utilise for his own scale of *imperfection*. Hilton, he remembered, had placed the bodily sins in a lesser category than the ghostly sins. '*I would*' wrote the good Canon, '*that thou knewest and chargest all, ilk a sin as it is, more the more, as are ghostly sins, less the less as are fleshly sins*' It had been Hilton's observation that men had more sorrow for their fleshly stirrings than their ghostly sins of envy and ire, yet the latter were the more serious.

The section had remained in Adam's memory since it had served as a cause for self-congratulation: he had been right in his decision not to waste his time, and indeed go counter to his present temper and inclination, and cultivate lechery and self-indulgence in drink.

But there must be more to Masterman, he thought uneasily, than a mere addiction to the more warm blooded sins. The besotted drunkard and the dreary mechanical fornicator were everywhere. He lacked pride, of course, the first of the deadly sins and the most serious. A humble man. *The meek shall inherit the earth.* He remembered again that the first pages of Hilton's book had been irritating reading for him because of their insistence on meekness. '*Be then busy to get meekness and hold it for it is the first and the last of the virtues*' It had been unpleasant to read this, for it suggested an unwelcome thought, that in the days when he had tried to mount upwards, he had hardly achieved the first rung, and had therefore not fallen so far as he had thought. And that thought must be put away for his own pride's sake! He put it away now, lying listening to Kathleen's breathing from the twin bed, and thinking instead of the article he would write for Rowton. It must be a good article.

— SEVEN —

I

It was his free half-day from the Library, and after lunching in his usual café, Adam decided to walk home. Not, he made haste to assure himself, because the sense of spring was all about him, riding high in the white clouds, whose shadows threw purple patches on the dream shapes of the mountains north of the city, but because the exercise would be good for him. Moreover he wished to savour the feeling of contentment that lay snug on his heart.

The most immediate cause of this contentment, he decided, was the self-consciousness to which he had reduced Dickinson that morning, by addressing several remarks to the pimple on his chin. It was all part of the day-to-day process of pricking the self-esteem of his assistant, so that the young man's natural cheerfulness was fast deserting him. Before his advent, Adam mused, Dickinson really felt rather pleased with himself over such matters as being able to follow the processes of political thought represented by the Leftist weeklies, and adopt them immediately for his own, so much so that he could quote whole tracts of the *New Statesman* almost verbally under the impression that he was repeating his own words. By congratulating him on his excellent memory Adam had impaired this fluency at least so far as he himself as a listener was concerned. And with regard to Dickinson's other ideas, and occasional raptures over a Beethoven Symphony, the greatness of some book, the benefits of Free Love—which actually he had not yet been fortunate enough to achieve—euthanasia, a rational agnosticism, and so on, Adam had perfected a kind of Rosa Dartle system of questioning. His method here was to treat Dickinson's views with apparent deference, and then, like Miss Dartle, his comments went to the tune of 'Live and learn, as they say. I had my doubts, I confess, but now you have cleared them up. I didn't know, and now I do know— and that shows the advantage of keeping myself abreast with modern opinion, doesn't it?'

And just as Miss Dartle had made David Copperfield feel that she must be very clever, so Dickinson felt that Adam was very clever, while disliking him very much. For the suggestion of much wider reading and of much wider experience that Adam was careful to give had had the result of shaking if not entirely removing Dickinson's landmarks. In a word, Adam made him feel that perhaps he was at least as much a fool as an up-to-date young man, and naturally that process was not an enjoyable one.

Yes, he was doing all right on the office front, Adam thought. His chief, who was an easy-going man, left him alone, but that didn't say he didn't approve of him. At least he had approved of the article on O'Hara's work pub- lished by the chief local paper under his assistant's name, and had come into the Department to congratulate him. Which reminded him that on the literary front he wasn't doing badly either. The intelligentsia were aware of him now as an influence ... he had praised O'Hara, for example, but he had made a very ambiguous reference to Norman which had delighted the novelist's enemies. Yet so far he had succeeded, or so he flattered himself, in maintaining an impression of impartiality. He was becoming quite a little master at the art of never saying quite what he thought, but of making the other fellow, especially after a few drinks, say what *he* thought. And that brought grist to the mill!

A baby running towards him on unsteady feet, pursued by its nurse, reminded him of the home front. Soon he, too, would have such a toddler. Kathleen had fulfilled with commendable promptitude the role he had allotted her and was already big with child. If he hadn't made her particularly happy, and he didn't think he had, she could shortly transfer the devotion of her heart into completely maternal channels. That would be a good thing for her, because she certainly had got much quieter lately: she was probably alone too much, since she had no capacity for easy friendliness with her next-door neighbours, and, of course, couldn't be said to be a pet of her mother-in-law. It would also be a good thing for him: children completed domesticity, and he liked to think of himself sallying forth from a snug little nest to sow his tiny seeds of ill. It was Charlie Peace, wasn't it, who had a snug little villa in Sheffield or some such place, and delighted in hymn singing and hymn playing. But he doubted if Peace was a conscious ironist, more probably Jekyll and Hyde sort of thing, whereas a higher intelligence, such as his own …
At this moment in his self-satisfaction, Adam, mounting the bridge which led over a canal, raised his eyes from the pavement, intending at this point to glance, as in his youth he had glanced so many times, toward the mountains. Instead his gaze was halted by a figure coming towards him. And with recognition, his heart was instantly deflated of satisfaction.

There was no doubt of it. The priest coming towards him was the man for whom during all those months that had followed his return he had kept a half-eye cocked, so to speak. So that he might be sure of avoiding him. How many times had he not crossed the road when any short-ish thick-shouldered man in clerical garb had appeared on his horizon. It had always been a false alarm, and so time had dulled his apprehensions into security. Most probably, he had decided, Father Mansfield, curate of the Church of Mary, Refuge of Sinners, had been moved elsewhere.

He had decided wrongly: all he could do was to keep his eyes averted, and hope that Father Mansfield wouldn't recognise him. But they had the pavement to themselves, and ...

'Well, well! I'm not wrong, am I? It's Adam Palmer?'

'Oh, Father! I never recognised you. How are you?'

'Fine, thank you. Are you back here for a holiday or something?'

'No, I'm back for good. Or ... The return of the mid-dle-aged failure!'

'Failure? Surely not. Wasn't I reading one of your arti-cles only the other day in where was it? About some poet or another?'

'O'Hara?'

'Yes, that was the name. And seeing your name I won-dered if you were back with us. I read you in that literary paper of yours from time to time. But that was some while ago. It must be going on two years.'

'Quite two years, Father. I had to give up that job. I was ill. That's why I've come back.'

'Ill! I'm sorry to hear that. Now that I look at you, I see.'

Adam forced himself to meet for a moment the blue-eyed scrutiny behind the glasses. Did a good man discern a bad man immediately? His eyes flickered away, as the priest said: 'You're much thinner. London can't have suited you.'

'Oh, I'm all right again now.'

'What was it that was wrong?'

'Oh, a kind of general breakdown, due to overwork, I suppose.'

'I'm sorry to hear that.'

He was waiting to hear more. What he probably didn't understand was that his own presence served as a mirror, making Adam's sense of his own corruption too painful to be borne.

'You haven't changed at all, Father. Well, I must be off. I'm married now, and I've got a wife waiting for me. I'm late already.'

'I mustn't keep you. Do you live near here?'

'Not far.'

At last, he had made his gesture. *What I have to do with thee, thou Son of David?* Out of the corner of his eye he observed the priest's impassivity of countenance, but it was as if a veil had come down between them.

'Well, maybe I shall see you another time. Good-bye now, and God bless you.'

'Good-bye, Father.'

It was over; he had turned away, making the first move, striding off as if in a great hurry. Every step he took bore him farther into safety. But it had happened! O God, it had happened! And therefore his heart was a stone in his breast. And when that stone melted, it would melt, he knew, in an agony of spirit.

Nonsense! Father Mansfield wasn't so much, after all. Not much of a preacher: no one went to hear his sermons the way they did to this or that glib Jesuit or bullying Redemptionist. *Oh, but he never said anything he shouldn't say, and what other priest was there of whom you could say that!* Nonsense! What did that mean? Did it mean anything? It was simply that in his youth he had made some sort of image out of Father Mansfield. He had probably done it just because other people didn't seem to be aware that … it was an image made out of … now he needn't go into that. There was no point in going into that.

In his unrest he walked so quickly that he was home almost before he knew it. When she heard his key in the lock Kathleen had just carried a jar of white narcissi from arranging them in the kitchen into their living-room. She had had a happy morning, because through all her cleaning, all her shopping, and despite some physical discomfort, she had been planning and dreaming of the future.

But one look at Adam's face struck away her welcoming smile. She said tensely: 'What's the matter? Has something happened?'

'What should happen? What's up with you?'

'I'm all right. It's just that you don't look well.'

'Of course I'm well.'

He sat down, drawing off his shoes. But she continued to stare at him, for he looked, what was the word that came into her consciousness? Stricken! And what misery had come into the room with him, the pretty clean room that she had worked so hard over.

'You look as if you'd had some bad news! Heard someone was dead, or seen someone run over, or something,' she said trying to speak lightly, as he gave her an impatient almost angry look.

Out of habit, his analytical mind stayed a moment on her words. Seen someone run over? He had seen an image of foulness. Himself.

'How imaginative you are getting. I'm just a bit tired, that's all. I walked home.'

'So I suppose you're too tired to want to go out this afternoon,' she said, trying to suppress her disappointment. 'I was thinking we might go up and sit by the Dargle stream.'

'Do you mind if I don't? I've got a bit of a headache. I think I shall take an Aspro, and lie down. Then we might go out later, after tea.'

'All right. I'm so sorry. Would you like a cup of tea?'

'No, thanks! It's nothing really.'

'You got your lunch, all right?'

'Yes … And you? You fed yourself properly and all that?'

'Yes, thank you,' said Kathleen quietly. His tone was as perfunctory as it generally was when he asked after her well-being. She didn't want to be treated as if she were an invalid, but if he cared for her welfare so little now when she was carrying his child, then would he, could he ever care at all? She had just been dreaming a dream. But she mustn't think bitter thoughts, because it might hurt the quickening of life within her. Turning away from him she looked steadily at the white flowers. Then she heard him say:

'I think I'll lie down for half an hour.'

'Very well.'

Still standing where he left her she heard him turn the key in the door of their bedroom. So it's like that, she thought. And supposing I want to go in I shall have to knock and beg cravenly for admittance. With hurt at her heart she curled herself up on the day couch, and tried to lose herself in the book on advice to expectant mothers that she had bought.

Adam had locked the door because the desire for privacy was overwhelming. Yet this internal fuss going on was all about nothing, he assured himself as he stared in the mirror at his face, wondering what Kathleen had seen amiss with it.

Abruptly he turned away, lighting a cigarette. Rationalise it! He had merely met a man whom once he knew, a priest to whom he had confessed, and by whom he had been shriven. And since all that had been over this many a day and many a year, why, what the hell!

Yes, it had been years. But, his heart insisted on replying, if it had been still more years, if Father Mansfield had become an old man with eyes sunken and white hair, he would still have recognised him instantly. Something perhaps in his aura, a mingling of innocence and charity, charity for this world, for unlike more ascetic-appearing priests one felt that Father Mansfield was keenly contemplative of the individual tragicomedy. That was why in the confessional one felt that he was really seeing one's soul, not listening to a mere mumble and waiting for it to be done. And then those little homilies of his, adapted to the liturgy of the year, but coming more or less to the same thing: '*Try and love God more!*'

Oh, once or twice, thought Adam, tense now, feeling his soul quiver within him at the recollection, because of Father Mansfield, he had been within an ace of the realisation of what it would mean to love God, to love God

185

more than he loved himself. That jewel of great price glittered afar off. From a great distance sounded the bells of the heavenly City … *If I forget thee, Jerusalem, Let my right hand forget its cunning.* The vision came when shriven he had gone out from the church into a street miraculously swept free from all sin and all weariness. Then for a little while he saw the world as God had made it, wherein all was joy and light and serenity, not only where his feet trod and where his eyes searched, but beyond sight to the very last horizon. '*Life seemed all calm as its last breath*'.

Long ago and far away, all that. He could trace as on a temperature chart the sequence from those first trembling intimations of the way to Jerusalem. The years of indifference and worldliness, full of petty fears. Then his heart opening again into love of a creature, sin, but sin which might, he now realised, have brought him back to God since once more his being was melted, the ramparts of cynicism borne away in a flood. We can learn by our sins, said St. Augustine, who had trodden that path himself. Instead he had chosen the presumption of despair, so that he had had to surrender his life into the ungentle hands of men. And then gathering vitality to take it back to himself, he had chosen deliberately to destroy whatever remained of his soul. Yet, even now—meeting Father Mansfield had told him that—even now it was not too late. Out of the depths he could cry to God.

The immediate path would be something like this … he would leave this room where he sat in such misery, go back to Kathleen, say: 'I feel all right now. You were right; something did upset me; let's go to the Dargle or wherever you want to go.' He would put his arms around her and kiss her.

The heaviness wouldn't go immediately, maybe wouldn't go for a long time, for he was too deeply bogged in mire, but as contrition increasingly came, God would sooner or later bestow His grace.

Sooner maybe than later. For, he remembered from those days when he had striven, that there was no predictability in the courtesy of God. When you were aware that you'd put a dozen, nay, twenty dozen things before Him, when you had done and thought almost everything that you should not have done or thought, yet at that very moment you felt the unmistakable joy of the stirrings of grace. As if God with His infinite delicacy would appear not to have seen your gaucherie.

There seemed an arrested stillness in the room, a reflection of the suspense in his own heart. It was the stillness, Adam suddenly recognised, which comes before a storm, a storm of repentance which might, yes, which *might* send him to his knees. He got up, walking the room, crackling his fingers, and then banged one fist against the other. Was this where his process of rationalisation had led him? All this, because he had met briefly a shabby little priest, with none of the reputation other priests had acquired for special sanctity or for great intellectual powers, with no following among the pious ... all right, yes, he knew he was really praising him, that a memory of Father Mansfield saying at Mass: '*Domine, non sum dignus*,' had even now the power to pierce his heart like a sword because of the true humility that went with it. Let that be. What it came to was that this priest was not spiritually unctuous, that like that chap whom physically he also resembled, Tommy Masterman, he was a humble man. But he, Adam Palmer, was not humble. He did not choose to accept the indignities that had been wrought upon him. No, he did not *choose*. Understand that, God!

He lit another cigarette, and sat down to smoke it, willing his heart to harden, watching its ramparts tighten once more. He fixed his intent firmly on the dark way: think of how he was deflating young Dickinson; think how he had troubled Norman, think how he had kept O'Hara thrilled to know if this were really a true disciple! So it must go on: let every room he entered become a little darker for his presence, as if it were darkened by the presence of the foul fiend himself. Ah, that thought did him good! To be a reflection of the foul fiend was no light ambition. Spreading darkness, as Tommy Masterman spread the light of a true conviviality in every bar he entered, as Father Mansfield sent every sensitive penitent away from his box with lightened soul. Let the devil have his due as well.

And was there not something he could do even now to be about his master's business? To efface that image of returning to Kathleen and making her happy with the suggestion of taking her for a walk? What was there he could do?

Asking the question he found himself only answered by an intense weariness. He could not expect to extract pleasure as yet, he reminded himself grimly, from the contemplation of evil, any more than the would-be virtuous person could extract pleasure from the thought of an act of charity that was not in conformity with the temperamental impulse. The goodness of the priest had acted as a refractor exhibiting to him the density of corruption with which already he had overlaid his soul, and for the time one had a natural inclination to shrink from adding to that density.

But it was just then that one must force oneself, that one must remind oneself not to weary of ill-doing.

Kathleen's face, he remembered, had looked serene and contented till she had seen him. She was at least looking forward to having her baby. Was there some way in which he could prick the very seat of this contentment. He meditated. Yes, yes … the fiend had come to the aid of his servant!

II

Kathleen hardly glanced up when Adam came back to the sitting-room. When he sat down in front of her, she asked in casual fashion, turning over a page as she did so: 'Is your headache better?'

'Yes, it's quite gone, thank you. What are you reading with so much attention?'

With an effect of being patient under an unnecessary question, she lifted the book with its cover towards him so that he could read the title.

'Oh, yes! *Advice to Expectant Mothers.* How interesting!'

'I dare say it wouldn't interest you. But it happens to interest me,' said Kathleen curtly.

'But how wrong you are,' he said after a few moments during which she had resumed reading. 'As a matter of fact, I'm exceedingly interested. In fact I'm very worried about the whole thing.'

'Are you? I hadn't noticed it,' she said, faintly sarcastic. Then the implication of his words began to sink in, and looking at him she asked: 'What do you mean, exactly?'

'Aren't you worried at all?'

'Why should I be? The doctor said everything was going according to specification.'

'Still that isn't all we have to worry about, is it?'

'What else is there? Do you mean money?'

'No, I don't mean money.'

'Suppose you drop this hinting game with me, Adam. Remember I'm not as clever as your friends at guessing.'

All right then. Blow for blow. It made it easier that she was in this mood.

'Sorry, but I should have thought it was fairly obvious. The child of a man who had been for a year in a lunatic asylum might not inherit a very stable temperament.'

'I think that's silly,' she said calmly, though her attitude now was a trifle tense. 'Everyone knows that a temporary nervous breakdown isn't hereditary.'

'Really? Does it say in your little book—well, perhaps it doesn't, but have you ever bothered to inquire whether my melancholia, which, any doctor is likely to tell you, is essentially a product of a morbid organism, is not due to my ancestors?'

'Do you mean that there is insanity in your family?' As he didn't reply, she repeated in a loud voice: 'Will you please answer me.'

'There's no need to shout. Most families have their skeletons, you know, and they don't much care about displaying them.'

'I'm not shouting. If there's anything to tell, please tell me.'

He blew out smoke through his nostrils. Then he extinguished the butt of his cigarette before answering: 'I don't think we'd better say any more. You are in too excited a state at the moment. I'm sure your little book does tell you that it isn't good for expectant mothers to excite themselves.'

Her control broke as she heard what seemed to her his jeering voice. Springing to her feet, and coming to stand over him, she said: 'Do you know what I think? I think you are saying all this just to torture me because you are a wicked man, and you're getting wickeder and wickeder every day. That's what I feel about you.'

She couldn't miss seeing the expression of satisfaction that crossed his face, as if he had heard something that greatly pleased him. It was gone as he shrugged his shoulder, and said: 'Well, take it that way if you like. Escapism, I think they call it in modem jargon.'

She looked at him fixedly for a moment and then turned to the door. 'Where are you going?' he asked her sharply.

'I'm going out.'

'Where?'

'I'm going to find Maureen and ask her.'

He rose and followed her into the hall. 'I really wouldn't go out in the state you're in.'

'I'm in no state.' He was standing in front of the bedroom door, so she went on to the hall door, deciding that the short jacket she was wearing would be sufficient covering.

'You're surely going to put on a hat or something, aren't you?'

He was still speaking in his jeering voice. She opened the front door and banged it loudly behind her. A moment later he re-opened it, and, thinking that he was going to follow her, she broke into a half-run. He caught a last glimpse of her set profile, and then she had disappeared.

All right, if she thought he was going to run after her and let her make a scene in the street, she was very much mistaken. He closed the door quietly and returned to the room. Maureen would of course reassure her, if she found her in. Though there had been a great aunt who had been 'put away' as the apt colloquialism had it. And Maureen was tactless enough to let that out. But she would also do her best to convince her that it was only a storm in a tea cup. As, of course, it was. And they'd both unite in vilifying his malevolence.

All the same he had certainly disturbed the maternal placidity. And there were more things especially in earth than science wot of. Any countrywoman could tell of those who bore odd marks because their mothers when bearing them had been suddenly frightened. He had put an ugly idea into her head, and ugly ideas bore fruit unto the third and fourth generation. In nature no rewards and no punishments, merely consequences! And what consequences, the hell that was in this world could testify! He sat on quietly directing his mind into strange lore: he meditated on Siamese twins, on artificial insemination, the making of robots, on the odd rites practised by certain tribes, on monsters hidden from human eyes; he recollected some of the fantasies of the madmen who had been his neighbours, the queerest pages of Havelock Ellis and Frazer, and other kindred matters.

But when an hour had passed, and Kathleen did not return, he began to look at the clock more frequently. Once he rose and went to the front door. He turned on the radio and turned it off again. It became more and more difficult to concentrate.

III

To the end of her life Kathleen never forgot the day she had run out of the flat, feeling that the secure foundations of the house she had begun to build for herself were shattered. That house had contained every promise she had of warmth and happiness. If she had in the Inishkill phrase married 'a queer man', a man not easy to live with, a man who left her in the dark groping for the key that would give her some true understanding of himself and the problem with which she sensed he was burdened, still she was now going to have a refuge of her own in a strange land. Whether it was boy or girl, and she thought it was going to be a girl, there would be no wall in that refuge between them. She could give what a helpless baby sought, her milk, her abiding care, her love. And when she started to toddle, to run about, to laugh, still there would be no wall between them, for a little child had no defences, only demands. Oh, if she hadn't been a good wife, and she had tried to be, at least she could be a good mother. Adam, she had often thought with resentment, didn't really require anything more from his wife than a woman about the place who did some housekeeping and could be relied on to make a cup of tea or perhaps set a glass that was properly washed before a friend. But with her new happiness she was beginning to put away all the little resentments that had gathered through the months.

And now he wanted to take this happiness from her, the rough snatching off of a rich covering revealing the shoddy and ugly. She slackened her pace after giving one long look behind her to make sure that he wasn't in sight, and tried to remember exactly what he had said. At least his meaning was clear: he had suggested that his offspring would inherit a diseased mind. Or perhaps, could he have meant that, a disease of the flesh? Now her mind in agony saw a tiny white face, whose eyes looked vacantly out on the world, who never spoke, who crawled instead of walking. Or, another picture: a baby who grew into cruelty, with hands that closed on everything in order to destroy it. Small wonder if that came true considering the man who had fathered it! She was glad she had told him that he was wicked. Yet, and her mind grew colder with a different horror at the recollection, he had been glad because she had said so, and glad in a different way from the mere pleasure of putting a woman in a rage. Glad because he *hoped* that what she said was true. Oh, but there must be some nightmare here, beyond all daylight probing ... yet there also seemed some gleam of hope here: if he delighted in cruelty for cruelty's sake, then her first reaction had been right, and he had just made things up in order to torment her. She would find Maureen and drag the truth out of her.

Once again she quickened her pace, and now that she had reached the main suburban shopping thoroughfare, she became conscious of curious glances directed at her. Women doing their Saturday afternoon shopping, women wheeling prams, women to whom shop-windows took the place of a picture gallery, prowling slowly and critically, all seemed suddenly observant of her. She supposed she was walking too fast for a woman in her condition: yes, she remembered: women who were big with child might if they were brazen go boldly, flaunting their fulfilment; or they drifted along ruminative and brooding, lost in themselves. She didn't match up with either.

She turned up a quiet road with pleasant mellow brick houses lying well behind tended gardens. Here lived the thousand or so a year professional class, whose lives seemed at a cursory glance so well ordered, a neat pattern of dignified labour, golf clubs, tennis in the summer, an occasional theatre and occasional bridge parties; Wimbledon and Ealing in Inishkill, and therefore rosier, more leisurely. No help for her here, thought Kathleen wildly; no help anywhere until she found Maureen.

After she had turned into the square where the Palmers lived, she instinctively desired to look at her face in her compact mirror and repowder it. But, of course, she hadn't got her handbag: that was what he had made her do, come out without her purse or anything! She must look a sight; and she breathed a prayer that Maureen would be in and Mrs. Palmer out.

But it was Mrs. Palmer who opened the door to her.

'Oh, Kathleen!' Her eyes went quickly past the girl and returned in disappointment. 'Adam's not with you, then?'

'No. I really just looked in to see Maureen.'

'Come in,' said Mrs. Palmer hastily, giving Kathleen the impression that she had just noticed her figure and didn't approve of her standing there in the porch for anyone to see. She closed the door as she said: 'Isn't that a pity now when Maureen's out. Is it a message from Adam you have?' Kathleen's heart had sunk. She said slowly: 'I wonder if she'll be long. No, I wanted to see her myself.'

'I see. Is it about the baby's robe she's making for you? It's not near done yet. But come in and rest yourself.'

Kathleen followed Mrs. Palmer into the living-room reluctantly. 'Will Maureen be back soon?'

'Ah, that's a thing I can't tell you. Not with the best will in the world. I can tell you this though. She went off as soon as she'd had her lunch. I told her she needn't wait to help with the dishes seeing that she was mad to see this new picture, what-ever's the name of it, you'd know, I'm sure. It's the one on at the Clifton. Sit down, won't you?'

'No, I don't know, Mrs. Palmer,' said Kathleen, sinking into the chair that her mother-in-law indicated for her.

'Don't you? Ah, well you've other things to be thinking of. How are you feeling? I can't say you look very well. Not as well as the last time I saw you. But you must expect that. It was the same with me. Ups and downs. One time I'd feel the world belonged to me; the next minute I felt it was on top of me.

'When do you think Maureen will be back, then?'

'Ah, that was what I was trying to work out for you. We finished our lunch, and it would be going on for two, because, of course, Maureen doesn't get home till nearly the half-hour. Then she went upstairs, and the queer thing with Maureen is that you'd never know how long she'll be in her bedroom. One day she'll hardly stop to put a lick of powder on her, but dash out anyhow; another day she'll take it into her head to be staring at herself side face, full face, hat on and hat off, and what not … by the way I've never seen you come out before without a hat on your head. You're not like Maureen in that; oftentimes she won't wear one.'

'I know. I usually do.'

'Perhaps you were in a great hurry thinking you'd catch Maureen before she went to the pictures?'

'No, I didn't know she was going or I wouldn't have come and bothered you.'

'Is Adam not at home with you this afternoon?'

'Yes, he is. He was tired and rested for a while. Maureen won't be back yet then?'

'Now let me see. As I was saying: This was one of the times I had to shout up the stairs to her, for I had done the dishes and not a sign of her. "Haven't you gone yet?" I called out. "Won't you miss the big picture?" Do you know the name of it was on the tip of my tongue and it's gone again. She said something, and down she came a minute after, and it must have been about twenty-past two, as near as I can say without actually looking at the clock. She should have been there well before three, quarter to three say, and you know as well as myself, and probably a good deal better, you being young and going the more often, I don't know when it was I was last at the pictures, how long the programme lasts.'

'Well, sometimes it lasts for two and a half hours, sometimes longer if there are two pictures.'

'As to that, I couldn't say,' said Mrs. Palmer. She watched Kathleen look at the clock, which said twenty-five to five, her mind exploring avenues which would give a clue to this sudden eagerness to see Maureen.

'I shouldn't think she'll be out before quarter-past five then. Do you expect her home to tea?'

'With Maureen you wouldn't know what she'd do. Expect her when I see her. That's what I always say. But you're welcome to wait if it's something important and no message I can give her?'

'It was just … I wanted to see her.'

'Adam could have told you she's generally out Saturday. After all it's her half-day, and do what she likes with it is the rule. But perhaps you didn't tell him you were coming over here.'

'Yes, I told him,' said Kathleen listlessly. Then she looked half-hopefully at the other woman, and Mrs. Palmer looked steadfastly back. Now something's coming, she told herself, and if she starts abusing Adam and trying to make me take sides in their quarrels, I shall just say: 'Well you chose him yourself, and if you expect to grab a man fresh from among lunatics, and not find him swearing and cursing at you or the moon or himself, then you've a lot to learn, my girl.' But when the question came it was different, it took her by surprise.

'Mrs. Palmer, I wonder if you'd mind telling me. When Adam was a little boy, was he happy?'

And what does she mean by that, the slut, thought Mrs. Palmer, and then, for a timeless instant, the shock of Kathleen's words loosened an agony of sub-conscious recollection: when he was a little boy, he had been hers and hers alone, in sickness: 'Your hand is so lovely and cool, mam,' in health crying proudly: 'Look, you're not looking,' as he made his engine go. And then later the look she had seen suddenly one morning at Mass on his face, so pure, so remote, that for her it had launched a dream, a dream that one day he might be a priest; that she might see her own son enter the highest vocation possible to man; that one day she would receive the holy wafer from his hands; that her name would always be first in the prayers he sent up to God at holy Mass. The dream had taken shape sufficiently to warm her whole life, to keep her on her knees praying fervently to God, to the Blessed Virgin, to one saint after another. Repeatedly he would shatter the dream: 'Oh, I don't know; I don't think

I'm as religious as all that,' and then patiently with infinite longing and in secrecy she would build it up again as she knelt by her bed or in church, offering up novena after novena, lighting candle after candle, for her intention. It was such a noble intention that God and His Blessed Mother and all His saints must hear her cry, and in raising him raise her also. But then he had started to scribble, and one day he showed her a poem he had accepted and printed for all Bailey to read under his name in the weekly newspaper. 'It's well enough,' she had said, and seen his face fall, and seen him turn from her. Oh, but she had still cherished her dream, and still said her prayers when they, his father and he between them had decided that for the time being, and while he did some free-lancing, he could pass the library examinations. For then what was he but a youth, stamping dates on books while dirty grubby people passed in and out day by day? And since he still went to Mass regularly, surely he must come to see that he was doing a mean and poor thing compared to what he might do, and she stinting and saving every penny she could put by for the time when he agreed to go to college. Once, her patience exhausted, she had dared ask him outright, tell him of the secret store of money, and what had he said but that he knew he couldn't be as good a priest as a Father at the big common church by the canal where only poor people went. 'And unless I'm a good priest, there's no point in my being a priest!' That's what he'd said. And that, she could see it now, had been his great fault, never wanting to do anything unless he thought he could do it better than anyone else. That was what had taken him to London when the chance had come, breaking her dream finally with his going, breaking her whole life when it was spilt, since savour and sweetness had gone. Of course she was still a good Catholic, but she prayed now to obscurer saints, whose names she had never previously invoked, saints whom she couldn't blame. And, of course, he'd never done anything in the big City, nothing really! It was true that for a while she could read articles by him about this or that book, but that was a poor satisfaction since books were, to her woman's heart, always detached from life and reality. You took them up and you put them down, and some were rubbish, and some were dull as ditch water. And in either case you went your way unchanged, and all they had done was to kill time when you were too tired to do anything else but read. Still she was a reasonable woman, and if he'd written some story that everyone asked for at the libraries, a book like *Gone With the Wind* that you had to read because everyone you knew was reading it, well, that would have been *something*.

But there was no *Gone With the Wind*; instead there came the day when a policeman, though he was not in uniform, knocked at the door of her house, her house to which no policeman had ever come before. Disgrace, and such disgrace as she had never thought possible could come the way of a woman like herself. And his father dead, and Maureen away on holiday. And now all that had surged up, starting with the beautiful shaping of the high dream, was dammed with the policeman's knock; the monster Reality banished the dream that had been, and Kathleen saw that the eyes which had gazed back at her unseeingly were now looking at her with hate, that the lips had compressed, and she looked away, and murmured: 'I'm sorry, I didn't mean to ...'

'Oh, he was quite happy as a little boy. I wonder. Why did you ask me that?'

'I was wondering. I was wondering if his father understood him; he never talks much about his father or his other relatives.'

'I don't know why he shouldn't. His father died when he was about twenty.'

'What did he die of?'

Well, really! Accustomed to the vast reticences which obtained among the Inishkill middle class, Mrs. Palmer's usually quickly moving mind was for a full moment paralysed at the audacity of the girl. She stared in silence. Then she said: 'I *beg* your pardon,' in a tone that convicted Kathleen of enormity. She faltered: 'I'm sorry if I shouldn't have asked.'

'If you are so curious about such things, surely your husband is the man to ask? If I'm being old-fashioned, well, then you'll have to excuse it, but I'm afraid I *am* old-fashioned, and never myself wishing to probe into other people's affairs, indeed being instructed by my religion that ...'

Kathleen was on her feet and fumbling with the door handle, so that Mrs. Palmer broke off to rise to her feet and ask sternly: 'Where are you going to now?'

Kathleen ignored the question. In the hall she turned to say: 'Please accept my apology for being tactless, Mrs. Palmer. Good-bye.'

'It's all right. I suppose you've got some bee in the bonnet. At such times, it's natural ... you should rest ... if I were you I'd go quietly ... I wouldn't rush ... go quietly back and lie down on your bed ... and get Adam to bring you a nice cup of tea ... that and an aspirin ...'

'Good-bye, Mrs. Palmer,' said Kathleen, who had now got the door open and was out on the steps. Without looking back she hastened into the square. She didn't hear the hall door close, so she assumed that Mrs. Palmer was standing watching her and walked steadily, looking through the railings with apparent interest at the newly-painted green boards of the tennis club-house. Mrs. Palmer standing inside the door watched, thinking at one and the same time: as bold as brass, so that's what she came for; Adam didn't like to tell her his father died of cancer and so she sneaked off behind his back to try and worm it out of me, and when I was as near my time as she is I certainly would never dream of going out except in the evening. Then, as Kathleen disappeared from her view, she closed the door firmly.

IV

How she hates me, thought Kathleen, beginning, now that she need no longer maintain the appearance of dignity, to walk faster. I knew she disliked me, but hatred, that was a different matter, and one which—however slight was regard for the person—brought with it a sensation of guilt. What have I done? she asked inevitably. The immediate causes seemed to have been her two questions, one surely harmless, as to whether Adam had been happy as a little boy, but her mother-in-law must have taken it as a suggestion of criticism toward herself; the second about the cause of Mr. Palmer's death was perhaps impertinent, though she certainly hadn't intended it to be. On the other hand, and wasn't this more reasonable, perhaps this was the skeleton in the cupboard to which Adam had alluded. Perhaps his father had been a lunatic. He had certainly told her that he had died years ago; he had also told it in a dismissing way. Other words that he had said came back into her head: a decent man, but a soft man. Mother was the person that counted. Oh, why hadn't her curiosity prompted her to ask more? If they had been an ordinary courting couple eager to lay everything that had ever happened to either of them before the other, confident in receiving tender interest in return; if he hadn't always made her feel that she must watch herself, that questions about personal matters were rather stupid if not in bad taste, then, oh, then she wouldn't have been as she was now, running about a strange city knocking at doors that banged in her face. But Maureen, at least Maureen wouldn't do that to her; what was it that Mrs. Palmer had said, something about her making a robe for the baby?

By now nearly back into the main street, she looked at her watch. If she took a tram now she would get to the Clifton fairly near the time when presumably Maureen should be coming out. But, of course, she hadn't got her handbag with her; if she walked she'd probably be too late; would it be better then to stand at the corner waiting for the trams back from the City, watching for Maureen to descend from one of them? But it might be hours: Mrs. Palmer had said that Maureen might have tea in town, or she might be meeting a friend, or anything. Besides people stared so; a policeman might come up and move her on, and all with the suggestion that she was somehow disgusting and obscene to be showing herself at all. And she was caught on a sudden into a wave of longing for dear familiar London, where people just took anything and everything for granted, but where you could also be certain of kindness, an easy kindness that didn't probe, that didn't immediately think your behaviour was extraordinary if you asked a simple question. It was all summed up, she thought suddenly, in the way the people serving in the shops called you 'dear', or even 'ducks', not *you* specially, but everybody who didn't come with a trail of expensive clothes or pompous airs. *Oh, dear, friendly, not-minding London, why did I ever leave you, and how I wish I could run back to you, and what am I to do now that I'm so tired, and that's why people commit suicide because they get so tired and so distraught and don't know what to do.*

For now she had stopped at the corner, and the trams were grinding past, and another woman was staring at her, and perhaps the sensible thing to do was to go back home and collect her purse, but there was Adam's jeering pale face to meet if so, and she'd probably miss Maureen if she did. And now somebody else standing near was looking at her, a man this time, and he probably thought she was disgusting too, so she turned away her head, but then a voice said: 'Good evening … it is Mrs. Palmer, isn't it?'

She turned sharply, and she seemed to know the face, but her mind was too confused to place it properly.

'The name's Masterman. We met at young Norman's flat, didn't we? Don't tell me I've got it wrong.'

'Of course, I'm so sorry. I didn't recognise you for the moment.'

'Lovely evening, isn't it? I'm just going up to town again.'

'Oh, are you? I was, too, only …' she paused and then rushed on because here was salvation. 'I'm so stupid, but I've come out without my bag, and I want to catch my sister-in-law when she comes out of the pictures, and I haven't my fare, so I wonder …' she stopped, her cheeks flaming. He'd think her mad; she was sure she looked mad, mad and disgusting, that's how she looked!

'But how splendid! Here's the tram coming now. We can go together.'

The tram came to a halt, and he stood on one side to let her mount first. She started to climb to the upper deck, thinking that was what he would do, and then thought, in another agony of shame, I should have asked him for the three ha'pence, and gone inside; he'll probably be ever so embarrassed sitting with me.

But stealing an agonised glance at him as he sat down beside her she received no sensation of his being embarrassed or even stiff. Of course he wouldn't be: this was the man who loved London, and the red buses swinging down Regent Street, who mixed with prostitutes and all sorts of people, and was supposed to have got drunk every night, and oh, thank God there were such people in the world, and how much nicer they were than Adam's mother. He said: 'I didn't realise you were a neighbour of mine.'

'Well, I'm not quite. I live higher up, in Church Road. You live in Grosvenor Road, then?'

He nodded. 'Number fourteen.'

'They're nice houses, aren't they?' And if he lived there, she was thinking, then some nice people who were not stiff shirts lived there, too, and she'd made up her mind that there was no help for her in those houses, but God had sent her help. Oh, if only God would now allow her to meet Maureen!

'The house is all right, but don't credit me with its possession. My mother, she's over eighty now, and my unmarried sister have the house, and I have the top back room sort of thing: no unkindness on their part, but, as my sister put it, anywhere I inhabit becomes festooned with empties which are better left unnoticed and unsung if the priest should call, or the doctor to see my mother.'

He paused, looking at her smilingly, but she wasn't listening. The enormity of what she'd done was suddenly to the fore in her mind and she said: 'You must be thinking it's very odd me doing this, Mr. Masterman. I'm very sorry; I mean I could have gone back and got my purse, and not bothered you.'

'But you're not bothering me. You're honouring me. When I saw you I thought where is this attractive young lady going, and it was an inspiration that I should recognise you.' He might have added that a noticeably pregnant young woman with eyes that stared unseeingly from a white face, and whom he had first noticed walking very fast in front of him, and who then came to a dead pause, and looked about her as if she were lost, was bound to attract attention. Here's somebody who wants help had been his resigned thought; then he was sure he had seen her before, and in a flash her name had come to his memory. Now before she could answer he went on: 'I wonder if you've been to the Hippodrome this week. Not a very good bill, but one or two turns weren't so bad.'

'No! Adam, that's my husband, is keen on the theatre chiefly. I mean the Repertory one.'

'Well, he's a high-brow, isn't he? Afraid I don't go there much myself. There isn't a bar, you see, and a theatre without a bar is Jerry-built, in my humble opinion.' Tommy broke off to say, as the conductor approached: 'By the way, where do you want to go to exactly?'

'The Clifton.'

After paying, Tommy asked cautiously: 'Did I get it wrong or did you say something about meeting your sister-in-law?' 'Yes, but she doesn't expect me. You see, she's been there, at the pictures, this afternoon, and I thought that if I caught her when she came out, then perhaps …'

'You could go and have a cup of tea together,' finished Tommy for her. 'I have a date for something a trifle stronger. Supposing you have missed your sister-in-law, well, then what happens?'

Kathleen didn't answer. She heard him say: 'I'd better lend you your bus fare, hadn't I? To take you back home.'

'Please, no. I can easily walk home. Oh, I get off here, don't I? Good-bye, and thank you so much.'

'Hold your horses. We're not quite there yet. Besides, I'm coming with you.'

This was dreadful, she thought, following him. He was getting off probably before his stop on her account. On the pavement, before she could speak, he said: 'I suppose she went to see the big picture, so the thing to do is for me to ask the commissionaire or at the box office when it's over. Now, don't worry, I'll see you through this.'

She stood waiting in the vestibule while he consulted the big man in uniform. He returned to her saying: 'I think you've managed it very nicely. *One Night of Love* is going to be over in just about five minutes time. What do you think of that?' He was laughing, so she smiled politely too. 'Thank you very, very much. I don't know what I'd have done without you.'

'That's nothing. Have a cigarette.'

She took one from him, and when he had lit it forced herself to speak: 'I know this must all seem very silly to you.

It's just that something rather worrying turned up, and I felt I ought to see Maureen to ask her about it.'

'The pleasure has been mine, but as to worrying, let me give you a word of advice. It's a great mistake to take anything too seriously. A lot of good men have come to a lot of harm through that: you'd be surprised!'

'I know. I'm silly. Anyhow, don't let me keep you any longer. You've been too good as it is.'

'I wouldn't dream of letting you stand here by yourself. Besides, I'm in no hurry.'

It wasn't true. Actually his appointment was with a prospective client, and clients were too few and far between these days to run any risk of missing them. As one or two people drifted out from the auditorium, he followed Kathleen's gaze, but evidently none of them was the sister-in-law. He asked abruptly because he hoped that this girl, whoever she was, would be a decent sort: 'You're fond of this Maureen, are you?'

'I really haven't got on very well with her, but it's been my fault,' said Kathleen, too exhausted and distrait to speak anything now but the simple truth.

'Has she a good heart to her, that's the main thing?'

'Oh, I think she has. She's not like ...' Kathleen stopped, horrified. She had been going to say 'Adam'. Where was her self-control? She looked desperately at the doors as they parted again. But no Maureen!

Tommy thought, she means her husband. What a swine the fellow must be, because this girl isn't a bitch. I ought to know. I've had experience enough of them by now. Nevertheless, as he met the disapproving stare now turned upon him by an elderly lady, and the curious one of her daughter, he wished that Kathleen didn't look quite so tragic, making for everyone who passed them a picture of a wicked old man and the innocent girl he had ruined! If he could only make her smile once!

'You know how some music-hall gags stay in your mind? Or perhaps you don't. But I'm an old-timer, and have seen all the old-timers. A gag that made me laugh thirty golden years ago always comes into my head when I'm bothered about anything. Are you listening?'

Kathleen turned obediently towards him: 'Yes?'

'Life's a terrible business, and you're lucky if you get out of it alive. You're lucky if you get out of it *alive*? See?'

She was smiling, and nodding her head. He resumed: 'Well, of course, in one way we don't, but in another sense you'd be surprised how much we can go through and still come out alive. Yes, and even kicking!'

But she wasn't listening any longer. Her face had changed; she made a movement forward: 'Maureen!'

Tommy thought he'd never seen anyone look so surprised as the tall girl whom Kathleen had singled out from the crowd now pouring through the doors. He stepped back, hearing: 'Kathleen! What on earth are you doing here? Has anything happened?'

'Not really, I just had to see you. I'll explain. But ...' she turned her head, and then they joined him: 'Maureen, this is Mr. Masterman who has been so kind to me, and insisted on waiting with me!'

Shaking hands, Tommy said: 'Well, how did the *Night of Love* go off? No hitches?' He met an answering twinkle as Maureen assured him: 'Marvellously. Songs, moonlight, champagne, *everything*.'

'My goodness! What I've missed!' Reassurance descended gratefully upon him. This girl was all right. If she'd been the vinegary sort, he'd have felt troubled about leaving little Mrs. Palmer with her. As it was: 'Well, I'll be off. I've got to see a man about a dog. Funnily enough it's really true. Almost unique. A dog did bite this chap, and he wants to get compensation. Good-bye now: you two girls will look after each other, won't you?'

He addressed the remark to Maureen, looking at her hard in the eyes, and received an answering look of comprehension. 'Surely. Thank you very much, Mr. Masterman.'

'It's I who should thank you,' said Kathleen extending her hands. 'It's no good apologising, but …'

'Good-bye,' said Maureen. 'You know I am delighted to have met you, Mr. Masterman, because I've heard an awful lot about you.'

Tommy threw up his hands in mock despair: 'Forget it. It's much exaggerated. Like the report of the man's death when he wasn't dead. So long.'

Kathleen looked at Maureen, who was staring after Tommy's retreating back: 'Now there's a man I could like,' she said regretfully. 'Trust me to pick out the wrong sort. Because I suppose in the whole of this City there isn't …'

'He's awfully kind. Maureen, could we go somewhere quiet and have tea? But I haven't got any money, no money at all. Mr. Masterman had to pay for my fare in the tram. Oh, I ought to have asked you to give it back to him.'

'Now don't worry,' said Maureen. 'Yes, of course. We'll go down the street to Richards. This place will be too crowded. And then you can tell your mother all your troubles.'

'Oh, Maureen, it's all … perhaps it's nothing, but …'

'Don't worry,' said Maureen leading the way.

They both had told her not to worry, thought Kathleen following. It didn't mean anything, because, of course, you had to worry. But *kind, kind* … there were kind people even in this horrid city.

'Well, now then, my pet,' said Maureen when she had guided Kathleen to an empty table, given the order for tea, taken further stock of her sister-in-law, thinking with apprehension as she saw a Kathleen who looked very different from her usual quiet neat English girl: 'My God, I believe something really is up.'

Kathleen said nothing, staring away, and Maureen, handing her a cigarette, decided to take the plunge—because I'm too nervous to sit round while she looks like that: 'I expect you've had a row with Adam. Is that it?'

'I suppose you could call it that. I don't know.'

Well, if you don't know, who the hell does? Maureen thought. Aloud she said: 'Ah, I wouldn't mind Adam. He's a queer fish, and doesn't know what he's talking about most of the time. You don't want to pay too much attention to him.'

'Why do you call him a queer fish?' Kathleen asked her in a strained voice.

'Well …' Maureen looked down at the table cloth. 'He's had a lot of trouble, hasn't he? And that makes people a bit queer and touchy and all that.'

'Do you think he might go mad again?'

'Of course not,' said Maureen quickly, unable to suppress a touch of something like her mother's horror at such plain speaking. In the next moment she thought, but, of course, I really believe he might. And the point is, has it

211

happened already, because he must have frightened her for her to come tearing out of the house with no bag and, for Kathleen who always wore a hat, hatless. 'Is he not well, or something?' she asked in a low voice.

But the waitress bringing their tea-tray stopped Kathleen from answering, and as soon as she had left them, Maureen started to pour out. 'You must be dying for a cup. Well, I am, too. Funny how going to the pictures makes you thirsty. Do you like it weak or strong, Kathleen? I've gone and forgotten. Oh, I haven't. Of course you like it weak.'

With their cups filled, and the toast on their plates, Kathleen was still silent. So Maureen asked:

'However did you know where to find me?'

'Your mother told me you'd gone to the pictures.'

'Oh, so you've been up to mother's?'

'Yes, I went there to find you. That's another thing. Your mother hates me.'

'Now Kathleen, what nonsense! Of course she doesn't.' Maureen looked across to see Kathleen looking back at her with complete disbelief, and decided that this was a case when a few grains of truth would do more good than harm. 'You have to make allowances for her, do you see? She's a disappointed woman.'

'Because Adam married me.'

'Not at all. She'd have been the same whoever he married. She thinks that if you had been a good Catholic and all that she wouldn't have minded so much, but that's all bilge. The real thing is that she never thought Adam would marry at all. You see, she wanted him to be a priest. And in a way she still sees him as a spoilt priest. It's just the way she has of looking at it, and you know how a mother is with a son. Do eat some of the toast, Kathleen dear. Or would you rather have a cake?'

Under the table Kathleen clenched her hands. When she hoped her voice would come out composed, she said, looking straight at Maureen: 'She hated me most of all when I asked her what your father died of. What did he die of, Maureen?'

'Why, he died of cancer of the spine, the poor darling,' said Maureen cheerfully and promptly, returning Kathleen's gaze directly.

'Are you sure?'

'Of course I'm sure. Why wouldn't I be? I was still at school at the time, but everyone knew about it. Of course mother mightn't like to tell you straight out. You know what that generation is! And then she'd think there was some reason why Adam hadn't told you.'

Kathleen picked up a piece of toast, and tried to swallow it. Maureen said in a voice of relief: 'So that was what was worrying you, was it?'

'Partly. Listen Maureen, I want to get the whole thing off my chest.'

'That's what I want you to do, isn't it?'

'Well, Adam seemed to imply that there was lunacy in your family and that I had no right to be having this baby ... oh, Maureen ...' Kathleen choked, and had to duck her head to hide the springing tears. The baby meant so much, and now that she had put into words her pent-up fear it was too monstrous even to look at. If I can't, if I shouldn't have this baby, I shall want to kill myself, she thought. And then heard Maureen say:

'Don't, Kathleen! Pull yourself together, and listen to me. It's all nonsense, nonsense, nonsense!'

In the distance, looked upon from the surging seas in which she was drowning, a vista of calm, the safety of land appeared. 'Maureen! Is that true?'

'Of course it's true.'

But one must not direct one's course too soon lest it proved a mirage. 'Supposing, though, they kept it from you?'

'I'm not a person that people keep things like that from,' said Maureen. 'I've lived with Mother for years, Kathleen, and she's always gabbling about relatives. Especially the grander ones, of course. But never mind that. I'm going to tell you absolutely everything Kathleen, just the same as if I were in the confession box telling my sins to the priest, and you know that means that we can't tell lies, don't you?'

Kathleen nodded. She felt that Maureen at least wouldn't tell lies in her confession.

'Well, then. Father had an aunt who went a bit queer; that is she didn't recognise people and so on when she was having her change of life. She went into a home run by nuns, and she died there. I'm telling you this because I'm trusting that you haven't lost all your common sense. Every family has something in it like that. It doesn't mean for one solitary single instant that your baby when it comes, the pet, will be affected one iota, and in any way whatsoever. So there.'

After a moment Kathleen said softly: 'No, it doesn't, does it?' A weakness, a blessed weakness such as one has after going through terrible pain when it has at last stopped, was overtaking her. She thought it was all right now; she believed it was all right, but also she felt drained of all strength. Still there was something left, a shadow:

'But why did Adam talk like that? Why did he suggest …?' Maureen's face closed up. Then she said slowly: 'I'm

afraid it was out of wickedness. Out of downright wickedness.' They both became aware of the waitress standing by
the table and scribbling out their bill. Maureen realised they
were almost the last people in the café, which closed at six.
'Oh, Kathleen, you haven't had anything to eat.'

Kathleen smiled back. It was all right now, she kept telling herself, and the more she looked at Maureen's candid
face the more reassured she became. The main point was all
right. She could still keep her baby!

But Maureen noticed chiefly how white and spent the
other girl looked, and anger allied with pity to load on
her heart a burden. It seemed ages ago that she'd been so
carefree at the pictures. That was, of course, she thought, as
she led the way out, because real life was so different from
the movies: you came out into the street to find it going
heavily, as it were walking on down-at-heel shoes. On the
counter which she was passing waitresses had loaded their
trays of soiled crockery, tea slopped in saucers, a plate with
a half-eaten cake, and for a moment she saw our common
pilgrimage as a trail leading past garbage bins, strewn with
discarded clutter and wastage packed away roughly, carelessly, impatiently, so that there were always traces. The sins
of one generation visited on the next, on and on and on.

Kathleen was waiting for her at the door. She said to
her: 'What about going to the Carlton and having a drink?
Wouldn't that do you good?'

'I'd rather go straight back, I think. I know it's silly: I feel
I just want to go to bed and close my eyes, and not think.'

'So then that will be the best thing for you. I'll come
with you.'

'Oh, will you?'

There was such relief in Kathleen's face that Maureen felt repaid. This, she decided as they sat later side by side in the tram, was a different Kathleen from the reserved girl who didn't like talking even about her motherhood, at least not to her, Maureen. A barrier had been swept away between them. Why, I believe we may become friends; I believe she won't mind me any more. And she said aloud: 'Do you know, Kathleen, I'm making one or two things that I think will come in handy for you next month.'

Kathleen said: 'Yes, your mother said something about a robe.' Her hand touched the other's arm for a moment. 'I'm so grateful. For that, and for everything.'

'Grateful for nothing. What rubbish!' said Maureen loudly. Inside herself she thought with joy, why, she's really the sweetest thing! And she also thought that she had been wrong when she saw life as just the wasteful repetition of pain and weariness bowing everybody's shoulders down. There was also always and everywhere the uprush of love, of charity, and then it went with a spring and with eyes that looked upwards.

'Now then,' she said, as they turned their steps towards Kathleen's flat, 'I'm taking charge. I'll deal with Mr. Adam. You must go straight to bed, and I'll bring you some hot milk. And you must try and go to sleep, and not think of anything at all. Promise me.'

'I promise you. I don't want to see Adam.'

They found the hall door open, and Adam standing in the hall. He ignored Maureen, saying in a faintly reproving voice to Kathleen: 'Well, well. You have been a time. I was beginning to think you had got lost.'

Maureen said coldly before Kathleen could speak: 'Kathleen's going straight up to bed. She's very tired. I'll see to her.'

'Certainly. Best thing she can do.'

Adam retreated from them back into the room. He knew from the expression on his sister's face that he was in for some hard words. Well, that didn't matter, for he had felt more relief than he cared to say when he saw the two girls come along the road. For an hour he'd been expecting a call from a police station. Or perhaps a hospital. And that would have been, well, inconvenient, was the word he insisted upon. He had been bothered. He could confess that he'd been dangerously near remorse. But now it was all right. And just to show that he didn't care he turned on the radio.

But then he turned it off, for, of course, it would disturb Kathleen! He was reading a book when after half an hour or so Maureen came back. She entered the room with that challenging walk of hers which presaged speaking her mind, and closed the door behind her.

'Now then, Adam. I want to know something.'

'Yes? Won't you sit down?'

She sat down, and he said smoothly, having rehearsed the words: 'It's been so kind of you to look after Kathleen. I was afraid she wouldn't find you at Mother's.'

'She didn't. She had to come up to town. Why did you tell Kathleen that there was insanity in our family?'

'I don't think I told her that. Aren't you exaggerating? Or perhaps she is exaggerating. In her state it's perhaps natural.'

'It's no good, Adam. You certainly implied at least that there was something murky in our past.'

'Well, isn't there?'

'Oh, I told her all about great-aunt Hannah, if that's what you mean.'

'Wasn't that rather tactless?'

'No. Kathleen is quite a sensible person. She didn't see anything in it any more than anyone else would. And all this, as you know, isn't the real point. Why did you want to frighten her, is what I want to find out.'

'I didn't want to frighten her. I was merely curious to know if she was worried because of my history. She got it all wrong. It did seem to me that if I were a woman who had married a man who had spent a year in the loony bin, I would be rather perturbed in case the child did inherit something mentally unstable. I must have put it all rather bluntly.'

'You are quite good at talking, but ...'

'The real point is,' said Adam interrupting, 'that both you and Mother hate to put into words that plain fact.'

'Not at all,' cried Maureen, angry now. 'If you want to have my plain opinion, Adam, it is that they let you out too soon.'

So that was out. Here was someone who wished him back in the inferno! He couldn't speak for a moment, then he rapped out: 'Thank you for revealing yourself! I like to know my enemies.'

'God forgive me for saying such a thing to my own brother, but if you are going to go round telling lies and trying to hurt your own wife, especially in the state she is in now, why then it seems to me that there is a devil in you.'

'You'd better send for a priest and have it exorcised.'

'I wish to God it were as easy as that.'

There was a silence, for they had both momentarily exhausted themselves. The chilly spring light was dying, and the room had faded into a half-light which a tone of voice could impress with nostalgic tenderness or a deep melancholy. But the current of bitterness which had surged up between brother and sister swept the melancholy on into gloom, and Adam looked restlessly round before he said:'Well, now you've got that off your chest. I'm possessed by a devil, or I'm in a state of mortal sin, or something, that's it, isn't it?'

'Yes, I do think you are in a state of mortal sin, and I don't think it's a thing to be laughed off.'

'No?' he queried, feeling a certain acquiescent approval. His pious Catholic sister had recognised a flower of evil, so that it must exist: she was a lamp lighting up a foul stew. A trifle Baudelairian, and self-conscious perhaps, but that was merely a phase before hardening set in. All the same he wished her gone. 'Have you anything more to say ?'

Maureen got up, and walking towards the door switched the light on with a decisive hand. Then she turned and faced him:'Nothing except that from now on I'm going to look after Kathleen. There's nothing fine or grand in going round committing dirty little cruelties, even though you may think there is. The real trouble with you is that you always wanted to be considered either a saint or a genius, and since you can't make the grade you've decided to try and be something special in the way of a sinner. I've watched you, and …'

She paused as he sprang up from his seat, his face suddenly distorted in a grimace of hate: 'Shut up, you bitch, and get out of here. Who do you think you are? Joan of Arc?'

'I don't think I'm anybody,' started Maureen, and then she opened the door quickly, for she was afraid that now he had come close up he was going to strike her. 'I'm going.'

'Yes, get out of here, and don't come back again.' He saw her eyes turn from him startled, and then he realised that Kathleen was standing in her nightgown in the hall. 'Oh, what is it?' she said. 'Why are you quarrelling?'

'It's nothing,' said Maureen quickly. 'Go back to bed, Kathleen.'

'What's happening between you?'

'What's happening?' said Adam, slowly striving for control, 'is merely that my dear sister wants me back in an asylum, and she is trying to goad me, trying to send me mad again.'

'Oh, no!' breathed Kathleen; she looked at Maureen with, the other felt, the old suspicion in her eyes.

'That's nonsense. I've just told him that he ought to be ashamed of himself for frightening you.'

'You said a good deal more than that. Never mind. It doesn't matter.' He stood thinking, watched intently by the two women. Then he said suddenly: 'You're not frightened of me, are you, Kathleen? You needn't be. I promise I shall never hurt you or the baby. You do believe me, don't you?'

'Yes,' said Kathleen listlessly. She turned back to the bedroom. At that moment she felt too exhausted to prolong any situation.

Adam followed her, patting her arm. 'Into bed with you, there's a good girl,' he said, turning back the bed covers. When she was in bed he stooped to kiss her mouth, but she turned her face to the pillow, so that he kissed her cheek. 'Good night.'

'Good night.'

'If there's anything you want, just give me a call. I'll leave the sitting-room door open so that I shall hear.'

'I shan't want anything.'

He closed the door behind him, and found Maureen still standing in the hall. 'I think she will be all right now,' he said in a matter-of-fact voice, for now that he knew where he was with Maureen, just as he'd got to know where he was with Dr. Canning, that they were both *enemies*, it was easy work. You had to palaver them along, that was all. 'I'm sorry if I shouted at you. I've been rather tired and nervy all day, I'm afraid.'

'I shall come in to-morrow and see how she is.'

'Do! That will be nice. Give my love to Mother.'

Maureen said nothing. She went to the front door and opened it. 'Good night,' he said genially, but she didn't answer, just closing the door very quietly behind her.

He went back to the sitting-room. His enemy had gone. It was just as well he'd got to know her. A man's enemies were those of his own household. He must watch Maureen very carefully. As he had watched Canning! He had been a trifle too zealous, that was what it came to. He must remember he was only an apprentice as yet.

PART FOUR

PART FOUR

— EIGHT —

I

KATHLEEN'S words, as for once she had stood at the front door waiting to see him off, kept echoing in Adam's mind throughout that day. 'Remember, Adam, I want to discuss this business of Sheila and the nuns seriously with you this evening. It can't be put off any longer.'

She had spoken in the crisp decisive voice she assumed nowadays when she had determined that, however vague and absent-minded Adam was, this at least must penetrate to his consciousness and be done. Sometimes she used it when she wanted him to bring something home with him from the city; sometimes it was a reminder that such and such a bill had to be paid immediately; such and such a letter had to be written; such and such a visit had to be made. Adam recognised that when this particular accent was used he must submit, since it was easier to submit. After all it was a small price to pay for the years of abstraction from household concerns, from herself, and, most important of all, from Sheila.

For it had been very difficult indeed to shut out the spectacle of one's own growing child, to suppress the uprush of spontaneous delight in the things she said, the things she did, turn of head, look of face, the indications of change from babyhood to little girlhood. Yet it had to be done. At first when he was but a tyro he had tried to do it by concentrating on the less pleasing aspects of Sheila: when she was a baby the nuisance of her crying; when she was older the ugly pig-headed expression she assumed when she didn't get her own way, or when she woke up in a bad temper increasing gradually to its crescendo as if determined to fight everybody and everything. But, no, that didn't work, for there came inevitably the aftermath of relief when she stopped crying and smiled; the surge of tenderness when she said: 'Sorry I've been a bad girl.' He had to make himself immune from Sheila, and immunity could only be purchased at the price of shutting her out completely, as he had had to shut out everything else that was lovely underneath God's sky.

And there were so many things, God damn it, so many things that one could go on cataloguing that inexhaustible treasury of beauty all one's life and never come to the end. One had never realised how many until it became necessary to close one's eyes and avert attention continuously from the little things that kept cropping up. Oh, those *little* things! It was easy to remember never to look toward the mountains, but the play of sunlight and shadow among trees, the flight of a bird across the evening sky, an expression of sweetness on some unknown person's face, a man whistling, ragged little children laughing at their games, these and a thousand thousand other things caught at one's eye and one's ear and one's understanding before one was even aware that it had happened, and that one's still living heart had responded. Only a blind man who had once seen could realise the mul-tiplicity of the seductions of beauty that now were a closed book, and the blind, of course, inevitably developed their other senses more acutely as compensation. Since blindness of the sight was no way for him, though there had been times when he had cried in his heart that his eyes might be put out, he had had to drug himself. That was what other men and other woman did, and he could still marvel at the aptitude they showed, an aptitude that was almost inno-cent in its ignorance that they had drugged themselves. The money-makers, for example, for whom figures were the only reality, who were truly lost when they were away from their desk and out of reach of the telephone; the women who played or talked bridge from morning to night not knowing, not caring, that outside their windows all the tragedy and all the hope of the sweet heart-breaking world was being enacted, that a million times Christ was born, Christ was crucified, and Christ rose again.

Well, his way of drugging himself had to be in confor-mity with the Little Way, and so he had chosen the easiest and the most obvious, drugging himself with the writ-ten word, drugging himself with print, so that he hardly ever sat down without dragging newspaper, magazine or book towards him. Good books mostly, or at least enter-taining books, for the reason that it was easier to hold one's attention bound to them. He had become what was known as 'a great reader'. How Kathleen had expostulated at first: 'Must you read so much, darling? It must be bad for your eyes.' And he had answered grimly: 'I know: that's why I do it.' And then from saying it to him, saying to other people: 'I never get a word out of him nowadays: he's always reading.' Other people, of course, smiled indul-gently: women because, of course, they knew all about the way husbands went on, and, as one woman had told Kathleen, she was lucky that her husband didn't drink, as her husband did, drinking all their money, all their home gradually away. Men, because they knew that Adam was one of these clever chaps, and clever people, they believed, did read a lot. And so he *was* clever, Adam had thought: cleverer than they ever knew!

So that was how it was Kathleen had developed the way she had in these eight years: a good and devoted mother, wrapped up in her child, as other people would also put it, making too a great friend of Maureen, and addressing him, when she wanted something done, in that peculiar bossy tone which meant insistence. As she had done that morning: '*This business of Sheila and the nuns.*'

By that she meant that at Sheila's convent school they had decided that now was the time when she should be prepared with the other children of her class for going to Confession and for her First Communion. 'Well, that's all right, isn't it?' he had said, and Kathleen had replied sharply: 'No, I'm not sure that it is all right. It's something that wants thinking over.' He had tried to wave the matter away as not worthy of his attention, as he had successfully waved so many matters away. But this time evidently thinking over meant talking over, and she intended to talk that evening, and therefore a comparatively pleasant stage in his reading would be interrupted. For he had recently purchased a second-hand set of the *Encyclopaedia Britannica,* and, still among the A's, had found its perusal most rewarding. That is to say it took him quite a long way away from Sheila, who wouldn't be found even when in months to come he arrived among the S's. It was evident, he decided, that in spite of Maureen's influence Kathleen was suffering from another of her recurrent bouts of anti-Papistry, and therefore that evening he would have to try and defend that Church all of whose commandments he had himself broken, and was determined for the rest of his life to go on breaking. For since it was no part of his design to harm Sheila, whomever else he harmed, she must pursue the normal course of one who had been born into a household whose tradition was Catholic on her father's side, and who had been baptised a Catholic. Afterwards she might do as she pleased. So far he had arrived in his thoughts when he was interrupted by one of the more difficult types of those seekers after facts who consult reference librarians. This one wished to know the provisions of a remote statute which required much consultation from one of the thick blue volumes of Butterworth's *Continuation of Halsbury,* and then another, and then yet another! For the rest of the afternoon Adam's domestic affairs disappeared from heart and mind.

II

Meanwhile at home Kathleen, taking her afternoon's rest with Sheila out of the flat, since she had gone to play and later have tea with a neighbour's child, was for the first time that day able to give her attention to the conversation she had planned for that evening. Lying on her bed she started to prepare her arguments, to plan her piece, to pose the question, for that was what it came to: actually what *was* the point of a non-practising Catholic wishing to have his child brought up as a Catholic?

Instead she found herself listening with some irritation to the footsteps which passed backwards and forwards in the room overhead. What could Caroline Wickham, usually a quiet enough occupant of the upper floor, be doing?

Caroline and John Wickham were the English couple who had taken the upstairs flat some two years ago. Wickham had some sort of a job with the Inishkill branch of an English tobacco company. Kathleen liked both of them, and believed that they liked her. Though sometimes she wondered if she would have been interested in either of them had not the three felt drawn by their sense of being exiles in this strange city of drift and melancholy, which expended anger and heat upon comparative trifles and appeared to view larger issues with a vast unconcern, a city of pious religious practices and merciless judgments.

If only John wouldn't sit round with his pipe in that self-conscious way and agree with everything Adam said, even when they were things he shouldn't agree with; if only Caroline wouldn't boss, and keep giving her advice as to how to bring up Sheila. Of course it was natural for her to think she knew about children as the job she had before she married was something to do with looking after the welfare of unruly and backward children, piloting the poor little devils off to approved schools when Caroline found, as apparently she had often found, that the parents were the wrong people to look after them. Now she was seeing Caroline's broad pink face, fine brown eyes, and the plait of fair hair she arranged in coronet fashion. She was kind really; also there was a suggestion of something appealingly helpless and soft about her until she spoke in that drawling voice of hers, which so often started earnestly with: 'But don't you think …?' And then when she, or more usually Adam, contradicted or questioned, she had a way of stiffening, like a cat suspicious that she was among enemies or had heard the sound of a dog barking; a slight frown appeared upon the broad smooth forehead, and the plump fingers holding her cigarette would twitch with impatience.

Kathleen sighed, and since the footsteps overhead had ceased, reached out her hand for a book which lay on the bedside table. Since Sheila had started going to school she had taken to re-reading the poems which used to be her special favourites when she was a girl. She was not wholly unaware that she read in very much the same baffled spirit of yearning for something that she felt poetry alone could give in which she had sought solace for the unsatisfactory nature of everyday life ten years ago. Now she read once more the Lament for *Adonais*. Gradually her mind tightened and took a grip on the words:

> He is a presence to be felt and known
> In darkness and in light, from herb and stone
> Spreading itself where'er that Power may move
> Which has withdrawn his being to its own;
> Which wields the world with never wearied love,
> Sustains it from beneath and kindles it above.

Kathleen paused to reflect. So even Shelley, the passionate questioner, the iconoclast, the knight errant, the advocate of free love, of free everything, had come before the end of his short and gallant life to a belief, to a faith in some sustaining Power, to that Power's unwearied love. Her eyes went quickly on to a passage which had once kindled her and also troubled her:

The One remains, the many change and pass;
Heaven's light forever shines, Earth's shadows fly;
Life like a dome of many-coloured glass
Stains the white radiance of eternity
Until Death tramples it to fragments.—Die
If thou wouldest be ...

Laying the book down Kathleen thought of Mitcham Fair, to which she and Eleanor had gone one Saturday in a mood of adventure. Riding one of the Merry-Go-Round horses she had looked down on dark moving crowds, on the flaring lights of the stalls, heard laughter and excited rough voices, and then had looked beyond these things to a clump of dark and silent trees under the great stretch of pale sky, and felt tensely the contrast of noise and colour against the still night of the countryside beyond. One had the same feeling looking at the gaudy pier at Brighton, bejewelled with necklaces of lights on a summer evening, flung out a little way from shore, a tiny futile but brave gesture against the dark infinity of sea which lapped it round.

Infinity, Eternity, God! These words mirroring such tremendous conceptions nagged at her, Kathleen thought, like an aching tooth. Not all the time, of course. Just occasionally. But most of the time she knew it was there. Maybe it wouldn't have nagged at all if she hadn't married Adam who had never loved her, if she hadn't come to live in this city where people crossed themselves when they passed a church, where one would suddenly espy a rosary dripping from a handbag where it kept company with lip-stick, powder compact and cigarette-case, where nobody lost anything without praying to St. Antony to find it for them, where the black flowing garb of nuns caught one's eyes as one turned from a shop window or from feeding the ducks when she took Sheila to the park: dark brides of Christ against the bright flower beds. Well, all this wasn't the point. What she would say to-night to Adam would be something like …

A knock at the outside door interrupted her thoughts, and impatiently she got out of bed and drawing her robe about her thought resentfully that it was always like this whenever she tried to get some rest and a little peace for thinking. Caroline Wickham stood outside:

'Oh, am I disturbing you? I'm afraid you were resting.'

'It doesn't matter a bit. Come in. I wasn't asleep or anything.'

Kathleen led the way back to the bedroom. Sometimes Caroline got into a lecturing habit of conversation, and if she wanted to lecture it was as well for the patient listener to make herself comfortable.

'Do sit down. You don't mind if I go back to my bed, do you? My back aches a bit to-day for some reason.'

Caroline sat down but in a bolt upright position, her eyes fixing Kathleen gravely. 'I wouldn't have dreamt of disturbing you like this except that I do want to get something off my mind.'

'Oh, do get it off your mind,' said Kathleen settling herself comfortably, and then thought remorsefully: 'I sounded just like Adam then, sort of sarcastic. And I certainly don't want to sound like him.' By way of apology she added: 'How nice you look. That blue is just your colour.'

'Is it?' Caroline looked down at the front of her dress in a meditative way. Then she looked up again, and started crisply: 'I hope you won't mind what I'm going to say, but I wish you'd ask Adam to lay off John.'

'Lay off John? I don't think I quite understand.'

'Well, John isn't a coward, Kathleen. Or perhaps you, too, think he is?'

'Of course I don't. Why should I?'

'I don't know. You don't say much about the war so I don't really know if you approve of it or not. But you may be one of those Imperialistic people who think he should go back to England and join up.'

Kathleen felt herself flushing. In a way it was precisely what she had thought, and that was why she generally turned the conversation when the war was mentioned. 'Of course I don't. It's not my business.'

'I can assure you it's not cowardice. He does happen to be a pacifist just as I am, of course, a pacifist. But he didn't come over here in '38 to escape the war, but because his firm sent him.'

'Of course I quite understand that. I think you're being rather silly, if you don't mind my saying so.'

'Oh, no, I'm not,' said Caroline in the voice that reminded Kathleen that she'd been to Roedean and taken her degree at Oxford whereas Kathleen had had neither of these social and intellectual advantages. She produced a packet of Player's cigarettes, then a box of matches from her bag, and lit up. As an afterthought, she said casually: 'Want one?'

'No, thank you,' said Kathleen firmly. 'I have my own here.'

She watched Caroline raise her chin and turn sideways looking out of the window, and realised that she wasn't feeling as comfortable—so poised, Caroline would call it, the necessity of poise being one of her articles of faith—as she wanted to appear. Of course John, who was a few years younger than herself, was her ewe lamb as well as her husband. She wanted to protect him. Why years ago she had felt something that way about Adam, she reminded herself.

'If you understand the position, and I give you the credit for thinking that you do, will you try and make Adam understand? Because John is getting rather tired of his continual gibes, and one day, though Adam is so much older, he might be tempted to hit him.'

'Really?' commented Kathleen. Her lips compressed.

'Yes,' said Caroline staring hard at her. 'John said to me last night: "If Palmer says to me once more that the war is going very badly for England with the Germans in possession of the whole of Europe, and that I am fortunate to be where I am, I shall knock him down." And I know he will. He may appear to you to be quiet and gentle, but he's not the sort of person to take insults lying down. And under his pretence of agreeing with the ideals of pacifism, Adam is continually sneering and implying that John is using this country as a hide-out. You know that's true, don't you?'

Yes, Kathleen thought, she did know it was true, but she had got so much in the habit of expecting Adam to say disagreeable odd things whenever he met the Wickhams, or for that matter when he met nearly everybody that she knew, that she merely changed the subject, and mostly steered him away from them. Now she said slowly: 'I know Adam has a very unfortunate way of expressing himself sometimes, but he doesn't really mean it. Why, the reason, or one of them, that Adam wanted us to live here years ago was so that we should be out of the way of the war he thought then was bound to come.'

'Quite. But then he belongs here. Quite a characteristic example of a native of this place, John and I have always thought. Also he's over military age. And like other self-centred middle-aged men he has quite a blood lust for other people being killed.'

'Now you're being very unfair ...'

'Oh, no, I'm not. You yourself told him the other evening when he was looking at the evening paper in the hall and commenting about all the people being killed in the London air-raid that he sounded quite pleased about it. You know you did ...'

'Yes, but I didn't *really* think anything so *ridiculous.*'

'If you didn't, I did. I happen to know something about individual psychiatry, as you know, and your husband is a destructive paranoiac if I ever saw one.'

Kathleen sat up. This was going too far. 'I think you are being rather offensive, and I object to your saying these things.'

'I don't mean to be offensive to *you*. We are both very sorry for you, if you want to know.'

'I don't want to know,' said Kathleen quietly. She looked at the watch on her wrist in a marked way, and then got off the bed, and disregarding Caroline walked to her dressing-table.

'I'm sorry if you are going to take it like this,' said Caroline watching her as she passed a comb through her hair. 'I hoped it wouldn't interfere with our friendship.'

Kathleen said nothing. She put down the comb, and reached for her powder-puff.

Caroline stood up. 'Well, perhaps you'll mention the matter to Adam,' she said, trying unsuccessfully to speak in a lighter voice. 'Then at least he'll know where we stand.'

'I may or I may not,' said Kathleen, also striving unsuccessfully for casualness. 'I really don't think it's my business.'

'Oh well, if you take that attitude ...' said Caroline moving towards the door. Just so, Kathleen thought, must she have moved away from some slum home and the back-chat of an erring but unrepentant parent.

'Well, good-bye,' said Caroline at the door.

'Good-bye.'

And that meant good-bye for ever, thought Kathleen, sitting down in the chair she had vacated, and trying to control the choking sensation in her breast and the tears that stung her eyelids. And Caroline had been very kind sometimes, so that it couldn't help being sad.

III

But there was no time to indulge the disturbances in her heart. Kathleen got herself a cup of tea, took two aspirin, and set out to bring Sheila home. As she had expected, Sheila was in the cantankerous mood which so frequently affects highly-strung children returning from other people's houses. They have been polite there; they have also been treated as dear little girls and guests who must have first choice: now there is Mummie and home and no such need to be polite, and the drag on the spirits of the return from rarefied air to familiar surroundings, unsanctified by use. There were some sharp interchanges, and finally a storm of angry tears from Sheila which at least justified Kathleen sending her off to bed before Adam's key turned in the lock, and she went into the kitchen to prepare the high tea they usually ate together on his return.

Adam aware of the atmosphere of storm and stress was more placatory than usual. 'Has Sheila been naughty?' he asked when Kathleen returned from a summons to the bedroom.

'Yes. She always comes back from the Hobsons in an over-excited state. That's why I sent her to bed early.'

'She's been playing you up as they say in dear old London,' suggested Adam, trying for a lighter tone.

'Yes, I told you,' almost snapped Kathleen. Then she added curtly: 'But she's all right now. She called for me to say she was sorry and ask to be kissed good night.'

'Fine,' said Adam, studying Kathleen's face, which suggested that though all might now be well so far as Sheila was concerned, other matters were not so satisfactory. And tired for once from his long wrestlings with Butterworth and Butterworth's extensions of war-time legislation, he felt his resolve to be patient with Kathleen's problems weaken. He knew from the closed look on her pale, tired face that she was unhappy; indeed he could feel her unhappiness. And he felt that irritation which human nature so often feels when other people's cares threaten to intrude upon our preferences for our own troubles. He turned to reach for the evening paper, saying by way of excuse: 'Not much news to-night. Nothing fresh really.'

'Isn't there?'

'No. At least there wasn't an air-raid.'

'Wasn't there? Do you want another cup of tea? Well then, I'll clear away.'

'You haven't eaten much.'

'I don't feel like it.'

It was some time before she came back from the kitchen. Adam had indeed begun to feel that the evening's conversation might be postponed, and he could venture to take down the Encyclopaedia. But this hope was dissipated when she sat down opposite him, and announced: 'If you've finished with the papers I'd like to talk to you.'

'Oh, yes? What about?'

'You know what about. I can't see the point of Sheila being prepared for her First Communion when neither of her parents are practising Catholics.'

'Can't you?'

'Do you?'

'Well, yes. As a matter of fact I do.'

'Perhaps you'll try and explain to my meaner intelligence then?'

'Certainly. I think it better for children to be taught, when their minds are plastic, what is right and what is wrong. Even if they do wrong afterwards—which, of course, they will do—they will at least know that they are doing wrong, and probably be sorry. They also know that they have the means of a return to grace in the Sacraments of Confession and the receiving of the Holy Eucharist.'

'Leaving out all this business of the Sacraments, don't you really think that Protestants know the difference between right and wrong, that if Sheila went on to the High School she wouldn't be instructed there, and given scripture lessons?'

'It is not only a question of being given scripture lessons; it is also a question of being given some understanding when one is at a receptive age of the great mysteries of the

Christian faith. Whenever Sheila goes to Mass she will be reminded of the Sacrifice of the Cross: the only way we poor human beings can honour God is to offer His Son once again on the altar through the ministry of His priests. It is the nearest approach we can make since we, of course, have nothing worthy to offer Him.' Kathleen stirred restlessly. She had heard something like this before. It might be true. If you believed that. It did show that Catholics really believed in the Atonement and all that. But ...

'It's not the Mass I really object to,' she started slowly. 'But those horrible sermons about hell, and the way the people go on, beggars cringing and saying they'll pray for you if you give them money, and cursing you if you don't, and ...'

'We've discussed all that before,' said Adam a trifle wearily. 'The whining and the cringing, the gaudy images, the storming of an angry peasant talking for the most part to peasants in the language they understand. All you are really saying is that as a middle-class woman you don't like the ways and the tastes of the common people. The common or rather vulgar touch which almost inevitably must debase everything which passes through its hands. Why don't you make allowances, and be less of a snob?'

'You can put it this way, if you like,' said Kathleen, angry now at what she thought was his unfairness. 'All I know is that when they debase God, in whom it may surprise you to know I do believe, making of Him a something to be sold in return for Masses, Thank Offerings, pious ejaculations, so many Indulgences as ordered by some Pope, so many visits to the tabernacle and so forth, I do object to Sheila learning what I myself consider blasphemy.'

'It isn't quite like that really,' said Adam quietly. 'Human nature, once again being human nature, has a tendency to clutch at the coin and forget of what that coin is a symbol. But a gleam may be caught even in exchange and barter.'

Disregarding, Kathleen said: 'I think of God differently. Austerity and strength as well as compassion.'

'In other words,' said Adam studying her smilingly, 'you have decided for a sober God, a God dressed in Quaker grey, a God who has nothing to do with drunkenness and excess, even if it be the excess of ecstasy.'

'Well, if I have, I think it is probably nearer the truth than a God to be propitiated by superstitions,' said Kathleen spiritedly.

'I know, I know. Generally we make God in the image of the virtues we most prefer,' said Adam slowly. He stopped, and she saw his face grow intent with thought. His own words were opening up an avenue of speculation which he realised was fraught with danger to his cherished project. The image in which he had made God was not indeed a glorified image of himself as he wanted to be, but it was very near indeed to a personification of Holy Church, speaking through the mouth of Holy Church, voicing merely the identical commandments of Holy Church. And since Holy Church herself was but the bride on earth, there remained still that cloud of unknowing which concealed the heavenly throne from us. *Who has known God at any time?* The Angelic Doctor himself had declared for the incomprehensible nature of the Supreme Being. Then might it not be that in that cloud of unknowing was concealed some branch to save or stay his fall to perdition, to the perdition to which the logic of Holy Church had certainly so far condemned him?

The thought was so troubling that he banged his knee with his hand, and Kathleen said surprised: 'What's the matter?'

He answered her strangely, after a moment's pause, during which he raised his hand and looked at it in a surprised way: 'I was thinking that perhaps I have loved the Church too much.' And, yes, his heart acknowledged with sadness and nostalgia, the Church had been his first love and always his greatest love.

'Well then,' said Kathleen after a moment or two for readjustment, 'why don't you go to Mass and so on? That's really the point. I wouldn't mind Sheila going if you really practised the things you apparently believe in. As it is, with neither of us going, it just seems ridiculous to me.'

He smiled at her with more tenderness than she had seen him smile at her for years, so that her heart contracted for a moment. 'Oh, Kathleen, don't you know yet how much we can reverence and believe in the things we don't do?'

'But why?' she said in a low voice looking down. 'I do understand that, yes, but in this case … why don't you?'

'That I can't tell you,' he said also in a low voice. He lit a cigarette before going on in a more business-like voice: 'But perhaps you do understand that since I *do* believe I'd like, at least as I don't want to hurt Sheila, I'd like her to be instructed by the nuns and so on. Let her do as she likes afterwards. It won't be my business.'

Kathleen meditated. She felt she was going to say yes, and yet he hadn't given her any real arguments, she thought. How had he persuaded her? She made a last effort: 'My real difficulty is that I don't want her to be taught a lot of things which I don't believe are true. That can't be good for her. Surely it's better that she should be brought up without any religion than that she should, well, let's put it this way, that she should be given bad or tainted spiritual food?'

He shook his head. 'Only the moralist, only the prig, only the reformer could believe that. The practical man, the artist, knows it's not true. If you have no food at all you die. If you eat tainted food, and most of the people in our industrial cities eat tainted or poor food out of tins, you do survive and you do live. The same applies to spiritual food. Let it be admitted that our people here are often given tainted spiritual food. It keeps them alive. It is better that a tired old woman with a long life of pain and struggle behind her should believe that she can partly buy her way into the bliss of heaven than that she should have no hope at all of any bliss. That for her, as she sits alone, there are only the lengthening shadows, and then the dark.'

Kathleen thought. 'I see what you mean,' she said at last. She gave him a long look, thinking it was strange that he could talk like that and yet be so without tenderness in all his personal relations. And that reminded her …

'Well, all right about Sheila. I'll let Mother what's-her-name know. As you really seem so keen. But there's something else that I have to talk to you about, and about that there's no question at all. I had a row with Caroline this afternoon on your account. And though I said it wasn't my business, I do think you've behaved very badly indeed.'

'Caroline Wickham? Good Heavens, I wouldn't touch her with a six-foot pole.' Adam sat up with animation. Thank Heavens, he was thinking, the matter of Sheila was disposed of. And now he needn't say anything more that was true for the rest of his life!

'It's not Caroline. Incidentally she dislikes you quite as much as you dislike her. She came to tell me that John resents your sneers at him for not joining up in the war.'

Adam smiled. 'Really? That's very interesting.'

'You can call it interesting. But she was quite serious. She said that if you go on sneering at him he'll knock you down.'

'Let him jolly well try. If he does I shall have him up for assault. He won't like that. Because it will bring it all up about his being a shirker, a young Englishman holding a soft job over here while his countrymen are being killed. He *is* a coward, you know. He calls his cowardice idealism, of course, as most conchies do. For their own self-respect's sake. He's enraged with me, because he knows that I see through him.'

'But what business is it of yours, Adam? Why can't you let people alone?'

'I have to be about my master's business, that's why.'

'Oh, now you are just being stupid clever. Why are you so delighted to hurt people? Why all this sadism?'

'Now I expect you're quoting dear clever Caroline. I suppose she said I was a sadist.'

'I don't know that she did actually. But she thinks you have a destructive mania.'

'Does she? Quite a bright girl, isn't she?'

'As a matter of fact she's not very bright. But she *is* kind. She's been very kind to me in heaps of ways. Doing the shopping for me when Sheila had measles that time, and all sorts of little things. But now because you've been so disagreeable to John I suppose our friendship is over.'

'Why, did you defend me?'

'I didn't like the way she put things so I told her it wasn't my business,' said Kathleen stiffly.

'Dear Kathleen! How sweet of you.' Adam put out a hand and touched her knee. She said, looking at him with cold directness:

'Don't make any mistake. I sympathise with her. I've often thought what rotten things you said at John, and I should have stopped you before. But I suppose I've got into the habit of expecting you to say rotten things, and I forget that other people don't take it that way.'

He looked at her, startled for a moment. Then he said: 'I see. I haven't been very clever about you, have I?'

'Haven't you? I thought you'd got me just where you wanted me.'

'Where's that?'

'Oh, the acquiescent housekeeper, the devoted mother to your child.'

She looked at him with eyes bright with hostility. It was odd: a few minutes ago when he had seemed to want to make her understand about religion, when he had spoken gently, they had seemed nearer to each other than they had done for years. Now they were far apart again. But a flame of anger, an unaccustomed flame, had spurted up. What would he say to that?

He said nothing. He watched her from a face that she saw was pale and strained, and embarrassed by his silence she got up, and went to draw the curtains. When she turned back to the room, she said, trying to speak easily: 'I don't expect either Caroline or John will want to speak to you again, so perhaps to avoid a breach of the peace you won't speak to them?'

'Very well.'

'Now I'll leave you in peace to go on with your reading. I'm afraid I've interrupted you for quite a while. I'm sorry.'

He still said nothing, and she went out of the room, closing the door behind her.

— NINE —

It was the day after Mrs. Palmer's funeral. Perhaps it was because the death of her mother had come so suddenly, so unexpectedly, Maureen thought as she stood looking out of the window, staring down at the street and away from the emptiness behind her, that her own feelings seemed so meagre, so dull. If she had loved her mother more, loved her as surely a daughter should love her mother, then her heart would have been swept by the nobler tide of grief. It wasn't so with her. Rather it was as if music which had been playing continuously, in the way some people kept their radios on as the inevitable background for conversation or reading, music which one hadn't noticed much had suddenly stopped, and first of all one was only conscious that something which should have been there was lacking. And the lacking expressed itself in prosaic terms: no one to get one's tea, so that coming home from the office she must fry her own egg and bacon, no long stories of shopping experiences that one must listen to with a scrap of one's attention when one would rather read, nobody to ask day by day how they were, if they had slept well, nobody who in return commented critically on one's appearance or reminded: 'Isn't it this evening you wanted to wash your hair?'

Yes, it was a lacking and a difference, all right, she thought, turning away from the window. Now she was a forty-three-year-old spinster left alone in the world—no, not quite alone because, of course, there was Adam, but then she didn't love her brother truly any more than she had truly loved her mother. And suddenly with the thought she was clenching her fist, her heart quivering in an intensity of sorrow for its lost youth, for the time when it had been eagerly open to all comers, intensely loyal to its kin. But little by little the cold mind encroached with its endless criticism of people and things. Nobody on a pedestal any more, mostly, alas, people whom perhaps one felt pity for but didn't really want to be with. God forgive her, she was nearly as carping as Adam, except that she did love one or two people, Kathleen and Sheila, the girls at the office ... Violet and Anna were grand, and, of course, there was always, all the time really, though one sometimes forgot, our Lord, and His Mother who was also our Mother.

But now it was her earthly mother of whom she should be thinking and for whom she should be praying, and so her thoughts fluttered among the past hours striving to bring herself a greater sense of their reality. It had started on the Friday when returning from the office she had found her mother in bed and complaining of pains in her stomach. The doctor had come, but Doctor Walsh hadn't seemed to think much about it, calling it an attack of gastric flu, of which he said there was quite a lot about. Mrs. Palmer had stayed in bed all Saturday, but had insisted on getting up on Sunday to go to ten o'clock Mass. Worried and expostulating, but after all it was only a step to the church, she had gone with her, and it had been all right till she had got back, and then when Maureen came into the room from peeling the potatoes in the kitchen, she had found her in a state of collapse on the couch, murmuring words that were hardly intelligible. The rush to the telephone, the calls for Doctor Walsh, for Adam, and then for Father O'Connor, who wasn't there, so they'd sent the curate, Father Cronin. And she had certainly recognised the priest, and understood that she was near the end, for the poor mouth had tried to murmur: '*Oh my God, I am heartily sorry,*' and then she could say no more, so that those were her last words.

And indeed though her senses were gone, and the heart soon ceased to beat, they were the only last words that counted for most of us, all any of us could say, thought Maureen, her eyes now full of tears, and it was right that Father Cronin had given her complete absolution. The end had come then, and by comparison the requiem Mass was an empty thing, a formal necessary rite, and that was all. It hadn't been a good funeral in the way that the last funeral she had been to, that of their neighbour Richard Hempall, had been a good funeral. For old Mr. Hempall had been a good man, who had loved his wife faithfully, cherished his children, considered his neighbour always with active friendliness, and thought so little of himself that the stupid had always adopted a slightly sneering attitude toward him. At that funeral one was convinced that God would not enter into judgment with his servant, since the path on toward the eternal light would be trodden with the same simple sureness as the dead man had made his earthly pilgrimage. From Mr. Hempall's funeral she had gone away with a light step, thinking with gladness that he was now come nearer to God.

But Mr. Hempall was a rare person, and most of us, including her own self, thought Maureen, are not rare, having fallen into the common state of cherishing ourselves or cherishing creatures more than God. So the pilgrimage is still unfulfilled; we watch the coffin as the holy water is sprinkled, and our prayers for the departed soul ask for God's mercy to be shown in Purgatory. Oh, it was easy and kind to agree that the dead man or woman would go straight to Heaven, but how could it be so with the most of us who not only were not saints, but who in our hearts didn't think that we were expected to be saints, who didn't really for one moment agree with the saying of Catherine of Siena: '*Do not be satisfied with little things, for God expects big ones.*' We were all satisfied with very little things, indeed pleased with ourselves for them, for having given sixpence to a beggar, for having visited a sick person, for even having kept our tempers with our neighbours when they had seemed to slight us. Her mother had been like that, just as she was like that, and Maureen moved towards the door, thinking she would go up to her bedroom and pray, looking toward her crucifix. But just as she reached the hall, the bell sounded, and she went to open the door.

It was Kathleen, whose arms came round her quickly. 'Maureen, I had to come, even though I know you didn't expect me to-day. I've been so worrying about you.'

'Oh, you needn't have, Kathleen, though I'm so glad to see you.'

Kathleen searched her friend's face as they stood in the living-room. 'Are you very unhappy, darling? Oh, I can see you are. You've been crying.'

'Yes, but I was crying for the wrong reason. Because I wasn't feeling sorry enough for losing Mother. Because I have such a cold, cold heart, Kathleen. I've been sitting in judgment on her instead, and thinking of all the funerals that are not good funerals, but only so sad, so unbearably sad.'

'But the funeral went off very well, I thought. In fact I thought it was most solemn. That's one thing I wanted to tell you. You see it was the first Roman Catholic funeral I've been to.'

Maureen smiled affectionately at her. 'Oh, it was all right. No one got drunk or fell into the grave as it is related *has* happened. And we took our place in the queue all right, and the corpse was despatched neatly and efficaciously, earth to earth, dust to dust. It was that it seemed just another death, one of the millions that are happening all the time, and several people were sorry, though one person at least, and that was me, Kathleen, God forgive me, was sorry, too, but the little niggling self also kept thinking, well, in some ways ... oh, well I don't have to say it, because I suppose there generally is one person who looks on the bright side of things! But, well, I hope I'm not doing Adam an injustice if I say that he wasn't broken-hearted, any more than I was broken-hearted. Her two children were not overcome by grief, and that seemed to me so sad, so pitifully sad. I mean it *is* sad that mostly we care so little about each other.'

Considering this, and a little puzzled, Kathleen looked round the room before replying. This was the room whose very chairs, sideboard, and tables had always before seemed so hostile to her. And now the hostility had gone. And so she, too, was glad that Mrs. Palmer wasn't there any more, that a house which actually had been closed to her would now have only a welcome.

'Maureen, I am truly sorry about your mother, though I admit that just because somehow we never got to be friends, it is really because of you that I'm sorry. So I see what you mean. But you have nothing to reproach yourself with. I've always thought you were an angel to her, because, after all …' She stopped. It was not perhaps the time to say that after all Mrs. Palmer had been a very prejudiced and selfish old woman.

'Oh, Kathleen, I'm not blaming *you*. How can you be expected to care when she was always so horrid to you? Right from the beginning. I'm just being broody about death generally, that's all. I'll just tell the woman I got in for the cleaning and washing-up to get us some tea. Excuse me a minute.'

By herself Kathleen thought with some resentment of what Adam had said when she told him that she would probably go in and see Maureen some time that afternoon. 'Try and find out, will you, what her plans are. She'd hardly speak to me yesterday. She can't go on living in the house by herself, but I don't want her to sell it, or anything like that. If she has any idea of that kind, you might try to curb it. Of course I shall see her in the evening.'

She had said: 'We must let Maureen do as she wants to, but I'd like to say that if she should want to come and live here with us, I'd love it.'

'How on earth could we squeeze her in here? That's ridiculous.'

And she would like Maureen to come and live with them, Kathleen thought, a little surprised at herself. At a time like this, one realised who were the people one really valued. And she valued Maureen because she was honest and outspoken. What a contrast to someone who was a compact of dark sayings and reticences!

While they drank their tea, Maureen answered Kathleen's questions about an elderly cousin who had unexpectedly appeared for the funeral, and had as speedily disappeared. He was an auctioneer from the north, she explained, according to her mother a distant cousin who had also been at one time an admirer and suitor. 'It was good of him to come, but I wish he'd stayed longer and talked more,' concluded Maureen with a sigh.

'All through lunch he kept looking at his watch. I suppose he was bothered about his train?'

'Yes, he told me it was most important he should catch his train.'

There was something so flat and tired about Maureen's voice that Kathleen decided to change the subject. And so she plunged.

'You know Adam's coming to you later when he gets back from the Library? I think he wants to sound you about your plans. Well, you probably haven't had time to think, Maureen, so all I want to say is that if you do feel you'd like to be with him, with us, you do know that I'd love it beyond everything. It's all right, don't say anything; it's just that I wanted you to be sure of that.'

'Sweet of you. You are a pet. Well, no, I haven't really thought. But … Well, anyhow Adam wouldn't want me, so we can rule that out.'

'Oh, no. I think he is thinking you will … oh, well, I can't say, of course, but I certainly got the impression.'

'Got what impression?'

'I had the feeling that he certainly didn't expect you to live alone.'

With some impatience Maureen asked:'What did Adam actually say?'

'He only said that he hoped you wouldn't sell the house.'

'Why, because he wants to live here?'

'Honestly, I don't know, Maureen. It was just when he was in a rush getting off to the Library, and I'd told him I would be along to see you.'

Maureen thought deeply. 'I bet he does want the house,' she said at last. 'Yes, I begin to understand that. I've heard him whining to Mother about how little space he has, living in the flat. Besides a house is more respectable, more established, than a flat. Adam has a great idea about being established, that's the only word I can think of.'

Kathleen observed the pain in her own heart as she listened to Maureen. Adam did want to be established, to settle down. That was why, after all, he had married her. She said a little coldly:'I don't think it's fair to discuss it till you and Adam have talked. I don't know what's in his mind, but naturally he wouldn't want you to be alone.'

'Oh, nonsense! Adam doesn't care what happens to me. It's himself he cares about.' She paused, and then said in repentance:'I'm sorry.There I go again. It's just that it seems to me to be the truth.'

'The house is yours, and nothing to do with him, is that right?'

'Mother left everything equally between us.The everything is really just this house and the furniture, since she had an annuity, and of course that goes with her death. We had no reading of the will, because both Adam and I know that. The will is with Carroll, the solicitor.'

'I think she should have left everything to you.'

'No. It was right of Mother, right in a logical way. She had been very fond of Adam, her son, her brilliant first-born: she never was really interested in me. Then Adam disappointed her, and so we were in fact both written off, as you might say. I thought she might leave it all to the Church, but I suppose she felt she couldn't quite ignore the old maid daughter who had to work in an office. And if she thought of me, why, then there was Adam she really deep down still loved, I'm sure. So it was natural to leave it between us, and not bother making alterations or anything. Actually I've a sort of plan in my head, to sell up, and then the money could be divided, and I should have enough to furnish a fairly large flat comfortably. And naturally I haven't discussed it, there's been no time, but I know a girl at the office, you've heard me talk of Violet, she'd be crazy to rent a room off me, because she wants to get away from her people.'

'It sounds thrilling,' said Kathleen warmly. And she thought, yes, but really I'm disappointed. I thought Maureen might like to be with me and Sheila, but she'd really rather be with Violet. And, of course, because Violet is the amusing one, and she'd have much more fun.

'Don't you think it would be a good plan?'

'Yes, I do, though I'm disappointed for myself. You'll have a grand time, Maureen: I can just see you, coming flying back from the office on your bike to your own place, and not giving a damn for anyone, and I'm so cheered up about you. Now I must go, because of Sheila, and it won't be very long before Adam will be knocking on your door.'

'Yes, bother!' said Maureen. 'Because he'll give me all the arguments about not selling the house, that it's the wrong time or something. And then we shall start quarrelling, with Mother's bones hardly cold in the grave as they say. You think how shocking it is when other people wrangle over property, and I believe it's going to happen.'

'Don't worry. Just try and be, well, patient with him, Maureen. Try not to dislike him so much.'

'I don't dislike him. It's just that whenever I think about him or see him, a cold weight comes down on me, so I try to think about him and see him as little as possible. I shouldn't be saying this to you, I know. I'm awfully sorry. I wish I didn't always say everything.'

'It's all right. It's a bit frightening sometimes, it used to frighten me, but now I understand you better, and I see you have to. Good-bye, and be sure to hold out for yourself, and do whatever you want.'

'I'm afraid, you know, I shall,' said Maureen, looking guilty. 'I felt miserable really till you came, and now I see all my future just glowing and happy, and I think I'm going to have such good times.'

'And you will,' said Kathleen, kissing her, 'but you must promise to come and be with me and Sheila a lot, because, you see, you are our best friend, our only friend really.'

'Of course I promise.'

And instead of thinking about her mother, Maureen found herself thinking, 'poor Kathleen', as she watched her disappear round the corner.

II

Adam was surprised by the Maureen who a couple of hours later opened the door to him. He had anticipated a suspicious Maureen, determined to make things difficult for him; or even more probably a Maureen dwelling with determination on the dead, resolved to maintain an atmosphere of pious gloom. But here was a smiling Maureen bestowing on him a sisterly kiss, telling him briskly: 'I've got sausages for your tea: I do hope you'll like them, because I've found an awfully good place near the office and they were just fresh in.'

Oh, so she's going to appear friendly, was Adam's underlying thought as he ate and drank, answered her questions about Sheila's cold, and agreed that Kathleen looked well. And beware the Greeks when they bring gifts, he also thought, for he was prepared for a tussle. He had now firmly made up his mind that he wanted to live in his mother's house, and that since his sister possessed a half share in the property she would have to be thrown in with the house. Not that he wanted her to live with them. A devout untidy middle-aged girl, who gave the impression of always rushing somewhere, to the office, to Mass, to the pictures, to Confession, to meet someone for a coffee and cigarette, or even daringly a drink in an hotel lounge, who would, unless she had changed her habits, talk too much and bang doors, was no adjunct to an intellectual's household.

Maureen had been right in her surmise. Adam, viewing the situation left by Mrs. Palmer's death, had decided that a house gave one status. He already had a disciple or two, young men impressed by his saturnine personality and the ease with which he punctured other men's reputations, other men's self-esteem. He needed to collect these disciples, to give occasional parties, to set his books out to greater advantage. As a flat-dweller he belonged merely to the Bohemian riff-raff who met in pubs rather than in drawing-rooms. His fancy had lingered, unchecked for once by the sardonic censor, upon a picture of himself watched a trifle uneasily as his long fingers pressed tobacco into the pipe he had lately cultivated, everything arrested until he chose to take up the last remark and either give it the weight of his approval or, in due course, reduce it to a manifold absurdity by the Socratic method of posing a question.

Yes, given the house in which he at that moment sat he could have his book-lined study, a garden, and, for that matter, another baby. One child caused a household to revolve about her; there was altogether too much of Sheila in the flat. Two children, or even three, made a real family one in which everything fell into place. And he must hurry up. Kathleen was now in her middle thirties, himself in his late forties. Moreover one could use Maureen. Maureen would be very useful with the next baby, giving Kathleen a much needed hand.

He watched his sister attentively as she prattled, observing the lipstick which, for once, appeared to be the right shade, noting a sense she gave him of a new interior firmness. It was certain that she was not overcome with grief at their mother's death, sudden as it had been. The bird let out of the cage, he thought. Quite a happy woman in fact. And happy people were the intolerable ones!

His gaze left her to go round the room, to check up on the furniture, which he was already rearranging in his mind. He noticed an omission on which he decided to comment.

'I see you've taken down the Sacred Heart picture.'

'Yes, I have. I did it this morning. It was really an atrocity, wasn't it?'

'You mean, I presume, from an aesthetic point of view.'

'Of course.'

'Oh, undoubtedly. But Mother liked it, if you remember?'

'I don't know that she liked it so much as she felt that it was a thing to have.'

As he merely raised his eyebrows she went on bravely: 'Anyhow, it doesn't help Mother any more, and as I never liked it, as I always thought it an insult to our Lord if one knows better to have such a tawdry travesty hanging here, I took it down. It's all right. I didn't burn it or anything. I gave it to Molly: she's the woman who's been so good helping with the tidying up and the lunch yesterday. She was delighted to have it.'

'Naturally.'

He decided to say no more. He had succeeded, he thought, in making Maureen feel guilty, in putting her on the defensive. It wasn't yet time to arouse her to hostility. He put his knife and fork together, shook his head when she made to pass some bread and butter towards him, and said: 'Well, I suppose there are quite a number of things we can send off to the auction rooms. There's a lot of junk that won't fetch much, but just as well to have it out of the way.'

'Will you have some more tea?'

'No, thank you.'

'What do you want to do about the house?'

So she wouldn't wait. Precipitate as usual. All right. If she wanted the direct counter she could have it.

'I think I will perhaps have another cup, after all. Thank you. About the house? Well, of course, the one obvious thing is to hold on to it. It would be madness to sell now. After the war property here will go up and up. Think of bombed London. English people will be rushing over to buy houses and we should get several thousand then. At present I doubt if we should get much more than a thousand.'

'Well then, couldn't we let it furnished? We'd get about three or four pounds a week: then we'd each have two pounds a week.'

'I see you've worked it all out. Well, well! So soon!'

'I haven't worked it out. It just came into my mind now. I had hoped we could sell it, divide the money and then what I want to do is to move into a flat of my own.'

'Do you? How enterprising of you! Well, I do want to live here if you don't. The flat is becoming quite impossible now Sheila is at the noisy stage. Besides that idea of letting never works out. All the furniture that, after all, Mother loved and has looked after so carefully would be ruined, and furniture is another thing which is going up in price. In fact, already it's worth double its pre-war value. Sorry to mention these sordid business details, but as a very poor man with a struggle to live and keep a wife and child I must mention them.'

'Oh, don't be silly, Adam. Of course we must go into business details. That's what you've come for, isn't it? But ... well, if you and Kathleen move in here, what about me? You won't be able to pay me anything for my share, will you?'

'I'm very much afraid I shan't. You see my balance in the bank at this moment is exactly twenty-four pounds, some odd shillings and pence. And when I pay my income-tax that will disappear, or almost disappear. I am sorry that I haven't been able to save so that I could buy you out, but probably as an independent woman you don't realise how difficult it is when one's salary is only …'

'Oh, of course, I realise, Adam. I see all that. But … what about me? I only get three pounds fifteen shillings a week, you know, and you can't get a flat under two pounds. Indeed I'd be lucky if I found one at that. And that doesn't leave much, does it, for food and clothes and all the other things?'

Adam was pleased to see that Maureen had lost her composure. She was flushed; she was talking rapidly; her attitude was tense. He took out his cigarette-case.

'Do smoke, won't you? Yes, and, of course, cigarettes count in a budget, too.'

'I've got my own, thanks,' said Maureen distantly. She left the table to find her handbag, thinking, oh, how horrible all this is. It's more horrible than I ever thought it could be.

Each waited for the other to speak first. At last Adam said: 'We had hoped, that is Kathleen and I had hoped—you do know, don't you, how fond Kathleen is of you—that we could all three share the same roof. That is what most people would, I think, in the circumstances naturally expect would be the sensible and indeed agreeable thing to do.'

'What does it matter what most people think?' muttered Maureen angrily, hearing herself with horror. She was behaving like a child. But he was making her behave that way.

'You mean you don't think so? That in fact you don't care for the idea of sharing quarters with Kathleen and Sheila and myself?'

'It's not that. You know I'm devoted to Kathleen and Sheila. But after all, well, can't we be truthful about it, I can't believe you'd want to have me around yourself!'

'I don't know why you've got such an extraordinary idea.'

He gazed with apparent amazement into her eyes, and saw them flinch under his wide-eyed look. And at that moment indeed he *wanted* Maureen to join his household, because it meant submission. The intent of his will toward darkness had brought him at least to the pass when it was a natural impulse to thwart rather than to help forward. If a dark cloud obscured the sun, he was on the side of the dark cloud. When it rained on a Bank Holiday he thought with keen pleasure of the upsetting of plans in a thousand thousand hard-working families. Whenever he heard of a human weakness, folly or vice, even if it were only that of a stranger reported impersonally in a newspaper, he experienced the satisfaction of one receiving confirmation of his faith. So that it only needed the certainty that Maureen was excitedly looking forward to a life of her own for his will toward frustration to go into action.

Maureen was thinking, I could tell him he's a liar, but that wouldn't do any good. He wants the house, so he's prepared to swallow me with it as the easiest thing. Oh, but there must be a way! People good at business would surely find a way? Wasn't there something about raising a mortgage on a house that would help? But if she said something like that he'd make her look a fool, telling her why that was absurd.

'I had no idea you had such an odd notion about me,' said Adam in a grieved voice, getting up from the table and going over to the marble mantelpiece, upon which he looked down with a proprietary air.

'It's just that you've always been the clever one, and I'm just an ordinary stupid person.' And that's true, anyhow, she thought bitterly.

'You really mean,' said Adam turning round, 'that you find me repellent in some way?'

Guilt flooded her being. Because it was true, and convicted her of lack of charity. *Judge not lest you be judged.* She ran away from the question, saying rapidly: 'It was just that I was thinking of sharing this flat with a girl at the office. Violet Marshall. She's my best friend and we have fun doing things together.' How schoolgirlish it sounded!

'Well, if it only could be managed for you. But I confess I can't quite think of a solution, can you? I admit I had really set my heart on this house, because of Kathleen quite as much as myself. You see ...' he hesitated for a moment, and then decided it was safe to anticipate the event by a little, 'she probably hasn't told you yet, we're not really sure yet, but I think, I hope, she may be going to have another child.'

'Oh, Adam!' Maureen wheeled round on him. 'How exciting. I am glad. She never said anything when she was here.'

'She wouldn't because we're not sure yet. So don't tell her I said anything. I know she'd rather tell you herself when we are sure.'

'Of course, I won't.'

Adam watched the glow fade from Maureen's face. Now her brain was getting to work, and she would get the sense that she was being ensnared in a web from which it would be difficult to escape. He decided on a slight change of the subject, and said: 'Also, of course, it's neither here nor there really, but I am sure Mother would have liked the idea of her grandchildren living here.'

There was a pause. Maureen thought, I needn't let him get away with that. She said: 'And of course her wishes have always been so important with you, haven't they?'

He noted the sarcasm, and decided since he was now practically certain of victory to return the soft answer.

'I suppose I deserve that. Well, I was rather fonder of Mother than perhaps you quite realise, Maureen, but I don't pretend to have been the devoted son. Still it is rather melancholy …' he paused to glance over at the lighter patch on the wall where the picture of the Sacred Heart had hung … 'that so soon after her death you and I should be discussing rather cold-bloodedly how to divide her things. Don't you think so?'

Yes, she did think so. Though she wasn't particularly cold-blooded about it. She nodded. He went on.

'I did expect to be more upset by her death. But we had grown apart, and there it was. She wasn't a specially good woman, nor certainly a bad woman. And she was seventy-five, wasn't she? She had passed the allotted time. It seemed to take its place in the procession of average deaths.'

Whereas when I die, he was thinking with satisfaction, it won't be an average death. It will be the death of a man who has entirely cut himself off from the hope of mercy. But to Maureen he was repeating what she herself had thought, and she heard him with horror.

'Oh, I know,' she cried out with pain. 'But we have no business to judge. It's dreadful to be so smug about other people. Oh, I am ashamed of myself for thinking just what you've said.'

Turning with surprise, Adam saw that her eyes were full of tears, that she was mopping them up with a handkerchief.

She tried to smile. 'I'm just hating myself for my lack of charity.'

'Oh, no, you, Maureen, are not at all uncharitable,' he assured her gravely. 'That's why I don't want to feel that I am taking advantage of you about the house. If you really feel you can't live with us, even though I was thinking we might make a separate flat for you, so that the children wouldn't disturb you, why then …'

'Don't let's talk about it any more,' Maureen implored. 'Not now. I am sure we can work it out some way. Of course you and Kathleen must come and live here. And Sheila and … I do hope that's true, because Kathleen makes such a lovely mother. And I'll help all I can. Of course, I will. But please …'

She was crying again. What an emotional girl she really is, thought Adam. He had thought he might have quite a job. But now everything would go smoothly. At the same time it was as well to make sure.

'Can I tell Kathleen, then, that at least she may think about making a move, and that perhaps, she's so very fond of you, Maureen … You are really her only friend here, you know …'

'Tell her everything is going to be all right,' said Maureen. 'Only don't let's talk any more. Please.'

'Good-bye, then. I'll be seeing you very soon. And thanks for the grand tea,' said Adam warmly. He kissed her wet cheek, and let himself out, thinking that now there must be soft words for Kathleen, while Maureen, with one agonised look round, ran upstairs to throw herself on the bed and cry her heart out, hardly knowing why she was crying, except that nothing was as it should be, and that she herself was revolting in her wicked selfishness.

PART FIVE

PART FIVE

— TEN —

I

BUT what a mistake it had been, Adam was thinking one evening rather more than two years later, to introduce Maureen into his household. The girl hadn't wanted to come, so why hadn't he left well alone, which was to say, what was well for him, and pushed her off to a flat with some furniture, and perhaps ten shillings a week to help out? To begin with she had insisted on having a kitchenette made for herself next to her attic bedroom, taking advantage of some words he was supposed to have said, and might have said but hadn't intended, since he had had to pay for the installation of water and gas-stove. And then it wasn't as if her separate quarters made her really separate. It seemed that either Kathleen and Sheila were always shouting up the stairs for her, or she was calling down to them. Certainly she was always rushing past his door, on her way to early Mass, on her way to the office, on her way to meet Violet.

And Violet was another person of whom there was a great deal too much. For Violet had turned out to be an unexpectedly dashing person who was always putting something on a horse and sharing her tips with Maureen, who when she came to spend an evening with Maureen laughed so heartily and seemed to walk about so much overhead that

Adam had complained of the noise she had made. And then Maureen with flashing eyes:

'I only came to live here on the condition that I could have my friends in to see me.'

'It's not that, but you have such a curious taste in friends, this noisy common girl.'

'Don't dare to speak of Violet in that way. She's not common. She's a very rare person as a matter of fact. And I certainly shan't tell her to be quieter. Tell her yourself if you like. I know she'd enjoy telling *you* what she thinks of *you*.'

And Kathleen trying to make peace, but inclining really to Maureen's side.

'After all it's never more than once a week that Violet comes, and if she disturbs you so, why don't you come and sit downstairs with me? I shan't disturb you.'

But he didn't want to sit downstairs. Downstairs one was disturbed by the baby crying, or having to be fed or something or other to do with the new king of the household. His book-lined study with its divan bed was a retreat from all that. For with the coming of Johnny, a new order of things, and, on the whole, a satisfactory order as far as it went, had begun. After his high tea Adam went straight up to his own room, the big first-floor room, stayed there and slept there. It was understood at first that the divan bed had been a temporary arrangement, that one day he would join Kathleen in the bedroom she shared with Sheila and, of course, Johnny. Then Sheila must have a room of her own. But that day could be put off indefinitely.

The sanctum apart from noise, dreary household talk and the smell of cooking, would in fact have worked well, Adam was thinking for the thousandth time, if it hadn't been for Maureen overhead, Maureen, who had brought such an increase of life with her into the household that one could no more remain unaware of her existence than one could of a perpetually buzzing wasp. At tea Kathleen was always quoting her: 'Maureen says …' 'Maureen is going to the races tomorrow,' 'Maureen is frightfully fed up because …' on and on it went, though he had told her quite plainly that really Maureen's doings and ideas were of no interest to him.

If it wasn't Kathleen, it was Sheila: 'Daddy, look what Auntie Maureen has bought me.' 'Auntie Maureen is going to take me to the pictures.' 'Wasn't it dreadful, Auntie Maureen's typewriter at the office went wrong to-day?' 'We are all going to have a picnic on Saturday because Auntie Maureen is having the whole day off. Are you coming, Daddy?'

He had made it clear that he wasn't coming to any picnic, that he had to be busy, that he always was too busy for household affairs, and so now he was left pretty much alone. Alone, that is to say, as much as a tiny island is left alone by the waters which swirl perpetually around it.

And which sometimes succeeded in encroaching. As for instance this evening when, solely owing to Maureen, he had agreed to meet this cousin of theirs, James Macmullen, whose arrival he was now expecting.

For the past few weeks this James had been one of Maureen's main topics. She shared other people's troubles around just as she shared their joys, a habit which, Adam had gathered, was prevalent in her singularly sociable office, to which all the employees contributed their personal dramas. But the case of James Macmullen could, Adam was thinking, hardly be called dramatic, and it certainly was not cheerful. For that very reason it had succeeded in engaging his attention. Not long ago a hard-working sober clerk, living in digs on the north side of the city, he had absented himself from work, at first through illness, later for no discernible reason. For though he had recovered, though the doctor no longer provided him with a certificate, he did not return to his office, but went instead for long solitary walks.

'And if it's raining,' Maureen had said impressively, 'he doesn't take an umbrella, or put on a mackintosh.'

As for eating: 'Well,' said Maureen, 'he's nothing but skin and bone. Because he never takes anything but cups of tea and a little bread and butter.'

Maureen had been informed of the odd case of James by a chance meeting with Mrs. Florence Purcell, a married sister of James. When he had been turned out of his digs she had taken him into her house. But it could only be a temporary arrangement, Mrs. Purcell had insisted, because Mr. Purcell was now objecting. Mr. Purcell was saying that something must be done, because if, as he was inclined to expect, James committed suicide, why then he might be held responsible. And it wasn't fair that he should be held responsible.

Of course Maureen had urged the odd case of James on his attention, because her mind had worked it out that a man who had been a lunatic and got over it might be of some help to a man who appeared to be on the verge of becoming a certified lunatic. My dear kind sister, he had thought, hatred for her stimulated once more. Nevertheless his curiosity had been aroused sufficiently for him to agree to see James, to give permission for the fellow to be pressed to call.

Not that he'll turn up, he was thinking, glancing at the clock. I wouldn't if I were he. At the same moment he heard the peal of the front-door bell, and after a moment got up, and going to the door, opened it slightly.

He heard Maureen say to someone she had just admitted in that over-quick effusive way she used when she was nervous: 'I'm so glad to see you. We were just afraid that you mightn't be coming. Adam's in his room upstairs. Let me take your hat.'

He closed the door softly, and went back to his chair. Then he glanced round the room. What impression would this James get as he came in? Chiefly of books. A poor seedy clerk belonging to the humbler branch of the family, he had probably never seen even a few hundreds gathered together before. He opened the lid of his cedar-wood cigarette-box, annoyed at feeling apprehension, and took one out.

Before he could light it, he heard the steps outside, and then Maureen's voice: 'May we come in, Adam?'

The young man who entered behind Maureen had a white bony face and much-lined forehead. His light brown hair was neatly parted but had been cut very badly, probably by his sister, Adam thought later, when he observed this. Tall and slight with high shoulders he wore a stiff white collar and a shabby blue suit, much shabbier than one would have expected from such an obvious, Adam thought, clerk. He recalled Maureen's words about James never using a mackintosh or overcoat as he put out his hand.

'So glad to see you. Won't you sit down?'

The cold dry hands fell away from Adam's clammier grasp as Maureen said: 'You'd never have known each other, would you? How long is it since you met. You did both meet when you were kids, didn't you?'

'Oh, but I'm much older than James.'

'I was a little boy with the Christian Brothers when you were a big boy with the Jesuits,' said James, a faint sneer in his voice. For a moment his light hazel eyes looked at Adam with a flicker of curiosity. Or was it disdain, Adam wondered. Inferiority complex, probably, since Adam had belonged to a socially superior side of the family.

Maureen, of course, was now assuring James that she remembered the times when they had played together. 'It seems so stupid that Mother and I never even realised that you were working here. Of course we knew Florence was living up north. Would she rather be there than here, do you know?'

As James made no reply to this, staring away from both of them, Adam said: 'What about a drink for James, Maureen? We've got some beer, haven't we?'

'Rather,' said Maureen. 'I'll go and bring it up to you.'

As she disappeared Adam said again: 'Do sit down. Yes, there! Have a cigarette? Or don't you smoke?'

'Not lately.'

'Well, have one now.'

For a few seconds the other man stared at the cigarette-box extended towards him in silence. Then he said, as if remembering an old formula: 'I don't mind if I do,' and took one. He added while Adam searched for matches, as if the words had struck him: 'They say that a lot in England, don't they?'

'What? "I don't mind if I do"?'

'Yes.'

'I suppose they do. I don't really know. You've been to England then?'

'Oh, yes.'

Adam found the matches and lit one, watching James inhale awkwardly.

'What part of England were you in?'

'I went to the Isle of Man for a holiday. And I was in Liverpool.'

'When were you in Liverpool?'

'I had to go for the firm. It was a year after the war had started.'

'Did you come in for any of the bombing?'

'Yes, a bit.'

'Must have been dreadful?'

'Yes.'

'You didn't like it?' persisted Adam. It sounded a stupid question but he was thinking, he *might* have liked it: having turned towards the dark by then, he might have thought of it as a way out.

'No, I didn't like it much,' said James staring away.

'The noise?'

'Yes, the noise was bad.'

Maureen came in with a tray. Adam stood up while James looked carefully away.

'You haven't brought a glass for yourself, Maureen. Won't you join us?'

'No thanks. Not just now. I'm doing some ironing downstairs. I'll see you after, won't I, James? Sheila says you must come and say good night to her before you go. Kathleen's just put her to bed.'

'Well, Sheila will be asleep, I expect, by then,' said Adam as James looked at her, apparently not understanding. 'Sheila's my little girl,' he added.

James gave a brief nod. He was watching Maureen's hands as she filled their glasses, watching them with that fixed barely seeing gaze with which very old men sitting on benches sometimes follow the movement of a passing car. It was a gaze which Adam had known well in his time, the gaze with which fellow patients sitting in chairs stared at the backs of their hands. A hard case, he thought, and rubbed his own hands nervously.

'Thank you so much, Maureen.'

'Good-bye for now.'

'Good-bye.'

He turned to James: 'Well, good luck.'

'Good luck,' said James after a pause. He sipped at his glass, and set it down almost untouched.

Something must be done to break this unaware indifference. Adam said, setting his glass down and forcing the words out, since the direct approach was always the most difficult for him: 'I gather you need a bit of good luck. You haven't been well?'

'No. I haven't been very well.'

'And you don't look very well now, are you?'

'No, I'm not well,' replied James after a few seconds during which he looked at Adam suspiciously.

'Pains in the head?'

James didn't answer.

'I asked you because I have had bad headaches occasionally.'

'Oh, yes?' said James with indifference. He glanced at the print that hung over the mantelpiece.

'I used to get them in London when I worked there. You knew I was in London, on a magazine, I suppose?'

James turned his head. 'Yes, I heard all about it,' he answered.

All about it? What did he mean? What had he heard? Now it was Adam looking at James with suspicion, the old suspicion. Had his mother talked, had she even written to relatives, judging that as they were relatives the shameful secret might be imparted? And then as James continued to look indifferent, continued to maintain the pose of some-one patiently waiting to be finished with and dismissed, a new notion came into his head. Why not tell James? Why not say casually: 'You may have heard I was in an asylum for a year. Better look out, mate, or that's what they'll do to you. That's what God will do to you.'

But the next moment he dismissed the notion as a moral temptation! Suppose that he did succeed in startling James for the first time into interest? It might do good! He didn't want to do James good. He was just curious about him.

'This country suits me better. But it may not suit you. The climate does tend to make one lethargic.'

No answer at all. He was merely boring his listener, who was now staring at the back of his hands again.

'You are not drinking your beer. Don't you like it?'

He spoke sharply, and James aroused looked at his glass, and then lifted it. But when he set it down it was still nearly full.

Adam said: 'I met my wife in London. You haven't mar-ried, have you? It's quite a sensible thing for a young man on his own to do, I think. Probably you need a woman.'

Ah, that had registered. He was going to answer.

'I'm not interested in women.'

'Aren't you! Lucky man. They are usually a bit of a bother to bachelors.'

'They don't bother me.' James hesitated and then made an effort: 'I'm no lady killer, as you can see.'

'Well, if you don't take any interest in them, you know …?'

James was looking away again. He evidently considered the subject closed.

'You prefer men friends?'

After a moment this got a doubtful nod of half assent. Adam let his imagination play about the tepid agreement. Perhaps at one time there had been another young man at the office with whom he had gone for a walk. Or perhaps the other man preferred watching football, and James had been bored. And so no real intimacy had sprung up. No, reflected Adam, watching the averted face almost dreamily now, this was no Tennysonian young man: no soul of the rose had gone into his blood, as the music clashed in the hall, no splendid tear had fallen from any passion flower at his gate, rather his life had trickled out in drops of water, no wine with that water, no agony of the Cross …

James stirred. It was evident that he felt the silence had been too prolonged. He said politely: 'You have a nice place here. This is a nice room.'

'Do you like it? I'm afraid it's chiefly books. Do you care for reading?'

'No, I'm not a great reader,' said James with some determination.

'Are you a practising Catholic? Do you go to Mass?'

James shook his head. 'It's a long time since I've been to Mass,' he said, as if noting the fact for the first time, though he did not find it an interesting fact.

'Well, as a matter of fact I don't either,' said Adam. 'Maureen now, she's the religious one.'

'My sister goes,' contributed James.

'But you've grown out of belief, shall we say?'

'I was never very religious, what you'd call religious,' said James with finality. He moved restlessly, and looked at Adam with a suggestion of a frown. You're not a priest, the frown seemed to say, so what's the point of all this?

There's no point, Adam silently assured him. He was proving himself a romantic, trying to fabricate adventures of the mind, the flesh and the spirit for a life barren of any adventure. A life for which routine had been the be all and the end all. At the end of each working day he might go now and then for a walk in the summer, and in the winter sit over a fire reading the evening paper eating his supper, smoking just so many cigarettes, and then going up quietly to bed. But, he thought again, that couldn't be the whole picture: resentments must have been born, strange angers which no one ever heard, but which in the end had caused him to decide to walk out, as he *had* walked out. If he could only find some key …

'I'm keeping you,' said James. He prepared to get up.

'No, no,' said Adam with unusual emphasis. 'Of course you're not keeping me. Have another cigarette? And let me fill your glass.'

'No, thank you,' said James, his hand going over the top of the glass, as Adam rose, bottle in hand. But he took the cigarette, and even found a match to light it himself.

'Please don't think me impertinent,' Adam said watching him as he inhaled, 'but, of course, you know Florence is worried about you. She feels, women are like that, you know, that you're not looking after yourself properly. And you are terribly thin, you know.'

'I can't help her being worried,' said James in a rougher voice than he had used before. He was scowling now. Adam rushed on:

'It's natural, isn't it. I mean there's her husband to consider, and the sordid question of finance. And as you don't work …'

James interrupted: 'I can't work when I'm ill.'

'It's not physical illness, she told Maureen. More of the mind, isn't it? Is something worrying you?'

'There's nothing worrying me, but I can't work,' said James. For the first time there was an accent of desperation in his voice, as if he was wondering how much more often he had to tell people the simple truth.

'I understand. I know that feeling,' said Adam in a sooth-ing voice. 'If you had a long rest in the country, perhaps … isn't there some sanatorium run by one of the Orders?'

'You mean, St. John's for nervous disorders? Florence asked about it. They want seven guineas a week, so that's out,' said James in a voice that betrayed some satisfaction. It was as if he himself knew, had always known, there was no solution, but that he expected other people would only find that out gradually.

'So for the present you're going to stay on with Florence?'

'She's written after a farm that advertised, and wants only two guineas a week for the winter months,' said James uninterestedly.

'So you'll go there?'

'If they'll have me.'

'Do you like the country?'

'Not particularly.' He flicked the ash off his cigarette, and then added: 'This place is miles from anywhere. That's why they are cheap, I reckon.'

Adam seemed to himself to be watching with him the set-ting in of the long dark evenings in the country. He sat in his chair, close up to the fire, because there wasn't much coal or wood or turf on the fire. The light was a poor lamp, but it didn't matter because you didn't want to read, and there was no one you wanted to write to. Sometimes you heard the wind outside, sometimes the farm dog barked. Or someone banged a door, and ran past your room, going upstairs, or coming downstairs. After a while you wondered if you wanted to go to the lavatory, but you put it off, because it was an effort to get up, and you didn't really want to go. When the clock said nine, or perhaps ten, then you would get up and go to bed. You'd undress by candle-light, and the candle-light flickered in the darkness when you lit it at first because of the cold air.

'If you'll let me have your address I'll send you some cigarettes,' said Adam, breaking another long pause.

'Florence has the address,' said James. Then he added: 'Thank you.'

'Do you think you'll like it down there?'

James looked at him with an irony which dismissed the question as a flippancy. 'It's what you can get,' he said after a moment, as Adam waited.

It's what you can get. If you did your work to your employer's satisfaction, you got your pay envelope. If not, then you got the sack. If you could pay the rent of a room, you got a room, if not, out into the street you went. That was the way of the world to the poor man, a matter of concrete practice, lightened by none of the dreams and faith of a Micawber. There came a time, now and then, to those who lived solely by this hard pursuit of putting a penny in and drawing a penny out, when it didn't seem worthwhile any longer. Was that what had happened to James? The robot didn't see the point of being a robot?

'I'd better be getting along,' said James, extinguishing his cigarette.

'No hurry. Don't you like your beer?'

Reminded, James took up his glass once more. Trying to speak lightly, Adam said: 'I can see that drink will never be your ruin anyhow. Do you like going to the pictures?'

'I used to go sometimes,' said James. He added: 'When I was in work.'

But the movies hadn't been enough. No pretty dancing girls on the films had kicked their way into his imagination, or, if they had, only to be set firmly aside.

'You're not specially keen? Maureen and my wife are great picture-goers.'

'No, I was never keen. They're mostly tosh, aren't they?'

'I suppose so. I don't go often myself, but now and then you get something good.'

Mostly tosh? And the warmth of the sun, and laughter and green trees weren't enough either. And goodness wasn't enough. Because if you hold a material creed strongly everything can be made to reinforce it. One greedy or shallow priest and you said: 'After all they are no better than the rest of us.' A few wives who betrayed their husbands, a few husbands who betrayed their wives and you said: 'That's marriage for you.' A few bullies set in authority, and you hated and suspected all top dogs. Why was he thinking like this? Because James just didn't believe in what he had given years of his life to fight, the goodness of God. If he explained his own campaign to James, James would believe that he was fighting not painted devils, but painted angels.

James, finding him staring at him in fascination, suddenly thrust up his chin and got to his feet. 'I must be going now.'

'Have a look at my books before you go,' said Adam, to gain time, though after all what else was there to say? 'Perhaps you'd like to borrow one or two to take down to the country with you.'

Politely James stood by his side. Picking a novel at random, Adam said: 'Would you like this?'

'I'd better not. Might lose it.'

'It doesn't matter if you do. Oh, here's a Hemingway. You know, the American?'

James didn't know. But he took the book in his hand and stared at the cover.

'Take them both. What about poetry? Not in your line?'

A shake of the head was the only answer. James was looking at the door. At least, thought Adam, he was still goaded by one human impulse, the impulse which says, 'this moment has lasted long enough: it's time to go'; the prick which drives us ever on into the future, even though James had said in effect: 'I don't want any future.' For him the minutes still ticked, driving him to walk in the rain, to get up from a chair, even if the passage of hours and days and weeks had lost their import.

But when you are in the asylum, so Adam silently addressed him, you'll have to learn to disregard even the inward minute imperative. You can go for a walk only when they tell you to go for a walk. And not by yourself. Never by yourself. Not in the rain, and not in the sun either, unless it's their time. In a minute you are going out of this door because you want to get away from here, but you won't be able to open certain doors when they've put you away. It's no good my telling you this, because it wouldn't matter to you, but it's surprising how it does matter even to the most deeply immersed melancholiac. At times it matters so much that you clench your fists to stop yourself from making a scene, from breaking the door down. At times having a cigarette matters so much that you have to steal one. And that's a bad mark against you.

'Well, good-bye, and thank you for having me,' said James.

Adam said: 'Not at all. It was very good of you to come. I'll let you out.'

He led the way, James following silently behind. The hall was quiet, and there was no light in the lounge. Maureen and Kathleen were in the kitchen at the end of the passage, and for a moment Adam meditated calling them. But *cui bono*? Why prolong the poor fellow's uneasiness, his awkward recollection of what he thought were the party manners required.

'Good night. If you have time, come in again and see us.'

'Thank you. Good night.'

He watched James go down the steps, and then closed the door quietly. There was something very important he had learnt that he must think about. But hardly was he back in his room when he realised that the women had heard. For he looked up to find Kathleen standing by him.

'Hello.'

'Has James gone?'

'Yes, just now.'

'We thought we heard the front door close. Why on earth didn't you call us?'

'Because he wanted to go, that's why.'

'But I cut sandwiches, and we had a kettle on ready. Maureen said that when you'd finished your talk you'd bring him downstairs.'

Before Adam could reply there was Maureen saying disappointedly: 'He *has* gone then?'

'As you see,' said Adam.

'I do think you might have told us, Adam. He didn't stay very long, did he? He hasn't even finished the ale.'

'Because he didn't want it.'

'I thought he was the sort who'd prefer tea. And we had it all ready. Well, I do think you might have given him the chance to say hello to Kathleen.'

'Even if you'd just brought him in to say good night,' said Kathleen. 'After all I've never even seen him.'

'I tell you he didn't want to stay. Can't you take in that plain fact?' said Adam speaking loudly and slowly.

'Or perhaps you decided you didn't want him any longer because the poor man wasn't entertaining enough,' said Maureen. 'And Sheila keeping awake so that she could see her new cousin.'

'That's not my fault. You shouldn't have promised her.'

'Even if she were asleep he might have wanted to look at her and the baby.'

'Sheila will be disappointed,' said Kathleen. 'She was rather sweet. She said: "Uncle James will like to meet my Teddy, won't he? I bet he's never seen such a big Teddy."'

'Very sweet, very touching, ha-ha,' said Adam.

Maureen rounded on him: 'And what's the point of that?'

'The point of that,' said Adam, allowing some of the turmoil within outlet by raising his voice, 'is that surely, Maureen, you, who pride yourself on not being sentimental, are not so stupid as to cherish the notion that the picture of a little girl in a white nightgown clasping her teddy bear is going so to move James that he will be immediately renewed in faith and get sufficient energy to sign on the dotted line, and go back to work tomorrow. If you and Kathleen really had some such notion I suggest you've been to the pictures a little too much lately. But James, remember, isn't a neglectful father. He hasn't any children. I doubt if he has ever wanted to have any children, surprising as you may find that.'

'Don't shout at me, please,' said Maureen.

'Now then, you two,' said Kathleen. 'We didn't have any such idea, Adam. We just wanted to give James a cup of tea.'

'I shall shout if I like,' said Adam to Maureen. 'It is still my own house, or this part of it's my own.'

'I'm aware of that. You're being ridiculous. Why did James go so soon, that's all *I* want to know?'

'Because he didn't like being here any longer, as I've told you over and over again. I don't think he enjoys paying calls, strange as it must seem to a sociable little thing like yourself.' 'Oh, you're very clever, we know that,' said Maureen angrily. 'What you mean to say is that now you, and you alone, understand all about James, and that we are too silly even to be allowed to speak to him.'

'Put it like that if you like. Ignore the fact that he mightn't have wanted to speak to you.'

'Don't let's quarrel,' said Kathleen. 'Maureen, sit down! I want to ask Adam something.' She turned to her husband.

'I can see you're upset about him. Tell me, do you think he's in a very bad nervous condition?'

'Well, it can be put that way, I suppose,' said Adam striving for control. 'He's the common or garden type of melancholiac. There were quite a number of them among my fellow patients in the good old days when we all sat round together.'

'For heaven's sake,' said Maureen. 'Do you really think it's as bad as that with poor James? Do you think he'll have to go into an asylum?'

'Such matters really depend on relatives, on the amount of time and money they are prepared to give. Surely *you* should know that?'

Maureen flushed. Kathleen said quickly: 'Is there anything we can do, do you think? Anything at all?'

Adam shook his head. 'Nothing. Anyhow he's probably going to a farm for the present. Florence found a cheap address.'

'Florence told me she had an address or two,' said Maureen to Kathleen. 'They can manage a bit longer because his unemployment money has only just run out. It's the future they are worrying about. Treatment is so terribly expensive.'

'Because even holy monks, fathers in God, and nuns who are Faithful Companions of Jesus, won't take him in without money,' said Adam. 'That is one of the things James knows.'

'And how can they, Adam?' inquired Maureen passionately. 'If the religious orders provided for everybody who can't or won't work, my God, they'd have half the country on their hands. And where's the money to come from for them? That's a pretty cheap sneer, isn't it?'

'My dear girl, I'm not blaming the religious. We don't live in the Middle Ages, fortunately or unfortunately, whichever you think. I was just telling you that James is not one of those who expect something for nothing. That's one of the things he knows. He doesn't expect anything.'

Adam said the last words in a remote way that made Kathleen look at him intently. She said to him gently: 'And how do you think he has come to be that way?'

'Because he has only seen what they call the hard facts of life, and he hasn't seen anything else.'

There was a silence. Adam added thoughtfully. 'A lot of people are like that, but mostly they are people who for that very reason make quite a lot of money and go hither and thither, spending it and impressing other people. James didn't, you see. He's not really very bright.'

'We all should have taken more interest in him,' said Maureen.

Adam moved impatiently. He was tired of the conversation. 'It's pointless discussing the poor fellow. If he gets a little more physical energy perhaps he may improve.' He got up and went over to the window, drawing back the curtain, so that apparently he looked down into the street. But he was thinking: *Poor fellow*? Not to me. For he has done what I've agonised to do, and now see I have failed to do. He has reached a complete stage of indifference toward God, Man, Self and the devil. Self is really the point. He had gone into No Man's Land, so what would there be left for either God or Mammon to collect when the flesh gave up the ghost? The ghost would surely be too thin and too wan to provide fuel for any cleansing fires of purgatory.

Behind his back the two women exchanged glances. Kathleen said: 'Well, I must go down and see to my baby. Will you come and have a cup of tea, Adam?'

'No, thank you,' he said without looking round. There was that text about the lukewarm and the tepid, those who neither blew hot nor cold, being spewn out by Jehovah. The Little Way didn't make one lukewarm. It required too much concentration in whichever direction it was followed.

'Quite sure you won't come?' said Kathleen at the door.

He turned round: 'No thank you, dear.' His gaze went from her to Maureen. Now that his anger had gone he saw them for a moment objectively as two really nice women. Kathleen had on a pretty fancy apron and looked becomingly flushed.

'Well, good night then. Sleep well. And don't worry about James.'

'Of course I won't worry. Good night, Maureen.'

'Good night,' said Maureen in a subdued voice.

II

It was curious that the Girl should come into the Reference Library again just after his great decision. He hadn't seen her at first; he had been too deeply absorbed in his thoughts, but looking up suddenly he saw her standing across from him, looking at the bookshelves, her back stiff with self-consciousness. She was hatless, and she was wearing a short green jacket over a blue dress, and, yes, she had greeted the coming of summer with bare legs. Pretty legs, pretty dark hair and, he knew from his former regard, quite an attractive warm-skinned oval face.

She has come too late, he reflected, observing her prettiness, and her self-consciousness—since he knew that the self-consciousness was due to him—with detachment. She had let too many days elapse since her last visit, when he had practically made up his mind to include a liaison with her as an incident of the Little Way. And now the Little Way was out, since James had, he had finally decided, been sent to show him that however efficient it was in the upward climb, it was inefficient as a method of killing the soul.

Now she was turning round, ready to catch his eye with a smile and bow, and he looked down at his desk determined to avoid any recognition. For now he was impatient with himself that he had ever harboured such a childish notion of folly.

Even though there was some irrational physical bond between them so that for the first time for many years his senses had been stimulated to consider that it would be agreeable as well as, of course, sinful, to have an *affaire* with this girl who, though he was old enough to be her father, was so obviously attracted by him. But already, so much had the making of the decision accomplished, he was far out of those moments. His one feeling was of bitter annoyance with himself that he had even thought of a commonplace intrigue as worthwhile. A sin of the flesh, ranking lower than all the other sins of the spirit he had painfully accomplished for the damnation of his soul. And there his soul still was, alive and kicking, even if its kicking was as the clicking of some machine which registered numbers. He had been like a child imagining that if he were only naughty a sufficient number of times he would go to hell. Not so James: James had known better than that: James had starved *his* soul: it had grown grey, not with the breath of the pale Galilean, but for want of belief in anything whatsoever. And though it was too late for him to adopt James's way, for time pressed and this night his soul might be required of him, James had taught him something. He had taught him something. He had taught him that he had been on the wrong track.

So that last night he had clearly realised that there were two alternatives. He could abandon the whole notion of damning himself as too difficult, and relapse into a dreary neutrality of life, or find another and more desperate path downwards. Of course there was still the third course: he might try and become a better man, a better husband to Kathleen, a better brother to Maureen, a better father to his children, even creeping back to Mass on an occasional Sunday. But at the thought his whole being had cried out. He was still too caught up in his dream.

For the dream, after all, had been a magnificent one. In it he was a new Moses who refused to go into the Promised Land, but turned his back on the Lord God by his own will. He was Judas who betrayed his Lord, but without remorse. He did not hang himself, but standing looked to the end. Even Christ Himself had merely refused all the kingdoms of the earth: it was left for Adam Palmer to conceive of refusing far more, of refusing the heights of Parnassus, the Isles of the Blest, the New Jerusalem, the company of the saints who would hunger no more, neither thirst any more … the refusal of the delights which eye hath not seen nor ear heard, the very splendour of God Whose image had caused Saint Thomas Aquinas to faint at the altar as he stood offering up the Sacrifice of the Mass. No, his last thought had been, as he lay tossing on his bed: he could not surrender his gesture, for without his gesture what was he? Just another poor devil who had been unluckier than most since he had known what an asylum was like, but again, people might say, luckier than most, since he had undoubtedly acquired an excellent wife, two healthy children, and at least earned enough money at easy if dull work to pay his way. Oh, an average life, that's what it would be in the summing up, and an average death, such as his mother had died. He'd belong to those half men who never deeply felt, nor clearly willed; he'd be indistinguishable from any of Arnold's 'vague half believers in our casual creeds'. And it wasn't true; he had ground his teeth at the notion. He *had* believed, and he *had* clearly willed.

Someone had approached his desk. A curt voice asked: 'Where do I find *Whitaker's Almanac?*'

With a wave of his hand Adam indicated the place on the Quick Reference shelves: 'Over there.'

The man turned without a 'thank you'. Before Adam could settle back to his thoughts he was in front of him again: 'It's not there.'

'Well then someone must be using it.' He glanced round. 'Oh, yes! That gentleman over there. You'll have to wait till he's finished with it.'

With a frown the man turned away. Adam watched his back. Well dressed and rude. Seeing me merely as a servant of the public, and *vox populi vox dei*. So of course he was. How could he have stood this life of being at the service of every Tom, Dick and Harry, meekly fetching books from the shelves for them; finding addresses for them in the *Street Directory*, even looking up telephone numbers for them, if he hadn't felt himself so much apart that it was only a feature of an innocuous mask. He had suffered men meekly because he had been fighting not with them, but with no less a person than the Archangel Michael, the angel with the flaming sword. Strive no more with gods and angels, and what a paltry mean existence his was, working to bring home the bacon. For the form mattered. James had proved that.

The house of the body could shape the soul. Those who seek the clear way to God live in monasteries and convents. The henpecked curate and his children, the busybody political Deans and Archbishops, running over to Russia and voicing political enthusiasms, had naturally brought the respectable middle way of the Anglican Church to its present ignominious plight. And all the little people living in their little flats with their radios, their little pleasures, their little pains …

'Well, well. Dare I interrupt this awful brooding?'

He looked up sharply, and then tried to smile.

'Oh, hello Norman. I didn't see you.'

'Such thunderclouds about your brow, that I'm not surprised. High Jove himself is not in it. Sorry to be a frivolous interrupter, but I hope you hadn't forgotten that we agreed that we should lunch together to-day. Perhaps I'm a little early.' Adam looked at the clock. He had forgotten the appointment with Norman, and now found it an intolerable interruption. But he said:

'I didn't expect you just yet. My relief doesn't come till one, you know, and it's not quite five to. How are you?'

'So-so. Full of divine discontent which I'm burning to reveal over a coffee. And you?'

'Oh, all right.' His eyes looking impatiently away from Norman saw that the Girl was closing her notebook, putting back a pencil into her bag. Her shoulders drooped. She had evidently sat there, just below his desk, deciding like Norman that he was in a bad temper. And now she had made up her mind that this morning at least nothing would happen. Nor ever, my dear. Nor ever, he silently told her. You see, I haven't time. I have really put away childish things.

Norman followed his gaze. 'Quite an attractive piece, don't you think?' he murmured under his breath.

'It's one of my rules never to notice my clients,' he answered. Had the Girl heard? She looked his way, but without meeting his eye. Feminine pride had obviously been aroused.

The door behind the desk opened, and Adam's relief, a serious spectacled young girl, Miss Wright, appeared. She had only lately come to the Library, but already Adam was one of her dislikes. 'He never tells you anything; he never tries to help you,' she had confided, and been answered with a chorus: 'He's like that. He only thinks of himself. Too high and mighty to have anything to do with the rest of the staff.'

'Good morning, Miss Wright. If you'd just stamp these new books. You know how, don't you? I'll meet you in front, Norman.'

'Oh, of course. You have your own staircase.'

'I have to sign out, that's the point,' said Adam. And how insufferable that one should have to, he was thinking for the first time.

The Girl, having restored the books she had been using to their places, passed by the desk on her way out. She looked at him straight in the eyes, and he looked back as if he didn't see her. And now that was that. And why should his heart sink ever so slightly, because he had pushed away a toy that he didn't really want? What a fool he had been!

He went down the stairs, nodded briefly to the librarian in the office, and scrawled his name in the book, and the time, 12.58, which the clock registered. And so on, and so on, for the rest of my life, he thought, as he pushed his way past two junior giggling assistants who entered as he left, and one of whom turned round to make a face at his unconscious back.

Out of habit Adam stood back at the door of the café to let the novelist enter first. This was part of his usual procedure with those who, he considered, believed themselves to be of more than average importance. When introduced he bowed more deeply; when they gave their opinion he listened with an expression of exaggerated deference; he stood back and opened doors for them. At first they were mildly flattered; later, as he hoped, they began to entertain doubts, to regard him with a suspicious eye. Was he or was he not laughing at them? This was the stage he had enjoyed. Such treatment he had given to Norman; Norman, he knew, had become very suspicious, and he had therefore been surprised by a recent outburst of friendliness. What is he after? he had thought to himself when the luncheon date had been fixed. Now Norman no longer seemed important.

Norman handed back the menu, he had automatically passed him. 'I've made up my mind. I'm having Welsh Rarebit. They do it very well here.'

This time Adam checked himself from saying: 'Oh, really? Then I must have some. Naturally.' For what was the point of understudying Rosa Dartle any more. That was all part of the Little Way which had been tried and proved wanting. He studied the menu carefully, and decided on fish-cakes. Then he said, coldly, abandoning his usual custom of waiting for the other's lead: 'You spoke of divine discontents? Still worried about the state of the country or something?'

'And you are not?' inquired Norman.

'Oh, no, I'm not. I'm not an idealist, you see, like you.'

295

'Does it make me an idealist, to possess social feeling, to want to be a good citizen?'

'Yes, I think so. Most estimable of you, of course. But rather unusual in an artist.'

Ah, so the hostility is quite out in the open for once, thought Norman. He said smoothly: 'How charmingly old-fashioned that term, "the artist", sounds. So sweetly redolent of the nineties and Oscar Wilde and green tea and absinthe, and making a living by cadging. I have always thought you at heart a romantic, my dear Adam.'

Adam looked into the mocking blue eyes, gathering his wits together. 'How interesting! You think me roman-tic because I don't believe that men who continue playing at being Boy Scouts after they are grown up are going to improve the world. And I think you're romantic because I believe you have that illusion.'

The waitress set their plates in front of them. Before replying to Adam, Norman called her back: 'Waitress, I'd like some mustard, please.' Then he turned to Adam. 'Oh no. I don't believe you are romantic because you lack a social sense. I just believe that temperamentally you belong to the school of Baudelaire and Van Gogh, and these intense people, and that therefore you are apt to scorn us matter-of-fact chaps who try and make our bread and butter by the exercise of our craft … you notice I don't say "art".'

Angered, Adam thought: 'No, and it's as well you don't, because you've put your talent out to usury.' Because he was angry he became careful. 'You exaggerate, I fear. I am actually a poor librarian and a dull domesticated family man. Perhaps for that reason I am inclined to exaggerate the importance of those who write the books I merely take down from the shelves for my customers. Tell me, by the way, you must find the paper shortage a nuisance?'

'It's more than a nuisance. I think it's a scandal,' said Norman. He took up his knife and fork. 'And not,' he went on, after eating, 'as I'm sure you think, because the great British and American public are therefore held up in their perusal of my works.'

'No?'

'No. I'm sure that surprises you. No, seriously, my dear chap, what we have to face is the plain fact that the generation growing up in this war is going to be deprived of any chance of reading the classics. When I was last in London I made it my business to look into several of the leading booksellers and inquire for this and that. Books which used to be in Everyman's Library. There was always the same answer:"out of print".' He looked over at Adam, who made no reply, and went on: 'It will take years, of course, before there is any real replenishment, before we are back to the days which we knew in our youth when any eager lad hungry for food of the mind ...'

'For all the best that has been thought and said,' interpolated Adam.

'Exactly. And when we do get paper again in plenty there will be years of starvation which cannot be made up for. If the war ...'

He went on talking, but Adam was too irritated to listen. He listened, as it were, instead, to the roar of the big guns, to the whizz of bombs hurling down from the skies on to Europe, on to the splendours of Christendom, destroying what it had taken centuries to build. There was the crash of falling building and there were the cries of the tortured and the suffocated. What a harvest of blood and tears! And after the funeral, the long grey drabness as men started once again to build up their lives and rebuild civilisation. And yet this fool could only prate about some books he had failed to get!

'Don't you agree with me?'

'Agree with what?'

'That as soon as it is all over the English Government should subsidise the printing of essential classics, and eliminate or at least control the printing of such pornographic rubbish as *No Orchids for Miss What's-her-name*?'

The man was insisting on an answer. Adam said: 'Is not the life more than the meat and the body more than the raiment?'

'I quite agree. That's really what I'm saying. I am talking about the starvation of the mind. But I gather from your tone that you are not quite in sympathy.'

Adam watched Norman push his plate away, and take out his cigarette-case. His hand went to his pocket to provide him with a match, the automatic reflex of the Little Way, and came out empty, and he turned to his coffee cup instead. What had mock subservience profited him? Maybe he had added a trifle to Norman's conceit of himself, and therefore prodded him an infinitesimal fraction of an inch on the downward path of those for whom the image of themselves obstructs the Image of God. But could he really flatter himself that he had done more than finally evoke the man's hostility?

'The name you forget is Miss Blandish. I think it's a very good book actually. It's the answer to those who sentimentalise lust.'

'Really? I haven't read it myself. I must do. But what is your feeling about my idea of a Government subsidy?'

'Merely that I don't fancy that the people in the concentration camps of Europe care very much whether thoughtful little Tommy Perkins who is such a bookworm can obtain or cannot obtain the works of D. H. Lawrence or Gibbon's *Decline and Fall of the Roman Empire*. You remind me of the women who knitted as they watched the heads of the aristocrats fall at the guillotine. And that was only a revolution: this is a world war.'

But what was the point of talking, he suddenly thought, turning away from his words with distaste. No orchids for Miss Blandish, no orchids for James, no orchids at present for Jews. Purgatory on earth, but doubtless they would have their reward when the saints and martyrs came marching in. Suddenly overcome with fatigue, he looked round the café, which was beginning to empty, and noticed vaguely how insubstantial it had all become, as if a blind had been drawn down. They were talking happily, some of them, but what did it matter what they were saying? It mattered no more than what he and Norman were saying. Norman was wasting his time, in the way a flea wasted your time by its irritation.

Norman was observing him with some care, seeing the dark pouches under the eyes, noticing how deeply grooved were the lines running from the nostrils, and extending now to the jaw-bone. What a queer fish, he thought. And as a novelist he wanted a solution. Not a happy man, and why not?

He said, passing his cigarette-case, since Adam had now pushed away his plate with unfinished food on it: 'Have

one. You make me feel quite guilty. I see you feel the tragedy of this war deeply. Whereas I merely selfishly cultivate
my garden.' You mean you like to tell other people how to
cultivate their gardens, thought Adam, taking the cigarette.

'Myself I feel pity is rather an enervating emotion. If we
can't do anything, why then …'

'I don't feel pity,' said Adam sharply. He closed his eyes
for a moment trying to focus his thoughts. 'What is the
definition of pity? Joyce quotes it somewhere. "Pity is the
feeling which arrests the mind in the presence of whatsoever is grave and constant in human suffering and unites it
with the sufferer." I have no sense of being united to the
war victims. Quite the contrary. Ergo I do not feel pity.'

'I thought, since you rebuked what you conceive as my
flippancy, my insistence on such trifles as good books for
the young …'

'Because I don't feel pity, it doesn't mean that my reason
and imagination have quite abdicated. I am still in possession of my intellect. Yes, I am still in possession of my
intelligence,' repeated Adam slowly as if to himself.

'My dear man, no one doubts it for a moment,' Norman
assured him, his perceptions darting like a dog on a bone. I
bet what I heard is true, that Palmer had been in the looney
bin at one time or another.

But for once Adam had no answering perception alert.
He was thinking that though he knew he was tired out he
could surely whip that intelligence up to find the right way,
not the Little Way any more, but the right way. Suppose he
had lost time, suppose he had lost years of time, in trying to
bank the fires for his damnation out of bits of straw. He was
not dead yet; the way was not irrevocable.

Norman watching him as he sat thinking was surprised to hear him suddenly ask, looking across at him with what seemed an almost childlike simplicity: 'Tell me, do you believe that Hitler is damned?'

'My dear fellow, why ask me? I'm not a theologian. Nor do I believe in the physical fire that is never quenched. But in any case you surely agree that Hitler is a symptom rather than a wicked man himself?'

'A symptom of what?' asked Adam, frowning as if he found this difficult.

'Oh, you know, that a superman must be born to set things aright, and he believes himself to be that superman. He is really quite a sincere individual, I think, don't you? After all most dictators believe that they are called by a divine or human destiny to set things aright for their bleeding countries. They need the help of thugs but they are not thugs themselves.'

'You believe he thinks he is doing right,' said Adam. He nodded his head slowly, thinking: so Hitler, too, will be numbered among those for whom our Lord prayed. '*Father forgive them; they know not what they do.*' That left him quite by himself. He passed a hand across his forehead and looked around him dazedly. Then he pushed back his chair. 'I must be getting along.'

'No hurry yet, surely. You haven't to be back till two, have you?'

'I must be about my master's business,' said Adam, forgetting to smile.

'Well, I'll get the bill then, and walk back to the Library with you.'

The waitress came up and asked: 'Separate or together?' and Norman replied: 'Together.' There was none of the expostulation he expected from Adam, the insistence on paying his share, or, failing that, an effusiveness savouring of irony, as if he would say: 'Oh you're the big man: and how kind to pay for a poor fellow like me!' Now, however, he didn't even say 'thanks'; he was staring about him as if he were half blind, Norman thought, genuinely puzzled, and it was indeed a full moment before Adam perceived that the novelist had risen and was waiting for him.

At the door Adam turned, and shot out a hand: 'Well, good-bye. I'll be seeing you soon, I suppose.'

'Oh, but I'll walk as far as the Library with you. I'm going to potter round for a bit. The missus wants me to do some shopping for her.'

Adam nodded: 'In that case,' he said, as one accepting a medicine.

Norman said, when it seemed as if his companion had again relapsed into complete inattentiveness: 'Do you mind my saying that I don't think you look at all well? Are you sleeping all right?'

'Yes, thanks.'

'Perhaps you are overworking?'

'There's nothing in the work that a child couldn't do.'

'Oh, come now. I can assure you that it is a relief for some of us to know that a literate man is in charge of one of our reference libraries.'

Norman spoke lightly, but the sideways glance he directed was keen. For, by no means an insensitive man, he was now aware that he was walking beside one who carried some crushing preoccupation. He had never thought of Adam Palmer either as a happy man or as a lively man; on the other hand one did not think of him as a gloomy or dull man, and therefore to be avoided. He was far too attentive to what one said: his comments at least on other men and their affairs were pertinent if barbed with malice. And certainly he was reckoned a personality in that section of the life of the town which eddied around the intelligentsia. Young men anxious as they stood in the Repertory Theatre's lobby to know what they should think about the play would, if they saw him, sidle up. Palmer could usually give them an idea or two as to why it was probably very bad! Or if the play was not bad, that is to say, if it were Tchehov or Turgenieff, then as to how far the interpretation had been at fault!

But at that moment there was no doubt to Norman that some component of the protective shell guarding his secret interior personality had cracked, leaving him less carefully guarded. Anxious to probe, anxious to press what might only be a temporary advantage, Norman said suddenly: 'Of course I've never felt that you were intended by nature to be a librarian. It's odd perhaps, but I always think of you as a spoilt priest.'

There was a moment's pause while the meaning of the words penetrated. Then Adam said tonelessly: 'But how dull! In a city that is full of spoilt priests, is it not?'

'Quite! But your question about Hitler, for example. One feels that theology is quite a preoccupation of yours, really?'

'And to you it doesn't exist? Did you have faith once?' Adam's tone was mildly curious. Norman said: 'Half and half, I suppose. Like most of us.'

'And how did you lose your half of the loaf?' But before Norman could reply, he went on swiftly, brushing away the flea as not really interesting: 'Oh, don't tell me. You had some literary success, and you preferred to give the credit to yourself.'

Norman held his breath for a moment. If Adam had not spoken so impatiently and at the same time uninterestedly, he would have thought, 'Well, here's the attack at long last out in the open. He loathes me.' But, no, it was a casual thrust, and he had leave to use his own rapier as casually. His mind working swiftly, he said:

'Whereas you prefer to maintain God on His throne so that you have someone to blame for your own, shall we say, decline into a librarian.'

While Norman waited not without apprehension for a reply, they had to divide to let two girls, their arms interlaced, walk between them. Adam said, rejoining him and looking at him without rancour: 'There is actually more to it than that. But a believer can really only discuss such things with a believer. As to *decline* into a librarian, you don't, I think, realise that we librarians take ourselves seriously as one of the learned professions.'

'Decline from being a priest was what I meant.'

'Oh, you still take that fancy of yours seriously, do you? More than I ever did. Save as a boy's dream of wielding mysterious powers, of being clad in ornate vestments donned with prayers, of swinging the thurible before the tabernacle, and so forth. Many Catholic boys surely cherish such dreams, as they and other boys cherish dreams of being an engine-driver: it is their hands which propel the long line of lighted carriages rushing through the night over immense distances. The thoughts of youth, you must remember, my dear Norman, are long long thoughts.'

Foiled, thought Norman, smiling amiably back. Your armour is now in place again, and in a minute you'll be back at your desk, and escaped. 'I suppose so,' he started, 'but …'

Adam interrupted him: 'But you, of course, always wanted to write, to express yourself through the pen?'

'Oh, no. I really wanted to be a Member of the Mother of Parliaments, and sway multitudes with my eloquence. I still do, now and then. Among other things, of course. By the way, I never asked after Kathleen.'

'Oh, she's very well. And Louise?'

They had come to a stop before the steps of the Library. Already as he made the perfunctory inquiry, Adam was looking away.

'All right. She's been raving about your new baby ever since Kathleen asked her to tea.'

Adam nodded. He gave the effect of waiting patiently for Norman to go. 'She's quite settled down now with us, hasn't she? Kathleen, I mean.'

'Oh, she's quite settled down. She has my sister, you know. They are great friends. And, of course, the baby and Sheila. Well, good-bye.'

'Good-bye. Louise is going to ring Kathleen and make a date. Perhaps we could all get together?'

'Oh, yes. Certainly! Good-bye. Thank you.'

Norman stood watching him go up the steps. Then he turned, and remembering he had run out of cigarettes went into a near-by tobacconist.

He had to wait to be served as there was no one behind the counter, and he stood patiently, for his mind was occupied with the echoes of the conversation. He was still preoccupied when he left the shop, but the next moment his eyes were once more brightly alert. For there, just in front of him, was the very man whose company he had so lately quitted, walking rapidly, head bent.

Puzzled, Norman followed. His curiosity was too lively to entertain any idea of a hail, a 'where are you off to now?' If Palmer, although he had said nothing, was having the afternoon off, where was he going? Was there here some solution to the man's odd behaviour?

The question was soon answered. Palmer rounded a corner, crossed a road and entered the gates that led into a small but much patronised public park. Norman followed only as far as the gates, and stood just outside, observing. A stone's throw away his quarry was sitting on an otherwise unoccupied bench, since the luncheon interval was over and the nursemaids had not yet arrived, and, reading something he had taken out of his pocket. Norman drew back, and walked slowly along the outside railings. In five minutes' time he had returned, and was again cautiously peering. Adam was still there, still reading. Norman saw him shake his head as if in impatience, and, as it seemed he was about to look up and about him, effaced himself from sight and walked rapidly away.

His steps took him back to the Library. Going up the staircase that led to the Reference Department he meditated his approach. Just ask for Mr. Palmer. That was all he need do.

At the desk sat the same spectacled girl he had seen come in when Adam had left for lunch. He approached her:

'Oh, excuse me, but is Mr. Palmer not here this afternoon?'

'He hasn't come back from his lunch yet.'

'I thought he was generally here by two?'

Her eyes followed his to the clock, which placed the time as a little after twenty-past two.

'Well, he's supposed to be,' she said in an aggrieved tone. Then remembering her status in life, and that after all this man was merely a member of the public, she said more primly:'He was expected at two, but something must have delayed him. Can I help you?'

'No. It doesn't matter. I really just wanted to have another word with Mr. Palmer about something. Let me see: you're not generally here, are you?'

'No, I'm generally downstairs. This isn't my job really up here. I just take over sometimes when Mr. Palmer goes to his lunch.'

'How do you like it up here?'

'I don't like it.' She hesitated for a moment, and then, her subconsciousness prepared, as naturally it is with most young girls, for the advent any day, any hour, of the knight on the shining charger, however disguised and looking per-haps not altogether what you were expecting, she became friendly. 'You see, it's dull sitting up here after being down-stairs with the others.'

'It's quiet up here, is it? Nothing much to do?'

'Oh, I wouldn't say that. I mean sometimes people come up and ask you difficult questions. Or they want books that I've never heard of ... after all, you can't know everything, can you? And I have to ring downstairs to ask. Or to get help. I mean you've got to be experienced. And I'm not really experienced. I've not been here long.'

'Haven't you? But I'm sure you manage beautifully. Well, you think Mr. Palmer will be back, do you?'

'Unless he's been run over or something. I've never known him late like this before.'

'He's pretty punctual as a rule, is he?'

'Oh, yes, he's punctual. Well, I mean we all have to be. Upsets all the time-table if he's not. I ought to be taking over the children's library, and they've had to send one of the downstairs girls, and that makes it a lot of work for the others.'

'Quite. I see. Well …' Norman gave her a sweet but vague smile, turning away.

'Shall I tell him you were asking for him if he comes in?' Miss Wright's voice intercepted him.

'No. Don't tell him anything. I'll be in another time.'

Miss Wright watched him leave, his mind already obviously departed from her. With a disappointment of which she was hardly aware she turned back to her desk, her subconsciousness accepting that so he wasn't the knight on the shining charger, and a bit oldish and a bit affected after all, the way he spoke. In fact he seemed to fancy himself rather. Which is what you might expect from any of Mr. Palmer's friends.

Unaware of the slight fluttering his advent had caused Norman was asking himself two questions as he went lightly down the stairs.

Why had Palmer played hookey; why had he left his desk unattended just to sit on a rather dull and damp afternoon in a park?

What was he reading of which apparently he so disapproved?

— ELEVEN —

I

Without any keys Norman would have been a long time in finding the answers to his questions. Indeed if given he would have found them inexplicable. For Adam Palmer was now near the centre of the labyrinth whose guiding thread was invisible to all eyes but his own. Of course the immediate clue was simpler. On entering the Library, Adam had glanced at his watch, as he had glanced at his watch so many times on going up the steps. And then, since he had already made some small beginnings in breaking with the Little Way, it occurred to him that this slavish subservience to punctuality which had become a habit over so many years was part of the frame he had devised for his way of life. Let him therefore that very day make a crack in the frame itself!

Neither of the two assistants who were stamping library books in their enclosed pen had observed him pausing in the lobby, and he returned cautiously outside, glancing this way and that from the top of the steps to make sure that Norman was no longer in sight. Assured of that, his lunch companion was banished from his mind, and descending he turned city-wards, making for the little central park as somewhere he could sit and reflect for a while.

The book that he drew out soon after sitting down on the nearest empty bench was the Gospel according to St.

Luke, pocket size, and bound in stiff brown paper, which for many years he had carried about with him. What he sought to find there was a pointer to a swifter broader downward path, some sin which had drawn our Lord's most signal condemnation. And the gesture he had made which the man watching him from the gate had translated as one of disapproval was nearer to despair.

For he had opened the gospel at chapter eighteen, and the first verses which had met his eyes had been those which record our Lord's sorrow for the rich, His saying that it was easier for a camel to go through a needle's eye than for a rich man to enter into the Kingdom of God, and then, when the disciples questioned, saying 'Who then can be saved?' His answer: '*The things which are impossible with men are possible with God.*' For these words pierced to the very core of his uncertainty, underlying, bringing into full light what had secretly troubled him many and many a time. Damn yourself in the regard of men; even, yes, even damn yourself as he had so carefully done according to the rules laid down by Holy Church, the Spouse of Christ, and there remained still the over-ruling Judge Whose ways were not our ways.

Clenching his hands, he looked away from the book and then about him, a feeling that his gesture had been observed putting him on guard. But he could see no one looking at him. Ah, but a priest was coming towards him, head down, reading his breviary, and for a moment he was doubly on guard. But it was not Father Mansfield, rather an ascetic-appearing man unknown to him. Looking at the intent profile as it passed he thought wildly, here no doubt is a learned theologian: why not ask him: why not say: 'Father, what must I do to be lost, lost eternally? You show us the way to be saved, surely you can tell, too, the way to perdition. I want a fool proof recipe, that's all!'

That's all, he thought, watching, forlornly now, the slowly retreating figure. But it was much, too much. For Holy Church herself, even at her most rigid, provided many loop-holes for the sinner. And his mind slid down a well-worn track. For example, even a Catholic dying in a state of mortal sin, unshriven, may in the final outcome be redeemed, since no man can know what at the very last moment passes between him and his Maker, what grace may be given from the infinite compassion of God.

He took up St. Luke once more, but now his fingers turned the pages at random, unseeingly. Yes, of course, he knew about the sin against the Holy Ghost, the only one unforgiven, whose mystery has shadowed men's minds for two thousand years, that crookedness which shall never be made straight. But to Adam at least this darkest spot of all had never been elucidated, the Catechism itself walking a long way round the enigma by defining not one sin, but six sins against the Holy Ghost, six neat parcels with two of which he was certainly well saddled: resisting the *known* truth and obstinacy in sin. But could one trust them to weigh one down the whole way to hell? He doubted it. At that moment, at least, he thought, sitting back in his seat and gazing despairingly up at the grey sky, he doubted it. And it was this doubt, this unsureness, that tortured and went on torturing. For what waste, what terrible futile waste all these dull venomous years had been if at the end no splendour of never quenched fires, no weeping throughout eternity.

More people were passing him now, but glances that rested upon him were quick to retreat, having gained the knowledge that this man was one of the moody broody ones with no quickened interest to spare for a good-looking girl, no friendliness to offer a fellow man who might want to pass the time of the day, or discuss likely winners.

But after a short while two middle-aged women, immersed in their conversation and seeking rest for their feet from the hard pavements, sank thankfully into this the first bench they saw. As they sat down, the sun suddenly grew brighter, burning its way through the cloud, and raising her eyes one murmured: 'It's going to be a grand afternoon, thank God.' And the other said: 'Aren't the flowers pretty; they're lovely, aren't they?'

In his own darkness he heard the words, but he heard them coldly, not even troubling to turn his head and observe his neighbours. For he had gone so far by now on his own lonely tortured track that for a long time James had been the only one to arouse in him the sense of human comradeship. In the main it seemed to him that nearly all the laity at least, except himself, were engaged whole-heartedly in undertakings whose frivolity and pettiness were such that, whether their trivial motions brought them joy or brought them grief, one could be moved as little as one was moved by the motions of puppets who, jerked this way and that on strings, played out their conventional drama or their conventional comedy. A grown man did not, after all, sit down and play with dolls, though since one was surrounded by animated dolls—Maureen, for example, was a lot too animated—one had to throw them words out of politeness. That is to say one ministered sardonically to their illusion of

being alive. The subtle pleasure of the Little Way he had followed was, of course, that he could use those polite words
to deflate their sense of life. But now, of course ...

So though the first scraps of conversation he overheard
entered his ears they did not enter his mind. He listened as
he listened to the quack-quack of the ducks:

'Would you say so?'

'I would say so, and you yourself know it's the truth. I'll
tell you why ...' the voice dropped.

A raised voice again in accents of disapproval: 'And to
think that a decent Christian woman should be setting such
an example to her children!'

And then later, approval: 'Ah, he's the decent man. Many
and many a kind thing I've known him do. And not asking
a thank you for it. Not asking a thank you.'

And then suddenly he was really listening as he heard:
'That reminds me! Corpus Christi to-morrow, and all the
children to get off to Mass. And it's the morning the sweep
is coming. It never rains but it pours, and that's a true word
for you.'

'Ah, indeed, so it is. Corpus Christi to-morrow, though
it had clean slipped out of my head. The way time passes,
and yesterday it was Easter, or that's the way it seems, and
now here we are in June, and it's Corpus Christi again.'

'But we've had no summer this year, no summer to
speak of. That's why it's queer thinking that we've got to
the height of the year, all unbeknownst ...'

But Adam had stopped listening, for his mind had stead-
ied itself over words thrice repeated, as a phrase in music
that catches at the emotions, obliterating all that follows. So
it was Corpus Christi to-morrow, and that meant, yes, that

in its liturgy the Church had arrived at the eve of the first Thursday after Trinity Sunday.

Corpus Christi, one of the most solemn, and yet to him once, he remembered, the music swelling, the most joyous feast of all, in celebration of the holy Eucharist, when God came down to earth in the symbol of bread and wine making these common things for ever holy, and so—as the imagination quickened seeing God Himself walking the roads of the world—sanctifying all common things. *Corpus Christi,* his mind repeated, and then came other words: *Who the day before He suffered took bread into His hands, and having lifted up His eyes towards Heaven, to Thee, O God, His Almighty Father … In like manner after He had supped taking also this excellent Chalice, he blessed and gave it to His disciples …*

And now, crouched low on the wooden bench, into his recollection came the bright pictures which had once hung about that glorious Feast, decking it as flowers and the golden flames of candles deck an altar. Dog-roses starred the hedges, the fields and ditches were yellow with buttercups, red with sorrel, white with cow-parsley and daisies; butterflies flitted while the bees drowsed and then, having taken their fill, buzzed on to another flower. Yes, 'all the live murmur of a summer day' accompanied the bell which heralded the tremendous act of God linking Himself with man.

His eyelids closed as he recalled these bright things, but he recalled them to his imagination without joy, as a woman in the autumn of her life, turning out by chance an old box, finds, surprised, verses once written by a lover in her praise, or reads an old letter written many years back, a cherished letter. But she has forgotten that she once

314

cherished the letter, that when she first read the poem her heart had leaped in gratification, in sweet and tender pride. For it has all gone by now, something that happened once upon a time, long ago and far away like a fairy story. Maybe she doesn't destroy those old bits of paper, but she puts the lid on the box, pushes it back to its briefly disturbed dust, and goes away to wash her hands.

But Adam did not go away so from the glowing images which the two words had conjured. Instead, vulture-like, his mind hovered over them. Because he had once celebrated Corpus Christi in a mood of rapturous worship, was there not now some way in which he could quite obliterate for himself even the most distant echoes of its music? At his call other words came to write themselves upon his mind: *He that eateth and drinketh unworthily, eateth and drinketh judgment to himself.*

His eyelids opened, for certainly now someone was looking at him. Yes, his neighbours had risen to go, and the nearer woman was giving him a full look of unabashed curiosity, curiosity carrying a meed of disapproval for she didn't care to see a man with a good suit of clothes on him idling in the middle of the afternoon, neither reading, nor paying the least attention to anybody about him, just slumped up anyhow. 'No rest for the wicked,' said the other woman, and then they turned towards the gates. His gaze followed them because of those words. Whether or no, he was thinking, she had really been sent by the devil, to remind him, those words were true. Be not weary in ill-doing. All right. Those two women had not wasted their half-hour, so far as he was concerned. He was resolved to defy the injunction of the Apostle Paul—presumably it was St. Paul's words upon which Holy Church had set also her seal of warning—and eat and drink unworthily.

He looked outwards once more, half wondering what he was doing in the gardens at this time of the day. Remembering how he had defaulted from the Library he decided to go and telephone them, explaining that a sudden attack of, say, giddiness had prevented his return. He had better sound apologetic as his future intent toward his daily work and daily bread was not yet clarified. Giddiness? Oh, well, he could make something up that sounded convincing as he went along.

A young man without collar or tie, seeing him rise, made for the empty seat. He, too, had a decision to make and he too wanted to make it in peace. He wanted to have a last long look at the papers he carried before going over to the turf accountant and putting a bob on the four-thirty.

II

Maureen got back home late that night. She had been to the movies with Violet, and then they had run into two men they knew who had insisted on standing them drinks at the new buttery which had just opened. The two men were a bit tight, of course, but possibly they wouldn't have stood the two girls drinks if they hadn't been a bit on. And it would be nice to tell everyone that she had been to the new bar, Maureen was thinking, composing commendations flavoured with some criticism such as 'They certainly know how to charge,' while she turned the corner. And then as she shut the gate she heard the neighbouring church strike eleven, and at the same time was surprised to see a light in the downstairs room. Did that mean that Kathleen hadn't gone to bed? Or was baby sick, or something?

But it was Adam and not Kathleen who came out of the sitting-room as she entered the hall. She saw him standing by the light he switched on.

'Oh, there you are, Maureen! I was wondering what had happened to you.'

'What would happen to me?' asked Maureen coldly. This sudden friendly tone made her suspicious.

'Have you been to the theatre, or something?'

'I've been to the pictures.'

'Oh, enjoy yourself?'

'Yes, thank you. I hope I didn't keep you up bothering about me,' she added sarcastically.

'Oh, no, I was just going to bed. Unless you'd care for a cigarette before you turn in.'

'No, thank you.' Maureen put her foot on the staircase.

She thought of asking him if he felt quite well, and then dismissed that as a childish underlining of his unusual behaviour. 'Good night,' she added.

'Good night. Oh ... Maureen. I suppose you'll be going to an early Mass in the morning?'

Turning and staring, she was now really surprised. 'And why should I be going to an early Mass?'

'Well, it's Corpus Christi, isn't it? Had you forgotten?'

For the moment Maureen had forgotten. But she was not going to admit that to Adam. She said sarcastically:

'This is a new thing for you, reminding me of my religious duties. Did you want to go with me, or something? Because as a matter of fact I prefer to go to Mass alone.'

317

He shook his head: 'No … no. I just wondered what time you would be going. Just an idle thought crossing an idle mind. I was wondering if you went before you go to the office, or if they give you time off.'

'I'm so grateful for your interest, but I'm afraid I can't tell you at the moment. I haven't made up my mind.' Maureen waited a moment, as he stared back at her in silence, and then said again: 'Well, good night.'

'Good night,' said Adam. He waited till she had got to the head of the staircase, and then went back to the sitting-room. So he hadn't got anything by that. He had wanted to know which Mass Maureen was going to in order to avoid the same one for himself. If she saw him receiving at the altar, knowing, as she must, how far he was from being in any state of grace, why then her mind would be full of questions. Perhaps she would try and make herself believe that he had repented, but at that best she would be watching him closely, praying for him …

Well, it just meant, he thought, dismissing her impatiently, that he had better avoid the near-by parish church, and go to an early Mass elsewhere, an early Mass because he wished for the support of others since he had decided to receive Holy Communion. He'd get a bus, and go to the almost country church of Newrath, a couple of miles outside. If Kathleen or Maureen heard him departing early he could say that he had got up to go for a walk before breakfast.

That decided and a bus guide consulted, he looked at his watch. It still lacked half an hour to midnight, and he was waiting downstairs till the hour had struck so that then he could get himself some food. The Church's law that forbade, without a dispensation, the breaking of the fast from mid-night, might merely be a technicality, but he was not going to disregard even the most minute part of the act of sacrilege he proposed to commit. He rubbed his hand across his hot forehead, trying to combat an urgent desire to sleep. To sleep for ever. Oh, that perpetual sleep in a perpetual night to which the fortunate pagan and stoic could look. How he longed for it, more and more and more. His longing for it must be, he thought ironically, at least as strong as that of the faithful pilgrim hastening towards the Beatific Vision. There was nothing at all that he could feel of himself left for Paradise, but oh, how his tired mind and body yearned for complete oblivion.

Upstairs Maureen was starting to reproach herself for coldness. Might it not be, her conscience had stirred itself to ask, that Adam's odd inquiry about when she was going to Mass had meant that he had thought of accompanying her, but was too shy to confess it straight out? It did not seem likely, and yet how was she to be sure? Lately, she had really seen very little of him. Perhaps the visit of James had made some impression on him, for he had acted rather strangely and emotionally. Suppose he had been moved, if only by some errant fancy, to attend the Sacrifice of the Mass on Corpus Christi; even supposing he wanted to kneel in a back pew in order to strengthen his own disbelief, might it not happen that some grace from the tabernacle might reach him?

She undressed with her door ajar so that she might hear his footsteps coming up the stairs. But no footsteps came. She went to the bathroom to brush her teeth, still listening, still hearing nothing. Then she knelt down by her bed to say her prayers.

And somehow having said her prayers, having prayed for him as she always did, she could not switch her light off and get into bed. At the same time she could not quite make up her mind to go downstairs and say—she rehearsed the casual tone she would use—'By the way, if by any chance you did think of going to Mass to-morrow, I'll go with you whenever you like.' Ridiculous, her mind said, as soon as the words were uttered. He'd stare at me, and say something very nasty. And I'd deserve it, too.

All the same she had to listen. At last she made up her mind. If he didn't come upstairs when her clock said twelve, she'd go downstairs. She'd make herself go downstairs. She'd say she felt hungry and had come to get something from the kitchen cupboard. She wouldn't receive the Eucharist whatever Mass she went to as she wasn't prepared.

The chimes of the outside clock startled Adam from his semi-torpor, and he got up hastily and went to the kitchen. He had just cut a slice of bread and was going to butter it when he heard a movement in the hall and then saw Maureen coming towards him in her blue dressing-gown. She looks young and rather attractive to-night, he thought, watching her as if she were a figure in a dream. His sister! Once he had loved, or almost loved, her. But that, too, was a long time ago.

'Hello,' said Maureen nervously. 'I see you're hungry, too.'

'Do you want some bread and butter?'

'I thought I'd like a cut,' she said, using the old childish phrase.

'Here you are,' he said, giving her the piece he had just cut, and shoving the butter towards her. Then he turned to the loaf and cut himself another slice.

'By the way,' said Maureen, swallowing in her nervous-
ness, 'I wondered ...' she stopped; he didn't seem to hear
her. It was as if he felt there was something very important
in what he was doing, which after all was only buttering a
piece of bread for himself. Now he was eating, thinking, in
that dream-like state, common bread, but He has blessed it
for ever to our use.

'You look awfully tired,' Maureen said, startled now by
his drawn look. 'You ought to have gone to bed before this.'

'I'm just going,' he told her. 'I think I'll have a drink
of milk, too.' As he poured from the bottle into a glass, he
added vaguely, 'do you want some?'

'No, thank you.' She stopped herself from adding: 'Don't
take too much or Kathleen will be short for breakfast.' She
half turned towards the door and then she heard herself
saying abruptly: 'By the way, if you do want to go to Mass
to-morrow, it's at seven, eight, nine and ten, at our church,
as you probably remember. And of course, if you want me
to go with you ...'

'But I never thought of such a thing. What are you talking about?'

She turned and stared at him. Why was his voice so angry?

'I'm sorry. It just came into my head. I didn't mean ...'

'No? I think it is rather late at night to start proselytis-
ing, isn't it?'

'I didn't mean to,' said Maureen quickly. 'Good night,'
she made herself say, going quickly from the room, going
up the stairs, thinking, what a fool I am. It must have been
the gin. They say it makes people go soft and weepy. And
now as she had turned from the reflection of herself as a
cold and callous woman, she turned with equal distaste

from the picture of herself as an interfering prig, imagining she was some ministering angel.

What a fool! she told herself again, staring at the reflection of herself in the long glass, and biting savagely into her bread and butter. As if I wasn't the last person Adam would turn to about anything!

III

Once in bed Adam became fully awake once more. Why had Maureen wondered if he were going to Mass? It was his own fault for mentioning the word. But at least she had no suspicion, and would, now that she had seen him eat, never dream that his real plan was to commit the sacrilege of going up to the altar rails, of taking the Sacred Host upon his tongue when he wilfully lacked all grace. He had not drawn the curtains, and he moved uneasily, aware that moonlight was striking on his pillowed head. The house and the square outside were very still, and across his fevered brain came the random thought that as he lay in the patch of white light he was being observed by the clear all-seeing eyes of God. How foul he must appear in that lucidity: it was as if getting out of bed to draw the curtains he tried to get away from the reflection of his own corruption by burying his head in the sand. But no, that was what he must not do, he thought later, seeking relief from the nausea which threatened. He alone had willed it to be so; he alone had never asked for his trespasses to be forgiven, he had never prayed to be delivered from evil. Remember that, God! I have willed it so!

Though he still lay tensely he had now the illusion of stoical calm, a calm in which he watched God turn away;

God Himself could do nothing against a conscious refusal. And to-morrow, indeed that very day, he was going to give further proof of his hardened will by eating unworthily. He reached out for his Latin Missal which he had unearthed earlier in the evening, and re-read the epistle for the day as a barrister might refresh his memory by a last glance at his brief, clutching at the final warning: *qui enim manducat, et bibit indigne, judicium sibi manducat et bibit: non dijudicans corpus Domini.* And, yes, and yes, his thoughts soared, even the Apostle Paul was out-reached: he would eat unworthily and therefore draw judgment to himself, but how much heavier that judgment must be, since he did discern the Lord's Body. Yes, St. Paul had not thought of that high degree of sacrilege!

So, stiffened in his pride, he fell asleep. But not for many hours. For the burden of his resolution was such that inevitably his being rose nearer to his consciousness and struggled into rehearsal. He saw himself in one dream in a large church kneeling at the rails, and then the priest passed him by, him alone, and everyone turned to look at him; in another he was struggling with someone, yes, he realised, he was struggling not with evil, but with good, for, of course, he was Jacob, and the shape he clutched was an angel: but if he killed the angel, if he could only slay the angel before he himself was slain, why then perhaps our Lord would never come down on earth as the prophecies said He would. So intense was the struggle that he awoke with a tremendous start to see the first light coming through the curtains.

As recollection came slowly back, he looked at his watch. It was not yet five, and his schedule had been to rise, dress and shave at six, and leave the house at six-thirty, which would give him time to catch the six-forty-five bus for the seven o'clock Mass. But to sleep again was impossible and for nearly an hour he lay listening to the twitterings of the first waking birds, increasing in number and then dying back to a solitary note. So had he lain in summer dawns long, long ago, when his boyish imagination had been that these bird chirrups were the joyous prelude to all awakening creation's praise of God. He heard, too, the clip-clop of the horses drawing carts laden with fruit and vegetables for the city market, and saw behind them the green country fields opening Danae to the light; then there was the windy rush of a distant train, and a little later the light-hearted whistling of a lad going to his early work. Oh, yes, all over the country, and over many a country in spite of the war, people were beginning to bestir themselves, to do whatever they had to do, often, consciously or unconsciously, preparing to do His will on earth as it was done in Heaven.

Yes, but there *was* the war! People were shaking sleep out of their eyes in order to go and kill and maim each other, and he, too, in this neutral place had his own discordant note to strike, and to strike firmly. Looking at his watch he saw that it was nearly six, and grinding his teeth he flung back the bed coverings. If he had been on a batter, if for days and nights he had been steadily drinking, he could hardly have felt worse. But no matter. And in a little while he was going quietly out of the still silent house.

He had to wait for the first bus of the day. He stood outside a red brick house whose blinds were, like most of the blinds, still drawn. The suburb was still asleep, and for that reason seemed sunk in an untouched innocence. Only a boy with bicycle, and satchel stuffed with papers for his morning's delivery, started to wheel down the road as the bus rounded the corner.

But as he came up to its railings, the bells had already started to peal out from the church, as they were pealing out from other churches all over Europe, and two old ladies dressed in old-fashioned long black skirts went up the path before him. They blessed themselves from the holy water stoup inside the door, and he followed their example. He would conform to every rite, inessential as well as essential, he told himself, bending his knee before the tabernacle and going down on both knees inside the pew he had chosen, near the back of the church. Let him appear as if he were praying, though all he was conscious of was the still familiar faint smell of stale incense, and the thrust of the silence, a hush which could not be broken by the clatter of feet because it lay deeper than a surface silence, having been created by many years' reverence of the human spirit.

The belief in Transubstantiation had done that much, he thought vaguely, as he sat back on the hard seat. Even suppose that the Protestants were right, as anyone could be right working within one set of formulae, and faith was but imagination creating in bright colours one possibility of the painted world, supplying it with a bridge to another dimension, to another and greater because perfect creation: even so, the effect of that imagination had lasted. And would last so long as the imaginative spirit endured, whether that spirit came from man or from God. For life is short, but art is long, reaching down from one century to another. Well, his own faith, *which could not be unseated,* was that that spirit came from God. If it were not so he wouldn't be here;

325

his presence would be but a meaningless act of discourtesy toward the belief of others.

And suppose, he thought in the next moment, that is all that it is. A curious new flicker of hope seemed to stir as he looked round for an increased clatter went up the aisle.

It was the children coming, little boys in knickerbockers, little girls in bright cotton dresses, some with bare legs, some with socks, ushered in by two nuns. No great display of reverence here, as they pushed and jostled; one did not expect it any more than one expected heavy decorum from butterflies: one boy was now sharing a private joke with another: it went down the pew causing suppressed laughter, lighting eyes and reddening cheeks: one little girl kneeling down was concerned only with pulling up a loose stocking; another patted her hair importantly. Then settling back on their seats, some stared about them, while others for the moment assumed a grave aspect which sat ludicrously and yet charmingly on their smooth little faces. For, whatever their physical diversity, innocence claimed them all, and therefore they were a spectacle to lighten the most frowning heart, if that frowning heart looked out upon them.

They made Adam think for a moment of his own little girl, of Sheila. So she too would come to Mass, rather importantly, that being her nature, till she tired of being important, and, as stray words had one day informed him, asked for a sweet to break the tedium. He broke off that thought impatiently, watching the children now resentfully. He hadn't bargained for children also coming to receive the Holy Eucharist on Corpus Christi. Surely they went usually to a later Mass? There was no real reason why their presence should disturb him, but he was disturbed as a general is disturbed by a rumour of an enemy approaching from an unexpected direction.

He heard the tinkle of the bell, and dropped with the rest to his knees. The Mass began; the priest was an old white-haired man who gabbled his way through the psalm and the Confiteor with the perfunctory ease of long practice in speed. After one swift look Adam had relaxed: nothing struck on his heart; he was feeling nothing; an old half-forgotten murmur came, signifying nothing, he told himself, except of course as prologue to the drama. And with that thought, his apprehension was diverted to the rapidity with which the Mass was approaching its culmination: already the priest was reading the Epistle, reading in one moment the very words which had sent him into the church. He had read them; he had already moved to the centre of the altar, and was bowing down. Now came the Gospel: yes, they were already standing up, and he stood with them, searching for the first time in his missal, finding the place and translating to himself: My flesh is true meat, meat *indeed*, that is how the translation went … and My blood … but the priest had already finished, and everyone was settling back into their seats, as he came down from the altar and stood facing them to read some notices.

Adam stared away, trying to find something to avert his attention from the heaviness in his heart and a mounting sense that could only be called fear. He stared at the crude colours and designs of the Stations of the Cross, from them to the gaudy statue of St. Teresa of Lisieux, and his gaze became fixed. Somehow she had misled him; for the moment he forgot and then remembered The Little Way, and let his glance pass on to a brown St. Anthony, and then to the meek and doll-like painted face of the bright blue Madonna; oh, yes, all quite dreadful, he thought with irony, remembering some criticism Kathleen had once made to him. But he was only playing a game, waiting to know if the celebrant was going to read the Epistle and Gospel for Corpus Christi in English. If someone else read the words in the vernacular with solemnity, he thought, it would convince him that they had really been said, were really true. But no, the priest was already turning from his final announcement that the Children of Mary would meet on Sunday afternoon at three o'clock, and they were all standing for the Creed: 'Credo in unum deum,' repeated Adam's mind, and then he stared at the pale flowers and golden flames of the candles on the altar, genuflecting a little late after the others: AND WAS MADE MAN.

And now they were all sitting again, and he didn't want to watch the movements of the ritual by which the celebrant prepared the altar and blessed the bread and the wine. He watched the children instead, and specially watched one little boy who, resting his elbow on his knee, had dropped his head on his hand in fatigue. That child had been awakened too soon, told to get up to go with the other schoolchildren to early Mass, and now he was drowsy, really back in his warm bed, indifferent to anybody and anything. And why did watching the sleepy little boy make him want to … not cry, of course, because there were no tears in him: he had been quite drained of all tears; indeed there was nothing in the world that could make him cry: he had at least accomplished that much.

The bell tinkled; they all went down on their knees. In a few moments Christ would truly appear among them, would be there seeing into his heart. But that was nothing, no—though he held his breath when the bell rang again— it was nothing.

And now the Elevation was all over, and already the children were moving out into the aisle ready to take their places before the altar rails. His glance passed from one tender profile to another, saw the droop of long dark eyelashes, watched small clasped hands, and slender childish neck. Once, he remembered, perhaps when he was seventeen, he had written a poem about a child's First Communion, a very bad sentimental poem it must have been, too, but probably, since the imagination wears tracks and repeats itself tediously, he had likened the child to a flower, for now he was seeing without emotion all these children kneeling with their clasped hands waiting for the priest to come down from the altar to them as wild flowers of the field, holding their petals very still before some mystery quite beyond their comprehension. And yet, of their courtesy, they were doing their best. And so creating an act of worship that held no alloy of the poison of self, whether that self was greedy of obtaining some magic remedy against all ills, or humbled in penitence and expectation. These children were neither humbled nor worshipping nor avid. They lifted their faces, and when the priest bent above them opened their mouths to receive the wafer as a tiny child receives an uncomprehended gift believing the grown-ups who tell her that it is a lovely present. Some of the children as they came back to their seats had already forgotten what they had been told, staring about them, looking for a friend's face; others more retentive still played the grown-ups game, their eyelids turned primly down, their hands clasped in front of them.

Now the grown-ups themselves were coming out into the aisle, and he forgot about the children, while his hands clenched in preparation. There were a couple of dirty women in shawls; there was a queer-looking old man who went up muttering loudly: 'Jesus! Jesus!' There was a younger man with a shock of thick black hair and a coloured scarf instead of a collar who went up the aisle with a sort of defiant strut and a half grin on his face as if he were saying: 'Why shouldn't I?' Then several pious-looking dowdy women who were obviously regular communicants, the trained regular guard who always wore the same expressions, made the same movements. Now he must go too.

But still he waited, looking round as if hoping to find someone whom it was intended he should follow, who would make it all quite easy. For of himself he felt he could not go; it was as if his body refused to obey, knowing quite well that it could not take part in this performance. His hands, which had been hot and clammy, were now quite cold: no life left in him, that was the trouble. He saw the old man slouching back towards him, still muttering: 'Jesus! Jesus!' He tried to stiffen his body to make it rise, looking toward the altar, hearing the priest's mutter: *'Corpus Domini Nostri …'* as he placed the Wafer.

'Go now,' he urged himself once again, and heard himself answer: 'I can't now: it's too late,' and he sat back on his seat, watching the priest's retreating back as he returned to the altar.

So the curtain had dropped, and he had failed. There was no point in waiting any more, and his body was now his servant again and took him out of the church, and made him walk fast, bringing him down to the bus stop in a few minutes. Later on, after taking food and drink, he did try and find the answer to the defection of his will, and it seemed to him that he had failed for a very simple reason, and yet one he had overlooked: that while it is easy, or not difficult, to commit a sacrilege, to utter a blasphemy, to call forth devils from the deep as presumably they tried to do at their idiot Black Masses, it is much less easy for the guilt-stricken to sit down among little children who are playing at making daisy chains, and hanging them round each other; to interrupt the secret rumblings of an old man's senility, to enter into kinship with an unwashed tinker who makes an embarrassed joke because his prayer had been over-heard. In that ugly little church the lambs had been fed, rather than the sheep; the simple had been satisfied, not the wise; the matter-of-factly pious had been given their small daily meed, and it all belonged to the pipings of Pan and the twitterings of birds, making an untouched Eden to which he could never come in order to desecrate. 'I went to the wrong church,' was the only way he could sum it up. 'I ought to have gone to one of the big city churches.'

— TWELVE —

I

THE prose dramas of everyday life, unlike poetic drama, have prologues which are always of more subtle interest, and often for that matter of tension, than the more widely reported scene which is their culmination. There is, for example, the transition between the time when a man is accepted rather than discussed, dismissed by his acquaintances in stereotyped phrases—unless such an acquaintance possesses more than the average interest in human nature—and the period when within his own circle or small town and village life his name seems to be on everyone's lips. A murmur here, a head turned there, a pursing of the lips, a meaning wink, and then the pack is off in full cry. The gradual swelling is something like the sounds which fall on the ears of a worshipper who lingers on after hearing one Mass, waiting for another; the last worshippers, slow to go, trickle out meeting the one or two early arrivals for the next Sacrifice. There are the coughs, the creaking of pew or chair, the echo of slow solitary footsteps, a few whispers: then, gradually the steps become more determined as the pews begin to fill up again; there is a rustling and heads looking this way and that to find the best places, till finally there is the hasty tramping of the late-comers, genuflecting swiftly, pushing perhaps into back pews, or marching boldly forward to the front. The waiting is over and in a wave of sound the people rise in unison as the servers and the priest enter.

So it was at this time with Adam Palmer. For years he had been settled in the esteem of those who knew him, who were mostly the so-called intelligentsia of the town. They thought of him as a quiet rather cranky fellow, but with a head-piece, capable of destructive wit at times. His dark mournful sallow face had impressed itself at first as being distinguished, and was then taken for granted, as a signature which first arouses curiosity is taken for granted after receiving several letters in the same hand. He had the quality that cats possess: even if they are curled up asleep, eyes stray in their direction, fascinated by the posture in which they take their temporary repose. The highly strung or those who are allergic to cats and aware of their sudden springs on to knee or lap are faintly uneasy, and at a literary party, even when saying little, Adam had that same capacity to excite uneasiness in his company. But the reaction lay in the nature of a nuance, a faint inflection, rather than of any definite feeling, and was therefore only remarked by the observant.

Moreover he had never provided any food for the gossips with a nose to scent out the most secret *affaire*, or to discover that relations between such and such a husband and wife were strained. That one, it might be reported, had made a scene; another in his cups had admitted that … this one wasn't speaking to that one and the reason was … And so forth and so on. But Palmer was consistent. His English wife might not be a social asset, but she was presentable if a little dull; he did not have *affaires*; if he occasionally drank more than usual he went home without creating any brawl or diversion, and if it were true that he was not always reliable as a confidant, that his finger had not been unknown to stir up mischief and bad feeling, well, that, after all, was the way of the town, a mark of sophistication on which it rather prided itself than not.

And then it had all changed. There had come the whisper here, the look there, those trickles that make a full stream, but whose origin is often difficult to trace. It could certainly be said that one source was the novelist, James Norman. Since the day he had followed Adam to the public park, his curiosity had played about the man sufficiently for him to make of him a psychological topic. And some of the things he had said were considered good enough for repetition in the pub or drawing-room:

'You can almost see the load Palmer carries on his back. A little disgusting to exhibit one's sores so openly …'

'But then he is medieval, an Abelard hating all his life because he once loved.'

And once near the mark:

'Palmer asked me whether I thought Hitler would be damned; he was inexpressibly delighted when I told him I doubted it. Then he knew he had no rival!'

'You *should* get Palmer at the Library. But don't be too sure. On one occasion I found a girl in tears because he hadn't come back when he should have done.'

All these things and others Norman said, rather pleased at the opportunity to avenge old scores. He said enough to make his listeners look more intently at Palmer when they saw him, to note that his manner was odd, that he appeared not to hear what they said, to answer at random. And so came the pursed-up lip, the meaning shake of the head.

At the Library, of course, there had been murmurs for a much longer time, but mostly a sneering murmur from the junior assistants who resented his entire lack of interest in themselves. Now there came into these murmurs the self-righteous joy of those who find themselves morally justified in their prejudices:

'Did you hear the latest about the balmy Palm? Miss Wright told me. She was studying for her exam, up in the Ref., and he stands by the bookshelves in a sort of daze. One of the public comes in and after waiting at the desk quite a while, to do him justice, rings the bell. Palm took no notice, and then the man rings again. So Miss Wright thought she ought to tell him, and she goes up and tells him he's wanted. He just stares at her, then at the desk, then has the nerve to say: 'Oh, will you attend to him?' Pretty cool when it's her off-duty time. What's he supposed to be there for? I ask you?'

'But he doesn't do *anything*. Honest! When I was last up there I looked up the cutting books, you know, because someone wanted to know about the rise in the wages of electricians. It ought to have been there, but it wasn't. And he hasn't entered ANYTHING for days!'

'A woman said to me, she said: "You seem to have a complete fool up there in your Reference Library." I didn't say anything, better not, but she was in a towering rage ...'

'That's nothing. I know someone who *has* complained. She wanted to see the Chief Librarian. I told her he was on holiday, and put her on to Mrs. Doyle.'

'How do you know it was about him?'

'I do know, that's all.'

The last speaker was right, though as she had obtained her information by discreet eavesdropping she preferred to let it be thought that it was due to hidden powers of divination. And Mrs. Doyle, who didn't like Mr. Palmer, decided not to mention the matter to him directly but to use her eyes, and report this and one or two other pieces of flagrant neglect on the Reference Librarian's part to Mr. Ferguson, the Chief Librarian, when he returned from his holiday in July.

It has already been said that Mr. Ferguson was an easy-going man, and one moreover with some respect for his assistant's literary qualifications. Still the evidence before him could not be neglected, and he at first decided that Palmer must be run down. Brainy people often got run down, or so he had heard. At his first visit to the Reference Department he said, almost apologetically:

'You know, I don't think you are very well, Palmer. One or two people have noticed it, and you don't *look* well if I may say so. What about taking your holiday soon? Yes, I know Dickinson, who is the one to take over from you, is down on the list for the first three weeks in August, but couldn't you change with him?'

Palmer had said to him with civility, after a pause, (but then the man generally seemed to think before he answered even the simplest remark) 'Yes, I think that would be a good idea. I am tired.'

But then Dickinson did mind changing. Dickinson had his rooms booked somewhere, and Dickinson was certain that it was quite impossible for him to change the date. Mr. Ferguson, seeing him so agitated, sighed, and gave in, hoping that all would be well.

But all was not well. Unfortunately for Adam, the annual checking of the Reference Library books had started, and, not without pleasure, Mrs. Doyle reported to him that more books, and those of the most expensive nature, had been lost, stolen, or strayed than the Library had known for ten years. 'Not,' said Mrs. Doyle, 'not since Mr. Purcell's time.'

Mr. Ferguson remembered Mr. Purcell. Mr. Purcell had been a secret drinker, and had exchanged the library desk for an inebriates' home. Mr. Purcell was suspected of stealing the books and exchanging them for the cash with which to buy hard liquor. Mr. Ferguson did not suspect Adam of thieving; he was certain by now that his assistant had not been sufficiently interested in the public to observe whether or not *they* stole. He paid a second visit to the Reference, and was pained to observe that Mr. Palmer was so deeply immersed in a book that he did not even look up at his entrance.

'I see you're reading,' he said in accents which expressed strong disapproval of such a course when Adam at last became aware that someone was standing by him.

'Yes. *The Brothers Karamazov.*'

'You seem to find it very interesting,' said Mr. Ferguson. Sarcasm seemed the obvious weapon, though it was not one he usually employed. Adam, unobservant now of everything exterior, did not notice the sarcasm. Mr. Ferguson as an employer was to him a dim figure, but the vague feeling that he was a sympathetic hearer rushed him into an unusual flow of speech. He felt the need to define:

'Very! It's years since I read this. Not since I was young. I was just thinking that while, though to say this is heresy, Dostoevsky is a great Christian novelist, he most definitely is not a Catholic novelist.'

337

Mr. Ferguson raised eyebrows. 'Really? Well …'

'There's no doctrine, no theology, you see. His rebellion is the old one, against human suffering, human cruelty. What it all comes to is that he believes that as soon as any feeling of love pierces a sinner's heart, he will inevitably be saved. Whereas, of course, the Catholic holds there must also be penitence. Then there is the Church's distinction between the Catholic, I mean the true believing Catholic, and the heretic or the pagan, agnostic, call them what you like. Within their cloak of invincible ignorance they can climb to Heaven almost minus judgment, saved by their natural grace. And most men, perhaps nearly all men, have some natural grace, some goodness. She is much, much harder on her own children, members of the Church Militant on earth. She will not allow us to have any doubt that, inspired by the Holy Ghost, her judgments and the judgments of God are co-equal; to doubt that is the first step toward heresy. Now that would be meaningless, in fact anathema, to Dostoevsky who, you will remember …'

Mr. Ferguson was at last successful in interrupting. 'All this may be very interesting, Mr. Palmer, but …'

'Of course you're not a Catholic,' said Adam, his employer becoming for the first time real to him. He stood up.

'No,' said Mr. Ferguson with some firmness. 'But I am a Librarian, and I came to tell you that, as you probably know, the books that have been stolen, *must* be stolen since they are missing, from this department are sixty-seven in number, including some very valuable ones that owing to the war we cannot replace. Now this is a very serious matter, as you must realise.'

Mr. Ferguson paused. Someone had come up to the desk, and he indicated that Adam should attend to him. It was a simple matter of passing over to him one of the medical dictionaries which were arranged on a shelf behind the desk, as a slight discouragement to the increase of hypochondriacs. But the moment's detachment gave him an opportunity of observing Palmer more closely. The flush which had come to his cheeks when he was talking about Dostoevsky had gone now. His face was grey and drawn; a pulse twitched below his right eye.

So instead of continuing his lecture Mr. Ferguson said with impulsive kindness: 'Look here, Palmer! You're not well, man. That's the root of the trouble. You must have a good holiday. That's what I said before, if you remember?'

'A holiday?' said Adam. He was finding it difficult to concentrate on what Mr. Ferguson was saying, and therefore automatically repeated the last word he had heard in order to give the appearance of understanding. His employer, however, construed it as an utterance of longing.

'It was a pity Dickinson was awkward about changing, but you must get away, or you're heading for a real sickness from the look of you. I've got an idea. There's a lad—oh, not so young as he looks, and quite decently educated; he's put himself through college—who wants a job here. I promised him he should come in soon, and I'll send him up here next Monday. If you give him a few days' training he ought to be able to take over till Dickinson is back. And then you should get right away. See a doctor, too.'

Adam managed a smile: 'Oh, I don't think it's as bad as that.'

'You're a sick man by the looks of you, and, of course, you can't do your work in that state.' Mr. Ferguson's eyes went round the room and he remembered the object of his visit. 'You must have been very absentminded, for example, over watching for the thieves that have been coming up here.' He sighed, thinking of the account he must render in his report to the Borough Council, and added in a more severe voice: 'Because that mustn't go on. It can't go on. One of us will lose our jobs if it does. I have to warn you of that.'

Adam momentarily realised the warning. It didn't matter much, he was thinking, because something would have to happen soon; something was going to happen soon, when the Library would sink away behind him. But Mr. Ferguson once again misconstrued his absorbed look.

'Well, we won't say anything more for the moment. I'll write this lad, and send him up to you. You should be able to leave for your holiday by the Thursday or Friday.'

'Thank you.'

Mr. Ferguson went out abruptly. He had caught sight of the open novel on the desk, but the words: 'And you must remember you are not supposed to read while you are on duty,' seemed too childish to utter. He decided that probably Palmer was writing something about the Russians for the local paper, and was taking the matter too seriously. All that stuff about theology, too. His face was grave as he returned to his own comfortable room. There was no doubt that the man had got himself in a very queer state of mind. He had always previously been inclined to think that Roman Catholics took their religion with a shocking lack of responsibility. But Palmer was evidently a very religious man; why, to hear him, he might almost, Mr. Ferguson thought, be a Calvinist.

II

Mr. Ferguson having gone, Adam sat at his desk, no longer reading, no longer, for a while, even thinking. That was how it had been with him for some weeks, ever since he had gone to Mass on the holiday of Corpus Christi. He thought hard along a certain new line of speculation; then his brain went quite blank. Again he would feel on seeing a familiar face the desire to talk, to sound out the acquaintance. Tap them hard enough, and long enough, and perhaps after all his neighbours could give him some clue. Surely they must, beneath their surface cynicism and apparent concern with trivialities, be concerned to know whether their course of life was leading them closer to God, or further away from Him. Unaware how his unusual garrulousness was being observed and added to other fuel, he had plunged into talk over a couple of glasses of whisky with an abandonment of his usual caution. It was true that not finding what he sought, not finding any real response, he soon grew silent again, and went home to his solitary reading. But the ironic gods looking down might have smiled at the spectacle of one who for years had been so suspicious, who had lived so much on the defensive against watchfulness, now, when there was some need to be on guard, throwing all caution to the winds and speaking his mind regardless to whom he spoke it. Because there was so much for him to think of. He thought he had at last discerned a true high road to hell.

The origin of this track lay in the thoughts which had followed upon his failure to commit sacrilege on the Feast of Corpus Christi. As he saw it, his will had been frustrated by innocence, chiefly the innocence of little children. You could interrupt prayer; you could never really stop little children from playing unless you made yourself not man but brute. Was that then what he must do? He went back to the Gospels, and found at last a text which confirmed:

But whoso shall offend one of these little ones which believe in me it were better for him that a millstone were hanged about his neck and that he were drowned in the depth of the sea.

No uncertain condemnation here. And since, in the context, Jesus had placed a little child in the midst of his disciples, His words could be taken literally as referring to the young in years. He went back to that, even when thinking of innocence he was reminded that it was a quality which a few rare grown-ups he had met also shared. Sometimes it could be possessed by the wise and the shrewd; for it hung about Father Mansfield like an aura; it could also be possessed by the simple; there was an old unlettered woman in an English country post office to whom he had talked when once on holiday, she, too, all unaware was so crowned, and he had never forgotten her for that reason. But mostly, of course, this childlike quality belonged to very little children, before they went to school, before their ambition was to be like the others, think as they thought, be as they were. Even Sheila had already become a trifle contaminated, he had decided, noting certain tones in her voice, observing certain coy gestures. There remained, however, baby John, not two years old, who crawled rather than walked, who made happy gurgling sounds that only Maureen and Kathleen insisted were perfectly intelligible speech. True belief had not yet entered the nascent spirit, but the potentialities were all there. Suppose he checked them at their source; suppose he killed or maimed? Yes, monstrous and diabolical, so that he sickened at the very thought. But monstrous and diabolical? Wasn't that what he wanted? Wasn't that what he must do in order to become a brute, and so cut himself off, beyond a peradventure, from the mercy of God which was shown to men and not to brutes? Anything after all better than standing at the impasse to which the Little Way had brought him, looking back at the laborious pettiness of the years behind him: the patient storage of little sins made out of cunning disparagement, of cleverly planted poison, but much, much more the vacuum, the hollow waste places to which he had refused to allow sun and air and beauty and friendship to enter. Could he go on, accompanied by that charnel smell? He was too tired for any more of it. So tired, and yet, strangely enough, Faith had not left him; Faith refused to leave him, as apparently it left others so easily, so apparently painlessly. Why, since he was so weary, had not this unwanted gift, defined by Aquinas as the first bridge to God, crumbled? Since it had not done so, he could not take the way of James, and starve out his soul. Therefore he must become brute beast, consciously become brute, and again and again he called up the words of the great condemnation! *Whoso* ...

So the obsession grew. As with other obsessions, it accompanied him through the day, it went to bed with him at night, and was there waiting for him as soon as his eyes opened on the new day. As others are haunted by an impossible love with whom they walk and talk in every waking dream, so was he haunted. But since his obsession was one which had no place in the main corridors of life, not to be recognised in the guise of human tenderness and human passion, but was a creature of hobgoblin fantasy, it needed much more dressing up. Robes must be put on the nightmare to give it a semblance of human shape.

And since the origin of the nightmare was pride gone insane, he had to find for it royal robes. He had to see his own project as more evil than anything to which the witches had lured Macbeth. Re-reading Macbeth's cry before he murdered Duncan: '*His virtues will plead like angels trumpet-tongued before the deep damnation of his taking-off,*' he asked himself, what were the virtues of Duncan, an old man and therefore like the rest of us a sinner, against the unstained innocence of his own little son? Iago had incited Othello to murder a near innocent, Desdemona, but even Iago was incited by some paltry feeling of human jealousy. The cruelty of Regan and Goneril had sent Lear mad, but Lear, too, was old and foolish, Lear should have learnt to be wiser in his judgments. Whereas his little child had not even eaten of the apple of knowledge of good and evil.

From Shakespeare he had gone in library hours to *The Brothers Karamazov.* Yes, Dostoevsky had realised this uttermost depth, for it was the crimes committed against little children which made it impossible for Ivan to accept this life as God has made it: '*Of the other tears of humanity with which the earth is soaked from its crust to its centre, I will say nothing.*' And even Alyosha had answered his brother's question as to whether he would accept perfection based on the tears of one tiny creature with: '*No, I would not consent.*'

But though he needed their shudders as part of the fabric he was weaving in his megalomania, Adam would turn frequently from the pages before him in a sort of impatience. For after all the rebellion of Ivan against God was not *his* rebellion. They were both believers, believing that one day all tears would be wiped away in the perfection of the Godhead, but whereas Ivan, *respectfully* in his own phrase, returned Him the ticket, because the price was too great for his stomach and nerves to pay, he, Adam, was merely returning the ticket because his *own* humiliations and sufferings were too much for his pride and stomach. All right then, that made Ivan the better man: one who really did love his neighbours even if he protested that it was only the innocent hurt children for whom he cared. Dostoevsky was right in saving him according to his own gospel of love. He, Adam Palmer, was cast in a meaner mould: let that be admitted, because even the gospel according to Dostoevsky, according to religious humanitarianism, couldn't avail for him. He loved no one, not even himself!

It was at this point in his reading and in his thoughts that Mr. Ferguson had entered, and had heard his excited speech. But Ferguson having gone it was not for a while that the thread could be resumed. He realised vaguely that there had been some talk of stolen books, and then of a holiday. And when finally his thought stiffened on the holiday, he looked about him furtively, and rubbed his cold fingers nervously together. For, of course, a holiday at home would give him more opportunity!

III

Alan Lane was not deeply disappointed to find that Adam Palmer was not particularly interested in him at his first appearance in the Reference Library. Some chaps might even have thought him standoffish. He initiated him into certain matters of daily routine, looking not at him but over his shoulder when he spoke. Finally, as he showed him round the shelves he remarked: 'Of course books actually are the last thing the public are interested in. They want facts out of them, that's all.'

'Of course they are literal-minded rather than imaginatively minded,' Alan interposed quickly. For he did want to show Mr. Palmer that he was not just the ordinary sort of fool. And he was pleased to notice that the librarian did look at him for the first time before he went on: 'So memorise the books on the Quick Reference shelves, and here is our old friend the *Encyclopaedia Britannica*. When in doubt about anything send them to that.'

'I see. Thank you very much. Yes, that's a good idea.'

'And I'd better find you the book of words about our numbering system.'

'That's all right. You see, I got the book as soon as I heard from Mr. Ferguson that I was to start to-day. I spent the whole week-end with it, and I think I've got the idea pretty well.'

Now Adam did look more carefully at his new assistant. He saw a thin lad of average height, but appearing smaller because of his slightness. The face was small, pale and rather peaked, and his dark hair, with an untidy lock hanging over his forehead, needed cutting. But the eyes were bright; at the moment, owing to Alan's excitement, the pupils were dilated, making them appear almost black.

'You're quite keen, I see.'

'Yes, I am.' Alan swallowed, perceiving that this was his opportunity. But his voice came out rather quaveringly as he made himself add: 'You see, sir, I feel it's a great opportunity working under you, if you don't mind my saying so. I've read all your articles, and I think, some of us, quite a lot of us, think that they are the most brilliant things in literary journalism that this city has produced for years. I hope you don't mind my saying this.'

'Not at all,' said Adam. Alan was not to know that the amused smile he gave him was the first spontaneous smile he had given anyone in years. There was something about this boy that reminded him of himself when he first started out:

'How old are you?'

'Twenty-seven.'

'You look much much younger.'

'I know,' said Alan dejectedly. 'I can't help it. Perhaps it is because I went in for sport a lot, running, you know, trying to harden myself. The mother of a friend of mine at college thinks that, and she says I ought to rest more. So I have given up sport to a great extent. My chief interests are literary.'

'Really. So you write yourself?'

'Try to. But I'm no good yet. I just practise and then throw everything I write away. Don't you think that's the best way?'

'Perhaps. But beware, lest you never recapture the first fine careless rapture.'

'That's Browning, isn't it?'

'But you've plenty of time. Are you a Catholic?'

'Yes.'

'Practising?'

Alan hesitated for a moment. Perhaps like a lot of clever men, like Voltaire, Mr. Palmer was contemptuous of religion. But he had to speak the truth. He said:

'Yes.' And then added frowningly: 'Though, of course, I see that a lot of people's religion isn't real religion or they couldn't do the things they do do.'

'So you go to Mass regularly?'

Mr. Palmer sounded approving rather than otherwise. 'Yes,' said Alan again. 'Well, I do miss it sometimes, but when I do I feel bad about it, so then I go on a week-day to make up. I know it doesn't make up theologically, but it makes up in my own heart till I go to Confession.'

Mr. Palmer seemed to be interested, waiting for more, so he went on bravely: 'You see, my father and mother died when I was only a kid, so I was educated by the Christian Brothers, at their orphanage. And I must say that though the other boys were a pretty rough lot most of them, those men were a very decent lot. The Father Superior was very good to me.'

'But you've been to college since?'

'Yes. I earned the money myself.' Alan stopped, for Mr. Palmer's face had suddenly gone blank, as if he weren't interested any more. At the same time two members of the public entered the room. One of them went up to the desk, and Mr. Palmer walked away to attend to him. Then he beckoned him over, and giving him the key of the filing-room asked him to see if he could find a certain back number of *The Times*. When he returned, elated because his search had been quickly successful, Mr. Palmer gave him a bundle of the morning's papers, and explained about going through them and making certain cuttings. Since now his voice was aloof and rather bored, Alan again became the assiduous understudy.

But sitting at one of the desks he thought happily that the ice had now been broken. Perhaps in time Mr.

Palmer might get really friendly with him, and he could report intimate discussions on literature to the other fellows. Something like: 'As Adam Palmer was saying to me the other day, and I am certainly inclined to agree with him, the Inishkill literary movement is exceedingly Provincial not to say Parochial.'

The ice had not been broken. Though Adam glancing across at him and observing how gravely he was taking his duties shocked himself by catching the thought: 'If I had a son I'd like him to be like this boy.'

For, of course, he had a son, a baby son, and his resolve toward him was either to kill him or better still, he had now decided, easier, to make him into an imbecile. And he drew away from the sense of something young, bright, eager and untouched in his vicinity that wanted his friendliness, as it might have been from a plague spot. Of course, he reflected grimly, his Guardian Angel who would soon, he hoped, be out of a job, must now be clutching at straws, hoping to make some last bid to save him through the agency of this lad who at the age of twenty-seven had somehow managed to remain unspotted from the world. He watched Alan, and threw him a question or a word occasionally just to make sure that his approach to life and to his work was really as disinterested as a child reading a fairy tale, finding adventure because the spirit of adventure was in his own mind. At the end of the afternoon, for example, he asked him abruptly:

'What about girls? Have you a girl friend?'

A shade, he observed, passed over Alan's face. 'I know one or two. There's one, a doctor's daughter that I play tennis with in the square. But, of course, she's only just left school.'

349

'No love-making, no heart-throbs?'

Alan shook his head, and grinned. 'Nothing like that.' Then, serious, he tried to explain: 'You see, being taken up with sport and then studying rather hard for my B.A., and having an office job at the same time, doesn't leave a man with much time.'

'I see,' said Adam, turning away. He did see. Alan was well aware that there was this exotic grown-up world of love-making; he had probably been teased because of his own lack of a girl, and felt inferior about it, in the same way as he felt inferior about his childish looks and lack of weight. But there still was, after all, so much else.

'Quite touching,' he told his Guardian Angel, as with a wave of his hand he went out of the office five minutes before his time, after asking Alan to sign off for him. 'All this and hero-worship, too. But I'm afraid, old man, you're too late.' And though Alan Lane was now disappointed that Mr. Palmer never really talked to him again before he left for his holiday on the Friday evening, merely saying as they parted: 'Well, I expect you'll do all right. Much better than myself,' he refused to admit any disappointment. For by that time he had decided that Mr. Palmer was suffering from some deep trouble. His wife, perhaps, was unfaithful to him! Alan had read about such things in literature and in the English papers. In any case he was obviously very unhappy, too unhappy to concentrate on anything, so that Alan's heart sank within him every time he stole a glance at the sallow deeply grooved face which he had decided was rather like Lord Byron must have looked when he was dying, and in sympathy his own boyish face took on a deep seriousness. Moreover his sense of loyalty was also kindled, since he soon found need to defend his hero. One of the girls downstairs remarked to him:

'How did you get on with old Palmer?'

'Very well, thank you.'

'Balmy Palmy, we call him. He's nuts, you know.'

'Nuts? I certainly don't know. Mr. Palmer is a very distinguished and a very interesting man.'

'Distinguished? Well I'll say he's distinguished. Distinguished for being crazy and doing no work. That's why the Chief got you in. Didn't you know?'

'No. And you're talking nonsense,' said Alan turning away with flushed face. He had thought that this particular girl, who was rather pretty, might be his first real girl friend. But now she was definitely off his map, and for ever.

And the girl herself looking after him with displeasure soon found an opportunity to say to her particular friend: 'You know that new kid, Lane, up in the Ref. Well, he's balmy too. Do you know he actually sticks up for old Palmer!'

IV

Though he did not know it, Adam returned to a home where the spirit of watchfulness was also now alert. It was particularly Maureen who was uneasily on guard. For some days ago a gentle elderly woman who worked in another branch of her office had come up to her and said eagerly: 'Oh, Miss Palmer, I was so glad to see your brother at Mass on Corpus Christi.' Maureen stared. Then she said: 'I think you're wrong, Miss White. He had breakfast at home that day and then went off to his work as usual. Besides, I didn't think you knew him.'

351

'Oh, but I've never forgotten him from the time when you were both young children, and Mother and I had rooms next door to your house. Such a nice-looking boy, he was. And I've seen his picture in the paper several times, and recognised him at the Library. Though, of course I never spoke because I knew he wouldn't remember me. And I've prayed for him, too.'

'Prayed for him! That's good of you, but …'

'Don't you remember the time you told me about his coming back to settle here, and saying you were afraid he had lapsed from his religion? Well, I asked you really because I so well remember your dear mother, God rest her, telling us one evening after Benediction how much she hoped he would be a priest. He'd have made a lovely one, I'm sure.'

'That's very good of you, but are you sure about seeing him at Mass, Miss White?'.

'Positive. He went all the way to seven o'clock at our church at Newrath. He sat just across from me, and the poor man, I was thinking, he didn't look well at all.'

'But you're not saying he took Holy Communion?'

'Well, I didn't actually see him. Because I went up myself and wasn't watching him. But why would he got out so early else? I thought maybe you didn't know, and he didn't want to go up in your church where people would notice more. It's often the way with them when they are returning, do you know? Oh, I felt so happy for you, and thought, well, I must tell his sister, so I must.'

'Yes, and thank you,' said Maureen. She pleased Miss White by asking with sudden warmth: 'Oh, and please will you go on praying for him, please do.'

'Indeed, I will.'

But the warmth soon died, leaving Maureen more frightened than anything else. She believed that Adam had gone to Mass on Corpus Christi, had gone all the way to Newrath, and therefore must have slipped secretly out of the house. But surely he hadn't gone up to the altar? Surely not, and she remembered his eating and drinking in the kitchen after midnight as if he were performing some rite. Had he some notion of committing sacrilege? If so, how pitifully childish! But dangerous, too, in the way that pitifully childish people are potentially dangerous. She took Kathleen into her confidence on his last Friday at the office.

'Do you know that Adam was seen at Newrath Church at early Mass on the Feast of Corpus Christi?'

'Was he? Oh, well! Perhaps he's going to be religious now.'

'But don't you think it very odd?'

'Why, I suppose he just felt like it,' said Kathleen in the impatient tone of one who had lived so long with an idiosyncratic that she has no longer any interest to spare.

Maureen sighed. It was difficult, perhaps impossible, to make a Protestant understand. Even if she told Kathleen that Adam had possibly received the Holy Sacrament of Communion, she would probably not blink an eyelid. Kathleen, feeling that her sister-in-law was finding her lacking, went on. 'After all, though it's queer after all these years, I suppose, it's no queerer than the other things he does.'

'What other things?' rapped out Maureen.

Kathleen, her baby on her lap, her fingers playing with his toes, hesitated. What she had in mind was Adam's general queerness, which made being married to him like being married, say, to a confirmed drunkard, whose addiction shut him off from being considered either as a real husband, or head of the house, or even a polite acquaintance. A little perplexed she wondered why it was that Adam no longer seemed to her a real person, and whether it was that any heart which has once opened widely to another and been turned away is henceforth faster locked against that individual, or at least as seeing him as an individual, than anyone else in the world. Only morbid people or lonely people, she thought, look back on ways that have led them into a dark forest of pain, and because, having her children, her heart and her head and her hands were full to overflowing, she actually took much more interest in the stray remarks of a shopkeeper than anything Adam ever said. Shrugging all this away because of a certain sensation of guilt, she said:

'Well, it's no good pretending that Adam is like other men and fathers who take an interest in their children. Sheila and Johnny here ...' she bent to caress the baby ... 'bless him, might not be alive for all the notice he takes of them. I thought he was going to take an interest in the garden when we first came, but after having dug up that bed, he walked off and left it to the weeds. Honestly, the way he goes on!'

'He doesn't look well, you know,' said Maureen, trying another tack. 'Everyone's noticing it. Even this woman at the office who saw him at Mass.'

'Nothing makes Adam look well,' said Kathleen. 'And now with this sudden change in his holiday we shall have to be at home most of the time he is here. But I shall stay with Sheila and baby at the sea when he has to go back. Because it's not fair to them.'

'They must have seen at the Library that he looks frightfully run down, and that's why they are giving him the holiday now,' said Maureen.

'He needn't have taken it just yet and upset all our plans.'
Maureen glanced at the clock. 'Well, he'll be back in a few
minutes. Don't say anything, will you, Kathleen?'

'About what?'

'About being seen at Mass.'

'Oh, that!'

Maureen was about to speak when she heard Adam's
key in the lock, and stopped. A moment later he came in;
they heard him pause in the hall, and then very slowly the
handle turned. Maureen was the first to receive his glance, a
puzzled stare. 'Hello, you're back early, aren't you?'

'You've forgotten; my holiday started last Monday.'

He came over and sat down near her, absorbing, as it
seemed, this information with some difficulty.

'You're not going away then?'

'Not till the week after next. And then, I told you, Violet
and I are going to blue all our money on one glorious week
in the West.'

'So you'll be about the house next week?'

'I'm afraid I shall.'

'And it's lovely having Auntie, isn't it, my pet?' Kathleen
addressed the baby on her knee. 'Look Adam, here is your
son all grand from his bath.'

Maureen noticed how he seemed to brace himself as his
attention went from her to the baby. Johnny was standing
up now, leaning on Kathleen's shoulder, laughing back at
her. But, Maureen observed, he won no smile from Adam.
Instead he stared and stared, and something in the quality of
that regard chilled her heart.

Kathleen, puzzled by the silence, glanced across at the
two grave faces opposite her. Maureen looked very queer,

she thought. Aloud she said: 'Well, Adam, so your holiday has started?'

After a moment he seemed to take in the sense of what she'd said, and nodded, but still his gaze was fixed on the laughing baby.

'It's a nuisance in a way about the change, because they can't have us at Whitestones till the beginning of the month.'

'It's all right. I'd rather be at home.' At last, looking away, Adam took his pipe out of his pocket and started filling it from his pouch.

'It would be better for you to have got straight away to the sea, though,' said Kathleen. 'Maureen here was saying how everyone thinks you are looking very run down.'

'Run down?' said Adam questioningly. He glanced at Maureen. 'Not quite,' he told her with a nod. 'Nearly perhaps, but not quite.' He looked round the room when he'd got his pipe going. 'Where's Sheila?'

'Playing somewhere,' said Kathleen. 'Well, now I'm going to put this young man to bed, and then I'll see to your tea.'

She went out of the room with the baby in her arms, expecting Maureen to follow. But Maureen stayed where she was. After a few moments' silence in which Adam appeared to have forgotten she was there, she asked him in a casual voice:

'Who's going to be Reference Librarian now that you're away? Dickinson?'

Adam shook his head. 'Not Dickinson.' He thought for a moment, and then added: 'His name's Alan Lane. A new chap they've just got in to replace me. He's very quick in the uptake.' He paused, and added dreamily: 'Rather a nice lad, really.'

As she listened Maureen felt the hands which were clasped on her knee grow tense. It was a long time since she had heard Adam praise anyone. Oh, yes, something was amiss, and badly amiss, she reflected without irony. Aloud she said, still carefully, keeping the casual tone in her voice: 'Replace you? Well, hardly that. I suppose he'll be your assistant when you go back?'

He said nothing for a moment. Then he made a sound of assent. In the room across the hall, Johnny had started to cry. Maureen watched how his head turned, how fixedly he listened. She felt that it was necessary to interrupt that listening, and said loudly: 'Do you know what I'm going to say? You look terribly tired. You ought to stay in bed for a few days, and let Dr. Morrissey look you over, make an examination.'

He looked at her frowningly, then got up and walked nearer to the door, nearer to Johnny, as if he wanted to hear him better. 'No need for that,' he said in a vague voice. Then he opened the door and went out. Maureen followed and, as she expected, the way led into the bedroom. But Johnny had stopped crying, and Kathleen was drawing down the blind at the window. Surprised at seeing them, she said: 'He's all right now,' in a whisper, and held up a warning finger. Then she passed them, going out of the room.

Standing by the wall Maureen watched Adam move over to the cot. He looked round, saw her, and moved away to Kathleen's dressing-table, where he started fingering a brush. Maureen said in a low but peremptory voice: 'I wouldn't stay here, Adam. You'll stop him from getting off to sleep.'

For a moment he stood motionless. Then he turned and went past her. She waited till she heard his steps go up the stairs to his own room, and then still waited, pondering. She didn't want to frighten Kathleen, but she must be warned, and warned immediately.

Kathleen was beating up eggs for an omelette when she went into the kitchen. She looked up and smiled, but then the smile went, and she said a little irritably: 'What's the matter?'

'Listen, Kathleen. Can't you see that Adam isn't at all well?'

'Well, what can I do about it?'

'We must get a doctor in, and try and keep him in bed.'

'You know very well that he'll only do what he wants to do. Does he want to see a doctor?'

'No. He's not thinking about that. But I think he's on the verge of a nervous breakdown.'

As Kathleen said nothing, she found herself adding: 'After all, you are his wife.'

Kathleen's lips came tightly together. Maureen had never interfered before but this looked like interfering. It was this Roman Catholic conception of marriage being a sacrament, and how could it be a sacrament when two people didn't care for each other? Seeing her expression Maureen said: 'I know it's not my business, but, Kathleen, didn't you see the way he watched Johnny just now?'

'How do you mean?'

'You didn't see, but I saw. It was such a strange terrible look. And I think there's something wrong at the Library ...'

But Kathleen had turned swiftly, and interrupted: 'Do you mean he wants to hurt my baby?'

Maureen wrung her hands: 'Oh, Kathleen, I don't know, but I'm frightened.'

As if fixed in a trance, the two women stood looking at each other.

V

And now at last he knew he was being watched, at least he knew he was being watched in his own home. For he didn't go out much because when he did he remembered there was something awful he had to do, and his steps took him back since at that very moment there might be the opportunity. It was Dr. Morrissey's questions on Monday morning that first made him aware that that awful thing had better be done quickly. After the examination, to which he submitted patiently, for, after all, what did it matter, the doctor asked:

'Anything on your mind, old man? Anything you don't want to tell the women about? If so, get it off your chest!'

Adam looked back at him intently. That hearty manner, that assumption of indifference, where had he met it before? Oh, yes. He remembered it all right from the old days.

'And what should be worrying me, Doctor?'

'Well, there are a lot of things that worry people. Money, for example.'

Adam reflected. From something odd Kathleen had said he realised that she suspected he'd got the sack from the Library. She was a little premature, that was all. But the money part would be her problem. And he had insured his life. That was one of the things he'd done soon after marrying her, when he was carefully building up the usual props.

'Of course we all want more cash, don't we? But so far I've managed, just managed, to pay my bills. Luckily the house belongs to my sister and myself.'

'Congratulations! I wish mine did. Well, nothing else? You haven't got a woman on your mind, have you?'

He was very late asking that question. Years and years ago he did have a woman on his mind, and he looked back on it smiling at such a childish and, worse, such a commonplace folly.

'My life is as chaste as the driven snow, I can assure you. Any other ideas?'

It was he who was smiling now, not the doctor, who abandoning his hearty manner said rather stiffly: 'You understand I'm just asking you these questions in the ordinary way. You're in very poor shape, you know, though there's nothing organically wrong. I should say you have been neglecting yourself. Not getting enough exercise, and perhaps not eating enough.'

'I haven't taken enough exercise, perhaps. And my room at the Library is very badly ventilated.'

'I see. Well, you want to look after yourself. Stay in bed more, and walk more, and eat more. That's what I usually tell my nervy patients. And I'll write you a prescription for a tonic.'

As he sat down and took out his fountain-pen, Morrissey added: 'You say you sleep all right, but do you dream much?'

'Well, now and then, of course. If I have a heavy supper, or have been to an exciting movie.'

'I see,' said the doctor starting to write. Adam watched the back of his bald head reminiscently. He was withdrawn now, just as what-was-his-name, oh, yes, Canning had withdrawn after an interview in which the patient had refused to co-operate! Everything changes; everything remains the same, he thought, with a fixed smile on his lips.

As he went into the hall with the doctor, Kathleen appeared from the kitchen. Adam turned his amused smile on her, feeling a glow of triumph because she was being stopped from getting a word in with Morrissey. 'Hello, there. I'm still alive, apparently.'

'But he wants looking after. Or at least he should look after himself better,' said Dr. Morrissey turning round. 'Why don't you take up golf, Palmer?'

'I'll think about it. I always do what you doctors tell me. The last one I had, or nearly the last one, told me to marry. I immediately went out and found this girl.'

'And I'm sure you did very well for yourself in following his advice.'

'Too well, as a matter of fact. Good-bye now, and thank you.'

'Good-bye. Good-bye, Mrs. Palmer. I'll be in again soon.'

So that was that. As he turned to look at her, Kathleen said in a rather breathless way: 'What did he really say, Adam?'

'Oh, nothing much. The usual things that all doctors say. But you'd better ring him up and ask him when I am out of the way, so then you can get the real low-down. Meanwhile there's this prescription to be made up. I may as well go along to the chemist; I must take more exercise, he says.'

'Don't go for a minute. I've got an egg nogg beaten up for you. Will you take it?'

'But, of course! How delightful!'

He enjoyed mystifying her for the moment. Then, as she went back to the kitchen, he walked over to the window which looked into the back garden. Immediately his attention was attracted by the sight of Johnny sprawling on a rug in the sun, various animal toys surrounding him. He looked long and steadfastly, and was still looking when she came in with the glass. After taking it he said in an assumed diffident tone: 'I wonder if you'd mind going to the chemist, dear, after all. I do feel a bit tired, so I think I'll just sit in the garden till lunch-time.'

'All right. I was going to do my shopping this afternoon, but I'll do it now.'

'And I'll stay in the garden and play with Johnny.'

'Oh, no, I'll take Johnny with me, I think. It will do him good.'

'I believe you don't trust me.'

'Of course I do.' She tried to laugh, and then turned away quickly.

Well, well, he said, half aloud, when she had disappeared. Yes, the old familiar pattern was hardly obscured at all. Eyes that looked sharply into his and flitted away as soon as they were met, voices that assumed brightness, and then went away and conferred in corners. For he heard someone coming down the stairs and assumed that it was Maureen coming to know from Kathleen what the doctor had said. Human beings had very little invention, he thought; their reactions were always so obvious. The only thing he wasn't quite certain about was whether Kathleen had any notion of his design toward Johnny, or whether she was just afraid he'd got himself sacked from the Library. No, no, the awful thing would be outside her range.

As soon as she had gone out, he dismissed her from his mind, and started to pace the garden, head down, as, he remembered, he had once paced the larger grounds of the asylum. But, he also recognised, he was much older and much wearier now. Too weary to raise any strength to struggle, to fight with his brain and his cunning. Near the end of my tether, he nodded to himself, pausing for a moment. Because for one thing he wasn't remembering anything very well. He could remember that he had to hurt the baby and hurt him badly, but it was difficult always to remember why, except that he knew a long way stretched behind him in which the why had all been worked out. 'I have received my orders,' he thought, 'and as Tennyson says, theirs not to reason why, theirs but to do and die.'

A sort of peace came into his heart and he picked up the deck-chair where it lay flat on the ground and arranged it carefully for himself. As he did so he heard a child's voice from the next-door garden say excitedly: 'And Daddy is coming with us, too, when we go. We shall all be at the sea together.'

He seemed to know that voice, he thought, and then forgot it picking up the last words, *the sea*. He closed his eyes and green waters came rushing up towards him, and then sank back stretching away to an infinite distance. Ah, yes, the sea, the great waters which had always been to him the image on earth of eternity, the sea which washed the shores of all the round, sometimes glittering, sometimes grey world. Lines of poetry drifted into his head:

And up the back garden.
The sound comes to me
Of the lapsing unsoilable
Whispering sea.

and then took possession of his mind, becoming the song of the siren. When he had done what he had to do, and there was some reason, he'd forgotten why, he must do it that very night while they slept, so perhaps the trams wouldn't be running, but anyhow he must run at first and then walk, and he knew the way and it wasn't so long, and he would get over the sea wall, and go down on the shore and on and on and on right into the cold murmuring lapping water, and let that suffocating embrace sweep over him; he wouldn't strive with her, nor wrestle with her, as Swinburne had written exultingly; there'd be no exultation; there'd been exultation in his life only in its beginning; it had gone, and would end in a different mood, a mood that Swinburne had also poeticised, something about:

> Out of the mystic and mournful garden
> Where all day through thy hands in barren ...
> Wove the sick flowers of secrecy ...

'Daddy!'

Someone was calling him. He opened his eyes, and saw Sheila at his side.

'Hello!'

'Were you asleep, Daddy? You weren't, because your lips were moving. Were you talking to yourself?'

'I was trying to remember some poetry.'

'What poetry?'

'It's called Ave atque Vale.'

'What does that mean?'

'It means "Hail and Farewell".'

And suddenly, without any volition of his own as it seemed, his hand went out, and gently smoothed the golden curls of the little girl standing puzzled beside him. Kathleen wheeling the pram along the side of the house was just in time to see the gesture, but her first impulse when she saw the child with her father was that of alarm, and she had called out before she could stop herself. 'Sheila, come here. What are you doing?' In a gentler tone she went on: 'You know you mustn't disturb Daddy when he's resting.'

'I'm not disturbing him. Am I, Daddy?'

'No.'

'I thought you were playing next door this morning.'

'I was. But Molly hit me, so I came away.'

'Well, go in and wash your hands now. Dinner'll soon be ready. I've got the bottle for you, Adam. You take it between meals.'

'Thank you.'

She undid the straps of the pram and lifted Johnny out. Yes, she thought, watching Adam out of the corners of her eye, he was staring oddly at the child in a sort of rapt way, but then it wasn't as if Adam was ever the smiling sort. She was beginning to believe, especially since she had seen his gesture towards Sheila, that Maureen had exaggerated. Perhaps they had both got him all wrong; perhaps he was really becoming interested in his children, but didn't want them to notice. And Dr. Morrissey, whom she had phoned, didn't think there was very much wrong. Also Adam seemed so amenable to any suggestion. When after their midday meal she suggested that he should lie down as the afternoon had clouded over, he agreed instantly. She did the washing-up with a much lighter heart, waiting eagerly for Maureen to come back from lunching with Violet in town to tell her that she was sure it would be a mistake for her to give up her idea of going away next week, as she, Kathleen, would be able to manage all right.

Adam went to sleep almost instantly. But whereas his sleep of late had been heavy but dreamless, now one dream

after another rushed in upon him breaking his false tranquillity. In the last nightmare he was crawling through a
narrow foul tunnel; every limb ached as he dragged himself
painfully through slime; he could hardly move one knee
after another, but he must go on, not towards any gleam of
light but towards complete darkness. And then suddenly he
knew he had reached the end of the tunnel, for everything
about him was black, and though he could see nothing he
knew that he crouched over an abyss; one movement and
he would be into the abyss. He had come to an expected
goal; yes, he knew that so far it was as he had expected, but
what he had not known was the immensity of distance that
lay below. He would fall and fall and fall; he would be ages
and ages and ages in falling, and he was frozen with antici-
patory terror. This isn't what I bargained for, he thought; a
drop out of a window on to a pavement as other men do,
not this. But at the same time he knew that *this* was what
he had bargained for, that he must do it, that now there was
no way back; yes, there was one hope; he could call on one
Name for aid, but no, he couldn't do that, that would make
him finally ridiculous, finally abject. So he had to go on;
he had to make just the one movement more forward, and
he screamed in fear as he felt the ground already slipping
beneath his knee, and awoke himself screaming.

No one heard him scream, for Kathleen was down at
the bottom of the back garden emptying some rubbish
into the dustbin. And sensing that he was alone he lay and
trembled and sweated. What he wanted to say was *O God,
O God, O God,* but, no, that was the Name that must not be
said, and he choked it back with all the strength he had. At
last he managed to stop shaking, and to prod his exhausted

hard-driven mind to mount its old wheel of ratiocination. You didn't need to be Adler to interpret that dream. Nor the other dream, that came back to him, in which intently he hammered at Johnny's skull, while the baby went on laughing, till the laugh changed to the hideous grinnings of an imbecile, and the head grew larger and larger. A rehearsal, but not an exact one, for what he was going to do, wasn't it, was just to seize the baby, bang his head hard against the wall, and then run, run down to the sea.

Could he do it, could he do it? he asked himself turning restlessly this way and that, still with his eyes closed. In his dream he hadn't been able to throw himself over the abyss. An anxiety dream, that was all, that was what they called it. But where, he asked feverishly, did the dream end, and action begin, life begin?—a dream couldn't go on forever. Not a man's dream. Only His dream went on for ever through all eternity. All men had their little temporary dreams with which to beguile the hard way, but all these petty dreams of love and money and benevolence and power and stamp-collecting ended with the husk of the body being lowered into grave or charnel house. Only his dream, like the dream of the religious stretched out a longer way. And he clutched the thought as a parched man clutches at cool water, making it vivify what he had never, never given up all the hard dark way, his pride. Yes, even as the saint acted out his dream of the Beatific Vision more resolutely than other men, shaping his whole life to run directly towards that eternal light, so he had shaped his dream more resolutely than the other petty sinners. Maybe he would scream as he fell into the last abyss: he was no mighty Lucifer, no bright son of the morning, but all the more should the devils in hell rejoice over him. They must know what a hard way he had made himself come, and maybe if he had known how difficult it was to serve either God or the devil, he would have chosen from the beginning the world's way, the *via media*. But he'd been too much of an artist, he assured himself excitedly. He hadn't written those poems he had meant to write, had in his youth felt it in him to write, but he had made his life into a work of art, and not Shelley's broken arc either but the complete circle, the approach and then the withdrawal.

Now was the moment when the dream must come to life in action, and so the circle would be completed and make something completely shapely and intelligible. No one would understand that in banging the baby's head against the wall he was putting the final necessary touch to his work of art, no, they wouldn't understand that, because mostly they understood nothing. But God would understand, and understanding turn finally away. Already in His infinite understanding He had pronounced the interdict: '*Better were it for that man that a millstone was hanged about his neck.*'

Because terror had left him, because he had taken a heady dose of the sad, ancient, so baleful stimulant, he imagined that now as the afternoon wore on he was lying quietly and calmly. When Maureen knocked at the door, he heard his voice say: 'Come in,' and admired himself for saying the two words with such coolness.

'We are making the tea, Adam. Shall I bring a tray up to you, or will you come down?'

'I'll come down,' he answered after a moment. Yes, he had better come down, for now was the interlude, the period of watchfulness.

'Are you sure? Did I disturb you? Were you asleep?'

'No, I wasn't asleep.'

He wondered why she didn't go, why she stood at the foot of the divan couch looking at him. Oh, of course, she was anxious. Now and then the little people turned from their shopping and getting cups of tea and fornications and washing the baby and playing golf, feeling disturbed. When they got disturbed, whoever disturbed them had to pay for it. They put one man into prison, or sent him to the gallows; another they 'put away' as they had once put him away. And when God came among them they crucified Him because that disturbance was much more than they could bear.

'What's the matter?'

'I was wondering if you have a temperature. Your eyes are very bright.'

'No, I haven't a temperature.'

He threw back the coverings, and put his feet to the ground. Instantly he felt so dizzy and tired that he had to pause. For a moment he considered that immense tiredness with a sort of anxiety. Suppose he couldn't run to-night; suppose he couldn't run down to the sea. No, his will had overcome his tiredness for a long long time. He really had a remarkable will. Look at what he was going to make himself do that very night! He rose to his feet, and then bent searching for his slippers. Immediately he felt so dizzy that he was glad that Maureen had turned to the door with: 'Well, I'll tell Kathleen you're coming.'

They seemed to want to chatter to him at tea, he noticed, and he was glad when at last they went away about their household duties. Vaguely he wondered why Maureen in particular seemed to want to talk so much to him, making an amusing story of what somebody had said. But he thought he managed very well, passing his cup up to the tea-pot, and once he told Sheila that she must drink up her milk and not be so faddy about not liking the jam. Because it was really very good jam. He had smiled at them knowing they were now his enemies, and would always throughout eternity be his enemies.

In the kitchen Maureen spoke urgently: 'Well, you can see for yourself that you were wrong now, Kathleen. I'm very glad I rang up Mr. Reardon and asked him to come along tomorrow. Morrissey is only the ordinary G.P., and no good for such a thing. This man is a first-rate specialist. I know he's done lots of people good.'

'I hope they get him into a nursing home,' said Kathleen. 'Because of the children. If I have to worry about not leaving either of them alone with him for a minute I shall be the one to go off my head.'

'I know,' said Maureen, 'I know.' She stopped herself from saying: 'But poor Adam, and his poor staring face, and those jerky movements.' Kathleen was only interested now as a mother. But for herself she wondered why all the love she had had for her brother had suddenly come springing back into her heart. Only with the difference that she was now the older sister, having, she knew, to care for someone helpless, as he had, she remembered, taken care of her once so many many years ago, and once crying, too, when she cried because she had hurt her knee and the blood had come, and asking: 'Does it hurt very much?'

VI

The three grown-up people who went to bed that night in the pleasant red-brick Victorian house to which fifty years ago Mrs. Palmer had come as an eager bride bent on doing her duty as a good wife and a good Catholic, did not have much expectation of a good night's rest. In the room at the top of the house, Maureen Palmer stayed long on her knees, directing her prayers sometimes in the familiar formulas, sometimes in a wordless appeal, not only to God, but also to the Mother of God, who was too her Mother and the Mother of all human creatures. Out of her prayers she won a certain tranquillity of heart, knowing that they had been heard, and surprisingly soon she fell asleep.

But at that she did not sleep as soon as Adam Palmer, whose frantic dream in the act of emerging from the long secret clutch of its begetter had shaped advance images of terror for the two women. He took off his coat, collar and tie, and then lay down on top of the divan bed, remembering that there was a reason why he should not fully undress. He knew he would wake up again soon, and when he awoke then he would know what it was he had to do, and go and do it. That was all.

It was Kathleen who tossed and turned in the half darkness of the summer night, listening to Sheila's soft breathing, alert to every movement Johnny made in his cot. While the clock struck the first quarters of the hours of the new day, she revolved plan after plan. She would go to England; she would find war work. But who would look after Johnny? Were the day nurseries really good places? Sheila could be taken as a boarder at the convent. This talk of a nursing

371

home for Adam was all very well, but a nursing home cost money. If Adam was really going to be ill for a long time, how would they afford to keep on paying when they had—how much was it in the bank? Not very much. Not a hundred pounds. And then she stopped thinking and lay just listening, listening to the old basket-chair creaking, to the clock ticking, to some sound, it must be a mouse, in the kitchen. Listening to her own apprehensions that informed her that the powers of darkness were abroad in this house which should be a happy house. And it is when he's not here, she thought, and resentment hardened in her mind as she thought back through the years, thought back to the bed-sitting-room in Pimlico. Right from the very beginning, she told herself, he arranged to spoil my whole life. But I shan't let him; I never have let him.

It was a few minutes after three o'clock when Adam awoke, and sitting up sought for the message which was contained in the urgency with which he felt the whole room was tense. Of course! They had been very patient with him, waiting, but now the waiting was at an end, and he must get up immediately, just as he had to make himself get up as soon as he awoke on a cold morning and remembered that this was the day he was going up to the altar to receive the Eucharist. His feet found his slippers, and he put on his coat, though still not quite sure whether he was awake or sleep. And still not knowing whether this was an imperative dream whose urge he was obeying he went to the door, for now the borderline which separates our consciousness of the exterior objective world from our interior life no longer existed for him. Outside the door and careless of muffling his tread he went down the stairs, so that

Maureen, waking as suddenly, and knowing too that she must get up immediately, heard him descend as she opened her door to listen. She waited only to grab her dressing-gown off its peg, before she followed.

Kathleen, who had just fallen into an uneasy slumber, did not hear him till he stumbled by her bed as he passed on his way to the cot. Waking she saw him in the act of lifting up the sleeping baby, and screamed as she was at his side in one wild rush.

But he knocked her back with his elbow as he made for the door. The kitchen, he told himself, and hit Its head against the wall hard, but there was someone at the foot of the stairs who was trying to take the burden away, so that he had to hold It high above his head where she couldn't reach. And they were screaming, and It was yelling, and he was falling over a chair, and now they had got It away. And he screamed, too, because he thought the awful thing had been done, just one scream, before collapsing on the ground.

Maureen heard the scream as she rushed away, her one idea being to get the baby out of the house. She found herself through the front door, and in the garden, before she remembered that she couldn't leave Kathleen and Sheila alone with a madman. But the next moment Kathleen called, and her voice seemed quite calm: 'Maureen, go to Mr. Fellowes next door; I must get Sheila.'

'But,' said Maureen desperately, starting to return to the house. Even as she did so an upstairs window in the adjacent house went up and a voice called: 'Anything the matter?'

'Oh, Mr. Fellowes, can you please come over.'

'Right. Won't be a minute.'

373

Mr. Fellowes, a portly chemist, found two women and two children waiting outside his gate when he came down. Kathleen said to him: 'My husband has gone mad, Mr. Fellowes. He tried to murder my baby. Could you take us in, and then telephone for the police?'

'No, not the police,' cried Maureen. 'The doctor.'

'Now, don't get upset,' said Mr. Fellowes to her in a soothing voice, for he saw she was shaking all over. While Mrs. Palmer showed that she was a true Englishwoman by appearing to be quite cool and collected from the way she spoke. Even though she had nothing on but her nightgown, and, of course, being an Englishwoman she wouldn't realise that some men might think her immodest, standing there giving her orders, for now she was saying: 'No, the police. He's mad, of course, but he's wicked, too. I've known that for a long time.'

'Both of you go into my wife; she heard the screaming and she's come down. She will let you have some clothes,' he said, and then half-turning paused. He was not a coward, but the idea of going into a dark house which apparently contained a madman was not a pleasant one. 'What's he doing now?' he asked them in a low voice. Sheila, who had just realised that exciting things were happening, said: 'It's my Daddy, isn't it? He tried to kill us all, didn't he?'

Kathleen ahead, having taken Johnny from Maureen, called from the other gate: 'There's a policeman at the end of the square, Mr. Fellowes.'

'Ah,' said Mr. Fellowes with relief. 'I think perhaps it would be just as well to have someone,' he added to Maureen, who had now lifted Sheila in her arms and was standing at the gate. 'If you'll only wait one moment I'll go in with you,' she said, but he disregarded this and went hastily over to meet the advancing steps of the law.

Anyway he could switch on the lights for the policeman because, of course, they were in the same places as in his own house. They found Adam crouched on the kitchen floor in a sort of huddle. But after the light had been on a moment or two, and they had spoken to him, he got up, and sat back in a chair. Relieved, Mr. Fellowes said: 'Feel better now? You know me, don't you? I'm Mr. Fellowes from next door.'

Adam looked at him hard, but without recognition. He said: 'Have you come to take me away to the sea?'

'Well, perhaps,' said Mr. Fellowes turning away to shake his head at the policeman, who said: 'I'll ring for an ambulance. That's the best thing. Can you stay with him? He seems pretty quiet.'

'All right,' said Mr. Fellowes, surveying Adam more distrustfully now. He was relieved when at that moment Maureen appeared. 'Dr. Morrissey is coming over,' she told them, and then to her brother: 'You had a bad dream, didn't you, Adam?'

He nodded at this, looking at her fixedly. But the dream was going on and in a different way, he thought, from the way he had meant it to go. 'I should be at the sea,' he told her pleadingly, and tried to get up. But he could hardly stand, and sank back again, closing his eyes.

A commotion about him made him open them again. He saw one or two faces that he seemed vaguely to recognise, but then his attention was arrested by the startling line between the partially drawn curtains of the kitchen window. It was the pearl white light of dawn he saw, and once again he was reminded of that other cleansing image which promised him surcease. He put both his hands on the table, and managed to rise, but immediately he was pressed back to his seat. 'Just a moment, old man,' said Dr. Morrissey soothingly. 'A cab's coming to take you to the sea, that's where you want to go, isn't it?'

He nodded. If they really understood that, it was all right.

'I'll get some things together,' said Maureen turning away. She felt her heart would break if she stayed there any longer watching him, so bewildered, so helpless, so completely lost once again.

The cab, it was a white ambulance, came in a few more minutes and took him away to the observation ward attached to the Hospital of the Mother of Mercy. The sky was light now, but there were few people abroad to mark its smooth and swift passage. But one man, a priest, saw it pass by as he hurried back over the canal bridge from a sick call in which he had administered the last Sacrament. As was his habit, whenever he saw an ambulance, Father Mansfield murmured a prayer for the distressed or suffering man, woman or child it contained. And for some reason beyond his ken, he found himself impelled to turn and watch the ambulance until it disappeared citywards, sending his good wishes after it.

— EPILOGUE —

As soon as she got back from work, Maureen noticed that there was something different about Kathleen, as if a tension had gone. This, she thought, as they were having tea and she postponed her anxious question till Sheila was out of the way, was the third change she had noticed in Kathleen's face. During those first months, those months in which she steadfastly refused to go and see Adam in the asylum, her face had been so set, the lips tightly pressed together. Then, when at last she agreed to go with Maureen, her face had grown softer again. She wasn't so much the practical business woman, occupied solely with ways and means. But now it was as if she had completely relaxed, as if the real Kathleen had come back. Half troubled, half hopeful, Maureen was able at last to put the question:

'Well, how was he?'

'I think *you'd* say better, Maureen.'

'Why me? You mean that you don't think so?'

'Yes, I think so, too,' said Kathleen slowly. 'In fact I'm sure. But I'm not certain that many people would understand.' She stopped to light a cigarette before she said: 'You see he was really much the same at first. Watching me, but not saying much so that talking was rather difficult. Though somehow I had the feeling that he wanted to ask me something, do you know? But that he couldn't get the words out. But at last they came. He caught me looking at my watch, I'm afraid,' Kathleen added apologetically.

'Yes?'

'He said: "Oh, by the way, Maureen told me that I didn't hurt the baby. I'd rather like to know if that's true." He said it in such a casual voice that for a moment I felt so angry that I wanted to hit him. And then I looked right in his eyes, and I understood that he really wanted to know, wanted to know desperately.'

'Well?'

'So I didn't speak casually back. I said very slowly: "I swear to you most solemnly that you never injured Johnny one tiny scrap."'

'I see. He couldn't really bring himself to believe me. Oh, Kathleen, what a good thing it was that at last you went by yourself!'

'I know. Because he wasn't quite sure whether to believe me at first. He said: "Why didn't you come and see me for so long then?" I said, well, I just said the truth. I said: "You know, Adam, that you've had things pent up in you for a long time. Well, I had, too. So that I couldn't bring myself to forgive you. But I'm sorry now." And he looked at me and nodded his head. And then, Maureen, this was the awful part, he looked away, and I thought he was going to sob. But at last he just drew a deep breath like a sigh, and said as if to himself: "I'm glad I was stopped from hurting the baby."'

'And then?'

'Then I thought I'd better go. I knew he wanted to be by himself. But, I want you to tell me if this is silly, Maureen. I did have at last the feeling that now he's going to get better, to get really better, I mean.'

'Of course he will. Because he's sorry. And so it will come right. Oh, I'm so glad.'

'I know what you mean. Because I felt so glad I told him I was sorry. I see I was very hard insisting that he should be certified and everything, with you doing your best to prevent me all the time. So that we had those horrid quarrels.'

'Oh, but I did so understand, Kathleen. It's very difficult not to be hard when, well, when that happened. Besides, you see, I had to try and make up for the first time, the time I never bothered to go and see him. Just sending him a few paltry cigarettes. Do you remember how, so rightly, you blew me up about that when first we met?'

Kathleen nodded. There was something else she wanted to ask Maureen, but she couldn't bring herself to say it yet. She remarked in a matter-of-fact voice: 'Oh, that young man, Lane, has been to see him again and left some books. He's a funny kid, isn't he? But I think he really distracts Adam, and it's nice of him.'

'He's a pet. I shall never forget the time he called on you, and said he hoped you understood that he was just keeping Adam's job warm for him.'

'I know,' said Kathleen. 'There's a lot of goodness about really. Kenneth Cooke has sent me another cheque. He's been sweet ever since I had to tell him the reason why Adam didn't answer his letters. Not that Adam ever wrote much. I'm afraid we both rather sneered at him.'

'Well, everything is going to get better from now,' said Maureen. She got up, and started to put the plates together. Kathleen wandered across to the window and stood for a moment looking out. At last she turned round.

'Maureen, do you remember that text, Saint Paul, I think it is, about his being persuaded that neither death, nor life, nor angels, nor principalities, nor powers, nor height, nor depth, can separate us from the love of God?'

'Yes. "Nor things present, nor things to come.'"

'Well, do you think we can believe that? Because some of the other texts say different things, so it's all rather difficult,' said Kathleen, turning back again. 'But are you Catholics *allowed* to believe that?'

For a moment Maureen hesitated, struggling with her sense of theology. She thought of informing Kathleen that it was never God Who separated Himself from us, but we who separated ourselves from God. Then she remembered, *Nor things present, nor things to come.* It might be a long way, in and out of time. But in the end ... perhaps. She said gently: 'I think we are all allowed to hope that, Kathleen.'

Kathleen left the window, and came over to help her at the table. 'Do you know, I was planning?' she said. 'We really ought to get this old room distempered ready for when Adam comes home again. I'm going to see about it straight off. And you must help me choose, Maureen.'